Praise for Laurie Graff's

You Have
to Kiss a Lot
of Frogs

"An ex-boyfriend of mine once said dating is a humbling experience, which I found out for myself right after he dumped me! Loved the book."
—*New York Times* bestselling author and actress Fran Drescher

"Ask anybody. There is nothing better than a book you have to sit up until 2:00 a.m. to finish. Follow Karrie Kline on her bumpy, witty, poignant road to happiness, and read this book— it will save you a date or two."
—Actress Finola Hughes

For my mother,
Lonnie
and for my brother,
Steve

You Have to Kiss a Lot of Frogs

Laurie Graff

**RED
DRESS
I N K**
™

First edition January 2004

YOU HAVE TO KISS A LOT OF FROGS

A Red Dress Ink novel

ISBN 0-373-89543-7

© 2004 by Laurie Graff.

www.RedDressInk.com

Printed in U.S.A.

ACKNOWLEDGMENTS

Thank you to…

All the family members, friends, peers and people who have inspired and encouraged me. You know who you are!

Margaret Marbury at Red Dress Ink for picking me out of the slush pile and saying "yes," and the RDI committee in New York, Toronto and the U.K. for agreeing with her.

My editor, Melissa Jeglinski, who is a joy to work with. Who helped me create a road map for Karrie Kline. Who has great ideas, and great taste in restaurants!

The entire RDI team for their wonderful and creative work on all aspects of this book, and special thanks to Zareen Jaffery for her help.

Robert Youdelman, Danielle Forte and Dianne Jude for their terrific work, and Mark Pedowitz for pointing me in that direction.

Nancy Kelton whose class, *Writing from Your Personal Experience,* started something. The "Los Angeles Writer's Bloc" and "The WorkShop Theater Company."

Lisa Forman and Ruth Kreitzman for pushing me to write.

Jill Cohen for the serendipitous act that led to publishing this book!

Jamie Callan for oh so much, for everything!

Nancy Giles for the delicious brainstorms!

Ellen Byron, Steve Keyes and Matt Graff for support from the beginning.

Stewart Zuckerbrod, Tracy Tofte, Sandy Eisenberg, Pam Clifford and Susan Donorjee for always listening to me read. Phyllis Heller for ideas. Mary Gordon Murray for living through the rewrite process with me, and Marlene Kaplan who's going in the white limo!

And in memory of David Stenstrom who was the first one to say, "Laurie, you should be writing this down."

CONTENTS

You Have to Kiss a Lot of Frogs

April Fools' Day
Hell's Kitchen, NYC 2003

I like being a woman. I also like being friends with other women. I don't, however, like feeling forced into participating in some ritual with an entire flock of them I've never even met. It's like having to wear those dumb party hats, and blow on those even dumber paper things at midnight with a bunch of strangers on New Year's Eve. You're thrown in with people you don't know and don't want to be with, but you're all going to share this intimate event with glee. If it kills you. And that's how I feel at this bridal shower.

Here I am. Tuesday. 6:00 p.m. Right after work, if you actually have a normal job, and I'm standing in a Mexican restaurant in midtown Manhattan, holding a mar-

garita I'm not drinking because I don't like the salt. I'm
stuck wearing gray wool slacks because I came from an
audition for a soup commercial, à la Winter in Vermont,
and realized way too late that the bag with my dress was
at home on my bed, and not with me. The bright fluorescents highlight the brown roots on my red head, and
a silver barrette is holding together a few strands of hair,
attempting to disguise a bad bang trim. That time-of-the-
month bloat is making my size-four pants feel tight, and
my hair feels hot around my neck. I can't help but compare myself to everyone around me. They seem perfectly
coiffed, and groomed, and excited to be here. I'm one
of fifty overeager women waiting for Marcy to arrive to
surprise her because, finally, after twenty-five years of dating, she's met some guy she's going to marry. And everyone's gabbing how they're sooooooo happy for her.
Frankly, I don't believe it.

The married ones must be remembering their showers. The too many toaster ovens and Crock-Pots, the
friction between the maid of honor and the other best
friends, and now the contemplation if the marriage has
lived up to the fanfare of the shower.

The single ones are standing with plastic smiles,
wondering if the person getting married is really better off than they are. That's me. I wonder, is Marcy really Happy Now? And is that to say she really never was
before? After the years of angst and dates and therapy

and plans for when The One arrives, when It happens, what does It feel like? What does it feel like to be with Mr. Right. Mr. It. Does it feel great? Does it? Does it feel better than it did before? Does it feel better than I feel standing in the middle of it? Watching. Comparing. Are other people unconditionally happy for this person or is it just me?

"*Sssshh,* she's coming."

"AAHHHHHH!!!"

"QUIET…QUIET…quiet…"

The lights in the restaurant are out, and there's chatter coming up the stairs to the balcony. Everyone pushes together in the middle to see. To see how Marcy will react. She thinks her mom and aunt are taking her to see *The Phantom of the Opera.* Aunt Tessie's visiting from Philadelphia and wants to see it, she's heard "The Music of the Night" sung so much over the years. Marcy thinks they're coming to Fajita Fajita for a bite before the show. Little does she expect that tonight, eight weeks before her wedding, years after attending God knows how many showers herself, instead of seeing *Phantom,* she would see every important female she knows tell her, "I'm so happy for you. I told you it would happen. It happens for everybody. It just has to be your time."

"Watch it, Marcy," I hear a gravelly voice say. "You stepped on my toe."

"Oops. Sorry, Mom."

"I can't see," says the other one. Obviously Tessie. "Go ahead of me, Marcy, dear. It's dark."

"SURPRISE!"

The lights snap on, and Marcy sees every woman she's ever known in her entire life before her—wide-eyed, drunk from waiting and wishing her well in her new life. Marcy is heroic, because Martin has found her. Marcy is elevated to another level, because Martin has picked her. Marcy is thrown to the other side. The side that is validated. She's no longer going to be Single. It's happened. It's happening now. And as a result, Marcy can't move.

I lift my five-foot-one-inch frame onto my toes so I can get a better look. Marcy's leaning against the banister of the balcony. She turns to face us. Her bright auburn hair falls back, and her smile spreads so far across her face it's inside her ears. She looks like she may faint. The banister is holding her up for dear life.

Marcy's face is frozen in terror. No. Not terror. Happiness. Terrorized happiness. Her small body's wobbling. Will all this happiness make her keel over?

"Ehhhhhhhh!" Marcy cries out. Her grotesque smile opens wider and wider, and her eyes bulge out. "Ehhhhhhhh!"

We are happy for Marcy. We are. But now we are worried. Our smiles are plastered to our faces as we watch her meld into the banister.

"You're getting maaarried!!!" a cousin calls out. Her

red nails wave at Marcy, and her gold-and-diamond rings catch the glimmer of the light shining above the picture of a bullfight that's painted on red velvet.

"Look at all your guests!" shouts her sister-in-law to be.

"Everyone sit!" says her maid of honor, who'd been spending the last few minutes at the banister trying to catch Marcy if she were to fall.

Marcy is walked over to a table by her mother and aunt Tessie, each holding half of her up. They smile at everyone, as if they were in a procession. Marcy remains in shock, until she passes the pile of one hundred beautifully wrapped presents that should cover almost every item on her registry. She is suddenly composed.

"Let's eat!" announces Marcy, taking her seat in the center.

We watch a moment. Marcy has caught her breath, and so we catch ours. We sit down to eat the guacamole. I take a seat near the gifts. I want to get a good look at what I'm missing.

Seven weeks later I wake up in the middle of the night. I have just turned forty-five and no Martin came and saved me from it. I am still in my apartment, or what I hope is still my apartment. The notice to buy me out of my rent-stabilized lease arrived the day before my birthday. My unemployment claim expired, and my acting prospects quietly disappeared in my forty-fourth year, just to make my forty-fifth as frightening as possible. I never bought that "Forty" was the "New Thirty," and feel petrified to find out that "Fifty" is the "New Forty." I am currently boyfriendless and in no shape to date.

Perhaps I should kill myself.

This seems like an interesting idea. I can kill myself tonight and just slip away. What am I supposed to do tomorrow anyway? Gynecologist appointment, gym, audition for a vacuum cleaner commercial… Now might be a good time. I have to slip away one day anyway. At least I'd have the say as to when and how.

I'd no longer have to worry about money. That would be a relief. I wouldn't be afraid I'd get raped running the reservoir, hit by a car or blown up by a terrorist. I wouldn't have to keep up with fashion trends, do laundry or search for the perfect haircut. I'd never have to overhear another ridiculous cell phone conversation on the bus, or waste my time running ridiculous errands. I wouldn't have to wait on hold for a representative to come on the line while simultaneously waiting for AOL to get me online, only to waste more time deleting junk e-mail when I finally got there. Never again would I have to press one for more options, or watch Dubya, looking oh so presidential in jeans and cowboy boots, give another inspiring speech recited off a TelePrompTer. I'd never have to hang around and watch people I love grow sick and die, or witness my young face and body turn old. I'd never get some awful disease, shrivel up in the hospital, and lose my dignity while chin hairs grew unruly and unattended. I wouldn't have to look for a new agent, and I could finally stop dating.

Good idea. Now. How?

Instantly every idea seems awful. No guns. No razors. No noose and no ovens. The only possibility would be pills, and who am I kidding? I don't have a prescription and I'm not going to get one, because I'm never going to do this. I don't want to die. I want to get a great acting job, and fall in love, and get married. I want to honeymoon in Italy, and buy a huge co-op on Central Park West. I want to go to Zabar's, and eat cherry cheese strudel.

With the exception of the cherry cheese strudel, dying seems easier to accomplish. But if I screwed up, which I would because I don't want to do it, it would only be interpreted as a call for help. Then I'd have to use the balance of my medical insurance to go to some kind of rehab and therapy, and for sure I would lose my apartment. By the time I got back rents would be even more expensive, even more of the good guys would be taken, and everyone would point at me as the one who tried to off herself. It would probably go on my permanent record. No. It's easier to take two Tylenol, warm up some hot milk, read a chapter of *Heartburn* and a few tarot cards until I fall back to sleep.

Forget that. I cannot sleep. I am obsessed. Forty and single. My God, wait, I'm forty-five and single! How did this happen? Oh, so what if I am forty-five and single. So was my mother when she married Henry. No, Millie was just forty. And she was Divorced With Child Single, not Never Been Down That Aisle Single. Still, how much worse is it than when I was thirty and single? Or thirty-five and single? Or fort— Oh… Ohh…

Much worse. Much, much worse.

Decades of people's good-intentioned sayings flash before me.

"It only takes one."

"There's lots of other fish in the sea."

"When it's right, you know."

"You're next."

"Every pot has a cover."

"When it's your time, it will just happen."

"Let go and it will come to you."

"You never know what a day brings."

"What's yours is still out there."

"Trust in the universe. All unfolds according to plan."

Decades of dates flash before me. I think about those men. What were their names? Oh yeah, I remember…and then there was that completely idiotic…and, OH!!, that was truly…

Hmmm… I can think about that. Those stories. Count them like sheep. Instead of feeling mortified, maybe I can laugh. Embrace it. Rejoice. This is it. This is my life!

Well, I don't have to go that far, but it wouldn't be such a bad idea to simply accept it as mine. I'm still here. I'm not dead and I can still date. And maybe it's really not so horrific. Maybe it's not such a big deal. Maybe you just have to kiss a lot of frogs.

Wake Me When We Get There

Flashback—Easter Week
Brooklyn, NY 1969

My mother took me to my favorite store, The Little Princess, on Queens Boulevard to buy the dress. It was dark-blue velvet with an empire waist, and a white satin ribbon that tied under the breasts, though I didn't have any yet. I wore it when she married Henry.

It was a nice wedding. I was the flower girl. I walked between the folding chairs, and threw rose petals on the hardwood floors of Rabbi Bernstein's study. Millie, my mother, thought that was a *goyishe* thing to do, but I had insisted since they always did it that way on TV. The rabbi forgot to pour the wine into the glass, and Henry pretended to drink it during the prayers so as not to hurt his feelings. My mother laughed so hard she shook, and my grandma Rose thought she was crying.

"Now she's finally taken care of," my grandma told me when she tucked me into bed that night. I got to stay with my grandma while my mother and Henry went to Miami for their honeymoon. I was sleeping in Grandpa Lou's bed. My grandparents had had single beds throughout their marriage. Grandpa Lou died three years ago. I was eight. The year before he died my mother brought me to Brooklyn for my Easter vacation to learn how to swim at the local YMCA. It was a special program that guaranteed that in just five days every child would learn how to swim. Faithfully every morning, Grandpa Lou and I walked what felt like miles to the Y. He waited in the lobby while I took my swimming lesson. The instructors called me Blue Eyes and told me I had the prettiest bathing suits. I wore a different one each day. But I hardly got them wet. I only sat on the ledge of the pool like a beauty queen or waded in the shallow end. I didn't want to go in the water. It was cold. I was scared. After every lesson I would see Grandpa Lou and cry. He didn't want me to go back. He and Grandma Rose had a big argument about it.

"*Gants gut meshuggeh* with the swimming lessons," I heard him tell Grandma Rose in the kitchen. "She's going to get pneumonia."

"*Sha!* The *kinder* will hear." Grandma Rose talked in a

loud hushed voice. She talked in English and Yiddish. "Millie wants her to learn how to swim," said my grandmother.

I didn't want to stop going. I just wanted to stop being scared, and I didn't know how to do that. So every day we went. Every day I cried. Every day they fought.

At the end of the week my grandmother came down with hives, and my mother came to the final class to see my progress. Every kid swam the length of the pool except me. With much coaxing I was able to do a ball float. I didn't learn how to swim until Henry taught me.

I lay in Grandpa Lou's bed and thought about how he would come in the locker room after each lesson. "Cover up," he said, while he took off his coat and put it over my bathing suit. I could tell Grandma Rose was thinking about him, too, as she tucked me in.

"Are you in tight, *mamala?*" she asked. She brushed a few wisps of hair off my face and stuck them behind my ear. "You'll see, Karrie, one day you'll be a bride. You'll marry a rich man. He'll buy you a big diamond ring, and he'll take care of you. And you'll do it right the first time. Not like your mother. Okay. That's finished. Henry's a good man. A *mensch.* Not like your father, that clown."

She wasn't joking. My real father had run off to join the circus when I was four. At least that's what I thought. For a few years we received postcards from around the country saying, "Hi, Cookie! What's doin' tips and all? The circus has come to town. Love, Mel."

My mother said he wasn't really at the circus, he just wrote that. And I wasn't sure if writing to "Cookie" meant writing to me or my mom. But I always pictured him eating fire and jumping through hoops. Traveling across the country, and putting up circus tents. After a while the cards stopped, and I forgot about him.

Then about a year after the swimming lessons, my mom told me one night that Maggie McGraw from the apartment upstairs would be watching me because she had to pay a *shiva* call. She told me that Henry Eisenberg's wife had died. I knew Henry Eisenberg from the neighborhood and he was always nice to me. He lived in the apartment building around the corner.

My mother went to his building that night and took the elevator to the sixth floor. When she got off the elevator she saw an open door. She looked at the name on the door and walked in. Millie said it was raining and she left her wet umbrella in the hall.

My mother went in the living room and sat down. A lit memorial candle burned on the end table. The only person there was an old man. He was sitting on a cardboard box that was supposed to look like a wood crate. That's what people sat on when they had to sit *shiva*.

"Where is everybody?" Millie asked. "Where's Henry?"

"Who's Henry?" the old man asked. He had an Eastern European accent.

"Who are you?" asked Millie.

"I'm Bernard Aisenberg. I just lost my wife. Who are you?"

"I'm Millie Klein. I was looking for Henry Eisenberg. He just lost his wife."

Bernard looked at my mother. Then he looked disappointed.

"Does this mean you're not staying?"

My mother collected her wet umbrella and went across the hall to pay the right *shiva* call. Apparently her story won a piece of Henry's heart. It happened slowly, but three years later they wed.

"You're a whole family now. A mother. A father. You have a stepbrother, Lenny. He's all grown up and away at college, but still…" said Grandma Rose as she slipped into the bed next to mine. "Better at that age he's away. The long hair and who knows what else."

She took out her teeth at night. It made her whole face sag, and her voice sound funny. Grandma Rose looked much, much older. I used to be scared when I was little, but now I was used to it.

"You have a brand-new apartment with your own bedroom," she said, turning off the night-light. The room was quiet. I heard her breathing and rearranging her blankets. "You have a normal life now. It's what I always wanted for your mother, and what I want for you."

A light from the street shone in through the cracks of

the venetian blinds. I heard the sound of a car driving by. Brooklyn seemed different to me than Queens. Older. They were both okay, but nothing like Manhattan.

Grandma Rose called Manhattan New York. My mother and I called it The City. I think that had something to do with being from Brooklyn or Queens, but I wasn't sure. Grandma Rose said when my mother and Henry got married, she would take me to New York to see Radio City and the Rockettes.

"You'll have to wear sunglasses," she had told me, "because there are so many bright lights in Radio City it hurts your eyes. Chandeliers there. And colored lights on the stage. Everything glistens. And all the girls are dancing, and wearing sequins, and everybody applauds when they kick their legs in the air. It's a whole line of girls, but when they kick it goes up like one leg."

We would be going tomorrow. Tomorrow. I couldn't wait. I would watch everything the girls did, because when I grew up I would be a Rockette and live in The City.

"A nice normal life for all my girls," Grandma Rose repeated. I heard her reach for a tissue and blow her nose. "Wouldn't you like that?"

I didn't want to lie, and I didn't want to tell her I was going to be a Rockette, so I didn't say anything.

"Are you sleeping *mamala?* She must be asleep. *Gai*

shlofn," I heard her say, and in the half-lit dark saw her put the tissue under her pillow.

I felt private and secretive as I drifted off to sleep, thinking of everything but a normal life in Queens.

Nottingham forest

"I bought extra just for you," said Henry, taking a slab of lox and tucking it into an onion-and-garlic bagel. "You know you can have another one. You're thin. You can afford it."

"I'm really not that hungry," I said, picking up the Sunday *Daily News* and fishing for the comics. The Parade section caught my eye and I started to read. "My husband and I are having a disagreement. I said that David Cassidy was the only son of Shirley Jones on *The Partridge Family*, but my husband insists that Shaun played the youngest Partridge. Life here hasn't been the same since. Who is right? Conflicted in Connecticut."

"I'm making eggs," my mother yelled out from inside the house. I positioned myself near the screen door to be able to carry on a conversation with both of them. I watched my mother pour the yellow liquid into the frying pan. "This is the best part about being up here," she said, stuffing the eggshells down the garbage disposal and flicking the switch. "I wish we had one of these in Queens."

"The modern miracles of the Catskills," I said, picking up the I Love My Grandparents mug Lenny's wife Sharon had sent from Boston. It had pictures of their two-year-old twin girls on it. "Good coffee, Ma."

"Henry made it."

"I love it up here," said Henry, setting up his bagel, cigar, paper, radio and fisherman's cap on a plastic table, ready to embark on a day of sitting out on the deck and watching the resort community of Nottingham Forest walk by.

"Maybe when you retire you guys should live here all year," I said.

"No, too cold," said Henry.

"The winters are too cold," yelled out my mother, who kept up her end of the conversation from the kitchen.

"Too much ice in the winter," said Henry.

"You know how icy it gets up here in winter?" said Millie.

"We'll stay in Queens, and when we retire we'll go to Florida," said Henry.

"We're going to Florida. I want to be near my brother. We'll live by Uncle Sy and Aunt Cookie," said Millie.

"We want to be near family," said Henry, from the deck. "In Florida it's warm."

"It's warm," said Millie, from the kitchen. "Why should I freeze?"

"We don't need to be cold," said Henry, getting up and sliding open the screen door in an attempt to hear.

"Shut it. The mosquitoes." Millie turned to me. "Karrie, come in here and help me carry this platter."

I nibbled at a piece of lox and stared down the whitefish with its bulging eyes before I went into the house.

"Have you called your machine since you're here?" Millie asked, removing the eggs from the frying pan and putting them on a Lucite platter. She handed it to me, then lifted the arm of the faucet and drew some water into the pan to unfasten the pieces of egg that stuck to the nonstick Teflon.

"No. Not since Friday." I brought the platter out to the deck and put it on the outside table.

"Maybe someone called. Maybe you have an audition," she said, wiping her hand with a dish towel as she joined me at the table outside. "Henry. Eggs?"

Henry looked up from his beach chair and shook his head.

"You just want to know if that doctor guy from the park called." I took a fork and started eating the eggs from the serving platter.

"Put it on a plate," said Millie.

"I don't want a lot."

"I don't care how much you want. But if you want some, put it on a plate. Don't eat like that, Karen, it's not nice." My mom put some eggs on my plate. I knew she meant it because she called me Karen, and not Karrie. "It doesn't matter if I care if the doctor called you or not. It matters if you care. It's your life." She took a bite of her eggs. "So, did he call?"

"Yes. He's working this weekend. He called to say he's on call. Don't get so excited. We've only been out a few times."

"Who's excited? I'm not excited. It doesn't matter to me."

It mattered to her. And it mattered to me but I didn't want to tell her. I had just turned thirty and I had met a Jewish doctor. I was a cliché. What's more, I really liked him, but he seemed a little remote. I was trying to be cool, something I wasn't very good at.

"I had a blind date last week," I said, opening up a new can of worms, giving more information than necessary, illustrating just how cool I was not. I needed to take the attention off the doctor guy because I didn't want to appear overly interested in case it didn't work out. I had enough trouble dealing with my own feelings about these things without having to worry about my mother's. "My voice coach set me up with his high school buddy."

"How was that?"

"Delightful." This was easy. A straight case of an idiot guy. I was off the hook. "We ate in Chinatown," I told my mother, "we walked around. Then we got on the subway, he said he'd take me home. When we were approaching Times Square he asked if he'd be able to come in when we got uptown. I told him if he wanted we could watch the news and I'd make some tea. He said he didn't want tea and he wasn't interested in the news. He wanted to make out with me on my couch. And if I had no interest in making out with him I should let him know, because Times Square was where he made his connection and he didn't want to wind up uptown and have to pay another token to go home if, ultimately, he wasn't going to get what he wanted."

My mother looked heartbroken. "I don't know what's wrong with these guys," she said, finishing her eggs. "I think the whole world's crazy." Millie paused. "You didn't go home and make out with him after that I hope."

"You want me to even answer you?"

"What can I tell you," Millie said, when there was really nothing to say.

"Let me clean up," I said.

"It's all right. I'll do it." Millie collected the dishes and brought them inside the house.

Henry waved to the neighbors across the way. Molly Berger, and her husband, Hal, were on their deck playing with their grandchildren. The kids saw Henry and waved back. Henry was a kid magnet. He started to play with them by throwing his cap in the air and pretending not to be able to catch it. The children watched from across the court. Whenever the cap seemed to almost touch bottom, they squealed with delight, only to get more excited when Henry actually caught it.

Molly motioned for Hal to keep both eyes on the kids when she saw me on the deck. She left hers and walked across to ours. Her gold sandals clacked against the wood as she made her way up the stairs.

"Karrie, hello," she said, pulling me into her large frame and hugging me. "How are you? When did you get up?"

"Two days ago."

"Really? I didn't see you. What have you been doing?"

"You want a cold drink?" Henry asked her. "It'll only take a minute. We've got iced tea, seltzer, sodas, whatever you want."

"No. I just had something with the kids. I'm running back," said Molly, pulling over a chair and sitting down.

"So tell me…" she said, as if I knew what it was I was supposed to tell.

"Tell you…?"

"Everything!"

"About?"

"You know…"

Molly and I were in cahoots. And the fact that I was clueless didn't seem to make any difference. She looked at me and crossed her arms. "Karrie, you're a smart girl. What do you think I'm talking about?"

"Molly, no offense. I have no idea."

"You seeing anybody? I love to talk with single girls," she confessed to Henry. "I know you just turned thirty so you must be interested in settling down."

I looked up at Henry and smiled a closemouthed smile. Actually it was much more like a grimace.

"How are your grandchildren?" I asked Molly, changing the subject. "They look cute. How old are they now?"

"Jessica's three and Zachary's five next month. Wendy has her hands full. But my Scotty does very well, thank God, and she has help. You know, they have a very big house in Roslyn. You should visit. Maybe Scott has some friends for you." She winked.

"Yeah," I said, standing up and walking a few feet away. I put my leg up against the edge of the deck and knelt over it, stretching my calves as I contemplated a run.

"Grandma Molly, come here." Molly turned her head to see Zachary on the deck calling her. "We're hungry."

"I should be getting back." Molly stood and waved to Millie through the glass door. "See you later," she said, walking to the edge of the deck and putting her hand on the handrail for support. "Don't worry, Karrie. In this world all you need is a little *mazel.*"

"What was that?" I said. Henry went back to his paper. He didn't want to get involved. "What was that, Henry? What's the matter with her?"

"Keep your voice down," he said, reaching to light his cigar. "She only meant well."

My mother came back outside wearing a green-and-black-striped bathing suit with a white chiffon kerchief wrapped around her head.

"Who meant well?" Millie asked as she unfolded a reclining beach chair. She lay down on the chair, pulled the straps of her bathing suit down and basked in the sun.

"Do me a favor and don't talk to anyone about me, Ma, okay?" I decided I would go for a run around the lake. I decided I might jump in.

"What did I say?"

"Nothing, no one said anything," said Henry.

"She comes over here," I said to my mother, pointing my head toward the Berger house, "and has a one-way dialogue with me, about my life. Asks the questions and even answers them herself."

"Don't pay attention," my mother said. "I just wouldn't answer her."

"Just don't pay attention," said Henry.

I stopped stretching, stood up and leaned over my mother in her reclining position.

"What do you mean? Just have someone sit and invade my privacy and not care? Not answer? Just sit and let people talk at me as if they were talking to a wall?"

"I don't know why you're getting so worked up about this," Henry said, flicking his cigar ashes into an ashtray. "She means well."

Millie folded her right hand across her chest, holding her bathing suit up, while she used her left to prop up her body.

"I don't know why you take everything so personally," she said.

"She's talking about me. It's personal."

"She doesn't mean anything by it. It's just conversation, Karrie."

"Mom. It's condescending."

"It's not condescending, it's talk. If you were happy it wouldn't bother you."

"What does that mean?"

"Just what I said. If you were happy it wouldn't bother you."

"What makes you think I'm not happy?"

"I don't want to talk anymore," Millie said, lying back down. "Talk to Henry."

"People just want to see you happy," he explained.

"People just want to gossip," I said.

"So what?" said Millie. "What do you care?"

"Would you like people to come to you and feel they can comment on your life?"

"There's nothing to comment on in my life," said my mother. "My life is normal."

"And what does that mean?"

"My life is a normal life," my mother said defiantly. "I have a normal job, a husband, a daughter, a house. Normal."

"By whose standards?" I was furious. "What makes you think anyone around here sets the standard for normalcy?" I made a grand gesture to the entire development of Nottingham Forest. It was just built and in its first year. I didn't know anyone there so it was doubtful Molly and Hal did set the standard, but it proved my point. Or at least it tried to prove the only point I had.

"All right," said Henry, putting out his cigar, "let's drop it."

"Let's not," I said.

"Let's," said my mother. "Let's not ruin this day. You're upset because you just turned thirty and you're not married."

"That's absolutely not true! You're upset that I just turned thirty and I'm not married. I'm not." I wasn't. But I was a little upset that I had just turned thirty. And

I was a little more upset that I didn't currently have a steady boyfriend. And I was really upset that I had just been released from being on hold for three national commercials. But that wasn't the point. None of this was. Molly Berger was an annoying *Yenta* and nobody came to my defense. Nobody would let me say what I feel.

"I'm not upset about anything. I'm completely happy," I said. "Completely."

"Good," said my mom. She resumed her reclining position on the beach chair. "Just keep in mind that it gets harder to meet someone as you get older. People meet when they're in college. That's the place to meet."

"That's where Lenny met Sharon," said Henry.

"First of all, Henry, Lenny met Sharon after college. After graduate school. Years after. In a bar in Boston. You may have college mixed up with college town. Second of all, I didn't want to get married to anybody in college. I don't even want to get married to anybody now. I'm an actress."

"So what does one thing have to do with the other?"

It was the first question my mother posed that made any sense and I started to think about it. I wanted to talk about it. What did one thing have to do with the other?

"Okay, I'll tell you something, Mom." I wasn't sure if this was an answer, but it felt like the beginning to understanding the question. "This is the thing." I looked across to see that the Bergers were safely ensconced in their house and out of earshot. "I have a much more interesting life than Wendy. I'm an actress. I live in the city. I go out all the time to concerts, theater. I take classes. I date all these guys. I'm single!"

"Keep your voice down," said Henry. "We don't need the neighbors to know our business."

"Why not? They know it anyway. They may as well hear it from the horse's mouth and get it straight."

"Do you want to go home?" my mother asked. "If you're going to be like this just go home and don't ruin my weekend."

"I'm trying to talk to you."

"And I'm talking to you. Wendy is a lucky girl that she met Scott. And Wendy has a very interesting life. She has a husband, Karrie. Children. A house."

"How interesting can that be? Come on, Ma. They live in the suburbs. They go to malls. She's a dental hygienist."

"Fine. Don't get married. Don't have children. Don't do anything normal. Stay in the city. Stay single. Just leave me alone and don't complain."

I walked away from the conversation and into the house. I didn't understand. I didn't understand my mother. I didn't understand Henry. I thought I understood Molly, but so what. I didn't understand why anyone thought there would be any consequences to not marrying by thirty. I didn't understand why anyone thought that was remotely important. I didn't understand why it all bothered me so much, and I certainly didn't understand how to understand it.

I always had a date. I met a lot of guys. I just assumed that by the time I was, oh, I don't know…thirty-seven or -eight, or my God, even forty, one of these guys would just work out. Meanwhile, all I wanted was to work and make money acting and have a boyfriend and have fun. I wanted to go with the flow. I admit it often felt like going against the tide, but I really wanted to enjoy my life and enjoy being me.

I bent down to put on my running shoes. I would run. I would run it out of my system. And I would feel. Better.

"Oh!!!" I turned around and saw Henry behind me. He had followed me into the house, but I didn't see.

"Don't say anything," said Henry as he slid the door closed. "Let's just drop it and keep the peace with you and your mother. But you'll see," he said, all-knowing. "One day you'll meet someone and you'll forget about the acting and the city. You'll have a change of heart. Settle down. You'll feel different."

I looked at my stepdad. I knew he meant well, and I knew he believed his theory. Perhaps for some it was that easy, and perhaps for others it was that true. But in my gut I knew he was wrong.

David's Dad

Rosh Hashana
Central Park West, NYC 1988

Rosh Hashana. One of the holiest days of the year in Judaism. And I was in rehearsal for a show. To be a nun, no less.

I was invited to spend the holiday with David's family and was pretty happy about this. I had met David a few months back in Central Park. We were both running the reservoir. We passed each other and smiled. When we passed each other on the second lap I gave him a flirtatious little wave, one finger at a time, then dashed out of the park. About five minutes later I heard, "Hey, wait up. Aren't you the woman who was running?" I turned around to see David standing on the corner of Fifth and

90th Street catching his breath and waiting for my response. David said he was a little out of shape. He was a first-year surgical intern at Lenox Hill Hospital and spent most of his time off call asleep.

The adrenaline was pumping as I showered and changed at the rehearsal studio downtown. The show was rehearsing in New York, but would be running in Philadelphia. I'd be leaving town the following week for an open-ended run. I was superexcited about spending the holiday with David and his family. I hadn't met anyone yet, and was told that everyone would be at his aunt and uncle's, including Grandpa Max who was a little deaf.

We were to meet at five o'clock at his parents' apartment off the park at West 92nd. Five o'clock sharp I arrived with a bottle of wine, a shopping bag filled with my tap shoes, and a big hand puppet that looked like a nun. A prop for one of my numbers.

His mother answered the door.

"Hi! I'm Kitty. Come in." I was taken with this very attractive and svelte woman. The apartment was open and pretty too.

"You can put your things over there. David tells me you do something creative. What is it?"

"I'm an actress," I said, hiding Sister Mary Annette. I stood for an awkward moment. "Uh—thanks for having me. It's real nice to be with a family on the holidays. I'm working, and my folks are in Florida with my aunt and uncle."

"A Jewish girl?" Kitty looked shocked. "With that light coloring and those blue eyes! Sid, come out here. Your son brought home a Jewish girl."

Sid bounded from the bedroom adjusting his bow tie.

"Hi, there," he beamed. "Welcome."

Kitty went into the kitchen to prepare some hors d'oeuvres, and suggested Sid and I get acquainted. We sat on the big beige sofa.

"David tells me you're a retired gynecologist," I said. "My doctor's on 79th and Park."

"My practice was across the street. You know, Karrie, lots of my patients were artists. Writers, actresses, painters. Sometimes they couldn't afford to pay me in money, so they paid me with their work."

He pointed to several beautiful paintings that hung in the living room.

"I love these. We had more, but when we sold the house in New Jersey we couldn't take everything. Actually, these mean more to me than the money."

Kitty came in with drinks. We talked about my show.

"May I see what you've got in that shopping bag?" she asked. "I'm dying of curiosity."

I pulled out "Sister" and let her sing a few bars.

"I love it when she projects her voice like that!" said Sid.

"You could give David some lessons," said Kitty. "Speaking of—where is he?"

"I bet he's asleep," I said.

Kitty went into the kitchen to call.

"David works hard," said Sid. "It was rough when I did it too. We've been getting lots of David's mail. All sorts of literature on orthopedic surgery. I've been reading it all, so in my spare time I can become an expert on orthopedics."

Sid was warm and proud.

"I know what's next for you, Karrie. A white picket fence, a couple of children…"

"Oh, God," I said. "I guess in time, but what would I do all day? I'd go crazy. I have to work."

"You're right," Sid agreed. "It's different now. A woman needs to work too. Right now Kitty works and I stay home. People need their own interests. Their own validation. A couple can't be together twenty-four hours a day all the time. But having kids is great. My three children were educated right from the start. And this is the result. My son Greg is a CPA, Stew is a dentist and David is following in my footsteps."

It was obvious his youngest was special to him. And David felt the same. The day I met David he told me he was having dinner with his "Daddy" that evening. He wanted to spend as much time with him as possible since his dad suffered a severe heart and kidney problem. Diabetes. Looking at this man aglow, I'd never have known it.

"I'm going to give David a buzz too," he said. "Knowing him, he fell back to sleep." As he moved toward the phone he looked at me. "Just wait. After tonight we'll have you married off!"

"Oh!" I wanted to sound surprised, as if the thought had not occurred to me. However, I'd been thinking about it a little more seriously all summer. Well—not that seriously, and not with much intensity. A boyfriend, a steady boyfriend, a relationship, that was important. That was imminent. But marriage? When college ended, I considered myself too young. I was always "just in my twenties." But now I was thirty. That was an age, as everyone made certain to keep reminding me. But more important, I liked how this felt. I liked David, his mother, and I was really liking his dad. They liked me, and art and culture. It was everything all rolled into one. And best of all, they lived in the city!

About half an hour later David arrived. His dad pulled him around in a big bear hug.

"How's my boy? Sit down next to me and tell me how you are. You look great."

I watched the two of them, side by side, and noticed similar mannerisms. Particularly a certain way they would convey comprehension.

"Uh-huh," nodded Sid.

"Uh-huh," nodded David.

I could see David thirty-five years from now. I began wanting to see David thirty-five years from now.

As we got ready to leave, David asked to borrow one of his father's ties. Sid and I watched him knot the tie in the mirror.

"He's the apple of my eye," his dad told me. "I love all my children very much and never played favorites, but my youngest, this one, he's the apple of my eye. I adore him."

We went across the street to David's aunt and uncle's apartment for dinner. The table in their dining room was surrounded by family. His cousin, Paul, was there with his wife, Judy, who was seven months pregnant with their first child. We ate and laughed and enjoyed ourselves. After dessert Sid sat next to me and looked to his dad, Max, a psychiatrist who was talking with David.

"That's Dr. Friedman Number One," he said, pointing to his father, "Dr. Friedman Number Two," he said, pointing to himself, "and Dr. Friedman Number Three," he finished, as he pointed to David. "Three Dr. Friedmans!"

"Isn't it nice to spend the holiday with your family, David?" Kitty asked several times during the meal.

"I remember when all these kids were little and running around this table," said Sid. "Now everyone's grown up and most of them live away. This is what's left of the New York contingent. It's up to this generation to carry on. Start the cycle all over again." It was a warm family.

Smart, cultured and most of all, welcoming. For the first time I realized the implications of being, virtually, an only child. I didn't have much of a relationship with my step-brother, Lenny, or his wife or kids. Unlike David's family, with siblings and the promise of nieces and nephews and generations to come, in mine it would be up to me to start the cycle all over again. I was feeling eager to oblige.

The evening came to an end. We rode down in the elevator and said our goodbyes on the street. Sid walked over to me and David. "Take care of her," he said. "She's bright, she's articulate, she's a nice kid. Take care of her."

Then Sid turned to face me. "Take care of him, okay?"

We all hugged goodbye. Sid looked at us once more. "Take care of each other."

"So…" I said, as David and I walked west towards the park. The evening was a complete success. I had been uncertain as to how things were progressing between us, and I thought tonight had clarified them. It certainly had for me. I knew where I wanted to stand. I turned to David, expecting him to put his arm around me with possession and pride. I had been completely accepted by his family. His dad. I smiled at him.

"That was fun," I said, breaking the silence. "Thank you."

"Yeah," he said, putting his hands in his pocket. "I don't make that much of these things. I'm glad you came though. I'm worried about my dad. Okay if we walk back to your place instead of a cab?"

There it was again. Nothing that said this is great and nothing that said it was over. We walked south on Central Park West toward my apartment on 78th Street. We walked in the relationship silence. Not the good kind where you know you can't wait to get each other home and into bed, but the ambivalent kind. The kind where one person has more power because they know they're the one who's holding back. But they're not telling you they're holding back, and since you don't really know this for sure, and you certainly don't want to make a big deal out of nothing and create a problem that may not even exist, you decide you're overly sensitive, paranoid, insecure. All of the above. You have no choice but to smile sweetly, keep your unspoken agreement in the relationship silence, and hope the other person will break it. That any second it will be broken by him seductively pushing you up against the bricks of the next building, off to the side of the burgundy awning, gently moving his hands across your cheeks, pulling back your hair and tenderly, deeply, passionately kissing you and kissing you and whispering in your ear, "Let's get out of here. Let's go home." On the other hand, you could suddenly find yourself on 78th Street turning right to Amsterdam Avenue and wonder how you got there.

"David, do you want to come up?" The telling moment that can make or break it.

"Sure, I'll stay."

We rang for the elevator and I thought about the summer. One night in July I had just gotten back home after a weekend on the Cape. I felt really good, my skin was a little tanned and my hair had that great windblown look from sailing. I was wearing a pair of white shorts and a short sleeveless green tank top. My best friend Jane had come over. I looked at her when the buzzer rang.

"Expecting someone?" she asked.

The abrupt sound of the buzzer caught us in the middle of "haircut interruptus." Jane had just gotten back from ten months on the road doing the lead in a national tour. She played a character in a fairy-tale musical where people appeared to be destined to live unhappily ever after. Despite her better judgment she got her hair cut in Detroit, just before returning to New York. We were in my bathroom pushing her thick black hair in every direction desperately trying to make it right. We had met on a national tour years earlier, rocking and rolling our way through high school in the fifties. Jane was full of passion and insight, loved her work and family. And even in the face of the haircut drama had the great vision to know that ultimately "it would grow." I really admired her for that. I pressed the intercom and heard David's sleepy voice.

"Hey—can I come up?"

"Yeah," I said, before even checking with Jane. "That's him! That's the doctor guy. You'll get to meet him."

David came up to my apartment and had his bike with him. He had been riding around the city and missed me. I was very excited he showed up. But the excitement of surprising me, meeting my friend and telling me I was beautiful quickly evaporated, and the three of us just sat there in an awkward quiet till Jane said it was time for her to leave.

"I'll walk you down to the lobby, Janey," I said. "David, hang out. I'll be right back."

I stood in the elevator with Jane waiting for approval. Nothing came.

"So?" I wanted her to say something great about him.

"He's cute," she said.

"Yeah. He is, isn't he? The dark hair and eyes."

"And he seems to like you a lot."

"Yeah? Yeah."

The elevator opened and a couple with a little terrier got in. We stood in front of the glass double doors.

"What, Jane. You can tell me."

Jane looked at me with eyes that said she wanted to be a good friend and didn't want to hurt me.

"I'm just not a fan of ambivalent relationships," she said.

"Oh. That." My heart sunk. I knew she was right. I wound up missing David even when I was with him. He was far away when he was right next to me. Was it the hospital, his schedule, his dad, me? Or was it just David? When I went back upstairs David was already asleep.

Now, almost two months later, nothing between us had become any more clear. Except now I would be working in Philadelphia for an unknown amount of time. I decided the distance would be good. Our visits would be great. Absence makes the heart grow fonder. And I decided it wasn't me, it wasn't David, it wasn't us and it wasn't work. I decided David was just concerned about Sid.

He talked about his father our last night together before I left town with the show. "You do know, David, that you're really lucky to have a dad like that."

David knew. David also knew his father's health was failing. So as the year progressed he did all he could to get through the intern program and make his father proud. But David was unhappy. He probably suffered more from sleep deprivation than unhappiness, but his undefined unhappiness gnawed at him. It colored our relationship gray. Murky. Ambivalent. Still, I wanted David. I wanted to belong to what seemed so appealing during the holiday. I spent the next six months in Philadelphia missing David, playing a nun and living like one.

In the spring David and I took a vacation to St. Barts. I had high hopes. The island was gorgeous and David and I were great travel partners. We rented a Jeep and he drove through the hills like James Bond. Every night we drank a bottle of wine on a new beach and brought in the sunset. We skinny-dipped and ate fabulous French food. We hiked and took a boat to St. Marten. We did everything you do on a vacation but make love. By the end of the week David went back into his ambivalent silence and we broke up on the plane coming home.

I was very sad to lose David and, as time went on, realized I was very sad to lose Sid. The night David brought me home from Philly, we stopped up to see Sid and Kitty. Sid had been in bed all day. His birthday party was canceled. He was not receiving guests. When we arrived, Sid came out of his room wearing a Dartmouth sweatshirt and jeans. He looked ten years older than when we had first met.

"Do you know how close Sid feels to you to be able to have you visit?" Kitty asked while I was helping her in the kitchen with the coffee.

Sid was quiet that night, but let me know how important I was. How good I was for David.

"I hope David thinks so," I told his father. I wanted to tell Sid to make David stop it. To wake up. To open up and let go. But a father cannot do that for a son. A person can only do that for himself. I needed to think about me and what I was really getting from David, and not what I hoped I would get from David "if only."

I called the Friedman house a few times after our breakup, and ran into Kitty once in H&H buying bagels. Then one night as I was drifting off to sleep, finally feeling better having turned the corner on David, he called.

"My father died," David cried into the phone. "He was in his bed at home, in his sleep. I just saw him that day. He told me his disappointment in our breakup. He had told me I could never do better than you. I miss my daddy."

David came over and we made love. Real love. Free and unencumbered, tender and a little wild. We decided to try again after Sid was buried. And it worked. For a little while. A very little, little while. Perhaps I represented a link David had to his dad. However, it did not make him more appreciative of me. He was just going through the motions. I was reactive. I would react to David's moods. His advances and withdrawals. I twisted into positions like a Gumby, until I finally made myself stop.

David missed his father. I missed his father too. And I missed my father. My idea of a father. I sure loved Henry, but it never was a substitute for not knowing my real father. Mel had become a fictional character in my life. The clown who threw all the emotions of my childhood up in the air and juggled them like colored balls, unconcerned if they stayed up there or crashed to the floor.

In my mind, David had had the perfect suburban childhood. I assumed the love David received from his dad made everything easy for him. I assumed anyone who had a dad like David's grew up happy. I didn't get David's darkness. I made an open-and-shut case that didn't hold water. Perfect father equals perfect life. Not true. Nonetheless, I kept to my theory and hoped it would turn David into who I wanted him to be. And I thought my connection to David and Sid would turn me into everything I wanted to be. That it would erase everything Mel was unable to be. Mel. An embarrassment. My secret. On dark days, the likes of Mel made me question myself. Made me think I could never get a guy like David. But what was a guy like David? Only over time could I see that a guy like David wasn't worth having.

Life moved on and I chose to keep David out of mine.

Whose Party Is This Anyway?

Daylight Saving Time Ends
Grand Central Station, NYC 1989

I stood at a pay phone on the corner of 42nd and Madison, checking my answering machine in the hope there would be a message that anyone called to hire me to do anything. New York City was in a recession. I suppose the rest of the country was too, but they were not my concern. I was concerned about me on the island of Manhattan. My unemployment claim was about to expire, I only had two regional commercials running and I needed a job. There were no messages. I thought I'd check again. My change fell back down into the slot and then dropped on the ground. I bent down to pick it up, but I couldn't see a thing. We had moved the clocks back last night and now I was well rested, but felt blind. I could barely see. It was so dark out and still so early! It couldn't be much past lunchtime, I thought. I tilted my watch up toward the streetlights and saw, in fact, that it was almost rush hour. As I gathered up my dimes and nickels, I noticed a pair of familiar feet walk by.

"Fred," I called out, stopping my friend in his tracks. "Where are you going?" I stood up, putting my change back in my purse.

"To work."

"Wow! Work. What do you do?" I asked.

"Oh, I'm working at Whiting and Ransom," he said. He was totally not excited. "They call it a law firm, but it seems more like a cover for white slavers to me. Ransom indeed... Right."

"Oh. So. Really. What do you do there?"

Fred paused for dramatic effect before he finally answered.

"Proofreading."

"Proofreading," I said. "Really! You know how to do that?" I was impressed.

"Any idiot can learn." Fred had just finished doing a showcase production Off-Off B'way where he played a woman. He looked pretty good with red lipstick and dangling earrings. It had gotten him great attention and an agent, but apparently it hadn't readily turned into income.

"Where are you going?" he asked.

"Me? No place. I have no job. Hey," I said, "I'll walk you to yours, okay?"

"Okay," he said. "We'll have to go through Grand Central. I'm working there two days and I already know all the shortcuts."

I loved rush hour in New York. Swarms of people moved by us in rapid succession. It was like a movie montage of people hurrying, scurrying to buses, trains and planes. Fred worked the graveyard shift and went to work at five o'clock when everyone else went home.

"This is great!" I said. "I don't get this in my apartment."

I accompanied Fred through Grand Central Station, onto the escalator into the Pan Am Building, and continued to ride the elevator with him to his office. I walked him down the hall and into reception, when he finally turned and blocked me with his hand.

"You have to stop! Now! You can't go farther than this. You can't come with me to work," said Fred.

"But what am I going to do?" I walked Fred to the end of the reception area, peeking through the archway into the long hallway. "Hey. How do the guys look here? Have you had time to check anyone out?"

Fred and I had met in acting class five years earlier. The teacher assigned us a scene where I played a girl whose plans to hang herself were put on hold until she met her new next-door neighbor. Just in case he turned out To Be Somebody.

A nice-looking guy whisked by us down the corridor. I followed him with my eyes until I saw the band of gold glittering from a stack of briefs. "Too bad," I told Fred. "So, any cute lawyers around here you can fix me up with?"

"I'm looking for the same thing myself," said Fred.

"Well, keep your eyes open! For both of us!"

"We'll double," said Fred, pointing for me to walk back to the direction of the elevator bank. "I don't want to be late."

"How are things going with Larry? Good? Maybe one night you and Larry, and me and a lawyer cou—"

"I'll talk to you later," said Fred, literally pushing me toward the elevator.

"Maybe tomorrow," I called out after him. "Maybe tonight," I said, getting into the elevator. "I can call you here. I bet I can get a job accompanying people to their jobs. What do you think?"

The elevator doors shut tight before I found out.

Earlier that day I tried to sign up with a Temp Agency. STAR TEMPS:YOU CAN STILL BE A STAR WHILE YOU WAIT FOR THAT BREAK! The moment I walked in the door I knew I did not want to be there. They gave me a written test.

Here are three numbers: 162, 539 and 287.

Which number is the biggest?

Which number is the second biggest?

Which number is the third biggest?

Not the smallest, the third biggest. There were thirty-five problems. That made a page of one hundred and five sets of numbers. My eyes were starting to cross. 1086975, 1097656, 1086456. There were no commas. I was losing my mind. I went to the guy at the desk. I did not want to take the test.

"I do not want to take this test," I said to the guy at the desk. "I am a college graduate. I know how to count."

"If you want to be a file clerk you have to take this test," he said.

"I don't want to file."

"Are you saying you don't want to be a clerk?"

"I'll be a clerk," I said. "But I don't want to file."

"All clerks have to file. Unless you type. You type?"

"I do. I'll be a typist."

"Clerk–Typist," said the guy. "Is that what you want to be?"

"Yes. Yes! That's *exactly* what I want to be. And Receptionist."

"What?"

"Receptionist," I said. "I can answer the phone."

"Well, which? Clerk–Typist or Receptionist?"

"Both."

"Both? What do you mean?"

"Clerk–Typist Slash Receptionist. That's what I mean. I can type. I can answer the phone."

"I don't get it."

"There's nothing to get. I can do both. I can type. I can answer the phone. Clerk-Typist Slash Receptionist," I said looking into his blank face, feeling the need to repeat it as if I was speaking Greek.

"Oh. Then you have to take a typing test."

I left.

It had started to rain. I reached into my bag for my umbrella and pulled out a recent copy of *Backstage*. There was an ad for an audition cross-town in Hell's Kitchen for a show. A nonpaying show. A showcase. A musical. The call was for WOMEN: TWENTIES AND THIR-TIES. I fit.

I walked from STAR TEMPS until I saw a small sign pounded into the brick wall along the side of an alley on 52nd Street near Ninth Avenue. The sign had the initials ACT. Artists Creating Theater.

I entered. The place looked like an old-fashioned casino in the Catskills that had been ransacked. An unkempt, overweight man sat next to his disheveled-looking ten-year-old son who was singing along with the out-of-tune piano. Finally the man playing the piano spoke.

"Would you like to sing something a cappella?" he asked me.

Actually, no…I did not want to sing something a cappella.

"What are my other options?" I asked.

"I can play a couple of chords," he said.

He kept his word and played a four-chord introduction. My song was from the musical *Fiorello*.

"What a situation, ain't it awful," I sang a cappella.

The phone rang.

"Keep singing," said the big guy. "Come on, Timmy," he said to his son. "Let's go answer it."

The guy at the piano who had played the four chords stopped my singing. He told me he was really a songwriter and began teaching me a song from the show.

"What's the piece about?" I asked.

"Well," he said. "I wrote 'It's No Party.' Remember that song? 'It's No Party.'"

"Sure, I remember," I said.

"This is a musical about that song," he said. "It's about all of those people."

"What do you know!" I was speechless.

"Oh, yeah," he said. "Remember Ditzy left with Donny? Well, they got married. Now it's over thirty years later and they're getting divorced."

"You don't say!"

"You'd be Ditzy's daughter who moved back with her mother because she's also getting divorced. She and her ex-husband-to-be have a great number together where they fight over who gets the furniture."

"Is it good furniture?"

The songwriter took a moment to chuckle at this. He looked to me to respond.

"Gee, what an interesting concept," I told him. "When do you open?"

"We are open. We're running," he said. "We play Monday nights. I'm double-casting the show. It's a big hit, you see, a really big hit, and the guy who plays your ex just got picked up for a new show. He's hot. They saw him in this show and everybody wants him. I can't afford to lose any more actors. That's why I'm double-casting. Everybody in this show is hot. Really hot."

"That's, um...great!" I said. "Really great."

"Hey, you've got to take this call," the big guy yelled across the casino. "It's California. Important. Someone who might want to do the show."

"Well, thanks," I said, gathering my music.

"Please don't go yet," he said. "I like your voice. You have a good sound. This will just take a minute." He walked over to the black dial phone that was mounted under the sign that read Things Go Better With Coke.

I sat a few minutes and waited.

"Hey, Timmy knows every song from the show," said the big guy. "Listen to him sing. He's terrific. Timmy, sing a couple of songs for the girl. You don't mind?"

"No," I said. "No, not at all."

Timmy sang. And sang. And sang. Timmy wasn't bad. Fifteen minutes later he pooped out. The songwriter was still on the phone. I bid Timmy adieu, wished him luck and headed for the door. I stopped by the phone and tapped the songwriter on the shoulder.

"It's getting late. I have to go," I said. "Thanks."

He stopped talking and cupped his hand over the mouthpiece. "I like your voice," he said. "You have a really good sound. I'll invite you to see the show. You'll get a call."

Out in the alley I could still hear him talking. Long-distance.

"Send me your tapes. I need to hear your sound. Can you send them overnight express? We're moving fast on this one. It's a big show. I wrote it. Remember the song 'It's No Party'? You do? Well, I wrote that. Yeah, 'It's No Party.' That's my song."

I hoped for the songwriter all would go well. It was, after all, the darkest day of the year.

A Clue in Time Saves Nine

Tisha B'av
Greenwich Village, NYC 1990

He was funny. At first, nothing special to look it. On a closer look—still nothing special to look at. But definitely funny. He had definite appeal.

Fred, and his boyfriend, Larry, were having a picnic in the park. It was supposed to be a big group, but turned out to be the three of us and a couple and their baby from the next blanket who visited for a while. Just as we were finishing the Brie, a friend of Larry's from his gym showed up. Some guy he recently met who decided to show Larry the proper way to use free weights.

"You're only two and half hours late," said Larry. He started to pack up the small remains of what had been a feast. You come late, you don't eat. He didn't say it, but he said it. "Where were you?"

The guy went into an elaborate explanation of not being able to find us.

"The Turtle Pond, in front of the rocks in the middle, directly to the side of the Delacorte Theater," said Larry. "How hard is that?" Larry was an accountant. Everything was black or white.

"Did you know all the lampposts have the street numbers written on them? If you can decode it you can never get lost in Central Park. It took me hours till I could find someone to break the code. By then I was at 105th Street, looking at the gardens—which by the way are really beautiful—before I figured it out and came down here."

I looked at him with his balding head and life jumping out of his pores. He was out of his mind. He could not have been that lost as to not realize he was miles out of his way. Still, I was interested to know about the lampposts.

"Come on," he said, looking at the two guys lounging on the blanket with all the food obviously eaten. "Take a walk with me and I'll show you."

We walked and talked. Andy told me a lot about himself. Too much in fact. He had just come back from Paris where a fortuneteller told him that he, Andrew Ackerman from Bayside, Queens, was a reincarnation of his former self. A French lieutenant. A hero.

He was very excited about this. He was very excited about everything. If Andy got turned on to an author he'd read everything he could and then move on. The same about a food, a place and a profession, which he seemed to have many. It stood to reason he would be like that about a person too. But he was a trip to be with.

Andy called the next day. After the park. The phone call was interrupted by six call-waiting beeps. He wouldn't answer any of them, because he said he knew it was his ex-fiancée from eight years ago.

"You know this?" I asked. "How do you know this?"

"It's a long story," said Andy. "You don't want to hear it."

"Okay."

"So let me tell you what happened. I wanted to go to Paris. I love to travel, you know, and I needed a place to stay. My ex-fiancée lives in Paris now, and she told me I could always call her and she'd put me up, so I did. Jesus, what a disaster. She was so crazy. She was furious with me because I didn't desire her anymore. She was attacking me. Finally, by the third night, I had to move out to the couch. And you know what I overheard her tell her neighbor? 'Stay away from him. He devours people.' Can you believe it?"

I think he had given me a clue to his personality. I was pretty certain he had given me a big, big clue.

"So," he went on, "you know what today is? I'm also into holidays."

"Uh, no," I said. "What am I missing?"

"Happy Tisha B'av!" said Andy.

"What is that again?" I asked. "All I know about it is that when I was a kid in day camp this girl in my group, Hope Moskowitz, said she couldn't go swimming because of that holiday. She was religious. It was a boiling hot day in July and I felt bad for her."

"Well," said Andy, "it was my favorite holiday to study when I was in Hebrew school, and believe me, I wasn't one of those nerdy guys or anything. But Tisha B'av was when not one, but two temples in Jerusalem were destroyed. Then for three weeks after that you go into this, like, period of mourning when all these tragedies can strike. Very cool. So—do you want to go out and do something sometime?"

"Ummm," I said, aware that "yes" should not be my first response, based on the information at hand. "Maybe," I mustered.

"Do you have someone specific in mind?"

He made me laugh. What the hell, Andy was alive and full of energy, and I thought he was funny.

A few nights later we had dinner. Andy was really nice. He took me to an Italian restaurant on Cornelia Street where he knew the chef.

"Let's order an appetizer. Maybe some clams," I suggested.

"Let's see what happens," said Andy.

"What can happen?" I didn't get it. But Andy had gone into the kitchen, and Mario agreed to surprise us. I liked the smoked mozzarella and tomatoes. I liked Andy trying to impress me.

We went on a tour of the handball courts in his neighborhood. Andy knew every punk personally. I got an introduction. They were really nice. I thought someone could lend us their paddle ball rackets. Fifteen minutes. Andy asked. He knew how to handle them.

"It's not cool," he told me. We split.

We went back to his apartment. He put on a jazz album. He put on the fan. He dimmed the lights. Then Andy turned to me.

"Wanna dance?"

Andy had taught dance at Fred Astaire studio before he was a boxing coach. He was a good dancer. The music stopped. We clapped.

"You want to dance another tune?"

"No, thank you. It's getting late."

"Yeah, it is our first date," he said, as he kissed me. Andy was aggressive but not pushy.

I went home. Andy paid for my taxi. He called me when I got home. I wanted to go rowboating in Central Park. He said we should rent the movie *The Lonely Guy*. Andy felt bad. I was going to Connecticut. I told him not to feel bad. I would be back from Connecticut. It was a visit not a move.

Andy called me when I returned. Many times. Too many times. Andy called from work. Now he was a trader. He traded at least fifteen stocks on each message he'd leave on my machine. The messages were long. It took a very long time when I beeped in.

Finally we talked. We made plans for Sunday. As we were about to hang up, he got a call-waiting beep.

"Damn, I know who this is and I don't want to talk to her," he said.

"The ex-fiancée from Paris?" I asked.

"No, someone else. Forget it. Look, call me tomorrow."

I was getting a headache. This wasn't so much fun anymore. "I can't call you tomorrow," I said, "but I'll talk to you early on Sunday."

I called him Sunday. His machine said it was Friday night at eight-thirty and he'd be back in half an hour. Andy called me Monday. Apologetic. He thought the plans were tentative. Could we try again?

I was tentative.

He called a bunch of times over the next ten days. We made plans for Saturday. Definite plans. I was to call him from my parents' home upstate and tell him what time I'd be back in the city. That morning I called in to my machine.

"Hi. It's Andy. I'm sick. I'm really, really sick and I won't be able to make it tonight. But call me."

I did. His machine said it was Friday night at eight-thirty and he was out.

"Gee, I'm sorry you're sick," I told his machine. "Maybe you went out to get some medicine or something."

I called him again that night when I got back to the city. His machine still said it was Friday night at eight-thirty and he was out. I wondered where?

I've never spoken to Andy Ackerman again so I don't know. However, several days later I wondered if perhaps he had died or something, death being the only really good excuse under the circumstances. I called his machine. It said it was Friday night at eight-thirty, and anyone who wanted to hang out at his apartment could show up at midnight.

I didn't go.

Roman Holiday

My Birthday
Gramercy Park, NYC 1991

Second Avenue. A rainy night. A night to remember. But more on that later.

His name was Roman. I had met him at the 86th Street bus stop a few weeks earlier. My scene partner from acting class was paying me forty dollars to feed his cats for a few days while he went up to Syracuse to see his girlfriend play Blanche in a production of *A Streetcar Named Desire*. I was waiting for the bus to take me across town, back to the Bohemian familiarity of the Upper West Side, when I heard someone talk to me. His friends talked to me first. His head was down. When he looked up I thought he was one of the cutest guys I'd ever seen.

I think he just asked me out on a dare. But when I got his message about a date, I immediately said yes. He was fairly new to the city. A stockbroker, a Yale grad. He'd gone to Yale on a soccer scholarship, stopped playing and wound up getting a great job on Wall Street. We would go all over New York. I showed him the city.

"Where would you like to go, young lady?" I got to pick the places and he got to pay. He set up the arrangement. I rather liked it. I'd go to Bloomingdale's and buy clothes to wear just for my dates with Roman. I remember a pair of short wide orange palazzo pants with a matching sash. I wore it with white pumps and a long-sleeved white tee. I thought it very chic. So did Roman. He was enamored of me. I was his first New York City girl. And Jewish to boot. And he wasn't. And it wasn't an issue, because he wasn't someone Jewish or Not Jewish. He was Roman. And that was perfect. However, he was still an East Sider, something bigger for me to overcome, but I was working on it.

The first night we went out, he told the waitress in Little Italy we were going to fly to Toronto for dessert. He knew a place that made great cannolis. I was wearing a purple scarf my friend, Fred, had brought back for me from Spain. Roman said it became a prop for me. A third hand. He thought it exciting that I was an actress. I thought it exciting that he made a living. That he was sensitive with a sincere edge. That he had big green eyes and wavy brown hair, and a voice that threaded together so many pieces of what the world had to offer.

"I tell the guy who comes by with the coffee in the morning that he and I are just the same," Roman told me one night over a Courvoisier.

He felt guilty about his success. He thought he didn't deserve it. That wasn't true. He wasn't on a free ride. He was working hard. He was trading the stocks. He was earning the money. It wasn't Roman's fault he got there by expertly kicking a ball instead of planning it out. It wasn't Roman's fault he came from a loving, not-well-to-do Catholic family in Boston and did well for himself. It also wasn't Roman's fault that he had outgrown his post-college girlfriend, Julie, who was still in Boston going back to nursing school. It wasn't his fault he was moving on.

A party. My acting class. Me in a short jean skirt, red tights. Roman in a purple-and-blue-striped shirt. A Heineken in one hand, the other wrapped around me. Us on a terrace that wrapped around Manhattan. A great night.

Now the night. The one to remember. My birthday. Roman said that there were two types of people. Those who liked to ignore their birthdays, and those who liked a big fuss. Which was I? When he found out it was decided that he'd pick out a fabulous place, while I went off to Bloomingdale's and picked out a fabulous dress.

I felt victorious as I combed through the racks of

dresses in the Nightlife department, remembering years of birthdays and birthday dresses. This one was going to take the cake!

My birthday had always been a big deal to me. An event. It started in elementary school with a birthday tradition in my class that was passed on from Joni Wolf's older sister, Debbie. We would take a bow used to decorate a package, attach pieces of ribbon to the back of it and put an ornament at the end of each ribbon. If a girl were turning eight, there would be eight ribbons with, let's say, Tootsie Rolls tied to the bottom of each ribbon. They were theme corsages. Candy, stationery, kitchenware. My favorite was from Rachel Smith the year I turned ten. Ten pink, plastic hair curlers at the ends of the ribbons with a little note saying, "After your birthday I want my rollers back." But by that time a girl could barely carry the weight of all those corsages, each with ten heavy ribbons and one for good luck. Especially when tent dresses were all the rave.

My mother and I had shopped and shopped until I found the perfect Kelly-green ultrapleated tent dress with white polka dots. When I put it on that morning, I spun round and round in front of the mirror watching the dress whirl. I looked like I was about to take off! I got to school and all my friends had made me great corsages. Bazooka Joe bubble gum, pencils, spoons. So now all of the very lovely, but *very* heavy corsages were pulling my dress forward, and when I stood up to answer a question, Murray Binder, who was seated behind me, screamed out, "Oooh, look, she has matching polka-dot panties too!"

"They're not panties," I turned around and screamed at Murray, totally embarrassed, bent over my dress, supporting it with my arms so the weight of the whole thing didn't make me fall over completely. "They came with it. It's part of the outfit."

"Where'd you get it?" Rina Biller snidely yelled out. "Alex or Bloomie's?" Rina knew full well that I had not gone shopping in The City at the wonderful and exclusive Bloomingdale's. Rina knew my mother always took me to Alexander's in Rego Park, Queens, where I invariably got nauseous from the ringing bells, the sales tables and the fights in the overcrowded parking lot.

"Stop this excitement," Mrs. Gorsky hollered. "This is stupidity."

I stood mortified and angry that our crazy teacher was ruining my birthday.

"Take those bows off and put them away. You can take them home at three o'clock. What's the matter with you kids? Doesn't anyone care about what's going on in this world?"

Mrs. Gorsky paused for a moment. I looked at her red hair standing up in the middle of her head like Bozo's. Her dress came to below her knee. There was a run in her stocking, and her black laced shoes looked like my grandmother's.

"Quiet!" Mrs. Gorsky went to her desk and picked up a small black transistor radio. She stood in the aisle between rows two and three, kept the radio to her ear and listened. The class was quiet. Watching. I was in the last seat of row three, soundlessly storing my corsages in the empty desk until the three o'clock freedom bell rang.

"No! No!" Mrs. Gorsky let out a scream. "ACHHH, NOOOO!!!" She threw the radio in the floor. We watched it break into pieces, the same as when she had thrown chalk, pointers and once Joshua Morris's eyeglasses. We were afraid of her. No one would speak.

"The world is insane. My son goes to Columbia. There are uprisings all over the campus. They took over the administration building. He can't get an education."

I carefully looked at my corsages inside the back desk as evidence of an innocent childhood. I was only ten years old and today was my birthday.

A week later Bobby Kennedy was shot. Every few years since I had been in kindergarten there were major assassinations. I watched other people mourn John and Malcolm and Martin. But this one, Bobby, felt different. This one felt real, and this one really hurt.

The following year we stopped making our own corsages and upgraded to the local florist. For seventy-five cents, the florist would make a little boutonniere out of a carnation. Now each girl looked like a bouquet on her birthday, but no one toppled over. By the time we went to junior high our birthday traditions had dissolved. It no longer mattered if I shopped at "Alex" or "Bloomie's." Girls were finally granted permission to wear pants. With all the marches and sit-ins and antiwar rallies I often felt like I'd never see another birthday. I'd never see another spring. But the world kept ticking and somehow it all kept going.

Looking at myself now while trying on these dresses, I was pleased with the woman who reflected back three times in the triangular mirror. I had grown up and I could do what I wanted, date whom I wanted and shop where I chose. Another spring was ending. Summer beginning. I left Bloomie's with the perfect dress. Baby blue. Silk. Bare shoulders. High heels. A matching shawl of pale blue chiffon.

My birthday night arrived with torrential weather. Rain. Pouring rain. Thunder and lightning. An emergency at work. A last-minute call.

"Jeans, okay?" he asked.

I looked at the blue silk dress laid out on the bed before I hung it back in the closet. Another time. The rain did not wash out Roman.

"Sure," I said into the cordless phone as I unhooked a pair of jeans from its hanger. I wore them with a white tank top. A fringe of lace over the bust. A peach cardigan. A yellow slicker. Roman was knocked out by the outfit.

"What outfit?" Rain clothes. I didn't see. I just felt. Beautiful.

After eating Mexican we walked up Second Avenue. People. Mist. Dogs. Restaurants. A taxi whizzing by.

"Come here, young lady." Roman pulled me to the side. Fluorescent light from a candy store. A kiss. Not just a kiss. A dissolve. Lips. So soft, hard, so warm, slow. Long and forever and so quickly a change. Between us. Together. Falling together into something else. A burrow that enveloped us.

"Is this how they do it in New York?" he whispered that night.

"This is how I do it with you," I said. "I will never forget this. Ever."

I cooked him dinners and he brought wine and flowers.

"I thought I should bring you something else," he said one night, handing me a bouquet of purple tulips. "I went into Barneys and looked around. I thought, 'Would she like this belt?' But then I decided to bring the flowers."

He helped me memorize a script. Roman hadn't acted since grade school. It was a good thing! But he loved doing it with me, and I loved sharing my world. He played hooky from work and we explored the city. We'd sit at an outdoor café sipping wine and watching the people pass. Roman was in awe of the city in the middle of the day in the middle of the week.

"I never see this," he said, sliding his hand up and down my thigh. "I'm inside at work, but the world is going on. The city never sleeps."

He saw Manhattan as if it were brand-new. I filled up with pride as if I had built it. We went boating in Central Park. We hiked up a path in the park that made us feel like we were backpacking together in Europe. At the top. Looking down on the city. Looking out. Green trim of the Plaza Hotel accented the lake like a picture frame. He stood behind me and moved his hands possessively over my body. I was happy and I told him. And then he told me.

"I'm being transferred back to Boston."

The weeks that followed were sad. Every great moment slipped into the next and it slipped into time that would move Roman from my present to my past. Unless.

"My agent called today to submit me for a role in a play," I told him over one of our last dinners. We were sharing a piece of apple pie, drinking decaf coffee and brandy. I went into the bathroom three times during dinner to splash water under my eyes to disguise the swelling from the tears.

"That's great. When is the audition?" Roman had learned the lingo.

"I don't know if I will actually get one. The casting

director has to select which actors they will give appointments to after they get the agent submissions. But I really, really want to read for this," I said.

"Is it a great part?"

"Who cares? The show would be six months of work. In Boston."

Silence.

Awkward.

Head down.

Shut down.

"What? I thought you'd be happy."

He took a long time to answer. "Don't give up your dreams for me, Karrie."

"Don't what?" I felt so betrayed. Misunderstood. "My agent submitted me for a role. For a job. A job! I'm not exactly chasing you to Boston. Are you afraid of that? What's going on?"

He felt guilty. He was supposed to stay at home and marry Julie and raise a family. Instead he came to New York. He loved it. He met someone new. No one approved.

"Did you ask for this transfer?" I needed to know.

"No," said Roman. "I didn't. But it happened. And it makes me wonder why."

"So do it. Go back. Trade stocks. Make money. And in a year ask to be transferred back here. It's not such a big deal."

Roman wasn't so sure. He was sure I was special. But

he was unsure how we fit. He was still pondering the question the day he left. Ninety-five-degree heat, a dog day of August, apartment packed, boxes picked up from UPS, two suitcases loaded into the trunk of cab, Roman ready for the airport.

"I'll miss you, young lady. Move on. And keep a little mystery when you meet someone new. Let them know you slowly. Be happy."

"I don't want to be mysterious. I don't want to meet someone new. I don't want to move on. I like you."

"Me, too," he said as the cab took off, and Roman flew away. I walked back home through the park. I knew time would turn Roman into a memory I could live with, and it would be some time before that happened. But it did.

Eleven months later he called from Boston.

"Do you remember me?" he asked.

Yes, I remembered. I remembered well. The voice. Those pieces. I hoped they would thread together the sound of Roman's transfer back to New York.

"Do you remember me?" I asked.

"I sure do."

"Tell me what you remember…."

Roman paused. "I wanted to tell you that I'm marrying Julie."

I paused.

"It's right for me," he said. "It's right for my life here,

with the company. Our families are here. I'm sorry. I don't feel I was fair to you."

I wondered if he had been fair to himself. There was so much in New York he had yet to discover. Inside the city. Inside himself.

"Do you love her?" I held my breath hoping the right answer would not hurt too much.

"She would follow me anywhere," he said. "Look, if you ever need anything. Money, anything, you can always contact me. Always. I'll always remember you."

"I'll never forget."

I never have. Sometimes on a moist and balmy New York night, when I take a walk, I can still see all the colors of the Roman rainbow.

My Worst Date... Almost

The day after the party he called. I was bedridden, feeling comatose from the twenty-four-hour bug that had hit six hours earlier.

"I was so glad you gave your card to my sister," he said.

I'd thought his sister was his wife. They were holding hands all night.

"Can we go out?"

"Okay," I mumbled in my delirium.

"I'm so anxious to see you," Arthur blathered. "I've never been this excited before. How's Thursday? What do you like to do for fun? Am I too forward?"

"No. No."

"Do you think it's a possibility we're going to have a great time?" he questioned. "I want you to come to this date really open with positive feelings. I'll talk to you before Thursday. I can't wait. This will be the best date of our lives."

We never went out. He never called.

Arthur must have literally burst from anticipation.

The Clan of the Cab Bears

"Need some help?" the homeless man asked while he watched me schlep my bags from the Airport Bus Center through the Port Authority.

"No, thanks," I said, kicking the flowered one that was bigger than me and wouldn't stay on my shoulder. The yellow cabs were all lined up on Eighth Avenue, just waiting to be hailed.

"We have to make a quick stop," I told the cabby while I stood to the side and watched him put my baggage in the back seat. He was a big, chubby guy with wild, messy brown hair in baggy jeans and flannel shirt.

"It better be fast," he said.

"Why? You have someplace to go?" I asked him, thinking that after he dropped me off, he'd probably like to go back twenty years, run over to the student union, lead a peace march and drop some acid.

"Well, no," he said. "I just don't feel like stopping."

I opened the door to get out.

"But I will," he said.

"Thanks a bunch."

We sped between the traffic up the avenue.

"You just get back from a trip?" he asked.

"Uh, yeah."

"Where'd you go?" he asked, stopping the cab at a red light.

Through the window, I watched a man shoving leaflets at passersby.

"Check it out. Check it out," he said, hoping to entice them into entering the House of Heavenly Delights. I looked up and saw an enlarged color photo of two women having their way with each other, while a man, dressed as the devil, held a pitchfork over their heads.

"Florida," I said.

"Vacation?"

He was turning out to be pretty chatty, this... I looked to the front seat to see the name on his identification card. Alan Cohen.

"Passover," I answered. Mom, Henry and I flew down to spend the holiday with Aunt Cookie and Uncle Sy.

It had become a new tradition since my aunt and uncle had retired there five years ago. Uncle Sy's Passover *seder* was so different from the holiday I remembered as a little girl when Grandpa Lou was still alive. He would recite the whole *haggadah* in Hebrew. My cousins and I would twist and turn in our seats for what seemed like a century until, finally, we could eat. After the meal, Grandpa Lou would hide the Afikoman, the magic piece of *matzoh,* and give a quarter to the kid who found it. All of us kids would search the Brooklyn apartment high and low only to find that, once again, our grandfather had hidden it in his suit jacket.

Some years later, after Grandpa Lou had passed on, Sy had stood at the head of his Long Island table and flipped on a small tape recorder. After a series of static sounds, Sy's voice had filled the room. "Your mission tonight, if you choose to accept, is to skip the formalities and go directly to the Passover meal catered à la Cookie." Everyone thought it was very funny, except for Grandma Rose, who was missing her husband and the days when "the holidays" meant her house.

"Yeah, Passover. Yeah," said the cabby with the recognition I expected. "The folks glad to see you?"

"Thrilled." There seemed no point explaining my folks didn't really live there.

"Boca?" Alan Cohen asked in shorthand.

"West Palm."

"Nice."

Alan Cohen probably had family in Boca, I thought, and wished that he had gone down for Passover to see his parents. They probably lived in a development with two swimming pools, four tennis courts and a clubhouse. Alan would always think he was going to play tennis when he visited, but it never happened. He probably never went to see them much, being the black sheep of the family. Alan had probably had great potential. He was probably the salutatorian of his graduating class at Midwood High School in Brooklyn. His parents had thought he would be a doctor, or at very least, a dentist. But he went away to college, did too many drugs and never got out of the Sixties.

"So…" he said. He was determined to keep the conversation going. "Does your family do a whole *seder* thing, or do you just eat?"

I pictured Sy standing at the head of the table wearing a blue satin yarmulke on his head, a gold Jewish star around his neck and a yellow-and-white kitchen apron tied behind his waist.

"Why is this night different from all other nights?" he asked. "Because tonight we're not going to ask the four questions. Every year you ask me the same questions, and for thirty years I'm giving the same answers. So, if you don't know the answers by now, you're out of luck."

"We did a little *seder*," I told Alan the interested cabdriver. "You know, the usual stuff."

Sy was in rare form this year. "Now I want everyone to listen to the instructions on how we will proceed with tonight's *seder*. First, this will be an abbreviated version of the abbreviated version we generally have. Only, I will say the blessing over the wine and that'll be it. There's no reason for us to go around the table and have everyone say the *kiddush*. So I will say the blessing and you all say Amen. Are you with me so far?"

"Like what's your usual?" asked Alan. "How many minutes is yours? Ours were like about fifteen minutes. Me and my cousin, Ricky, always tried to sneak in some decent wine. That Manisohewitz crap is not anybody's idea of a great vintage year."

"I know," I said. "You know what else is funny? They always have the yarmulkes from all the affairs they went to over the years. There were three white velvet ones that said 'Wedding of Mark and Mindy Sokoloff, May 15, 1982,' written in gold and nobody knew who the Sokoloffs were!"

"I wonder if anybody still has the ones from my Bar Mitzvah?" Alan Cohen wondered aloud. "Oh. Did you use the coffee books?"

"Yes! What is that about?" This was turning into a fun cab ride. "How appropriate is it that a coffee company publishes the most popular Haggadah! You read this horrific tale of the Jews fleeing Egypt with a picture of a piece of *matzoh* on the front of the book, and a cup of hot coffee on the back!"

"Well, we as a people like to eat!"

"No kidding," I said, glimpsing a look at Alan's back taking up a broad part of the front seat.

"So, what do you do?" he asked me.

"Well, Alan," I said, feeling it might be a little personal to use his name, but also as if I knew the cloth from which he was cut. "Why don't you guess?"

"Drugs?"

"That's it! You got it on the first try. Amazing!"

"Really? You're kidding."

"Of course I'm kidding. Do I look like a drug dealer? Look, we're here," I said, pointing to the white doorman building on Eighth Avenue. "Stop. I'll be just a second." The cab stopped near 52nd Street. I ran in and picked up the yellow manila envelope that said FOR PICKUP—K. KLINE from the doorman.

"What'd you get?" he asked when I got back into the cab.

"I had to pick up a script."

"An actress!" he said, driving up Eighth Avenue.

I received a last-minute call from a casting director asking me to fill in for an actress who wasn't going to be able to do the reading. I pulled out the script and started to read. The play was a political farce about a presidential campaign that totally revolved around junk food.

It was called *Eat This*. I flipped to where Mac, the campaign manager, and the candidate come into the diner where they always eat and come up with their campaign strategies. In this scene, Mac and the waitress, Addie— that would be me—try to convince the candidate to hold rap sessions at fast-food chains across the country and give the voters free food. The casting director said they hoped to bring the show to Broadway. It was a stroke of luck that I got in on the project.

"I'm sorry," said Alan, breaking the silence.

I realized I had suddenly stopped talking after having that whole Passover conversation. Now I felt guilty. Well, that was ridiculous. I didn't have to entertain the cab-driver. I was a passenger, he was doing his job and now I wanted to read my script.

"Sorry for what?" I looked up at the back of Alan's wavy head

"For thinking you were dealing."

"Don't worry about it. It happens all the time." I held the script high so he would see me reading in his rear-view mirror. I was way too involved in this relationship.

"So… Uh… You're an actress?"

"Uh-huh." I didn't want to talk anymore.

"What have you been in lately?"

"Nothing. Really." I always hated that question.

"You have an audition?"

"Uh-huh." Here we go. Why was I so friendly before?

"What's it for?"

I put the script down. It seemed easier to have the conversation than not to. I'd be home in a few minutes and I could read then. What could it hurt to talk a little more to Alan Cohen. I was sure I had known him all my life. He seemed like a boy who would have summered at my bungalow colony in the Catskills when we were kids. Someone a few years older than me, I would have looked up to for a while just because he was there and he was older. Someone who would have been a counselor at the day camp and led you in Color War when you were little, then put that stuff down, grew his hair long and tried to get you to smoke when you were big. Someone whose mother would say she didn't understand him, as she played her Bingo card in the casino on Wednesday nights, and waited for her husband to come back upstate after working in the city all week, because she couldn't handle Alan alone.

"Do you do anything in addition to driving a cab?" I asked, curious to see if I did have him all cut out.

"What do you mean?"

"Anything particular that you aspire to do?" I figured him for a comic book collector.

"Does anybody ever get what they want?" he said. "An actor, a musician. Even a doctor or lawyer. Does anybody really get what they aspire to in life? Does it really pay to even care?"

"I'm sorry. Just making conversation. I didn't mean to be condescending," I said. We were gliding past 72nd Street, a few blocks from my apartment. "Driving a cab is great. Anything you want to do is great. Really."

"You think so?" he asked, turning the corner on my block.

"Oh sure," I said. "People should do whatever makes them happy."

"Do you have a boyfriend?" he asked.

"YES," I said. "Yes. Yes, I do!"

He pulled up in front of my building. The meter clicked off.

Alan Cohen turned and faced me. "You have a steady boyfriend?" he asked. His eyes looked vacant behind the dirty divider that was meant to protect the people in the front seat from the people in the back.

"Very steady," I said. I took a ten from my wallet, shoved it in the tray and dipped it toward the front. "Can I have back three dollars?"

Alan Cohen didn't move.

"How about you keep your money and have a date with me instead?"

"I really can't do that. I have this boyfriend. I can't. May I have my change?" That's what you get for being friendly, I thought. The change wasn't forthcoming, so I collected my bags and opened the door. Alan Cohen was standing in the gutter, blocking my exit from his cab.

"Are you going to go out with me or not?"

My eyes came level with his stomach. It was protruding through the buttons on his dirty navy-and-green flannel shirt.

"I need to get out of this cab," I said as calmly as possible.

"Oh yeah?" he said, getting in the back seat and slamming the door behind him. He threw my flowered bag to the floor of the cab. It had been the only thing between us.

"So, you think you could go for a guy like me?" he asked, leaning over me.

"Alan…" I didn't know what the hell to do.

"I really like how you say my name." Alan Cohen leaned in closer. I could tell he had consumed a few beers. "Say it again."

I inched backward against the other door, hoping I could open it behind me. He pulled my hands into his and gripped them tightly.

"Say it again. You're really hot. Say it again."

"Uh, Alan," I said, trying to grasp what was happening. A few possible scenarios crossed my mind, none of them particularly appealing. "Alan," I repeated, trying to appease rather than seduce.

"Kiss me," he said, moving closer toward me. I could feel his breath on my neck. I thought I would puke. "Come on…"

"Stop it, Alan. Just stop! What's the matter with you? Get off me. Leave me alone!"

He didn't move away, but he didn't move closer.

I tried to figure out how much trouble I was in. I didn't know what to do when I found out, but I searched his eyes trying to assess if Alan Cohen was Nebish Gone Astray or On Track Psychopath. I opted for number one. We were both breathing harder. Obviously for different reasons.

"You were flirting with me," he said.

"I was talking to you."

"Bullshit."

"I was…friendly."

We were face-to-face in a stare-off. No one was winning.

"Why won't you go out with me? Don't you like me?"

"I've known you fifteen minutes. That's not long enough to like or dislike you. I just got home from Florida. I hailed a cab. Please…be a *mensch* and just let me out of here."

"If you weren't going out with that guy would you go out with me?"

"Perhaps," I said, wondering if someone had once dropped him on his head for him to wind up like this. "Perhaps if you asked like a gentleman instead of scaring the shit out of me."

"Are you scared?"

"Yes! Of course I'm scared. I'd have to be lobotomized not to be scared."

"I didn't mean to scare you," Alan Cohen said. He sat up straight and tucked his shirttails into his khaki pants. "I just wanted you to like me."

"I think you can use some improvement on your courtship skills, Alan," I said, feeling out of danger although I was not yet out of the woods. "Some men bring flowers and candy. Wine and dine a girl. You trap me in the back seat of your taxi, act like you're going to rape me, and, by the way, now you owe me money because suddenly I don't feel like tipping."

He looked right through me and got out of the cab. I grabbed my bags and bolted out the door. I could feel my hands shaking underneath my bravado. I approached the first step down into my building. A hand touched the back of my neck.

"AHHHHHHHHHH," I screamed. My bags rolled down the cement stairs. I could see my tampons tumbling over my curling iron.

"Don't scream. I won't hurt you. I'm sorry," he said, putting his pudgy hand in his pocket. "Really."

"It's okay," I said. My heart beat so hard I thought I'd find it on the stairs next to the tampons and the curling iron. "I have to go."

"I just don't want you to think bad of me," he said. "Do you like me?"

Out of my right eye I watched my blow-dryer fall out of my bag and cascade down. I heard a small crash.

"Yeah, Alan, I like you. In fact, I'm crazy about you. Jesus Christ!" I screamed. "JUST LEAVE ME ALONE!"

He ran into the street back to his cab. The engine had been going all this time. I knelt to pick up my broken belongings. My script was still in the cab. Fortunately, the envelope with my name on it was in my purse.

"Are you absolutely sure?" I heard him yell from the street. "I live in Park Slope. We probably won't ever see each other again. I can leave my number on the car over here or, if you…"

Alan Cohen was still yelling when I rang for the elevator. I couldn't make out the end of the sentence.

wherefore Art Thou?

Valentine's Day
Upper East Side, NYC 1994

"Have whatever you want," Henry told me. "You're our little girl, it's Valentine's Day, and your mother and I don't want you to be alone."

"Look, Karrie," Millie said. "There's a Valentine's Day Special. You can have a tender, juicy chicken breast à la Romeo with artichokes and mushrooms. You're the artichoke eater here, and an Idaho baked potato with fresh asparagus and hollandaise. I don't like hollandaise sauce, it has no taste, but you like that. And it comes with dessert. Juliet Surprise: A chocolate brownie topped with whipped cream and a cherry. How does that sound?"

"Chicken and artichokes make me think of Jack," I

said. I reached for the miniature blackboard that had the daily specials written in pink chalk.

"Why are we talking about Jack?" asked Millie.

"Oh, I don't know," I said, contemplating the chicken breast. "Maybe because he was my boyfriend for a year, and it's only six weeks since we broke up and I'm despondent about the whole thing. Maybe that's why. But I could be wrong."

"It's Valentine's Day," said Henry. "We're all together. Why are you even thinking about him when you're with us?"

"I don't know. I can't imagine what came over me."

We were seated in a corner nook of the heated indoor café. A candle illuminated the table. Outside on Second Avenue couples walked by, huddled in down coats, romping through the gray of the city, hailing cabs and kissing. I turned to my parents. "What are you going to have?"

"I'm going to have the fish," Henry said.

"Me too," echoed Millie.

"So will I." I made it unanimous.

"Since when do you eat fish?" asked Henry.

"Always. I always eat fish. What is the fish tonight?"

"Snapper," Henry said. "Red snapper. You like that?" I nodded.

"You're sure now?" Henry grilled me. "I don't mind ordering anything you want, but I want to make sure you like it. Don't do it on my account."

I took a deep breath. This would have been Jack's and

my second Valentine's Day. Last year at this time I was so excited. It was still early, we'd only been dating two months. Jack surprised me with a warm blanket, a cold bottle of champagne and an easy climb in Central Park to a rock that overlooked the lake. It was a little cold, but totally romantic! This year I thought I'd cook an indoor dinner, but we broke up soon after Christmas. That disaster. Somehow I knew from the start it could never work. A Jewish actress and a born-again Christian comedian. It would have been easier to not have the relationship and to have just sold the movie rights.

Jack and I met at a second staged reading of *Eat This* just before Christmas in 1992. *Eat This* still looked like it could happen for Broadway, but the money the producers thought was there was not. In almost two years, there had been four readings with one more to go. My part had been cut to shreds, but I was still a contender so I was happy. Anyway, the second reading, the one where I met Jack, was the best. I say this objectively, even though my part *was* a lot bigger in that version! I was flying that night, and really up when we all went out after for a drink. My friend, Jane, was dating Philip Moore, an actor in the show, and came to the reading. And Philip invited his stand-up friend, Jack Whitney, whom I'd once seen emcee at The Comic Corner. The four of us got a booth and a round of drinks. Jane and Philip were pretty cozy, and I thought Jack was cute and funny. It was a pretty instant attraction. After they left, we lingered over a glass of Merlot and the rest, as they like to say, was history.

"It comes with dessert," said Henry. "You'll have the dessert too?" he asked, bringing me back.

"Yes, she'll have the dessert," my mother answered for me. "She needs to put on a little weight. I think you lost some weight. What do you think? Your face looks thin."

"I think I lost some weight." It felt easier to agree.

The waiter came over to our table. He was a tall, gangly-looking man with an earring in his left ear. He wore wire glasses and a befuddled expression.

"Three snappers," Henry told him. "And make them all on the special."

The waiter smiled pleasantly and looked at me.

"Don't I know you from The Comic Corner?"

I had no recollection of him whatsoever.

"I took Jack Whitney's 'Intro to Stand-Up' class at the Learning Annex and we went to see him perform. You're his girlfriend, aren't you?"

"Well..."

"I wasn't sure at first it was you. We went again last night and it looked like your hair was lighter, but you were sitting close to the stage with Jack and we were in the back. It's hard to see at night. Up close, though, I remember you. He was great, wasn't he? All that new material about all the bad relationship stuff that happens on the holidays, and accepting Santa into your heart."

I twisted the swizzle stick from my drink.

"Well, let me put your order in. I'm sure you want to get over to the club early for the special Valentine's Day show."

I stared at my place setting and took a sip of my Virgin Mary.

"That was unnecessary," said Millie.

"He obviously found a new one," said Henry.

"Did you change the message on your machine yet?" my mother asked.

"I'll do it soon. It's funny," I said.

"It's not funny, Karrie. It's pathetic. Change it tonight."

The message played in my ear.

Hi, this is Karrie. Jack and I just broke up so I can't come to the phone right now. Actually, I can't even get out of bed. But if you leave your name and number, someday I'll get back to you.

Beeeeep.

"And after you change your message, set your alarm so you wake up at a decent hour tomorrow," Millie continued.

I had made the mistake of confessing to my mom that unless I had an audition I'd been sleeping half the day away, waking at 12:59 p.m. in order to make it into the living room by one, just in time to watch my favorite soap, *All My Problems*.

"Maybe she was just a date," I said. "Or it could have been a friend. Who says he has a new girlfriend? Anyway, what's the difference?"

Silence.

"I spoke with Aunt Cookie," said Millie. "She said she spoke to her friend, Phyllis, and her son Seth, the chiropractor, is still talking about you from last Passover. I know he's not exactly your type…"

"No."

"Just for an evening out," Henry chimed in. "No one's saying marriage, but just to get out. There's no reason for a young girl like yourself to stay home alone staring at the four walls."

"I'm not staring at anything. Besides, he's a geek. He's a nerd. He even liked the Manischewitz wine. No."

The waiter came by and served the salads. Henry reached for the pepper.

"No salt," said Millie.

"No salt," said Henry. "Pepper. I'm just using pepper."

"He's not allowed to have salt," she told me.

"He's not having salt," I said.

"I'm having pepper, Millie."

"See, he's having pepper, Ma."

"That's okay. Pepper he's allowed to have."

"I have an audition tomorrow," I said as the food arrived. The fish stared up at me, alongside the baby red potatoes, the stewed zucchini and the waiter. "For a commercial."

"What's it for?" asked the waiter. My new best friend.

"Some fast-food chicken chain. I'm a perky waitress." I smiled at him to prove my point.

"Well, *bon appetit* and *bon chance*," said the waiter. He winked at me before he walked away.

"This is good," I said.

"Very good," said Henry.

"I like mine too," said Millie.

"Anyway, I have to make it an early night," I said before I barely started my meal, let alone finished it. "You know, with the audition in the morning."

"It's all right," said Millie. "I'm tired too. I don't mind an early night myself."

I watched my mother delicately mash her potatoes. Her pink nail polish shone under the candlelight, and her diamond ring glimmered. She was trying so hard to be nice to me. So was Henry. I was so unhappy about Jack. I just felt so bad.

"No, Ma. No rush. Really."

"It's okay," Millie said through knowing eyes. "We don't have to get indigestion, but I am tired."

"I'm tired too," I said.

I took my fork and mashed the baby red potatoes, pasting them together with some of the snapper. I was tired, I thought. I really, truly was.

That's All, Folks

I walked my parents to the garage to get the car and watched them take off down Second Avenue, the fumes from the engine trailing behind. I walked south to get the crosstown bus back to my apartment, but felt a tug that pulled me in the opposite direction.

My oversized orange fake fur wrapped around me like a warm blanket and I pulled my black earmuffs down around my neck so I could hear the street sounds. I walked past liquor stores selling wines to woo with. Past a Hallmark gift shop where the window displayed the little redheaded girl sending Charlie Brown a valentine. The next thing I knew I was standing in front of The

Comic Corner. I looked up at The Comic Corner logo. To go or to stay?

I was about to go. I was about to stay. For a moment I felt like I lost my balance. I was in the circus, walking a tightrope. I was struggling to keep on a straight course, but I could not. I looked around for help. I saw a man below me. I waved. I kept waving and waving, but he never looked up. It was clear that I was going to fall. But I didn't. I was at the end of the rope. It was over and it became instantly clear I had to get out of there. I had to escape before I found out what more there was to lose.

I turned away and the door slammed against my back.

"Ouch!"

I spun around and came face-to-face with Jack.

I stood, frozen, taking him in. Jack's blond hair was longer in the back, and he had started growing a beard. The beard was darker than the hair on his head. It looked like he had dyed either one or the other.

"Oh my God. Hi. Hello. Jack. I never expected to run into you."

Jack stood and looked at me. Actually, he stared.

"It was an accident," I said. "Kind of."

He smiled as if he understood that it was. A collision of sorts. Of which sort, he was uncertain.

Being in Jack's presence for the first time in almost six weeks was like finding that glove you gave up on. You had lost one so you couldn't wear the other. You could try, but one hand was always left out in the cold. Even though there were new gloves to be bought in stores all over the city, some of them even on sale, none would ever be that pair. None of them would be broken in. Comfortable. But you wouldn't throw out the mate. You just kept it with your hats and scarves as a reminder. A hope. And then one day, when you were moving the couch to get the pen that had dropped behind it, there it was. Your glove. Your favorite one. It had been waiting for you to reclaim it, you just didn't know where to look. And later that day, when you went to the deli, you slipped the pair on in the elevator, and a warmth and familiarity consoled your body. You were only going out for a container of milk, but however far you went, you felt fine.

I smiled in spite of myself. Then I laughed.

"What's so funny?" asked Jack.

"You!"

"Me? I thought we broke up because you didn't laugh anymore."

"Did I say that?"

Jack nodded yes.

"When did I say that? You're lying," I chided.

I waited for him to laugh, like in the old days, but he didn't. I waited for him to do something, anything, so I could feel normal.

"How was your set?"

"Great. They loved me."

"They always do, Jack."

"You always used to laugh at my stuff and then you stopped."

"No."

"Yeah. That last time you were here."

"Well, we were breaking up. I was upset. I think you're the best."

"You do? You really do?"

His eyes softened and his lips turned up into a smile. "So, little Miss Orange Coat, you think I'm the best?" He extended his arm and spun me into him like I was Ginger Rogers. He dipped me over the cracks in the sidewalk, then dramatically pulled me up. He parodied the song "You Don't Send Me Flowers Anymore." Looking deliberately into my eyes, he sang from his heart.

You don't think I'm funny anymore—

I threw my arms around his neck. He picked me up.

"Oooo, Ouch, Oooo!" Jack mimicked Curly from the Three Stooges. "It's a giant Twinkie," he said, poking at my coat.

"What goes good with Twinkies?" I whispered in his ear.

Jack's eyes looked at me. Then he looked through me, as if to answer a question without having to actually ask it. Again his lips broke into a smile. I laughed.

"I haven't felt this good since we broke up," I said, laughing.

"Which time?" he asked.

"This time. The last time. How many times did we break up?"

"Altogether? Over the whole year?" he asked.

"Uh-huh." I nuzzled my head into him so that my hair warmed his neck.

"We broke up three times," Jack said.

"Right. But that would be counting the time in the Chinese restaurant and I thought we said we weren't going to count that time."

"Didn't we break up twice in a Chinese restaurant?" he asked me.

"Yes."

"I thought so. Once in ChowFun in Chinatown, and once somewhere around here."

"Szechuan East."

"Szechuan East. So which one doesn't count? Szechuan East?"

"No. ChowFun," I said. "Szechuan East counts."

"Remember we got those great fortunes." He put me down as he recalled them. "Mine said, 'You will soon go from rags to riches,' and yours said, 'Something you don't think is possible will soon surprise you!'"

"Right! So we figured why break up? This was an omen for everything to change."

"What were we fighting about again, hon?" he asked.

"Oh, your career, my career, competition, money, marriage, religion, children. The usual."

"I knew it wasn't anything important." Jack moved into me and put his arms around my waist. He rested his chin on top of my head. His lower lip was slightly chapped and his red scarf hung loosely around his neck.

"This is new," I said as I untied and retied it.

"Yep. My mom made it for me. Remember. For Christmas. This was the gift that wasn't finished that she said she'd send. She made one for you, too. She sent it even though I told her we broke up. You know, just in case we got back together. Mom's a real optimist."

"How's your dad?" I asked while I pictured Jack's mother sitting in her kitchen, shucking oysters for her famous oyster dressing.

"Good. Still a gentleman farmer. He also sent a book for you on Jews for Jesus."

Oy gevalt, I thought. "So, Jack... You've got a lot of stuff for me in your apartment!"

"I guess I do."

We took a breather. We let it all sink in. Whatever it was, and looked at each other a long while before we kissed. My lips brushed his cheeks inside his right dimple. They moved down his straight nose and back up to his green eyes to gently tug on his long lashes. Jack's breath felt warm on my neck. His hands were inside my hair.

"Let's get a cab home," said Jack, and before I could blink we were sailing through the park going west on 79th Street. We were silent until we got out of the cab on Amsterdam Avenue. I turned to Jack, put my hands in my pockets and started to walk to my apartment. He took my left hand out from inside my orange coat and held it tightly as he walked, quietly, alongside me. Saying anything would spoil the moment. This moment was swell. I didn't want to spoil it about thinking about what would happen next, because it was "the moment after" I was afraid of. I thought I had come too far in the healing process to blow it all just for one night of delicious, passionate, uninterrupted, erotic love.

Then again…

Actually, I hadn't healed that much. Quite frankly, I had been pining. Obsessing. I'd practically been carrying Jack around in my pocket. If I spent the night with Jack, I would still wake up with yearning as I watched happy couples stand in movie lines, but at least I would have a memory of a nourishing, tactile and filling night.

And what if I got hit by a truck on the way to my audition tomorrow? Then I would have given up the last Valentine's Day of my whole entire life with my best male friend and lover, to date, just because it wasn't permanent. What was permanent in this world? Hardly anything. This was the moment to take and to seize. Spending the night with Jack Whitney was not only the smartest thing I could do, in fact, it was my only option.

I turned to him as we passed an open deli.

"You want me to get those Chips Ahoys you like?"

"I'm cutting back on sweets," said Jack, placing his free hand on his stomach.

"Oh. That's nice."

I took out my keys and opened the double door leading into the lobby.

Gomez, the super, was wheeling out a barrel of garbage with a hand truck. He was wearing a red bandana around his neck and used it to periodically wipe his moustache.

"I fix the kitchen sink for you, Miss Karrie," he said. "It won't be leaky anymore."

"Thanks, Gomez."

"Nice to see you again, Mr. Jack. You been away making people laugh?"

"I like to think so," he said, opening the elevator door for me to get in.

He pressed the button numbered three, with the assurance of someone who knew where he was going and where he had been. I stood on the other side of the elevator. Leaning against the banister I took solace in deciding that I really wasn't in my life, I was just watching the dailies.

Jack unbuttoned the big, black buttons on my coat. I unzipped his leather jacket and slipped my cold hands up the back of his sweater. His skin felt warm against my palms. He pressed close to me and filled the gap between us.

With a sudden burst, I jumped onto Jack, straddling

his waist with my legs. He fell backward, me on top of him. Our bodies made a loud thump as we landed. I fell all over him, my body pressing into Jack's under the canopy of my fake fur. Jack pulled me toward him, massaging my shoulders as my breasts dangled over his face. Our mouths seemed to search each others for reasons why they had been apart these weeks.

"Not that I care, but I don't remember the elevator being so slow," Jack murmured as he nibbled on my upper lip.

"It isn't."

"It is," he said while expertly moving his hands under my sweater to unhook my bra. Jack knew all of my bras hooked in the front, except for the strapless, which hooked on the third set of clasps in the back.

I waited to feel his fingers cup my left breast before I spoke. I knew you didn't have to be a rocket scientist to figure out if didn't take more than forty seconds to ride from the lobby to the third floor.

"We're stuck," I said, allowing my body to move into the swirling motion of his hands. By this time his two hands had successfully located my two breasts.

"I guess we are," Jack said. "I love your body. Let's put our differences aside tonight. You're right. We're stuck with each other."

"Not us. The elevator. We haven't moved in a while."

"What do you mean?"

I removed my tongue from Jack's ear and whispered, "I think we did something when we fell. We're not moving. The elevator is stuck."

He looked up at me, his brown eyes dancing.

"You're kidding." He laughed. "This is great. Let's not call for help. Let's do it here."

He went to unzip my jeans.

"Wait," I said, stopping him. "Gomez will be back to get more garbage any minute. He'll find us. I'd be mortified."

"Well." Jack tried to salvage the idea. "Maybe just a quickie. Under your coat."

I didn't want that. "I like when we have time for a whole, you know…"

"We can have another session in the apartment. But how many times can you say you had sex in an elevator?" he asked.

"Six hundred fifty-three. At least."

"This will be exciting. Come on. Let's do it fast. Before Gomez gets back."

We unzipped each other's pants. He slid his right hand beneath my pink lace panties.

"Wait. We can't." I stopped him again. "We don't have anything."

Jack's face lit up. He reached into his coat pocket. "I've got," he said, pulling out a brand-new package of three lubricated latex condoms.

My body came to an involuntary halt as I stared at the

man and woman embracing on the misty blue box. The Natural Way To Love That Special Someone, it read.

Jack opened the box and took one out.

"When did you buy these?"

"Today. Come on, there's not much time."

Jack tried to remove my panties but my hand said no. "The last time we made love was in your apartment and you still had two left."

Jack froze in his tracks. He looked like a little boy whose mother had found dipping into the cookie jar.

"So I had two left," he said. "So what are you saying?"

"What do you think?"

I was embarrassed. I knew not to pursue the conversation; I just didn't know how not to pursue the conversation.

"Jack, remember where we broke up?"

"Yes, I remember. On 57th Street. At Duane Reade Drugstore."

"Do you remember why we went to Duane Reade?"

"Yes, yes, I do," he said. "To buy condoms."

"Right. I asked you why you didn't just buy a dozen, and you said you would only buy three at a time and you never bought a new box…"

"…until I used up the old one."

We lay on top of each other, breathing as if we had finished what we barely started. A tear dropped from my left eye onto Jack's face.

"I'm sorry," I inaudibly said. I was just sorry I knew something I really didn't want to know. Jack reached and held me.

"It was so ironic," he recalled. "Breaking up while we were condom shopping. I remember we broke up at the counter when I went to pay for them."

"I paid for them," I said, just pulling back slightly from his embrace.

"Well, hon, you had just shot a commercial."

"But, Jack, we had decided each person was in charge of the condoms at their apartment and we were in your neighborhood. Besides, I bought most of them anyway because you stayed here most of the time."

"Well, hon, you have the one-bedroom."

"Well, I asked you to move in."

"I told you I would when my career took off."

"When your career takes off we could buy. And we deserve a life even if no one's career ever takes off."

I sat up. I felt dizzy. I zipped up my pants and took off that big, crazy-colored coat.

"We wouldn't need a house," Jack said. "We're only two people."

"Maybe we would have a pet," I said. "A dog."

"Dogs belong in the country."

"Well, maybe," I said slowly, "we would've had a child. Another person."

Jack stood up and zipped his pants. He ran his fingers

through his wavy hair. "I told you, in the afterlife I want to go to heaven with my wife and family, and we can't go unless you accept Jesus into your heart."

"Jack Whitney, I don't care where I go after here. I think it would've been terrific if we found heaven in this life," I said, knowing we were stuck. Individually stuck, stuck in the elevator, and we stuck close together as the walls closed in around us.

Again.

12

Joy to the World

Last Christmas
Charlottesville, VA 1993

We stood in the barn. Although it was empty, I was petrified of getting trampled by a cow. I was not comfortable walking outside with animals meandering around right next to us. It was a zoo on the loose and I was very unsettled. Not to mention the mud.

Charlottesville, however, was charming. Red clay dirt roads, just like they talk about in *Gone With the Wind*. I was no Miss Scarlett from Queens, but it was a fun getaway and a real departure from the city. Jack's parents were very sweet. They had a condo in Arlington, but loved their time on the farm. They made me feel welcome, and insisted I bring my *menorah* down to their farm. Christmas was nice, even though they spent a lot of time trying to talk me into becoming a Jew for Jesus.

Christmas morning they had gone shopping in town, and Jack and I were alone in the house. I fell asleep on the living room floor, in front of a roaring fire. At some point I heard my name. I jolted up, looked around and gasped. One of the walls was a floor-to-ceiling window. Outside, in front of me, was Jack, sitting on top of Smokey, the family horse.

"Hello, darlin'," he called out. I hadn't seen Jack that happy in a long time. We'd been dating a year, and the past six months our differences were driving more of a wedge between us. In that moment I knew this was not a boy who wanted to live out his days on New York's Upper West Side.

The day after Christmas we all went for a ride in the country. Me, Jack and his parents had driven through the red clay dirt to a small church off the beaten path. At first it was empty. Then it filled with a congregation that looked like it had been handpicked from Central Casting. The services that began slowly blew up into a full-scale revival meeting with a Gospel choir, the likes of which I had only sneaked glimpses of when watching *Guys and Dolls.*

Jack's mom had wanted to stay. And it was very interesting. For a while.

However, three hours later Jack, his parents and the

entire congregation were on their feet clapping and singing song after song praising Jesus, while I sat by myself.
It was a full-out revival meeting. Any second I thought
everyone would start speaking in tongues. I finally ex-
cused myself to the bathroom. And didn't come out. I
just stayed inside the stall trying to figure out how Jack
and I could fit together as a family. Part of the problem
was religion, but it was bigger than religion. It was how
we saw things, what we wanted from life, how we wanted
to live it. And everything between us out of bed was out
of sync.

Jack and I were now in the barn. We knew we should
be talking but didn't feel like it. I watched Jack take
some metal thing and poke at the hay. He told me the
name of the hay stick pole thing at least three times and
I still couldn't remember it. I couldn't concentrate. I
knew where this conversation was heading.

"You could've joined in," said Jack for the fourth time
that day, while moving hay from one side of the barn to
the other. "Why didn't you come out of the bathroom?"

"I didn't know any of the tunes. Besides, I felt out of
my element."

"You didn't have to hide in the ladies' room."

"It was three hours, Jack. My family never made you
sit in a temple for three hours."

"No, they just served me that gold-colored fish with
the bulging eyes that glared at me. What is that again, hon?"

"Whitefish."

"Why do they call it white when it's gold and scaly and bony? And why don't they remove the eyes?" He shivered at the memory. "They cut the fish in half so one part has a head but no body... Why? Why?"

"I don't know why."

"You don't know anything about your religion," Jack told me.

"You're the most unreligious person I know. Aside from today, here in Virginia, I've never even seen you step foot inside a church!"

"Well, at least I know everything there is to know about my religion. Unlike you."

"We were talking about food, not Judaism."

"It's the same thing in New York. You look at every holiday based on what you're going to eat."

"There are traditions, Jack."

"That's true. You even have your own traditional Christmas dinner."

Jack finally came into the ladies' room and knocked on the bathroom stall looking for me. I wanted to be a good sport, but I just felt so uncomfortable. I felt too embarrassed to come out.   "I don't know what I'm doing here," I cried to Jack through the closed bathroom door.

"Why can't you go with the flow?"

"I'm flowing as best I can. What am I doing here? I'm from Queens. I'm Jewish. What do I know from Christmas? Traditionally, I'm supposed to see a movie and eat Chinese food today."

He laughed but we both knew it wasn't so funny.

"What are we going to do, Jack?" I carried some pieces of hay over to his side of the barn. "I mean, if we just forget the problems with our careers and money and the city and the country thing for a second, could you see having a child of yours get Bar or Bat Mitzvahed?"

"Hon. Karrie, listen." Jack came up close and put his hands on my face. "In the afterlife, I want to go to heaven with my wife and family, and we can't go unless you accept Jesus into your heart."

I was stunned. "You think I'm going to hell?"

"Well, you haven't accepted Jesus so you're not going to heaven."

I heard what he said. Then I started laughing. I threw my arms around his neck and kissed his nose.

"I'm glad you're happy again, Karrie," he said, suddenly kissing me. And then he stopped. "But what's so funny?"

"You! You just reduced this whole thing to something so crazy. Heaven and hell. No wonder you're a stand-up." It was all ridiculous and silly. Just words and posturing, and none of it meant anything. I slipped my hands down the back of his pants and felt the warmth of his skin.

"I'll make love with you here in the barn, hon, but understand that I'm not joking. I am dead serious that I will be going to heaven in the afterlife, and from what I can see, you won't."

I didn't answer. I looked at him and he looked back. Nothing broke this silence. This look. This was for real. He meant it. I was so astonished I couldn't discuss it. I couldn't even digest it. The expiration date on our relationship was about to be stamped. It would take a few more days or weeks or months for the ink to dry, but an end date was near. And the words, the ones to nail the end, would soon be spoken. They were out there, and would catch up with us. Soon. But not just yet. Right now all was quiet.

I continued to kiss him, and he kissed back. All you could hear was kissing and breathing. Sighs and moans. The rustling of clothing. The crinkle of a blanket on hay, of bodies on a blanket. The sounds of people coming and coming together. We were on vacation and we were making love in this barn. It was what we did best and we were going to do it. After all, it was Christmas, goddammit!

That's Really All

"Jack Whitney, I don't care where I go after here. I think it would've been terrific if we found heaven in this life."

"Somebody stuck in the elevator?" Gomez shouted up.

"Yes, it's me. Karrie. Help," I yelled from my soul.

"I get you out in five minutes, Miss Karrie. Is Mr. Jack with you?"

"I'm here," yelled Jack.

"Then you okay," Gomez shouted back.

I looked at my official ex-boyfriend.

"I'm okay, you're okay," I said.

"Okay."

"I wish…"

"It'll be okay, hon." He put his arms around me. We kissed. The kiss grew. And grew.

"Oh no," I said. "We can't. History can't keep repeating itself like this."

Six weeks ago, when we left Duane Reade together, we walked down the block toward Carnegie Hall. On the corner of 57th Street, the Homeless Wanna-be Opera Singer serenaded us with the death aria from *Madama Butterfly*. Crying, we walked back to Jack's apartment and used one of the newly purchased condoms.

"I'll be sorry I asked, but who was the lucky recipient of the remaining two?"

"A cute little actress I met handing out fliers down at TKTS."

"Oh, Jack. I don't know what hurts more. That this is over, or that you moved on so quickly. I feel so replaceable."

"Look, she's only twenty-five and not looking for any commitments. It's someone to be with. Besides, she's from Indiana."

"Jack, is it special? And what does that mean, Indiana? What is that?"

"Karrie, don't make me say things I don't want to say. I just don't like to be alone. You're great, but you're a tidal wave, Karrie. Carla's a lake."

"Sounds more like a puddle to me."

The elevator door moaned as it got cranked open. Gomez extended his hand. We climbed out. The super stood proudly before us, having successfully rescued his party.

"You have some fun in the elevator while you wait?"

"A barrel of laughs," said Jack.

"Good. You both a nice couple. I go now. I have more garbage."

"Thanks, Gomez," I said. "See you tomorrow."

The hallway was empty. 1940s movie music came from inside Mrs. Fudge's apartment.

Jack took my hand. "Want to dance, Ginger?"

"I think I'm going to retire, Fred."

"What? And break up the act?"

I knew the sooner I ended these moments, the sooner I'd be in my apartment alone. I didn't want to face that, but I knew it was inevitable.

"You don't have to use the bathroom or anything, do you?" I asked.

He shook his head.

"Good. I don't want to see what you look like in my apartment."

"I probably look like I always did."

"You feel like you look the same, but you look different."

"What does that mean?"

"I don't know. Maybe I'll know tomorrow."

He bent into me and pressed his lips on my hair.

"I guess I should be going, hon."

"Yeah."

"I guess I should take the stairs."

"Yeah."

I knew there were only seconds left.

"See ya, hon."

"Yeah."

I watched Jack walk to the stairway at the end of the hall. Then I walked to the door, anticipating the safety of my aloneness.

The Truth About Men and Astrology

Flag Day
The Upper West Side, NYC 1994

I met him in the racks at the neighborhood Barnes & Noble before I even knew it was the new, hip place to meet in the city. The *New York Times* wrote an article saying the bookstore was to the nineties what Laundromats were to the seventies and singles bars were to the eighties. I didn't even read the article and I met him anyway.

Barnes & Noble is a place where I get to do a few of my favorite things. Read, eat and talk. Once when I was there with a friend who was visiting from Canada, we went upstairs to the New Age section and I showed her a book.

"Shhhh," she whispered.

"What's the matter?"

"People are reading," she said.

"It's okay," I said. "We can talk. It's not a library. It's a store."

Anyway, the night I met him I was upstairs in Self-Help, looking for that new book that had just taken the town by storm. It was called something like *Men Are From Mercury, Women Are From Saturn,* or *Women Are From Somewhere, Men Are From Somewhere Else.* The point being, however you look at it, men and women are from two different planets.

I picked up the book and began to read. It said that when a woman has a problem she wants to talk about her feelings. When a man has one he wants to revert into his cave. I skipped around. I read a little more. The book seemed to be talking about couples. People already in intimate, ongoing relationships. I was searching for a different chapter. The chapter that told you how to find the man to be in the intimate relationship with, who won't talk about his feelings and wants to go into his cave. And come to think of it, where was the chapter before that? Where was the one that explained six phone conversations, four dinners, two-and-a-half make-out sessions, one night of sex, and the man permanently disappearing into his cave, never to call again? Where was the chapter to explain my affair?

Calling my affair an affair was giving it more weight

than it warranted, but I figured if something could cause me that much grief, it certainly carried a lot of weight. Earlier that year, I had met a young theater director at the gym. It was instant rapport, instant attraction and instant chemistry. We were both traveling a lot at the time, so our dates were limited to one a month. January, February, March. We slept together in April. There was no date in May.

It was now June and I was completely over him, except that I was devastated. It was shocking to me this had happened. I hadn't been in a situation like that in years and was taking it very hard. I could not accept that I had misjudged him, and move on. I kept replaying the tape, and going over the scenario again and again. Prior to the main event, I had told him my feelings.

"You're very brave to talk to me like this," he had said. It was easy. He was lying on his couch with a busted knee preparing to go for surgery the next day. He had to listen. What was he going to do? Run?

"I know we've been seeing each other infrequently," I said. "But if we spend the night and don't see each other for a month, it won't feel okay to me."

"I'm not ready for a commitment now," he said. "I'm not afraid of it, and I want it, but I'm not ready right now."

"That's okay, as long as we can see each other and just see. And you are open to commitment. I want to make sure this is not a one-night stand."

"I'm very, very attracted to you," he said, outlining my lips with the tips of his fingers. The gentleness of his touch set off a little fireworks demo in my tummy. Still, I needed to make sure. I opened my mouth to talk, but he kissed me. Tenderly. Deeply. Passionately. I knew I didn't exactly have all my answers, but I could no longer talk. My mouth was doing something far more engaging.

I thought, "He's kissing me. He's telling me it won't be a one-night stand."

He thought, "I'm kissing her. She's finally stopped talking about one-night stands."

We kissed some more. We spent the night. The only night we spent. It was a one-night stand.

Now, almost two months later, I was combing through *Women Are From Pluto, Men Are From New Jersey,* trying to find out why that had happened to me and how. There was nothing in the book. The only thing I was able to surmise was a) don't sleep with a man you're not seeing regularly, b) don't sleep with a man who has put out any disclaimers, c) don't sleep with a man for the first time on the eve of any major surgery and d) if you're really that unsure, don't sleep with that man.

Unless you really want to.

"Why do you think you need to read this book?"

I heard a voice out of the walls of Barnes & Noble. I looked up. The voice belonged to a hippie, intellectual type. Blond curly hair, wire glasses, black jeans, ripped

BVD and black sneakers like the boys in my class used to wear to go out and play.

"What did you say?" I asked.

"Why do you think you need to read this book?" he repeated.

"Maybe you can tell me," I said, figuring the guy in the high-tops who knew me from Adam would probably know all.

"So, how long were you going out?" he asked, sitting down next to me at a square wood table.

"Four months," I said, trying to find out what this opposite sex from an opposite planet knew.

"Really?"

He seemed impressed. Yeah, four months was a decent amount of time.

"And you saw each other how often?" he asked.

I decided not to tell him it was only four times in four months.

"Well… We were both traveling a lot. So we saw each other…uh…not that much."

"Did you live far away?"

"Seven blocks. But in the winter it was very icy."

"Oh, yes. It was a very icy winter."

Donald was a writer. He had a Ph.D. from NYU in literature, and had run an alternative movie theater in the village for a decade when he had been married. He was very interested in solving my problem. He wasn't solving it, but I was talking about it to someone new, which was almost the same thing for me.

The announcement was made. The store was closing.

"Are you getting the book?" asked Donald.

"Nah. I'm going to wait to see the movie."

We left the store. It was raining. Donald had an umbrella so he walked me to my building. We said good-night.

A few days later I received a call from him.

"I took the liberty of checking to see if you were listed," said Donald. "Would you like to go out for dessert?"

At first I was surprised. I had spent the entire time in the bookstore talking about another man. I was very self-involved, and very down in the dumps. I couldn't figure out on what level I had been appealing.

"I think you're pretty," said Donald on the phone.

Ah. That's how!

The night we met was a beautiful one. Warm and breezy. Donald suggested we meet at an outdoor garden that served desserts. I wanted to look nice. I wanted to leave all my baggage at home. Travel light. Find out about the writer who thought I was pretty and invited me out for dessert.

Entering the garden, I saw a table with two young women, and at the table next to them was Donald, already seated and drinking a cup of tea. He was wearing the same outfit I had met him in last Sunday.

"Wow," said Donald when he saw me. "It doesn't even look like you. What'd you do?"

I wasn't sure if that response still qualified me as pretty. I had put on a summer shift over black leggings, a little makeup and a smile.

"You're wearing white!" he said. "I don't care for it, but it's interesting on you. What did you do to your hair?"

"Combed it."

"You're kind of like a chameleon."

"Thanks," I said, choosing to take it as a compliment.

"I wear the same clothes over and over," he said. "I can wear the same outfit for a week. I like to stick with one outfit at a time. Then I change."

"Really? *Everything* the same?" I asked, suddenly unsettled. Quickly. Just like that. Feeling the evening turning weird in that very quick, unsettled way.

"I do change my underwear. And I can add a sweater if it's cold. But otherwise, the same."

The waiter approached with two glasses of water.

"Nothing for me," said Donald.

"You're not having anything?" I said, wondering if I was supposed to take a cue from him.

"Well," said Donald, "I'll take some more hot water for the tea."

"I'll have a cappuccino and the tiramisu."

"You don't want the tiramisu."

"Yes, I do."

"No, that's too… Get a piece of pie. Or a cookie."

I didn't know why he was doing this. I was embarrassed. The two women at the next table looked at me as if to say, "Get what you want. Get the pie. Better yet, get out!"

"Umm…just the cappuccino for now," I said to the waiter, who also rolled his eyes before he walked away.

"Tiramisu is too much," said Donald.

"Too much what?" I asked. Too much to eat, too much calories, too much money?

"They have cookies inside. In the front," he said. "I'll get you two of those. Okay?" Donald left the table before I could answer.

The cappuccino arrived. I looked at my watch. This was a waste of my time. If I drank my coffee quickly I could be home by *Seinfeld*.

"Why doesn't he want you to have the tiramisu?" asked the dark-haired woman at the next table. "Does he think it's too fattening?"

"I don't know what he thinks. I don't know him," I said.

"See, I told you," said the blonde in the ponytail to her friend. "I could tell it was a first date," she said to me. "It's strange. Maybe he's allerg—"

I saw Donald walking back into the garden.

"Shhhh, he's back," I told the women.

"These are very good," he said, placing two butter cookies in front of me.

"Thanks," I said, happy for something sweet.

"I like these," he said. "Generally, I don't like to vary

my meals," said Donald, adding more hot water to his tea. He had picked that up inside with the cookies.

"Oh?" I said, sipping my coffee and crunching my cookies. "Tell me what you do."

"At the beginning of the week I cook one meal and then I eat it for three or four days. When that's finished, I cook another."

"Really? What do you cook?"

"Beans. Mainly beans."

"Really? Beans."

"Rice and beans. Sometimes. Or beans and greens."

"How does that work out?" I asked, eating my other butter cookie. I was hungry for something sweet. Hungry for something that would fill me up. Hungry for the communication I'd had with the director, for those feelings. It wasn't happening here.

The girls at the next table were clearly eavesdropping. I couldn't blame them. I didn't want to look in their direction for fear I'd laugh.

"One week I had broccoli the whole week," continued Donald.

I caught the eye of the blonde.

"I'd write all day and then take broccoli breaks," he said.

The blonde looked back at me. She was smiling. Giggling. I began to giggle. I began to laugh.

"What's so funny?" asked Donald.

"Don't you ever get bored?" I said, catching my

breath. "One food the whole week. How can you just eat one food?"

"Why? What do you do?"

"Me? I vary my meals. I eat different foods for different meals. I'm kind of out there. Zany. Why, I've been known to eat eggs for breakfast, a tuna sandwich for lunch, and pasta for dinner."

"That would make me crazy," said Donald. "That would keep me from my writing. My way it's in the pot on the stove, and I can concentrate on my work."

"You sound very disciplined. What are you writing?" I asked, hoping to find some variety in the conversation. Now I understood why we had stayed on my topic the whole time in the bookstore. It didn't matter that it was about another man. It was one topic.

"Well, right now I'm working on this paragraph," said Donald.

"What paragraph?" I asked.

"A paragraph. On page three. It's almost done."

"How long have you been working on it?"

"About four days now."

"Really?" This was unbelievable to me. "One paragraph? Four days on one paragraph? The same paragraph?" The minutia was astounding.

"Yes," said Donald.

"And how long do you work on it?"

"About eight hours a day."

"Eight hours? EIGHT hours?? You've spent thirty-two hours on one paragraph? Oh my God. What's it about?"

"Snow," said Donald. "I can't get the description just right. See, it's not exactly white. It's almost iridescent."

"That sounds good," I said. "Why don't you write that? Just write what you said and keep writing. Then go back later."

"Oh no," said Donald. "I can't write that way. You see…"

Donald was extolling the virtues of spending thirty-two hours on a paragraph, and I was in bed with the theater director. The director was touching me exquisitely, he was saying something funny, he was sharing a child-hood intimacy and then he wasn't calling.

I sat in the garden, nodding my head at Donald, and hearing the sounds of heavy breathing, laughter and silence. The silence was the loudest sound I heard. The sound of the phone not ringing was deafening. I still didn't understand how two people shared a night like that, and one felt sure to never repeat it again. I didn't understand how someone could tell you his fear of being seen naked in the boys' locker room, his fear of not measuring up, but have too much fear to say he can't see you.

The waiter put down the check.

"Do you want to split this?" asked Donald, showing me the check. It came to six dollars and eighty-one cents.

I looked at him before answering.

"I don't generally like to pay for women, but I'd actually like to this time. You can pay next time."

Next time. Right. This exchange was not lost on the two women next to us. Donald left the exact change on the table.

"I just have to use the rest room," he said.

He waited for me.

"Are you coming?" he asked.

"There's no tip," I said, looking down.

"That's all right," said Donald. "I got the cookies and the water myself."

"I'll meet you in front," I said, waiting until he was on his way to reach into my purse and put a few dollars on the table.

"That was crazy," said the brunette. "He's on another planet."

"It was pretty funny, though," said the blonde.

"It was," I said. "What a character."

"You're not going to see him again, are you?" asked the brunette.

"Deborah!" said the blonde.

"It's okay," I told her. "No. Of course not. But what can you do? It takes all kinds. You have to laugh. Right? You have to laugh."

I stood in front of the restaurant near the cashier, waiting for Donald to come out of the bathroom. *Tosca* was playing through the speakers. It sounded like a climactic operatic moment. Donald made his way through the small marble tables and black ice-cream chairs. He tapped me on the shoulder.

"Come on," he said, taking his right hand up to his ear and covering it. "Boy. I wish they'd turn it down." Puccini's music was apparently wasted on Donald. Had Puccini thought to compose the same passage over and over, maybe, by a week from next Thursday, Donald would have developed an appreciation for it.

"Do you want me to walk you home?" he asked. "It is a few blocks out of my way, but I had a good time with you so I'm willing to do it."

"Hmm, that's quite an offer, Donald," I said. I wanted to walk myself home. I was out of conversation and out of patience. The only possible joy left in the evening would be that lonesome stroll up Columbus Avenue, reviewing the idiocy of the night and filing it away in the date box under the heading: Don't Worry. Just Another Night. Better Things To Come.

"I think you must want to get back to your writing," I said, "so I'm going to walk myself. Thanks."

"I'll call you," he said.

I nodded my head, wished him luck and left.

"Karrie!" His voice stopped me just as I had reached the corner.

I turned around to see Donald still standing in front of the restaurant. "I had a good time tonight."

"Oh!" I paused a moment and looked at him in his current outfit. "I'm glad!"

I went directly to a candy store and treated myself to a large vanilla frozen yogurt with chocolate sprinkles. I felt free walking home in the night, eating the frozen yogurt and thinking. I certainly was disappointed in the evening but kind of amazed by it. We all come out of the womb and enter the world, and I could not get over how different everyone was. But I could not understand Donald's socialization. Or lack thereof. Where did he grow up? Who were that guy's parents? How do people get like that? That brunette was right. He was on another planet.

I curled up on my couch when I got home, and turned on *Seinfeld*. They were in the coffee shop. Kramer had just left. He's on another planet too. George was telling Jerry he's in a rut. Instead of eating the same thing every day for lunch, he's going to dare to be different. Instead of tuna on toast with coffee, he's switching to chicken salad on rye with tea.

I'm laughing. I'm laughing with George.

George told Jerry he's eating broccoli for an entire week. He's staying in the same outfit. He's going to write a book about weather and spend thirty-two hours working on a paragraph about snow.

I'm laughing. I'm laughing with George.

George saw a pretty girl sitting at the counter. He told

Jerry to watch. He walked up to her and asked her out. She said yes.

George looked through the television. George looked at me. George is looking at me. George is asking me.

"Good night," I say. Laughing.

George is still asking.

"Good night. No," I say, turning off the TV. Laughing.

"Good night," I say, laughing. Still laughing.

15

from the Top

Election Day
The Theater District, NYC 1994

Jane and I were finishing breakfast at an old-fashioned coffee shop in the theater district. It was legendary as a place where writers came to eat and hang out through the sixties and seventies, and it was one of the few coffee shops left where you could get a breakfast special. I had just polished off bacon and eggs, French fries and an English muffin, while Jane was having fruit. She had just come back from spending a week at the fat farm upstate, and was really watching it. Jane had a great figure. She was far from fat and she certainly didn't need a farm, but she liked the idea of cleaning out her system and starting anew. I liked the idea too. But just the idea. We were seated near the window and I could see the marquees of all the Broadway shows. Although I was seated, I was walking on air. Today was the first rehearsal of my play. My play. I had an acting job!

"So what has it been?" asked Jane. She was adding another Equal to her coffee and stirring. "Almost two years since the reading that I saw?"

"Exactly," I said, tearing at the last strip of bacon. "Want half?" I pointed to a perfectly crisp but juicy piece.

"Sure." Jane picked it up and popped it in her mouth. That's what I liked about Jane. She could eat the fruit, but she'd still bring home the bacon.

The producers had finally raised the money for an Off-B'way production of *Eat This* at a great theater uptown, just a few blocks from my apartment. Not only did I have an acting job that would pay me a weekly salary and earn medical benefits through Actors' Equity, I would be able to walk to work in five minutes and never get stuck in traffic.

"I think I like bacon strips better than Canadian. Except for when I have eggs Benedict. What do you like?"

"I like them all," she answered. "Not picky."

I always thought you could tell a lot about a person by their relationship to food. Were they open to trying new things? Did they like bland or spicy? Did they cook or order in? Were they open to sharing? Maybe I would just give the next guy a food survey instead of a date.

"So how are your rehearsals going?" I asked.

"The harmonies are impossible, the music is scored really high and the choreography is heavily propped with ropes and knives, but other than that it's FABulous!" Jane was in rehearsal for a musical version of an Edgar Allan Poe short story. It was going to tour a bunch of schools in the hopes of getting kids excited to read.

"Will Philip be coming in for Thanksgiving?"

"His show is closing the weekend before so he'll be here. He'll be here for Christmas this year, too. Unless he immediately gets another job."

"Yeah. The actor's life. I hate going out of town. We'll be going into previews in January. You know, the busiest month for theater!"

"Don't worry. An Alan Starkman comedy. You'll have an audience." Jane looked at her watch. "Let's go. We don't want to be late."

We walked down to Eighth Avenue and climbed the stairs two flights to the Tipton Studios where we were both rehearsing. We looked at the big white board directing her to Studio Four, and me down a long and winding corridor to Studio Seven. The place was jam-packed. Every studio was booked for either rehearsals or auditions. To the right and left of me actors were preparing for auditions. Jane and I looked at each other watching the anxious, hopeful faces go by.

"I'm so glad I have a job," said Jane.

"*Oy!* Me too!"

Somewhere at Tipton there was an open call, and people of all shapes and sizes were signed up for an appointment. The dancers, clad in leotards, were stretching their legs.

"Okay, dahling! Go be brilliant!" Jane gave me a hug and disappeared.

I walked down the corridor toward my studio and passed tons of singers warming up. Bits of lyrics and scales were quietly sung a cappella in the corners. Actors were passionately speaking their audition monologues to themselves.

"Hey. Karrie. Hi!" I turned around and saw Jack standing next to a petite blonde in black tights and a short pink chiffon dance skirt.

"This is Carla," he said, possessively placing his arm around his current belle. "This is Karrie. I told you about her."

"Hello, Carla," I said, trying to take her in on a glance. As I extended my hand, I wondered what exactly Jack had told her, and why Carla was still wearing sea-blue eye shadow in the nineties.

"Nice to meet you," Carla said. Sweetly smiling.

"Carla's auditioning for *Oklahoma!* for the Skylight Outdoor Theater. She's a wonderful little singer-dancer."

"How nice. Jack likes to rewrite lyrics. Could be fun," I said.

"Oh, it is." Carla swooned and looked up at Jack

through her starry eyes. He beamed. I could see this "little singer-dancer" made Jack feel like a very big man on campus.

"Are you auditioning, too?" she asked me.

"Yeah, Karrie. I see there's some good stuff in their season for you," said Jack.

I took a moment before I answered. Whoever said living well was the best revenge had no idea exactly how right they were. I looked at the two of them. Blondes from other parts of this country. The real America. Time had really made things clear. It was almost two years ago that I had met Jack, and now close to a year that we were broken up. Almost a year that he was with Carla. Even though it was a fast first impression, Carla seemed better for Jack than me. I knew it and I accepted it, but it still hurt.

"I'm starting rehearsal today. *Eat This.*" Sure it hurt, but that made it hurt a whole lot less.

"It finally happened!" said Jack. "That's so great, Karrie. I'm happy for you."

"Eat what?" asked Carla.

"*Eat This.* Alan Starkman's new comedy," Jack told her. I saw the look in Carla's wide Maybelline eyes. I could also see the look in his. Jack was the big man in this relationship. The man of wisdom. The leader. I could see he was happy with her.

"Broadway?" he asked.

"Off," I said.

"I'm really happy for you, hon," he said. "You deserve it."

"I never knew anyone in an Off-B'way show before," Carla said. "Can we go?" she asked Jack through her big, blind, dewy eyes.

I stood in the middle of this triangle, trying to have the perspective one can only gain from a distance. It seemed fairly obvious that Carla wasn't much competition for Jack in the funny area, but then that probably worked out for the best. Jack had gotten into an occupational habit. At the club, the comics were so competitive with each other, instead of laughing when they heard something funny, they would ponder the joke and then respond with, "That's funny," as if it was a commentary. If a joke was truly inspiring, they would say, "That's really funny. Funny stuff." Carla didn't seem to be much competition for Jack in any area. But she seemed to be there for him, and to be accepting of him in a way I wasn't ever able to be.

"It'll be crazy during previews," I said, "but sometimes they paper the house. If there are any freebies I'll let you know, okay?"

"Sounds good," he said.

"You're so lucky," said Carla. "Jack says if we just hang in there, it'll happen."

Jack and I looked at each other for a quick second that

encompassed one-hundred-and-one conversations we'd had about our careers.

"Jack's right," I told her. "Good luck in there. I hope you get it."

"Number sixty-four," the monitor for the Skylight auditions called out. "Sixty-four on deck."

"Hahhhhhhhh!" It sounded like Carla had sucked up all the available air in the room in one giant gulp. "That's me!"

"Go get 'em," Jack cheered her on, punching his fist in the air like he was leading a pack of cattle across the prairie. "I'll be waiting for you out here."

He gave her a quick kiss. She picked up her music and soundlessly pranced down the hall in her black Capezio dance shoes. I watched their exchange and tried to remember when Jack had ever accompanied me to an audition. He had always said he was too tired to get up early because the comedy clubs always ran so late. Either the clubs had changed their hours, or Jack required a lot less sleep.

"Sorry, hon," he said, turning to a water fountain behind him for a drink.

"What?" I said. "No big deal. Of course you want to wish her luck."

We stood together for an uncomfortable moment while I checked my watch. It was nine forty-six. Rehearsal began at ten. I figured it was time to get to where I belonged.

"I have to…" I pointed to my watch and nodded my head in the direction of Studio Seven as a way of completing the sentence.

"I'll walk you."

Fortunately, it wasn't that long a walk.

The high I had felt walking in with Jane was doing a quick dissolve as I walked the few yards to the studio with Jack. I had a great job. My life was good. So why did I feel, well, that undefinable blah thing? That, "I know I'm okay but there's a little something pulling at me and it goes away but here it is and is it a thing about Jack? or is it a thing about not having a new Jack? or is it some other completely different thing that makes me feel that yechy, undefinable blah thing?" Jack looked good. He looked comfortable with himself. I was happy for him. In spite of myself.

"She's, uh…lovely," I told him. "Very sweet. And obviously crazy about you." I smiled. I forced myself, but I did it.

"It's good. It's different from us. But it's good for me," he said, somewhat apologetically.

"I can see." We had gotten a few feet in front of the studio. We stood.

"I think you're great," he said, reaching his hand up as if to touch me, but running it through his hair instead. "You must be pretty happy…" he went on, pointing to the door that would start a new chapter.

"I am."

"Are you…?" Without finishing the question, Jack had asked it.

"As a matter of fact, yeah."

"Really?"

"Well…yeah!"

"Anyone…?" asked Jack.

"No, you don't know him. Not in the business. Lawyer," I said. Eric and I had only had dinner once, but what the hell. A girl had to have her dignity.

"That's just what you wanted," said Jack. "I'm glad you got everything you wanted. See, I did you a great favor by breaking up with you, Karrie. Look how your life has improved."

"That's not so and you know it," I said, not knowing if I meant it or not, not knowing if a lawyer was just what I wanted or not, not knowing many lawyers and hardly knowing Eric.

"Well, you know my theory. I think people have already been at the happiest that they can be," said Jack. "The people you're with may change, the events may change. The stakes may get higher. But I bet you'll be as happy during the rehearsals for this Off-B'way show as you were when you got the lead in your high school play."

I looked at him and wondered why he suddenly looked wise. I wondered if he was right, and, if he was, if people were wasting their money going to therapy.

I checked my watch.

"You've got to go," said Jack, "and I want to be there when Carla finishes."

"Okay." I took stock of my life, again, and didn't know why it hurt to hear him say that.

"Let me know if those tickets happen," said Jack. "Good luck."

"Okay."

I pulled out my compact and powdered my nose. I didn't remember when I'd actually started to carry a compact and literally powder my nose, but I liked doing it. It made me feel like I was in a Doris Day movie from 1963. A madcap romp through a new phase of life. It was unpredictable and alive and something good was bound to happen.

Eating out of His Hand

Veterans' Day
SoHo, NYC 1994

A small woman huddled under a blue blanket was seated on a stool beneath the awning of a brownstone. The sign above her read SPECIAL PALM READING—$5.

"I'm such a sucker for those," I told Eric. It was our third date. We had just left a jazz club on Greene Street, and were walking over to Eric's favorite place on Spring. Nouvelle cuisine.

"Oh yeah?" Eric handed a five-dollar bill to the tiny woman. "Knock yourself out," he said. "I'll be over there." He pointed to a leather shop a few doors down. I sat down on a crate and offered my palm to the gypsy.

"I can read your aura by looking in your eyes," she

said, giving my hand back to me. "You recently had broken heart. Yes?"

"Yes!" I thought that was truly amazing. On the other hand, this fortuneteller could probably go up to any single woman in New York City, tell her she had her heart broken recently, and be on the money. I'd been trying to wipe my broken heart slate clean. Every time I felt like I did, someone wrote on it. I was doing really well until I ran into Jack and Carla. I was completely over Jack, but apparently I wasn't over Jack and Carla. Now I couldn't stop thinking about him, and it was about time I did.

"You have new love coming." She took a breath. "But…"

"But what?"

"I cannot say at this time," the palmist said. "I still see a few dark clouds covering your aura. If you give me money, I will pray for you to be free from the blackness."

I went back to Eric, who was gazing at the store window, fixated on the mannequins dressed in leather pants, jackets and boots. They looked like they lived at a sidewalk café where they spent eternity drinking caffe lattes.

"How'd it go? What do you think of these cowboy boots?" he asked, pointing to a pair of crinkled brown ones. "I like them."

I flashed on Eric Epstein—Jewish Cowboy galloping through the city on the 104 bus. We had met a few weeks ago on that bus. Eric got off at my stop, and then asked me to join him for dinner. I thought I should be cautious, but I was flattered, and I had been eyeing him on the ride uptown. He was handsome in an off-beat kind of way. His dark hair, which had obviously been slicked back that morning, fell over the left side of his face, while his black wire glasses slid down his nose. He was impressive in a charcoal-gray suit and London Fog overcoat, while carrying a black leather briefcase embossed with his initials. He had introduced himself on the street, when we got off at the same stop.

"Eric Epstein, tax attorney. Noticed you on the bus. You're pretty cute. Hi." Eric had a client in my neighborhood.

"Karrie Kline. Actress. Noticed you too. I think we're part of an alliteration epidemic."

I looked up at Eric now. He was still fixated on the cowboy boots. "What do you think? Should I get them? I just bought a pair. I think two pairs in one month is a bit over-the-top."

I didn't answer. I was thinking about what the gypsy said, and wondered if he was just another guy that wouldn't make the dark clouds go away.

"So," he said, shifting all his attention to me, something Eric seemed to be very good at. "Did she tell you anything interesting?"

"Well, she gave with one hand and took away with the other."

"You know, Karrie, I'm a little psychic too," he said. He took my right hand in his, pulled off my mitten and put it into my pocket.

"Oh, really? What do you predict?"

Eric brought my hand towards his eyes to study it. He gently ran his fingers over each one of mine. Then he licked the center of my palm with his tongue. Eric slipped my index finger into his mouth and released it between his lips. Then he spread my fingers apart with his, and kissed each one.

I'm not over Jack, I thought as I responded to Eric. The tips of his long fingers combed through my hair. His strong hands massaged the back of my neck. He repositioned himself as he set the scene. Eric lifted my chin with his hand and brushed the hair out of my eyes. He nibbled on my lower lip and outlined my mouth with his tongue. He took my face in his hands like he had read a book on the art of kissing.

"Oh," I moaned, giving myself a little permission to get swept up, even though I thought it was too soon to get swept away.

Dinner conversation of that evening popped into my head.

"What does your dad do?" Eric had asked.

"My stepfather works in the garment center."

"Ah, the *garment center.*" Eric rolled the words over in

his mouth like they were a new flavor he was trying to identify. "And your real dad?"

"Hmm?"

"Did he go to school?"

"School of hard knocks," I said.

"What does he do?"

"He's a clown."

"Aren't they all?"

The waiter came by at that moment to see if we wanted dessert.

"It looks like they come around with a miniature Viennese table," I said, noting the selection wheeled by on a two-tier cart.

"A what?"

"A Viennese table. Didn't you have one at your Bar Mitzvah, Eric? It was very popular. After hours of eating, in addition to a gigantic cake, the waiters rolled around this table that was stacked with tons of desserts."

"I wasn't Bar Mitzvahed. We were only cultural Jews."

"Oh, how nice." I paused. "What's that?"

"We're aware of our heritage, but my family is very assimilated. Princeton. You know."

"I guess that's why you pronounce your name Epstine, as opposed to my mother's friend Dottie Epsteen who used to bring over sliced pineapple when it was her turn to hostess the weekly mah-jongg game. Oh—speaking of, I have a callback for a commercial for Kole's Pineapples on Monday. It's a network spot. I play a waitress."

"Well, you are definitely going to book this spot," said Eric, who had already learned the lingo.

"I hope."

"You have to."

"If you say so," I said. He was so dramatic about my career, but so much more interested than Jack. And not in competition with me, either. I liked having my own cheerleader. Especially a sexy one.

"The spot takes place in, where else, a diner, but I think they'd be better off setting it in Brooklyn at a mah-jongg game!"

"You're very funny, Karrie. Your life sounds quaint. Like a Neil Simon play."

"Or an Alan Starkman." Eric was an avid theatergoer and really impressed when I told him I was in rehearsals for *Eat This.*

"That is wonderful! I read about that. He's terrific. Most of his plays turn out to be hits," he had said, with a seductive intensity. "This has to be a hit. And that is key!"

Eric pulled me in closer. I tried to think why that should be key, but as I was enveloped by his tall, lean frame it was kind of hard to remember. He broke away for a moment, as if he needed to check how he was doing. Then he pulled me into him again. His hands moved under my coat and dress to caress my shoulders while he licked my lips.

"Ohhh…" I moaned. Just when I was ready to go with it, Jack came back in my head.

Eric put his tongue in my mouth.

"Ohhhh…" Jack was watching.

Eric reached down under my coat and grabbed my buttocks with his hands. His tongue reached deeper into my mouth. My body melted into his.

"Ohhhhh…" Jack was. Jack…was… Jack who?

"Would you think it was too forward for me to ask you to spend the night?" asked Eric.

"Yes."

We were both attracted. We were both unattached, but we did not know each other well. Eric seemed great. He went for what he wanted. It was the opposite of being with Jack. Eric could seem a little slick, but I think it was just confidence. Again, the opposite of Jack. I had to admit I liked it. Eric loved that I was an actress. He hardly even knew me and yet he took such an interest in my career. Come to think of it, why? Oh, he was a gem. A supportive gem. Everything seemed good, but maybe I should just wait and get to know him better before… I thought, while his hands expertly stroked my buttocks and his tongue found new nooks inside my mouth. I should just wait. I was wounded, I was too vulnerable, I was…

…lying down in the back seat of a cab, with Eric's hand stroking the insides of my thighs.

Feast Your Eyes

Twenty Minutes Later
Fifth Avenue, NYC 1994

His doorman nodded hello. Eric owned a one-bedroom apartment on Tenth Street just off Fifth. It was an exquisite prewar building. He took his hands off me long enough to enter the building.

"I thought you were sexy the first second I saw you," he said. His left hand fumbled for his keys, while his right was wrapped around my waist. I was pressed up against the frame of his apartment door, standing on the doormat that said WELCOME.

Eric pushed the door open with his arm and kicked it closed with his foot. Then he swooped me up and carried me toward his bedroom. I had one eye closed, envisioning romance. The other was wide-open, trying to catch a glimpse of his apartment.

He carried me through the black leather couches and modern art paintings of the high-ceilinged living room, down the hall with the red-and-gold Persian runner, and dropped me on his queen-size bed with the black lacquered headboard and the geometric print sheets.

He tossed his suede jacket on the soft gray carpet and threw my coat on top of his. He pulled off his boots. It seemed like his socks, sweater and pants came off in one grand gesture. Eric leaned over me with a pair of red Calvin Klein briefs and a huge bulge that hung above my eyes.

"Now I can undress you," he said, running his hands down my legs and removing my black suede pumps. He reached under my dress and rolled down my black panty hose. Then he lifted me up and pulled my dress off over my head. My black lace bra sailed across the bed, and I saw my matching panties dangling around my ankles before they vanished.

I moved to pull off his briefs.

He shook his head no.

"I don't want to be naked by myself," I said. "I've had enough of that recently, thank you." I tried to take off his underwear again.

"Not yet," said Eric, in complete control.

It was the Eric Epstein show. I thought we'd be sharing this feast together. Maybe a few appetizers before dinner. I wondered what he was going to do next, but one thing was certain. He had whet my appetite.

Eric rubbed his hands down the length of my body. One hand at my feet, the other at the top of my chest. Each hand inched slowly toward each other until they met in the middle. He spread my legs apart with his fingers. He was like an explorer in unknown terrain who could not leave the site until every stone had been turned. As if to get a better look, he moved his hands to the side and peered in with his eyes. Eric moved in closer with his nose, his mouth, his teeth…his tongue.

It was the Sex Olympics!

Eric was well trained. Strong. He had stamina. I thought he would have put my name on the sign-up sheet next to his. Like a team. Instead, I was there as the pool to be swum, the slope to be skied.

I felt left out. Taken over. And crazy. Dizzy with desire. Eric dazzled me with those right-hand moves, the tip-of-the-tongue action, and what was that thing he did with his toes? He stopped for a split second and came back with a startling intensity. I was with him all the way. Heaving. Panting. So close. Wanting to go the distance, enjoying the ride too much to get off. I didn't want to stop. I wanted to go and keep going and going and…

"OHMYGOD!!" I screamed, quivering and shaking as I crossed the finish line.

I reached out for Eric. I didn't see it happen, but his

briefs were off, the condom was on, and he was in. If I thought he'd read a book on the art of kissing, he must have done an intensive weekend seminar on the art of fucking. It was aerobic. Original. I was overwhelmed.

Up. Over. In the air. We tumbled across the sheets onto the floor. Eric picked me up and straddled me across his waist. Then he laid me down on the bed. He got serious.

"Yes," he seriously groaned as he competed with himself for the gold medal. "Yes—yes—yes—yes—" He was coming to the end. "YEESSSSSSS!!!" he cried out, falling all over me.

We lay sweating in each other's arms. My face was tangled underneath his left armpit. I saw my brown hair wrapped around his elbow. I rearranged myself, and gasped for any available air.

"I knew this would work out rather well," he said, carefully removing the condom. He wrapped it in a tissue and shot it across the room into a gray wicker trash basket.

"I have perfect aim," he said.

"No kidding."

Eric leaned up against the black lacquered headboard.

"Why do you think you've never been married?" he asked, propping up the pillows behind him.

"Now there's a postcoital question for you," I said, laying my head down on his chest.

"Were you ever close?"

Talking about commitment after sex was definite compensation for lack of intimacy when in it. Eric was even slick in sex, but I was hooked. It was not too slick for me.

"Close to what?" I asked, still composing my new theory.

"Karrie, answer my question."

"Gee." I was so unused to a man who had it so together. "It's been over a while, but my last major relationship was with a comedian who made a joke every time the subject remotely came up. I guess I'm just not used to talking about *C* words."

"*C* words?"

"You know. Commitment. Closeness. Confusion. Competition."

Eric reached over to the night table and put on his glasses as if they might shed some light on the conversation. "Come here," he said, picking me up and laying me down on top of him. "Are you saying the men you've dated have had trouble with *C* words?"

"Uh-huh."

"Maybe you've been dating the wrong men."

"Maybe that's the answer to your question."

"Tell me more of these words," he said. His hands were gently circling my rear. I would tell him anything.

"Crisis. Conflict. Corn dogs."

"Where did you learn all these words?"

"From the comedian."

"Well, there you go," said Eric, removing his glasses. "The comedian obviously knew *C* words. I'm a lawyer."

"So…"

"I know *L* words."

"Such as…" I could feel him growing beneath me.

"Like. Love. Longevity." He massaged his long fingers into my rear as he said each one. "Litigation."

"Mmmmm," I said, thinking it over. "I like *L* words."

"But there are several *C* words I want you to pay attention to." Eric lifted me up by my shoulders to make his point. "Career. Comedy. Callback. It's very important you do well at your rehearsals and you get that *commercial* next week." He ran his fingertips down my front before he put me back on top of him. He wrapped his legs around me and pushed his body into mine.

"OHHHHH!" I sighed.

"Condoms. Copulation," said Eric, sliding his hand inside the top drawer of his night table.

"You're pretty *cocky*," I said, wondering why it was all so important to him.

"I like that word too. I like part of it a lot," he said, filling me up again.

"Me, too." So much so, I would really concentrate on career and callback to keep those condoms coming.

The Lightbulb at
the End of the Tunnel

Three Months After That
Midtown, NYC 1995

"Could you pull over on the next corner?" I asked Henry. "I see an open newsstand." My folks were navigating their way through the late-night traffic on Broadway. The opening night and, I had the distinct feeling, closing-night party was held at a hotel in midtown, just like real political campaigns. The party, ironically, happened to be at the same hotel where, some years back, I watched the election returns in defeat and watched the Republicans take office. I vowed to never go back there again. In fact, I vowed to never even walk on that block.

Henry and Millie insisted on driving uptown, and dropping me and Eric off after the party. The party. It wasn't much of a celebration. The show worked for the first fifteen minutes. It was all downhill from there. In the final scene, the audience was to vote for the new President and join the cast on stage for a victory party that included complementary wingdings. The candidate in our show lost, and the script had never developed a character running against him. The audience not only passed on the Prez, but on the wingdings too and went home after the curtain call, which they also pretty much passed on. I hadn't thought that being steadily employed would be so short-lived.

"Maybe you should just go upstairs and take yourself a nice hot bath, Kar, and read them in the morning," said Millie.

"Why, Ma? You think the reviews are going to be horrible, don't you?"

"I didn't say they were going to be horrible. Eric, did I say I thought they would be horrible?"

"No, you did not exactly say that."

"See," said Millie. "I'm glad somebody knows what I'm talking about."

"Well…" Henry looked into his rearview mirror to catch my eye before he spoke. "I, for one, thought it was a very enjoyable show. Really."

"Thank you, Henry," I said. I looked to Eric to punctuate the moment, but he was looking out the window.

"I love a musical," said my stepdad as he drove up Broadway to Columbus Circle.

"It wasn't a musical, Henry. It was a straight play."

"There was music."

"But it wasn't a musical. It was a straight play. A comedy." I reconsidered the audience reaction. "Well, maybe not, but it wasn't a musical."

"What was all the singing?"

"One chorus of 'For He's a Jolly Good Fellow' does not make *Funny Girl*."

"Well, I heard your voice above everyone else's in that section. I even poked Mother."

We stopped at a red light at the newsstand at Columbus Circle.

"I'll jump out and get the papers," said Eric.

My parents turned to face me as soon as the car door shut.

"Now, he's a nice one. Very nice," said Millie.

"Lovely young man," echoed Henry. "Really."

"A *mensch*."

"I, myself, was very impressed."

"And nice looking."

"Makes a good living, too, from what I can tell."

"And he likes you?"

Eric opened the car door. I took the papers from his hand and flipped through the *Times* until I got to the review.

"Here it is." Everyone waited for me to say something. "Okay, here we go." I angled the paper so I could get more light from the street lamps. I was hoping there was a good word missing I couldn't see. "Don't *EAT THIS!* Save The Calories."

Silence hung over the car.

"I'm not going to read this one now. Eric, can I have the *Daily News?*"

I turned to the theater page and read aloud, "*EAT THIS*—Half Baked Theater." The unemployment line loomed ahead. "Great. This is just great."

Eric had opened the *Post.* "Undercooked and Raw—Eat Something Else. Well," he said, "I suppose these are not exactly encouraging."

"I'm sorry," said Millie. "Something better will come along. Always remember, what's yours is still out there."

They pulled up to my building.

"Well, it was nice meeting you both," Eric said, cordially, before walking into the building.

"Yes," said Henry. "Very nice."

"I hope we'll see each other again," said Millie. My mother pulled me close to her and whispered. "See, something good came out of all of this. Let's hope," she said, moving her eyes in Eric's direction.

I hugged my parents and dashed down the steps to catch up with Eric. Gomez, the superintendent, was exiting the vestibule.

"I saw you on the news tonight, Miss Karrie," he said. He was carrying a stack of recycled newspapers.

"What did they say?"

"They repeat it now," he said, looking at his watch. "You see it yourself if you hurry."

We raced into my apartment and turned on the TV. They flashed a picture of the cast as I caught the reviewer's tag line.

"…and so, for my money I would not *Eat This!* I'd send it back. This is Gerry Goodman live from New…"

I shut off the set, kicked off my shoes, and slumped on the sofa.

"Whewwwww… Brutal!" I felt like if I breathed out loud enough, I could dispel some of the awful feelings. "What a disappointment. What a huge disappointment! On a scale of one to ten, it's somewhere around a thousand."

Eric stood in front of me. He was still wearing his coat.

"Eric, come sit with me," I offered my hand to him. "Thank you for being with me," I said, snuggling around him on the sofa. He felt good. I was grateful to be with him. At least my personal life would be moving forward. "Thank you for the beautiful flowers, and all your enthusiasm, and for being such a good sport. You had to meet my folks, not to mention my mother's whole Hadassah group, on such a miserable night. You were wonderful. Thank goodness I have you." I moved to kiss him.

His body stiffened. I noticed he was sitting on his hands. I looked into Eric's eyes for the first time that whole, long evening. He was so somber. He truly cared. He understood my feelings and he was taking this very seriously.

"Eric, oh, Eric. If you aren't the most compassionate, sensitive… It's okay. Don't feel bad for me. It'll be okay. I'll get another job. The good news is I'll have more time to see you, and now I have enough weeks to file for unemployment."

I touched his cheeks. I ran my hand through his hair. He was here for me. I was disappointed about work, but I was happy about him.

"Talk to me."

Eric remained silent. Then he quickened his breathing as he made several false starts to speak.

"You're going to hate me," he began, his words dripping out one at a time. "You're really going to hate me."

"How could I hate you? You've been terrific. I—"

"Let me finish," he said. "I don't know what's going on. I wish Dr. Dean made house calls."

He removed his hands from under his thighs and positioned himself to face me. I wondered why he was still wearing his coat.

"I don't understand your new haircut," he blurted out.

"My new haircut? What? They trimmed my hair for the show."

"Well, I think you looked better with it two inches longer. It doesn't work well with the shape of your face. I really noticed it during the second act."

Okay. I was waiting for the punch line. So far the conversation was absurd, and more so because Eric continued that halting stop-start thing while he spoke.

"And I've noticed you never wear makeup unless you have an audition, and you're not auditioning that much. You didn't get the Kole's Pineapple spot, and you're not even making regular trips to the gym."

"I've been working, I've—"

"I didn't think you were funny enough in your bit scene with Mac. You said you were going to do it the way I suggested."

"Excuse me, Teddy was the director." I could not believe I was participating in this dialogue. This was clearly not the way this wretched night was going to end. Eric was going to defend the play, praise my talent, sweep me up in his arms and make the part he could make better, better!

"Everything would have been okay if the show was a hit. I could have overlooked—things. Even that your part was not that big. But with the show obviously closing, you're just a girl from…QUEENS!" He punctuated the name of the borough as if it were a poison that was released from his mouth.

"You, your family, you're all too…Jewish…for me.

Your mother invited me to visit them at their summer house in the CATSKILLS! I can't go to the CATSKILLS! My family is very assimilated. You're just not my type."

By this point Eric had stopped any hesitancy. He was sure of what he was saying and was gaining strength with every word.

"You never took a share house, you don't even know how to ski," he said.

My mouth, which had dropped several inches, seemed to be locked in that position.

"I'm so disappointed. I miss my Off-B'way Baby," he said, reaching for a tissue to blow his nose.

"Eric…are you…you're not serious?"

"I'm afraid so. I've known for a long time. Since the beginning. It went away, but then it came back. I thought…with the play… I was so excited about dating an actress in an Alan Starkman play. My mother was an actress, you know. She was very popular in Princeton community theater. My mother may not be a pro, but she is really good! I always wanted to be with an actress. But that didn't work out for me, now, did it? And I kind of met this other woman a few weeks ago and, well, you know I'm a sexually monogamous person."

I felt like I had just been in a head-on collision and there were no witnesses. I was stuck to the sofa like someone had glued me there, my face hot with flashes of humiliation and disbelief.

"When were you going to tell me this?" I was livid. Hurt. Disbelieving.

"Well, if the play was a hit I wouldn't have had to. But since it isn't, I'm going to break up with you and sleep with her."

Now it was my turn to be silent. But it didn't last more than a fraction of a second because I was enraged.

"You're not that shallow, Eric. Are you?" I thought he would say something, anything to defend his honor. Redeem himself.

"I am talking to you! Are you that shallow? Please tell me you're not." I wanted to slug him, I wanted to hurt him and make him feel as awful as he made me. But mainly I wanted it all to not be true. Closing notices were being pasted in all areas of my life. It was too much to take in. I wanted it to be a mistake. A big, terrible mistake where the tape would be erased and it would all be taken back.

"ARE YOU THAT SHALLOW? ANSWER ME!"

At first he did not respond. Eric stood silent. Then he appeared taller, proud, confident and—oh my God—slick! Slick. Not in the cool, appealing way I had always perceived, but in a consciously duplicitous, detached, manipulative, ugly, good-at-getting-what-he-wanted-for-the-moment way.

"Why did you go out with me, Eric? Just tell me why! If you knew from the beginning, why were you on a mission to seduce me? Because you could?" I was seeing him for the first time and it was not pretty.

"Hey, I'm a nice guy," he said. "I just feel when it comes to women, I deserve ten out of ten on my list. Don't turn this around on me. I'm nice."

"You are not nice. You are mean, you are deluded and you are shallow." The evening that began with the fulfillment of my personal and professional dreams may have crashed, but this guy was not leaving the crash site unscathed.

"I may be a little shallow, but at least I'm honest about it. I'm working through some stuff with Dr. Dean. Look, I'm not even sure what will happen with us. I don't want you to get your hopes up or anything, but maybe, in a few months—"

"Eric. Enough. It's time for you to get out."

He didn't move.

"Get out," I said. My voice was breaking. I wanted him to leave before my anger broke and tears spilled out. I marched to the door and opened it.

"Okay, I should go." He buttoned up his coat, and reached into his pocket for his cashmere scarf. "I'm getting kind of busy at work. Tax season. But I'll call you later in the week. We can stay friends."

"I have no intention of being your buddy. Get out."

"Oh, you say that now, but you'll change your mind."

"I most certainly will not. I'd really like for you to leave. Get out!"

"You'll see. You'll change your mind. I'm sure of it. I stay friends with all the women I've gone out with for a few months."

"Eric—" My voice came steady and quiet out of a very hollow cavity in my chest. "Get the fuck out of here, you hear me!" I pushed him out with both of my hands. He was unprepared, and fell against the door of the opposite apartment. It was a fairly narrow hall. "Get out now!"

I slammed the apartment door, twisted the top bolt and the bottom lock. I was miserable, but at least I was alone with these feelings. These unexpected brand-new surprising horrible feelings. I threw my clothes on the bathroom floor, and turned on the shower. I stood underneath the hot water, shaking and crying until I'd emptied the well. The phone had been ringing off the hook. There were more than a dozen messages on the machine. I poured a glass of wine and picked up the newspapers.

My stomach was in a knot. I skimmed the reviews to see if anything kind had been written about the show. I found a copy of *Newsday* hidden under the stack of papers and turned to the reviews. It was the Queens edition. I opened to the Entertainment section and there it was! Like manna from heaven, my name jumped out. My name! I ran my index finger down the page until I saw in print. "…as the quirky waitress, Karrie Kline, a Queens native, is a real bright spot with her sharp comedic timing." I read it again. And again. I continued to read while the phone rang and rang, until finally the machine made it stop.

"It's Jane. Oh, honey. I'm sorry it wasn't all you wanted but I'm so proud of you. I bet you looked beautiful tonight and I'm sure Eric was thrilled with you and the whole thing anyway. Theater. What can you do? It'll be okay. You'll get another job. Call me tomorrow. We'll talk. Bye."

The machine clicked and hummed and returned the apartment to silence. I sipped the wine and stared at the good review that was wet with the water that had dropped down from my eyes.

Cheesecake Delight

Labor Day
The Great Lawn, NYC 1995

He had a hearty laugh. And smiling eyes. Fred saw him in the hallway when he came out of the elevator, and told me he was hiding the dozen red roses he bought for me behind his back, before he even got down the hall to our apartment. Our apartment! Fred was going to sublet my place when I moved to Los Angeles. It would be a permanent temporary move. I had to see how it went. However, one thing was clear. I would not give up my apartment. I mean, it's practically a law. *Never* give up your New York apartment.

After all these years, I just decided to do it. To go to L.A. To get on a plane and go. Jane would be out there, too, getting ready to audition for pilot season. Pilot season was that time of year when they cast the new TV pilots. Actors crossed their fingers and toes hoping to get the audition that would turn into the job that would turn into a series that would run for six seasons, making them a permanent part of television land, with reruns and residuals for all of eternity.

Fred was currently *between* apartments, jobs and boyfriends. Fred had been on the road for eight months, touring with a children's show and playing a wolf. When he got back to the city the real wolf turned out to be Larry, who had found a new boyfriend. Fred moved out of Larry's and kind of in with me. He was now working part-time at a florist in the plant district and counting the days until I would leave and leave him with some privacy.

"I wanted to say hi to him, but I didn't," Fred told me several days later. "He looked so sweet, hiding the flowers like that."

He and I met at a wine-and-cheese thing thrown after a reading of a play written by some guy from my acting class. It was a rainy night and I wasn't really up for it, but I felt that tremendous need to get out of the house. The play was so-so, but I liked seeing theater and I definitely liked cheese. When I reached across the table for a cracker, I looked up and saw Bradley. Bradley was warm and strong and striking. And he was dressed in a suit. I always think where there's a man in a suit there's a job nearby. We started to date. I figured out fast that Bradley liked food, and I liked Bradley. I bought a cookbook and invited him for dinner.

"What do you like to eat, Bradley?" I asked.

"Beef stroganoff, meat loaf, salad. Regular salads. Nothing fancy. Just a plain dinner salad, some lettuce, tomatoes, maybe some cucumbers."

I decided to make a meat loaf. I only made it once before. It came out a little bready. Bradley didn't notice.

"This is good," he said. "I haven't had a meal like this in ages. Except from my mom."

"Don't the girls you date cook you dinner sometimes?" I asked him.

Bradley thought.

"Not this past year."

He thought some more.

"Not last year either."

He's obviously been dating the wrong girls.

Bradley owned a magazine that tells tourists where to eat when visiting New York City. He knew lots of good places.

The first time we ate together we went Italian. Northern Italian. I enjoyed watching Bradley order food.

"What do you like?" he asked.

"Pasta," I said.

"Pick a pasta dish you like."

I did.

"What else? Veal, chicken, lobster?" asked Bradley.

We picked a few. It was an Italian potpourri.

"The Napoleons here are terrific," he said.

"Great," I said, knowing this guy knew what he was talking about. "Let's get one."

"Only one?"

"Oh, yeah," I said, resting my hand on my stomach. "One is plenty."

It was nothing short of heaven!

"Waiter," called out my friend. "I think we need another one of these."

It was a nice moment. Our heads bent over the flaky crumbs. Whipped cream melting in our respective mouths.

"Ever been married?" Bradley asked me.

"Nope." I knew he was divorced.

"Do you want to ever?"

"Yes," I told him. "You?"

Bradley shrugged. At first I couldn't decipher if it was a good shrug or a bad shrug. But I decided it was a good shrug because Bradley was leaning into me in such a seductive way. I guessed he just didn't want to be too obvious. His body was obvious! But the words, well, he probably didn't want to come on too strong.

"Do you want children?" he asked.

But he did. He was coming on strong! Oh boy, I was right. I was thrilled. He was interested. Really interested.

I wanted to give him truthful answers, but felt I should also seem a little reserved. Not in a rush for marriage and kids, but open.

"I'm not quite ready yet, but… It will depend on all the circumstances. But yes, with the right man, of course, I do want them."

The groundwork was laid. This relationship would progress. Nicely. Slowly working up to speed. I was already thinking of my L.A. plans, but I figured I could go out there for a few months, he could come visit, and if nothing connected for me I'd come back. See! *Never* give up your New York apartment. You just don't know what's around the corner. As Henry would say, "You never know what a day brings."

"So," I asked. "How about you, Bradley? Do you want children?"

"No," said Bradley. "Well, just this past year I had an inkling that maybe I would, but a child changes everything. I don't know that I'll ever get married again." He leaned in toward me and picked up a luscious piece of the pastry, then parted my mouth and put a dollop of whipped cream on my lower lip that he licked off with his tongue. "Let's face it," he said in a sultry tone. "After spending a lot of time with one person, you do kind of get sick of them."

"Excuse me," I said. Somewhere between the mention of children and the whipped cream I'd stopped breathing, and practically choked on the damn Napoleon. "I have to use the…"

I went downstairs and looked in the mirror.

"Smart Women, Smart Choices," I told my reflection. You have your plans for L.A. You have your friends, and you have you. It's a nice night out on the town. Enjoy it and go home. Alone.

A few weeks went by. Bradley called. We spoke.

"Do you want to get together?" Bradley asked.

"Umm…"

I did. I went to his apartment. He introduced me to his dogs, Emma and Clyde. His stuffed bears. He had lots of plants.

"What can I get for you? I have some strudel."

"Nothing," I said. "Really. I shouldn't."

I looked inside Bradley's refrigerator. "Cherry cheese from Zabar's! That's another story." Bradley heated it up in the microwave. It was really good. I noticed a Bible on the chair and he shared some of his spiritual philosophies with me.

Another night Bradley took me to his friends' for dinner. He brought a game for us to play. After eating a great meal of turkey meat chili, we played Life. I watched Bradley get a spouse. He picked up the little pink peg that fit in the little toy car piece that made its way around the board and made a life. Bradley's toss of the dice had him winding up with two kids. First a girl, then a boy.

When the game was over, I watched Bradley pull the pink peg out of the car and drop it back in the box. It was just a game, but it made me sad to see the little pink peg coveted and discarded. When it was over we ate two pints of vanilla-chocolate-chip-and-coffee ice cream that Bradley had bought when we'd stopped at the deli, ending the evening on a sweet note.

One Friday evening he picked me up after a workout at my health club. We went for Chinese.

"Do you like lobster Cantonese, spare ribs? How about the Oceanic Bouillabaisse?"

"Yes! Yes! Okay!!" I was catching on. This was fun. "And some egg drop soup."

We strolled uptown after dinner. We got to my building. He came inside. The apartment was still. Fred was crashing on another friend's couch who was out of town doing summer stock.

"Well," Bradley said, standing in the middle of my living room. "Good night."

"Thank you," I said, massaging my left shoulder.

"Would you like me to rub your neck for you?" he asked.

"Uh—only if you let me rub yours first."

I did.

He did.

I started to feel good. Really good. I started to worry. Remember the conversation you had with yourself weeks ago in the bathroom of that restaurant. Remember everything Bradley said that's making you remember the conversation you had with yourself in the bathroom of that restaurant. You're going to L.A. You're not available. Anyway, what's the difference. He's not available. He doesn't even want a—

I looked up at him. His eyes were intense and smiling. I wondered if Bradley made love like he ordered food. A feast of all kinds of tastes. With spirit. Generosity. And definite know-how. He kissed me. I had to find out. I let go. I kissed him back. And back again.

Dessert!

The next morning we went to the bagel place for breakfast. Bradley ordered.

"You like bialys?" he asked.

I just nodded. I knew for certain I was in good hands!

"We'll have a couple of those toasted with lox spread and cream cheese with chives," Bradley told the guy behind the counter. "Oh—and two of those blueberry cheese Danish heated up."

We were on a roll. I invited him to come to my friend Hank's barbecue. It was an annual event held in the park. Hank brought a few hibachis, a ton of hamburgers and hot dogs, and everyone invited brought everything else. On our way uptown, I asked what he thought we should bring.

Bradley led me into Carnegie Deli and picked out a perfect cheesecake. Standing at the cashier, I noticed an architect's drawing of an elaborate art deco corner building. Underneath the sketch it said Coming Soon—Carnegie Deli—Beverly Hills, California.

"L.A.'s answer to a deli looks like a Hollywood studio from the forties!" I said.

"That's what I'm going to do," Bradley said. "Go to California and raise the money to produce movies in the studio system like they used to."

"What about the magazine?" I asked.

"What about it? For the right price I'm on the next plane out of here."

After the barbecue we headed to Bradley's apartment. He turned to me.

"I'm concerned," he said, "that we're going to get close and you're leaving. Perhaps it'd be best to keep things casual."

"I thought that's what they were anyway," I said. "You as much as said so from the start. I wasn't even going to see you again, but I changed my mind."

"Why?"

"I found out I like you," I said. "I feel open to you." It was scary to say but it was the truth. I was glad it was out. I was glad I said it.

"I can't have a long-distance relationship and you can't have reasons to want to come back here," Bradley shot back. "You're so ambivalent about L.A. and you belong there for your work."

"Believe me," I said, "my conflicts about being in L.A. have been going on long before I met you. Leaving is hard for me. I grew up here."

I looked around. A perfect end-of-the-summer, breezy Manhattan night. Good or bad, New York was my city. I saw me not being here. My eyes welled up with tears.

Bradley looked at me.

"Oh, don't take this too seriously," I said, wiping my eyes. "I just have very severe separation anxiety. Really. The other day a man at work got fired and I cried when he said goodbye to me and I'm just a temp and I'm only working there a week and we never even spoke."

Bradley seemed unconvinced. So was I, but if I could manage to convince Bradley, perhaps I would convince myself. I'd been down this road before and knew that the door was closed on Bradley's desire to be in a relationship with me. I could do it with him, but he couldn't do it with me. I didn't want to feel bad about this and I didn't want to feel those "if only" feelings, so I didn't ask why. I didn't want to know.

"Look," he said. "Maybe I only have clarity about this situation because of California."

I didn't want to know, but I was going to find out.

"Maybe I don't want to fall in love now," said Bradley. "Maybe if you were staying here, a month from now I'd pull away and say it's because you limp on your left side when you walk down the street. Look, maybe you shouldn't spend the night."

Maybe, we agreed, it'd be a good idea if I got a cab home.

"I'll call you tomorrow," Bradley said, waving good-bye to me as if his puppy was going away to the vet.

When I got home Fred was stretched out on the pull-out sofa where he crashed until I left for L.A.

"What's the matter, honey?" he asked. "You look so sad."

We spoke.

"And when he tells me why, it's not even a reason. Limp on my left side! What is that? If we were fighting, I would get it. If we were having bad sex, I would get it. You know what else he told me, Fred?"

"What?" Fred was in the "has moved on but not completely" stage, and his relationship had lasted a lot, lot longer than mine. He was being a good friend listening to my war stories. I never seemed to run out.

"He told me I was his type. That if he had to choose exactly the type of person that he likes, it's me. I guess I'm his kind of person but not his kind of woman." I suddenly remembered being in a restaurant with him a few weeks back and watching him watch a tall, Connecticut-looking blonde walk by.

"I think he likes *Shiksa*s," I said.

"What?"

"Well, he may be into the New Testament but he's still a Jewish boy from Long Island, and I think he goes for

Shiksa girls. You know, Fred, those perfect non-Jewish-looking women with the little noses and everything."

"Well, you've got one of those," he said, pointing to my kind-of-perfect, cute little nose.

"Well, I've got one because I paid to get it. Doesn't count."

"Does count. Plastic surgery counts even more. Believe me!" said Fred.

"And I've got this stupid brown hair. Maybe I should dye it blond or red or something. Maybe when I'm in L.A."

"Don't pick yourself apart, Karrie. You know these guys, they don't know what they want. Imagine being me. A guy dating guys! The blind dating the blinder!"

"Well, you're doing better in the long-term relationship department than I am." We looked at each other a moment.

"To be honest, for a minute there I was worried," said Fred. "I was afraid you'd fall in love with the guy and you wouldn't leave," he said, eyeing the bedroom door.

"Don't worry," I said. "I'm still going and you're still staying. I'll even add your name to the mailbox tomorrow. I'll make a little sign that says Kline/Grennon. Happy?"

"Delirious."

I called my friends the following morning to thank them for the barbecue.

"By the way," said Hank, as we were about to hang

up, "that cheesecake was incredible. People raved about it all night. Whose idea was it to bring that anyway?"

A few days later Bradley called again. He was at work eating a chicken salad on rye with lettuce, tomatoes and mayonnaise. It came from The Fluffy Donut. "They make a perfect little sandwich there, and not many people know about it."

He asked me to get together one last time before I left. I hedged.

"The movies?" asked Bradley.

I knew I should decline.

"Sunday?"

I had no plans, it would just be a movie. But still, I knew how I felt and...

"Buttered popcorn. Large."

Oh??!!

"We can share."

What the hell. I am going to go. I'm still in New York and I still like Bradley. Besides, Carnegie Deli will be opening in Beverly Hills, and let's face it, even movie moguls have to eat.

Life in the Fast Lane

First Day of Autumn
Los Angeles, CA 1995

At first glance I'd have guessed my new agent to be no more than forty-five. Forty-six—tops. However, on second glance…

I was here. I had just relocated to Los Angeles and was interviewing with Jordy's talent agency, GSP&T TALENT. They were the best commercial agents in town. Going out to California was risky, but I had always wanted to check out the business on the other coast. Who knew what might happen? When I flew out of Kennedy airport, I knew I was leaving New York with an open heart, an open mind and an illegal tenant in my apartment, so my options would also be open.

Sitting on the posh leather sofa in the conference room, waiting for P. to come in and meet with me, I was struck by how much fancier this office was compared to what I was used to in New York. L.A. felt lush. Opulent. Pristine and perfect. Not to mention everything was sunnier than back east.

Jordy Parker walked into the conference room and sat down on the sofa opposite me. I thought he was the living end. Beautiful dark hair, impeccably groomed, really tanned. Great taste. Shiny shoes.

I was nervous meeting him. I made a joke. Nothing terribly funny but he laughed.

"You're adorable," he said. Having already interviewed with G,S&T, Jordy was the last person I had to meet. The meeting was great and we agreed to sign a one-year contract for me to be represented by his agency.

I was excited and flattered, and naturally assumed Jordy meant I was adorable in a completely professional way—until he asked me to go out. I had never dated an agent of mine in New York. True, they were all either women or gay, but this was new. It seemed a little dangerous, but he was quite intriguing.

About a month later, I went to the office for a radio audition. In Los Angeles practically all of the radio auditions were held at your agent's office. GSP&T had built a beautiful sound studio especially for this purpose. When I was finished, I dropped by Jordy's desk to say hi. We had gone for coffee two weeks before when I was at the office for an audition. We had run into each other in the reception area, just as he was going out for lunch. It just happened. Now I was taking the initiative. I know they say, "Don't mix business with pleasure," and I also know they say, "Don't shit where you eat," but I had already booked two radio spots and Jordy and I hadn't actually eaten, and besides I knew I had a sort of crush on him. The sort that's sort of huge.

Jordy was sitting in his green leather swivel chair, hunched over his antique pine desk, fidgeting with the right cuff of his crisp white shirt. Brown leather suspenders accented the front of the shirt, and the initials JP embroidered in navy blue surrounded a gold pair of dignified cuff links.

"What's the matter?" I asked.

"There's a thread hanging from here," he said. Jordy brushed his forefinger over it.

"Where?" I allowed myself to lightly touch his hand as I looked for it. After a minute I found the minuscule, practically invisible thread.

"I really hate this," he said.

"You just need a cuticle scissor," I told him, squinting my twenty-twenty eyesight in order to keep my eye on it.

"Do you have one?"

"Yeah."

"If I took you to dinner tonight out at the beach, would you bring your scissor and fix my shirt?"

I was flying as I sat beside him in the car on the way to the restaurant. Pacific Coast Highway whizzed by. The Golden Hour lit the road, the sand, the ocean. What a smooth ride.

"I'm usually not that excited about cars," I said, "but this one's really nice. What's it called?"

"A Mercedes."

"Even I've heard of that," I said. Oh, I was very cool. I was very in.

Dinner was divine. Glamour. Class. The Hollywood life. I threw caution to the wind. Not only was I living in L.A. and valet-parking my car, I was dating my agent.

Jordy called me every day and took me out most nights. I was on a high and felt lucky to have fallen into the good life so quickly. And to top it off, Jordy was originally from the east.

Born and bred in Newark, New Jersey, Jordy was now a native Californian equipped with the house in the Hollywood Hills, a Mercedes and an MG, and an outdoor Jacuzzi.

Jordy loved the California lifestyle. He loved his days because he loved his routine. Jordy's leather-skinned face did not come from Jacuzzi alone. Oh, no. No. It came from running. Ten miles a day. Every day. For years. Day in, day out, up at five-thirty every morning. To run.

5:30 to 6:30 A.M.—Running.

6:30 to 7:00 A.M.—Walk the dogs. Two Irish setters named Noah and Noelle. Two very large Irish setters.

7:00—7:30 A.M.—Shower and shave.

7:30—8:00 A.M.—Breakfast with the *L.A. Times.*

8:00—8:30 A.M.—Dressing.

Then off to the office in Beverly Hills until six o'-clock. Dinner plans always ended early so the dogs would be walked before his ten-thirty bedtime, so Jordy could wake up at five-thirty to run.

"Jordy, let's go to a movie tonight." It was now our sixth week going out, and in the past two we had not gotten together during the work week at all.

"I can't. They end too late and I won't be able to get to bed by ten-thirty."

"Come on, a seven-thirty movie."

"No. I've tried it, and it never works."

"Then let's rent a movie." I'd show him we didn't have to go out. I would go to his house. "You have a VCR."

"My ex-wife took it. It was part of the property set-tlement."

"Sally? Sally stole your VCR?"

"No. Nancy. My second wife."

"Your second wife. Nancy. I see," I said, only seeing how much of Jordy I didn't know. "Of course."

Saturdays arrived with more flexibility.

Up at eight o'clock to run.

8:00—9:00 A.M.—Running.

9:00—9:30 A.M.—Walk the dogs.

9:30—10:00 A.M.—Jacuzzi.

10:00—12:00 P.M.—Breakfast with friends and the
L.A. Times.

12:00—3:00 P.M.—Housecleaning.

"Jordy, don't you want to take a ride? Go to Malibu?
Farmers' Market? Make love?" I understood the workweek
thing, but couldn't the weekends be kind of freewheeling?

"Then who's going to clean?"

"Grace, your housekeeper. She comes here five days
a week. She cleans."

"No. I've tried it before and it never works. If anyone
ever wants to know how a big shot Hollywood agent
spends his Saturdays, tell them you've got the inside scoop."

I sure did, I thought, as I watched him exchange the
feather duster for the Windex. I watched him clean the
glass shelves hanging in the breakfast nook in the kitchen.
His kitchen! You could fit my entire New York apartment
in his kitchen. I glanced over at the stove and saw an
apron hanging on a hook on the brick wall just to the
left. I took the apron, turned around, grabbed the feather
duster from Jordy's hand and ran upstairs.

"What are you doing, Karrie?" he called, chasing me
up the stairs.

I went into his room and took the pair of black pumps
I had worn the night before, and ran across into a guest
bedroom. I slammed the door.

"Karrie, come on." I heard Jordy look for me in his room, then in his adjoining bathroom.

"I am in here!" I said, with a singsong lilt, in a really not-so-great French accent. I hoped I would properly distract Jordy and he wouldn't notice the not-so-great accent, him being my agent and all. Worst-case scenario was that I would not be sent out to audition for any commercials requiring someone with a French accent. Not that there was such a big market for French accents in voice-over work in the States. I opened the door to the guest room wearing only black high-heeled shoes and the little gingham apron. I held the feather duster.

"You have zees problem wanting zings clean?" I pulled Jordy inside the room by the drawstring on his sweatpants and pushed him down on the bed. "Perhaps you like to dust? Watch zees!"

I took the feather duster and lazily, delicately, dusted my neck, my breasts and my belly.

"You like, *monsieur?*"

Jordy looked at me. Something had gotten turned on, but I didn't know if it was his libido or not. I unbuttoned his shirt, took the feather duster and let the tips of the feathers lightly caress his chest. He began to relax. Jordy started to moan. He lay down on the bed. I did it some more.

"Oooh, baby," he said. "I like this."

Okay. This was more like it, I thought. This was just

what I had in mind. This is how you spend a weekend afternoon. I straddled myself over him and handed him the feather duster. I lifted my arms in the air so he would sensually run the feathers over me, my breasts and my belly.

"You're my maid," he said, throwing the feather duster to the side and pulling me down on him. "You're my slave," he said. And suddenly, the apron was off, the sweatpants were down, he was in, he was out and it was over.

I took it back. This was not *exactly* what I had in mind.

People can sure be deceiving. On the outside the package seemed so sensual. Witty, charming, well-dressed, sexy, inquisitive, charming, dark, handsome, charming...did I already mention charming?

He was adorable. Really. Very Irish.

"Parker is a pretty generic name for an Irishman," I once said.

"My real name is O'Malley. Jimmy O'Malley."

"Why'd you change it?"

"I started out as an actor."

"What happened?" I asked.

Jordy pointed to his chin. The lower right-side portion of it was patched together with a piece from his stomach.

"My chin," he said. "I lost part of it in a knife fight in Newark."

"Jesus Christ," I said. "Thank God you were okay."

Vacation time rolled around for Jordy who would be

gone for a month to Mt. Everest. Trekking in Nepal. He took me out for an early dinner a few days before he left, and brought me a bouquet of yellow and white roses for the holidays he would be missing. It was the last act of a suitor. Without any discussion, we both knew the next time I saw Jordy he'd be just my agent. I knew it wasn't right, but all the attention from Jordy had spoiled me. He certainly made my initial transition to "La-La Land" easy and painless. Jordy was a package I wanted to open, but I could not find my way underneath the glossy wrapping. I never figured out what made him tick.

Waiting at an audition one day, I overheard some actors talking. Who was making it, who wasn't. Fate. The punches life throws us that change our destiny. Suddenly my ears perked up. I heard a familiar name.

"He's a terrific agent, but you know he started out as an actor," said the man.

"Really, how interesting. I wonder what happened?" asked the woman.

"Well, I heard he was teasing his brother's dog and all of a sudden the dog bit him. Took a big chunk out of his chin. They fixed it, but he never felt he was good-looking enough to make it anymore."

"That's pretty amazing!" said the woman.

It sure the hell is, I thought. It sure the hell is.

The Lion's Share

We were on line when we started talking. In a Safeway in Los Angeles. West Los Angeles to be exact.

One of the major differences between NYC and L.A. is that no one in L.A. will speak to each other on line. On line as in standing in one, not to be confused with being online with your computer, which I am not because I don't even own one.

"What's that? Pie à la mode?" asked the guy in the running shorts as he watched me purchase a Sara Lee apple pie and a container of Bryers, which only proves you don't need to say a line, as in something catchy to initiate a dialogue. All you need to say is something.

"Fattening," I said, putting my change in my wallet.

"That's okay once in a while," he said, watching his fruit and juice sail down the conveyor belt. Another difference between the two cities is that the conveyor belts in this one work.

"I'm going to a barbecue in the Marina and I'm bringing dessert," I said, picking up my package that was bagged in paper, or plastic, or paper in plastic, or maybe it was just double-bagged. You know you're not on the East Coast anymore when you're asked the question, "How would you like this packed?" The first shock is that the checkout person in the supermarket is actually speaking to you, and the second is that they're the ones who'll be packing your groceries and not you. Although making the paper plastic decision requires vision, as well as practice, if you stay in L.A. long enough, believe me, you will adjust.

Anyway, the guy behind me, in line, with the gray running shorts was cute. On the short side, but so am I. Dark, in good shape—but who isn't in California?—and friendly. He walked me to my car.

"Where are you from?" I asked. "Brooklyn?"

"The Bronx," he said. "How'd you know?"

I smiled. I knew. The cadences. The point of view.

"I'm from Queens," I said, answering his question.

His name was Ron. He was a musician. He'd been in L.A. seventeen years. A long time.

"Too long," he said.

That's what everyone said.

"I have a few gigs but I'm free on Friday," said Ron. "Would you like to go out?"

"Sure," I said. Ron reached into his pocket for a pen and pointed to a spot on his grocery bag for me to write my number. We chatted a bit more.

"I don't want the ice cream to melt," I said, signaling it was time to go.

"I'll call you," said Ron as I drove away.

"You gave your number to who at where?" said Leslie, when I got to her apartment in the marina. She was marinating the chicken. "Isn't that dangerous?"

"I don't think so," I said, putting some franks on a platter to give to Dan to grill. "How else do people meet people?"

"What do you think, honey?" she asked her husband who came in from the terrace in time to hear the conversation.

Dan had been transferred from Wall Street to downtown Los Angeles, and every morning he had to be at work when the market opened and the bell rang in New York. Dan and Leslie found it easier to live in Los Angeles on New York time. They had two clocks set for both coasts in every room. Right now we were trying to finish dinner so they could get to bed by seven-thirty.

"I don't think she has to worry," said Dan. "It's fine. Where else are two crazy kids going to meet?"

Leslie married Dan for his sense of humor.

The pie à la mode was a success, and when I got home there was a message from Ron. Thanks to Dan and Leslie it was still early enough to call back, even by L.A. standards. I had two comp tickets to a show for Friday night and invited him.

"A show. Wow," said Ron.

"I don't think it's anything great," I said. "I've been working for someone that has a magazine, well, not working exactly, and not all that long. Just since, well, yesterday, and he, the boss, also has a theater company and the lead in this show. He gave me tickets."

"Oh," said Ron, "it's nice that you'd like to share these tickets."

"It's their opening and there's a little reception."

"This really sounds like something," said Ron.

"Ron, it's a small little company."

"Like Off-B'way?"

"It's so far off Broadway it's out here. I have a strong feeling it's not going to be anything memorable, but you never know. I would like to see it."

"It doesn't matter. And since you're taking care of the entertainment, I'll take care of dinner. I want to do my share."

"Oh. That's nice."

It was. Sort of. Ron wanted to do his share. It wasn't as romantic as it was…dutiful. He'd do his share, like picking the corn in his section of the field. Or dusting while I vacuumed. "Please," he'd say. "You did the dishes, let me take out the garbage. I insist on doing my share."

Ooooh! I was having domestic daydreams. "I met him at the Safeway on Pico," I'd say. "He was buying papaya and I was buying an apple pie…"

Well, you never know. As Dan had said, "Where else are two crazy kids going to meet?"

Friday night came and Ron arrived. I opened the door and he was standing on the porch in jeans and sneakers holding a plastic Safeway bag.

"Hi!" he said. "This is a really nice house."

It was. I had lucked out and lived on Coldwater Canyon with a young TV star that decided after furnishing the house she'd put it on the market because she didn't want to live in the house alone. Fortunately, we hooked up before someone bought it. Now she mostly stayed with her boyfriend and I lived in the house alone. It was my Hollywood story and worked out well for everyone except the two cats, whose preference I clearly was not.

"Come on in," I said to Ron, motioning to the living room.

"Wow, is this yours?" he asked, looking around.

I explained.

"Boy, this is really nice," he said, sitting on the oversized Southwest-print chair with the big, white overstuffed pillows.

"Yeah, I kind of love it here," I said. He was sitting. I was standing. I was starving.

"I'm broke," said Ron.

"Oh," I said. I felt a story coming on. I moved across the room and sat on the oversized Southwest-print sofa with the bigger, white overstuffed pillows.

"I don't live like this," Ron confided. "I live in a bachelor apartment in West L.A. My gigs aren't really paying. I was working in a music store but I got fired. I'm trying to get office temp work but I can't type. I'm really in debt. It's hard on my ego. I'm forty-six."

First I felt bad for him. Then I just felt bad. I wanted to go out and have fun. I needed it. I had plenty of my own problems. Life in L.A. was not going as well as initially expected. In the land of the have and have-nots, I was not having much luck. Instead, I was having car accidents. It seemed I had a much greater affinity for sitting on the subway than behind the wheel. Despite the fact I had found allies in Herman at Jake's Auto Body Shop, and Christopher at the Comedy and Pizza Traffic School, it was still taking its toll. I looked at Ron. He looked sad. I wondered what was in the Safeway bag.

"Gee," I said. "That's hard. Sorry to hear all that. I don't know if this is any consolation, but you only look around thirty-eight."

"Hey—thanks... Anyway, I can't afford to go out to dinner," said Ron. "I called all around and even a cheap

Thai dinner was going to be around seven dollars a person, including tax and tip. But I promised I'd do my share, so I brought these. They're already cooked. You just have to heat it up. You must have a microwave."

Ron reached into the Safeway bag and pulled out three freezer bags of cooked vegetables.

"You like vegetables?" he asked.

"Uh…yeah…pretty much. It kind of depends on how they're prepared."

Ron took his vegetables and found his way into my kitchen.

"I'll take care of the cooking," he called out. "I want to do that. You know I really want…"

"…to do my share," I mouthed along with him from the living room.

Okay. It's okay, I thought. Just regroup. Walk into the kitchen and say, "Ron, take your zucchini and take your squash and please leave." That seemed plausible. I didn't want him in my house. I especially didn't want him cooking in my house. I didn't want to sit with him in this intimate setting, eating dinner in my house. Eating these stupid vegetables from the Safeway in West L.A., and then having to do the dishes and take out the garbage like we were a couple making believe that this evening was the beginning of anything. I practiced on the cats who had witnessed the whole scene. They were snuggled up on the other oversized Southwest chair with the big, white overstuffed pillows. "Ron," I whispered to Marilyn and Clark, "take your carrots and take your cauliflower…"

I heard singing. Ron was puttering around my kitchen while singing "I Won't Grow Up" from the score of *Peter Pan*. "Where do you keep the spices?" he called out. "Oh, wow, a pantry! Never mind."

This was probably a treat for Ron. He probably didn't have a pantry. He probably didn't even have a separate kitchen. Oh. What the heck? It was one evening. He was harmless, I was hungry and I wanted to go to the play.

But I couldn't bear to sit down in the dining room and eat those vegetables. Cheap Thai had sounded good to me. It seemed I was always eating at home in Los Angeles. I attributed part of that to being broke, and the other part to living actual walking distance to Ralphs supermarket. Unlike my kitchen in New York, the one in L.A. always had food. I cut up some tomatoes with balsamic vinegar and olive oil and heated up a little sourdough bread. Ron appreciated my pitching in and doing what he considered to be more than my share.

We got to the play. The neighborhood was on the very eastern edge of Hollywood. We drove in circles till I finally spotted a little door in an alley we realized was the theater. Then we drove around and around until we could get a spot right near it so we wouldn't be afraid to walk from the car. Ron seemed less than happy. I asked if he wanted to leave, but he felt it could be the key to that lucky break.

"This is the great thing about living out here," said Ron, as we walked to the theater. "You never know where it's going to come from."

"Where what's going to come from?" I looked down at my shoe. Some gum was stuck to the heel.

"I might be able to meet somebody here tonight who could really help my career. Thanks for asking me."

"You can't be serious," I said, stopping a moment to rub my shoe against the dirt surrounding a small palm tree. "Who do you think can help your career?"

"Maybe your boss," he said, entering the untidy, tiny, depressing gray theater. "Oh," Ron sighed. "Maybe not."

Despite my explanation, Ron still chose to see the glamour version.

My "boss," which Ron insisted on referring to him as, was the lead actor in the play. Joe, an ex–New Yorker near sixty, seemed like someone who'd be sitting at the counter in the Hopper picture of broken Hollywood dreams. He had done a few lines in B movies in the fifties and sixties, and somehow lost his way. Joe had a little literary magazine and had advertised for someone to sell advertising space to bookstores. I had never sold before but I needed money and answered his ad. I had gone down to his office earlier in the week. It was chaotic, topsy-turvy and clearly nothing valuable was happening there. But I did it for three days. I thought I'd learn *something,* and then I could go to a real magazine and say I had experience. When I gave Joe my "notice," he told me all about his play and asked if I'd come. I was curious to see Joe playing Roy Cohn in yet another piece about the lawyer's demise and his illness with AIDS.

Joe was such an egomaniac he had the playwright alter history to make his part big, bigger and biggest. In this play, Roy Cohn was single-handedly responsible for the spread of AIDS throughout the entire United States, and forget McCarthy. In this play, Roy Cohn was the McCarthy era. Even though someone dying of AIDS would become weaker and weaker, in Joe's performance he was getting stronger and stronger. From his hospital deathbed he was screaming and crying and *kvetching.* His arms were flailing. The theater sat forty-nine. Joe acted like he was playing the Paramount, and we were sitting in the first row. Ron had wanted a good seat.

The opening-night reception was on the stage, since there was no lobby. Ron would not stay. He gave me one minute to say hello and goodbye to Joe and would not speak to me on the way to the car. He would not speak to me in the car. We sat in silence on the 101 going east or west, or some direction back to the Valley. I looked out at the Freeway and caught my reflection in the lit-

tle side-view mirror. I didn't recognize myself, having just
dyed my hair L.A. blond. It wasn't bad on me, but it
wasn't good. I was looking like everyone else, and I didn't
necessarily know that I wanted to. We passed a sign that
read Adopt A Highway—Bette Midler. I didn't know
what that meant except that it had to have something to
do with money, roads, traffic and the car. I was so sick of
the car. I hated dating in L.A. I hated dating in the
damned car. I hated being strapped in next to someone
I didn't know when I had to go on dates in the car. I
wanted to be free. I wanted to have my own space and
walk down the street. I wanted to say, "See ya," and make
a clean getaway into a cab.

When we turned off the Coldwater Canyon exit,
Ron started to speak. I realized he was timing his speech
to coincide with the drop-off at my house.

"I could not believe that," he said.

"I knew it wouldn't be good," I said. "But I really
couldn't believe it could be that bad." It was so bad it actually made me nostalgic for the vegetable portion of the
evening.

"Where is your self-esteem?"

"My what?"

"How could you do it?" he asked.

"Do what?"

"You're a smart woman. You seem like a talented
woman, and you stooped so low."

"I stooped so…what are you talking about?"

"How could you misjudge like that?"

I had certainly made an error in judgment that evening, but it wasn't on the theatrical end.

"If you saw the way he ran a magazine, why would you think he ran a top-notch theater company?"

"I didn't," I said, "but it was fun, don't you think? In a dreadful, macabre sort of way."

"I cannot believe you would take me to a place like that. How could you do that to me?"

I chose not to answer as we pulled up in front of my house. I got out of the car and felt sheer and utter relief. I wanted to get away from Ron, but, walking up the driveway, he stopped me.

"I just want to be clear," said Ron, in a tone of voice that sounded as if he had taken EST and every workshop spun off it. He was standing in front of the rear tire of my blue, dented '89 Toyota. "I want you to know I won't be asking you out again."

He waited for my response. Inside I was doing flip-flops and yelping for joy, but at the same time I was incredulous that he thought he was rejecting me! I looked at Ron. It had been a horrible night, but I was curious to hear his explanation.

"I believe in honesty, you know," said Ron. "I believe in doing my share. I had really high hopes for this evening. I did everything I could do to make it nice. I dressed up. I was on time. I brought dinner. I have no money, and I made sure to honor my agreement and we had a wonderful dinner. You even said it was. And you said you were taking me to an opening. I drove you and escorted you and you made me go to a horrible neighborhood and sit through an embarrassing and amateurish show."

"A play is live. It's not a movie you can prescreen."

"You should have known better. You've worked. You've been on tours. You've been Off-B'way. I thought you were taking me to something great. A great event with great people I could meet. An opening. I thought you wanted to network with your boss. An older actor who could pull strings for you out here."

"He is not my boss. And why would you think that? I never told you that."

"I just thought you were modest."

"I was honest."

"Well, if you knew he couldn't do anything to help you, why would you want to see his play?"

And if you knew I couldn't do anything to help you, why would you want to see me? I thought.

"I love to see theater," I said. "Good stuff. Bad stuff. I love to see people do their thing. I like that. And you can learn a lot from bad theater. A great advantage to being here in L.A., because there's certainly no shortage of it."

Ron didn't laugh. What did he know from theater?

"This was one of the worst nights," said Ron. "You should take better care of yourself. Next time you make a commitment to do your share, I think you should keep it."

I turned my back. I was not going to answer him. He didn't deserve a moment more of my time. A complete imbecile! Clueless *and* pompous. A real winning combo! He didn't matter enough to make me angry. I would look ahead. Be positive. Spring would be just around the corner. Not that you'd notice it in L.A.

I walked into the beautiful house and heard the wind chimes singing outside. I was catching on. In Los Angeles it all looked nice on the surface, but I was beginning to see you didn't even have to look closely to see the cracks. Appearances. Lifestyle.

I lived the fancy L.A. life in a house, but it wasn't mine. I had expensive haircuts in the best salons, but they were the worst I'd ever had. I couldn't begin to talk about the shmooze factor in getting acting work, and even the concept of a bad date had to be redefined. Everything revolved around The Industry. Tonight was supposed to be a night out. A little fun. And although I had read Ron the book version of *Joe's Magazine & Theater Company,* he spent the whole night desperately trying to see the overblown Hollywood movie. I was an actress on his arm. The costar in Ron's bomb.

"That's why they call it Tinseltown, huh?" I asked Marilyn and Clark. They didn't answer. They were smart. They hadn't left their spot the whole night.

What's the Big Deal?

Christmas. Again. If the holidays didn't bring up enough conflict, now it was Christmas conflict, Los Angeles style. Lots of glitz and no chance of a white one. But I decided to just stay put. It wasn't such a big deal.

Jane was going back to New Jersey to be with her family. She and Philip had broken up and she was not spending it alone out west. Christmas was a big deal in the Murphy family, and her holiday always sounded Norman Rockwell perfect to me. Millie and Henry had retired and now lived in Florida, and since we didn't actually celebrate anything on Christmas Day, I'd only be trading the warm weather west for the warm weather east if I went there.

Christmas, ever since I could remember, was a club I could not join. The neighborhood where I grew up in Queens was half Jewish and half Irish. All of the kids got along well throughout nursery school and kindergarten. When it came time for first grade the Jewish kids stayed on at P.S.150, the public school, and the Irish kids transferred over to the Catholic school, Queen of Angels. The kids I had played with all my young life were now the very ones I would argue with on street corners.

"Well, we don't have to wear uniforms. We can wear whatever we want to school."

"Oh yeah? Well, we got beautiful white dresses with veils for our communion. And we get off Saint Patrick's Day and you don't."

"Oh yeah?? Well, on Jewish holidays we're not allowed to write and we don't even get homework."

"Oh yeah??? Well, we get Christmas!"

"Oh yeah????"

There it was. Christmas. The magic club. I couldn't come up with anything better. I could stammer something about getting lots of checks when I'd be Bat Mitzvahed, but every Jewish kid knew that money was going to be put toward college, so it wasn't such a big deal.

I remember being in our living room one Christmas when I was seven years old, watching my mother iron while playing with one of my Barbie dolls.

"Can I go up to Maggie McGraw and ask her to come play with me?"

Maggie was my baby-sitter and lived upstairs in our apartment building. She was probably about fifteen at that time. She was blond with freckles, and used to sing the song "Red Rubber Ball."

"Not today," my mother said. "It's Christmas. Don't disturb them."

"Why? What are they doing?"

"It's a big holiday for them. Irene probably has the whole family over. She's been cooking all week. Not today."

I had to go. I had to know what was going on up there. I snuck up the stairs to 5K and knocked on the door. The apartment was filled with food, laughter, presents and a big, beautiful Christmas tree. Everyone was dressed up. John, Maggie's father, was wearing a tie. So was his son, Johnny, who was my age, and little Tom. Maggie was in a red dress with a big red-and-white bow. She did come downstairs, later, to play with me. I stared at her the whole time, hoping her Christmas magic would rub off and initiate me into the club.

"Why can't we celebrate Christmas?" I asked.

"Because it's not our holiday. We're Jewish."

"So what? It's just a seasonal thing. It's just a time to spend money. It's not religious. Jesus, you're so narrow-minded."

I was sixteen and had just finished reading Meir Kahane's book, *Never Again*.

"You don't do anything religious all year, but God-forbid I would ever marry out of the religion, you'd make such a stink. You're such a hypocrite, Mother. I'll never be like you when I grow up!"

"When you were little, didn't we light the electric *menorah* every night? Didn't I hide a different gift for you every night? And I made latkes and we played with the dreidel. What do you want from me?"

"I want a tree."

"Not in my house. Not with Grandma Rose coming over."

"I want a tree! You're depriving me of everything. I swear to God, I'll never deprive my children like you do!"

"Go. Get a tree. Get a tree, go to church, raise your children any way you want. Just leave me alone."

I got a tree. It was two feet high. I covered it with candy canes and silver tinsel. My grandmother came over to visit, and I hid it in the closet. I had a tree, but it didn't feel great. It wasn't a very big deal.

In my junior year, when I was away at college, my school sponsored a trip to Florida over the winter intercession. But first I spent Christmas week at home in Queens.

For a few days in a row, I ran into Johnny McGraw on the street, in the lobby of our building and in the elevator. He kept flirting with me. I thought he looked really cute, and I flirted back. I always liked Johnny. I had known him all my life, but I didn't think anything really would happen between us. The flirting kept getting more and more intense, and the day we were alone in the elevator he kissed me.

"I want to see you before you go back to school," said Johnny. "Maybe we can go over to Hannihan's for a beer."

"Is this a date?" I asked that night, sitting on a bar stool next to Johnny, drinking my first beer from the tap.

"Why do you have to label everything?" he asked. "Just enjoy the beer and feel good."

When we went home and got in the elevator, Johnny pressed the button that said 5 for the floor he lived on, instead of 2 for me. I looked at him with a question. As an answer, he kissed me.

"So, are you coming in?" he asked when the elevator stopped at 5. He used one hand to stop the elevator from going, and the other to stop me from going with it.

"I don't think this would be right," I said. "I feel good with you but it's not like you're my boyfriend. Are you?"

Johnny pulled me out of the elevator and kissed me.

"Do you want to think or do you want to enjoy your life?" he asked.

I went with him and slept with Johnny in his bed while everyone in his family was out. It was the first time I had ever slept with a boy who wasn't my boyfriend. I

liked it, so I assumed I liked Johnny and he liked me. I
assumed I had been wrong, and something really could
happen between us. I would be his girlfriend now. It was
Christmas, and I would go shopping and buy presents
for all of the McGraws.

"I guess I'll come up to your house on Christmas
Day," I said to Johnny after.

"No," he said. "I don't think so."

"Why not?"

"Doesn't the Jewish college girl have something better to do before you go to Fort Lauderdale?" His remark
was very mean, but I knew it wasn't meant to hurt me.
Johnny was feeling the differences between us. Jewish and
Not Jewish. College and No College. Christmas and No
Christmas. It was a division with a boy who was at my
birthday party when I turned three. A boy I had grown
up with in the same building. And though his comment
made me feel bad, Johnny was the one who looked hurt.

"Huh? What does me going on a vacation have to do
with anything, Johnny?"

"You know we're different, Karrie. Don't make this
into a big deal."

We just slept together. It was nice. I thought he liked
me. Was he embarrassed about me? Or embarrassed
about himself?

"Well, do you feel bad because you didn't go to college? Johnny, you could go to college if you wanted. I

could help you apply. And no one ever has to know what just happened. Can't I come to Christmas? What's the big deal?"

"I've got to be at work in an hour," he said, getting out of bed and tossing me my jeans. "My dad will be home soon. We had fun, okay?"

I ran down the three flights to my house. My house. Growing up, I always called our apartment a house. The phone was ringing. Millie and Henry weren't home. I picked it up and heard Grandma Rose's voice and started to cry.

"*Mamala,* what is it? What happened? Did somebody hurt you?"

"Yes, Grandma. Somebody did. A boy."

"What did he do? Tell me, Karrie, tell Grandma."

What could I tell her? I slept with a boy in my building and I felt used and confused. That he would not be buying me a big diamond ring or breaking the fast with us on Yom Kippur.

"I like a non-Jewish boy, Grandma, but he doesn't seem to like me that much, and he won't let me come to his house for Christmas."

"Oh." Grandma Rose sounded a little relieved. "Try to forget about it. You'll go to Florida and you'll meet other boys. If he doesn't like you, he doesn't know what he's missing. And Christmas is not our holiday. They all make such a big deal. Who needs it?"

A few years later Grandma Rose died. It was two days before Christmas. Now the time of year has me thinking of her, and not the holiday I thought I was missing. I missed Grandma Rose and the clarity of her life. Her clarity of what was right for you, and what was not. Who was good for you, and who was not. Her world may have been more limited than mine, but it was a lot less confused. Her purpose was her heritage and her family. I wanted that clarity. I wanted *that* sense of home. That, to me, would be a very big deal.

I was really a grown-up. Living in Manhattan. An actress, dating a comedian. At Jack's parents' farm in Virginia I had my first real Christmas ever. As Born-Agains the Whitneys embraced both the Old Testament and me, and even felt this was a positive step on the road to my becoming a Jew for Jesus.

I had shopped for weeks in preparation for that trip. I bought gifts for Jack and his parents and his sister and his brother-in-law and his brother and his sister-in-law and his five nieces and nephews. When it was all over, both Christmas and our relationship, I was overcome with how much work it had been. If Jack and I had worked out, it would have been fine. But since we didn't, I was able to admit it was a lot of shopping and a lot of shlepping. Three years had passed and it was becoming clear that a magical Christmas was not the club I was searching for.

* * *

"I miss the change of seasons," I've been telling people when they want to know what I miss most about New York, now that I'm living in Los Angeles. I drove down Wilshire Boulevard and found the seasonal disparity between the Christmas lights and the palm trees too wide to make any sense of.

"No, I'm not going back east for the holidays," I told my agents when they asked if I'd be booking out. "My grandmother's gone, and my folks moved to Florida," I explained. "Maybe I'll have some people over, or just go to a movie. For me, Christmas is not such a big deal."

Hanukkah came early this year. I took out my grandmother's *menorah* and put it in the window facing Coldwater Canyon. The Eight Days of Hanukkah met the Twelve Days of Christmas. When I lit a candle, I wished for something I wanted. I repeated all the wishes each night, before lighting the newest candle.

Then I opened my *siddur*. The small, black prayer book has my name embossed in gold on the cover. The Sunnyside Jewish Center had presented it to me at my Bat Mitzvah. I read in Hebrew, while I kindled the lights from left to right. I felt pride in my heritage, reading each Hebrew word while each candle was made to glow. Then I read the passage in English.

"We light these lights on account of the miracles and wonders, triumphs and battles thou didst perform for our fathers through thy holy priests in those days at this season. These lights are sacred throughout the eight days of Hanukkah; we are not permitted to make any other use of them except watching them, in order to praise thy great name for thy miracles, thy wonders and thy triumphs."

I realized I am not a religious person, but I am traditional. Jewish tradition is a part of my culture, and a part of my soul. It is the part of my childhood that remains in my adulthood, and the part I will pass on.

I watched the candles burn. They reflected in the bay window. Cars drove by the house, north and south over the Canyon. As they passed homes decorated with colored lights and snowmen, they also passed this one, with eight lights shining in the window. Lights that signified that through it all, Judaism prevails. In L.A. In me.

This is a pretty big deal.

The Call of the Wild

Mother's Day
Beverly Hills, CA 1997

The Famous Television Star poured himself another glass of wine. His house was ensconced in a wooded road, just north of Sunset Boulevard. The location gave it a very east coast, New England feel. The brown leather sofas and plain wood furniture helped make it the tasteful bachelor pad it was. The only real Hollywood giveaways were the telephones in every room, and, yes, a gym. It was night, but the oval swimming pool was visible through the huge picture window.

"You want some more?" The Famous Television Star asked me.

"Hmm." I looked at the bottle of Chardonnay sitting on the antique oak coffee table. "Let me think."

"Oh yes, you dainty little lightweight girls have to watch it."

Earlier that evening, The Famous Television Star had come to see my show. It was a sketch comedy show I did with some people I knew from New York. It was funny and we performed on Melrose Avenue in a bar. The Famous Television Star said he would come and he did. We had met years ago when we were both doing shows Off-B'way, back in the days when he was just a terrific actor turning into The Famous Television Star. I had followed his career, and seen him when we did shows in the same cities.

Tonight, after my show, The Famous Television Star invited me to his house for dinner. It would be the very first time in ten years I would be with him in private. Alone. I was nervous following his black BMW on Sunset. I was less nervous when we arrived. I liked his house. The high ceilings. The steps. The levels. I used the bathroom, and called my machine from that room. I had no messages. When I came out, The Famous Television Star had gotten a fire going and opened a bottle of wine.

"You sure you don't want some more?" he asked again.

"Well, maybe just a drop. Have to drive," I said, hoping I wouldn't. I looked at the mantel over the fireplace where his two Tonys, Emmy and Golden Globe awards were prominently displayed.

I liked being there with him. In his sweatpants. In his kitchen. He cut kiwis for fruit salad, while I microwaved Stouffer's tuna lasagna and put together a salad.

I was cold, even though it was May. The California desert air. The anticipation in it. He was old enough to be my father, but I didn't care. He showed me pictures of him from college, from high school and from his Bar Mitzvah. He talked to me about his mother. She lived in Palm Springs and they were very close. He turned on classical music. He turned off the lights. We sat in front of the roaring fire—wine, food, two forks and the fruit salad in one bowl.

"Can I give you a hug?" he finally asked. It was warm. Sexy. The famous hand of The Famous Television Star played with my hair, as he tried to define the word interested. As in what makes him interested in someone. What made him *interested* in me. Snuggling into his shoulder I told him I liked him.

"I don't know what will happen with us," said The Famous Television Star, his famous brown eyes looking straight into my blue ones.

"What do you want to happen?"

"I don't know. Maybe you can write this. In your diary. Do girls still keep diaries?"

"Little girls do. Big ones keep journals," I said, wondering where this was going.

"Write in your journal and find out what happens,"

he said. The thought of my journal with its overanxious scribble was anything but promising.

"Maybe one of your staff writers will do it," I said. The Famous Television Star had a show that was a midseason replacement for what he hoped would be another famous television series. "Or better yet, how would you write it?" I wanted to know. I searched his famous face to find out.

My body unwound as The Famous Television Star moved in closer. I put down the wine, I put down the fork. I was ready to receive his high TV-Q.

The Famous Television Star bent over me, on his knees. He raised his hands, as if to gently stroke me. Then he barked.

"Huh?" I turned to see if he had a pet I had neglected to meet.

The Famous Television Star barked again. He cupped his hands like little paws. Then The Famous Television Star growled. Was this some kind of famous foreplay? Or an unaired episode of his famous, funny show?

I giggled. My nerves were back. Nervous laughter. Very nervous, in fact. The Famous Television Star thought I liked it. He got down on all fours. He started to lick my nose. He howled.

I scampered across the floor and picked up my purse.

"Let's go for a walk," I suggested, wondering if he'd like to be put on a leash. "You'd like that, wouldn't you?" I went to the glass door, slid it open and ran.

The Famous Television Star followed me.

"Where're you running to?" He looked so innocent, panting, chasing me, his tongue going up and down.

"Exercise," I called out. "Figured you wanted some." I got to my car and flipped open the door, anxiously awaiting my escape. The Famous Television Star caught up and faced me. I wondered if he thought his behavior odd.

"Well," I said, relieved to be safely inside my car. "It was great." The Famous Television Star barked in approval. "Have fun on your trip to Hawaii," I said, turning on the ignition. "Have fun on your hiatus."

"Yes," he said, happily. "Bye, bye." The Famous Television Star put his face up against the open car window and pulled my hand to his ear. He moved his face up and down so it appeared I was nuzzling him like a little puppy. He let out a sigh.

"We'll have to do this again," he said. Romantically, I think.

"Hmm." I placed my hand on the wheel. I couldn't see where I was going. I closed my eyes, backed up a few feet and prayed I wouldn't have another accident. Then I cut a hard right. All the while my face was frozen in a superficial smile.

"Wait," he said, as I was pulling away. "Did you have fun?"

"My tail is wagging!" I called out. I drove down the

gravel driveway. He stood at the top of the hill jumping up and down, waving after me. Then The Famous Television Star let out one last bark. Just for the thrill of it.

Weight-Listed

First Day of Summer
Los Feliz, CA 1997

The traffic on the freeway was, as they say back east, bumper-to-bumper. In L.A. they called it gridlock. Whatever they called it, it wasn't moving. I looked at my watch. At this rate I was going to be late. We'd been crawling since Highland. We were barely moving. I was tired of sitting there. In New York when there was some sort of city traffic crisis everyone would band together to talk about it. People would look at each other on the subway or bus and scream, "What the hell is goin' on here? Why aren't we moving?" It didn't make us move any faster, but it kept us busy and bonded.

For lack of camaraderie, I tuned in to talk radio and

talked back. I looked at the car on my left. The guy next to me was engrossed in a conversation. With himself. On my right the woman in the Porsche was on her car phone. And the person in the passenger seat was wearing a headset and having a sing-along with his Walkman. I suddenly figured out where the traffic jam was. It wasn't. No one was driving. Everyone was talking.

Jane and I were meeting at the gym in her hood for a quick workout. She had news! We were meeting at Not Just Aerobics, a chain in L.A. that had reciprocity with our health club in New York. I finally pulled up to the place just before dusk. Only fifteen minutes late. The smell of jasmine coated the air. There was a peacefulness, as if the hills were a little village getting ready for sleep. Summer was approaching. I knew it by the calendar. You could not sense it in the air. The feeling on the west coast was so different from that of the east. It was quiet. Soft. Nice. But there was never any holiday spirit.

After being in L.A. for almost two years I could honestly say that every day in Southern California was the same as the one before. This is not to say that the weather didn't change some. There were low clouds that burned off to sun. And sun that was hidden by clouds. And sometimes clouds that made rain. But there was a sameness to the days. There was never an electricity buzz just because it was a Monday morning, a Friday night.

In Manhattan now the city would be clearing out. It

was Friday, and you could probably feel the division on the streets of who would be staying for the weekend and who would be going. People leaving rushed around with the anticipation of fleeing the cement for greener pastures. And those staying walked the streets territorially waiting for everyone to go, eyeing the cafés, the parks and the movie lines, knowing they would soon have full ownership. No one cleared out of the streets in L.A. because no one was on them to begin with.

Big holidays like Christmas, Easter and even Fourth of July blended together in Los Angeles. I would never be woken from a deep sleep in L.A. because the Puerto Rican Day parade danced outside my window. The only day I felt a buzz in the air was the day of the Oscars, the national holiday of Hollywood.

I parked the car, walked inside and looked at the enormous classroom that practically took up the entire main floor. It was carpeted in a garish orange industrial carpet. Nautilus equipment and stationary bikes surrounded the perimeter of the room.

"AND ONE—AND TWO—AND UP—AND TWO, AND ONE—AND TWO—AND UP—AND TWO," the aerobics instructor called out. She wore tight black spandex biker shorts and a hot-pink sports bra. "TURN LEFT!" she shouted as she jumped off the platform onto the workout floor. Her long blond braid bounced underneath her Lakers baseball cap. "TURN

RIGHT!" She spoke into a hand mike in order to be heard over the music that banged against the walls. The Stairmasters surrounded the perimeter of the gym floor, and everyone working out was watching the aerobics class as if it were a movie.

I walked into the small office. "Good afternoon. It's a beautiful day here today at Not Just Aerobics. How can I help you?" The phones were ringing off the hook.

"Hi. I'm from the Manhattan Sports and Racquet. I've been going to Not Just Aerobics in Studio City. We have reciprocity with this club and I just want to work out here for the day." I pulled out all my membership cards as I approached a hefty, muscular man at the desk. He wore tight black gym shorts and a white tank with the logo Not Just Aerobics scrawled across the back and J.D. sewn onto the shirt on the front.

"Gym."

"What?"

"We're not a club," he informed me. "We're a gym."

"Same difference."

His eyes narrowed. "They're not the same at all," he said, crossing his arms, standing a little taller.

"Sure they are. Fundamentally, they are."

"I'll tell you what," he said, reaching into the desk drawer and pulling out a day pass. "I'll give you a free One-on-One today at the gym. Then you tell me if you see a difference."

"You're on," I said.

"Meet you at the Stairmaster in an hour."

"Perfect," I said.

I went into the locker room and found Jane changing into her workout clothes. I opened my mouth to explain the time when she stopped me.

"Just got here five minutes ago. God, look at me," she said. "I'm wearing these horrible torn gym things and everyone else is dressed in outfits."

"I know," I said. "Same in my neighborhood. I won't give in. I'm not getting all dressed up to sweat."

Jane and I went out to the mats. We stretched and I looked around, observing the clientele. This was a place where everybody clearly took their body seriously. Very, very seriously. In Los Angeles, it seemed that going to the gym could be one's work. It could be one's job. Full-time. An all-day full-time affair.

The gym was certainly not the place where you just threw on some sweats and dropped by to work out. The gym was certainly not the place where you dropped by to keep in shape. It didn't even appear it was the place you dropped by to get in shape. To be here was to have already arrived. A lifestyle. An event. Everyone here was outfitted. The right attire. Spandex, Lycra, hats and bandannas in every imaginable color and design adorned the bodies around me. It was a walking catalog for workout clothes. Tight clothes. Skinny clothes. Skinny, little workout clothes. Workout clothes that showed just how much you worked out so that you could show skin. Tight, taut skin. Skin that dripped with sweat. Tons and tons of sweat that dripped from everyone's tanned, skinny pores. I passed my image in the floor-to-ceiling mirror and saw a woman with no makeup wearing a pair of running shorts that stuck out under an oversized New York Mets T-shirt, and wondered what could have possibly gone through my mind when I selected my workout ensemble.

"So, Kar," Jane finally said. I was waiting for her news. I knew she had two callbacks for a soap and I was hoping she got it.

"Yeah?"

"I'm moving back east. I'm going to leave next week."

"What?" I was shattered. I didn't want to stay out here without Jane. "You're doing so well." Jane had just done a major guest spot playing a jewelry thief on a crime show and did two national diaper commercials. "Why are you leaving?"

She looked at me and smiled. I knew that smile well.

"What's his name?" I asked.

"William. William Harris."

"Who is this? What's going on?" I felt so out of the loop.

"Well, remember the Christmas I didn't go home? When I stayed out here and went to Mass at that tiny little church on Beachwood Canyon?"

I did remember. I was going to join her, but I went to a party instead.

"Remember I told you I sat next to that litigation lawyer, the tall good-looking blonde who lived in Manhattan and came back to see his family."

"Yeah, the guy you were in touch with for a while."

"Well, he's been out here on vacation. We got together and it feels so right. I also miss real theater more than I can say. I can't do musical theater out here the way I want. My parents are getting older, I want to be close. I gave notice on my apartment, bought a ticket and I'll be gone a week from tomorrow."

"Oh my God, Jane! I'm going to miss you so much."

I was happy for her and knew she had to feel good to have made a decision. We frequently debated the merits of The Coasts and The Business and we were each waiting for something to help make a firm decision. For Jane it was made, and I was glad.

"You'll be back too, Kar," she said. "When you're ready. Let's have dinner at the Vietnamese place on Franklin next Tuesday. You'll get to meet William."

Our friendship traveled through national tours, regional theater work, stock and bicoastal living. I knew this wasn't goodbye, but Jane's L.A. chapter was ending, and she was being written out of mine. Her absence was going to make me think twice about staying.

"I keep waiting for things to get settled and stay that way," I said, "but they insist on changing. What is that?"

"I think they call it life."

"Life," I said. "There's a concept."

Our reflections stared back at us as we finished stretching on the mats. Jane picked up a piece of my hair and talked straight ahead into the mirror.

"I like this. Red is a very good color on you, dahling!" she said.

The blond was getting that dyed, brittle look and the hairdresser talked me into red. "With your pale skin it'll make those blue eyes pop!" he exclaimed.

"They say this stuff to you, and before you know it you've got tinfoil all over your head and you're in for over three digits." I wove my fingers through my scalp and lifted my hair up to the light. "It is kind of fun, don't you think?"

"*I Love Lucy!*" said Jane. "Listen," she said, getting up and taking the mat with her, "I have to get going, meeting William, but I'll call you tomorrow and we'll figure out Tuesday."

"No problem. I have a training session in twenty-five minutes."

"Are you okay about this?" she asked.

We had never promised each other we'd stay together in L.A. forever. It was unspoken that we'd do our own thing, and fate would do the rest. And it did.

"Yes, Janey," I said. "Go home. Be happy! Ride the subways and sing."

Jane and I hugged. She went back to the locker room and I did some free weights before I met up with J.D. by the Stairmaster. I found my way to the machine. I punched in my program, put my book on one of the Lucite reading stands and climbed onto the pedals. My trainer came up from behind. He looked at my reading material.

"Where do you think you are?" he asked, picking up the *New York Times* bestseller I was reading. "The beach?"

"I like to read on the Stairmaster."

"You're here to work out," he said.

"I am working out," I said, pedaling up and down as I spoke.

"You need to concentrate. No reading."

I stopped the machine.

"You know, I could concentrate if you'd stop talking." I stepped down from the Stairmaster. "At home, people read through their whole workouts," I said, gathering up my literature. "If you look around you can see people lined up doing push-ups over the *Wall Street Journal*."

"Well, those people are probably not their absolute perfect body weight," he said, leading me towards a weight room.

"Those people probably don't even care."

"I'm going to determine your overall body fat content," J.D. told me as he sat me down on a bench facing another floor-to-ceiling mirror.

"Have you ever used this before?" he asked, reaching for a contraption that looked like it was supposed to cut the fat directly from your body.

"No."

"Now we'll see what they're doing for you at that *club* of yours."

I sat confidently and watched him clump up sections of my skin and measure it with the contraption.

"Hmm," he said, writing down the score from my waist. "Uh-huh," he declared, grabbing the backs of my thighs.

I felt like I was in that commercial, "Can You Pinch An Inch?" only I wasn't doing the pinching. I sat quietly watching J.D. pinch, measure, mumble and write. When the results were in, he sat down cross-legged in front of me and pulled his clipboard to his chest.

"All right," he said, looking down at his notes for positive reinforcement. "I don't know how to break this to you."

I snuck a peek at my reflection in the mirror. Unless something drastic had happened within the last four minutes, everything looked the same to me.

"Now, these results are compared throughout the country," he began. "So you must bear in mind that my findings here are accurately based on women your age throughout America."

"Okay," I said, getting annoyed. Doing this One-on-One wasn't a great idea. I couldn't stop thinking about Jane's news and I just wanted to finish my workout, get some steam and go home. "Tell me what you found. I'm all ears."

"Well, on a nationwide scale your body fat content is on the low side of poor."

"Poor meaning there's not much fat so it's poor?" I asked.

"Hell no!" J.D. was triumphant! "Poor as in Excellent, Good, Average, Below Average and Poor. You are in terrible shape. You're on the low side of poor."

I pulled off my Mets T-shirt revealing a tight little tank top. Lifting my arms I saw definite definition. My clavicles protruded under a slender neck. My waist slimly tucked into my shorts. Well, slimly enough! I stood and looked at my fairly firm leg muscles.

"This is the low side of poor?" I asked.

"Yes."

"In the entire United States of America?"

"Yes."

"This is one of the worst female bodies in this country?"

"Yes," answered J.D., pulling the skin around my stomach area. "See," he said, tugging at my sides. "It's not perfectly flat and tight," he said, proving his point.

"It's not exactly a Rubenesque painting either," I said, pushing his hand away. "I know what a lot of women in this country look like. I see them. Many of them would be very happy to change bodies with me, thank you very much," I said, staring at my hundred-and-five-pound reflection.

"You know those two-hundred-pound women you see on *Oprah?*" J.D. asked.

"Yeah?"

"Well, they don't think they're fat either."

"So you think I'm fat? Is that what you're saying?"

"Yeah."

"Yeah?"

"Yeah," J.D. said, clapping his hands.

"And what do you want to do about it?" I asked. Now I was angry. I was insulted. But I was curious because suddenly I was something I had never been before. I was fat.

"Well, since you are a new member," he told me, "I can give you the special new-member-only discount on our special One-on-One training."

An application form materialized in his hands as if he were Houdini.

"Ten individual one-hour workout sessions with me, of course, will run you only six hundred dollars. That's a savings of one hundred dollars by doing this today."

J.D. produced a pen as magically as he had the application. He grinned from ear to ear waiting for me to sign on the dotted line. I looked at him blankly.

"So?" he finally said.

"So," I repeated. "Do you think I'm crazy? FORGET-ABOUDID!!!"

"What?"

"That's New Yorkese for Forget About It!" I picked up my T-shirt and headed for the door.

"You need to do this," he called after me. "You really do."

I stopped under the doorway and turned to face him. A weight chart hung to my right and a regulation scale stood to my left.

"Maybe I do need to do this. I'm not perfect, but I'm also not unhappy. Let me tell you something about people," I said, taking two steps closer to J.D. "They respond more to positives than negatives."

Now it was J.D.'s turn to look blank.

"Had you told me I was in pretty good shape, that I had a nice body but with a few tips and some individual attention I could have a really great body, I might've actually considered this. I am a woman. I like compliments. But you insulted me. You hurt my feelings and made me feel bad, so now hell would have to freeze over before I'd do One-on-One training with you."

I marched out the door only to remember I forgot

my book. Despite my big exit I reentered the room. J.D. was standing next to the bench holding the paperback.

"Thanks," I said, taking it from his hands. I saw the national edition of the *New York Times* on the floor. "You know, reading is good. Reading can teach you a lot about people," I said, glancing down at the paper. "Yep. If I were you I'd read."

I made a beeline to the ladies' locker room, passing two blondes in matching blue Lycra bodysuits and faces full of makeup on their way to a step class. I hugged my book to my body, gabbed a towel, tore off my clothes and hid myself under the steam.

Starry, Starry Night

Last Day of Summer
Hollywood, CA 1997

"Hi!"

I looked up and saw a man behind a camera. Not a big one for television, but a small one for Kodak moments.

"On vacation?" I asked.

"No, I'm the still photographer on the show," he explained. "I take shots for publicity and stuff."

"Oh, I never knew they did that."

"Well, some of the shows do."

"I don't know. This is my first time at a taping."

The Famous Television Star had invited me to watch a rehearsal and taping of *Deli*. They were several episodes into the season. This was The Famous Television Star's

first TV stint since his seven successful seasons on the
hit TV series *Subway*. He played Harry, the owner of the
deli, and he was the star. People came in and out of the
deli and confided in Harry. Harry would lend a sympa-
thetic ear while customers drowned their sorrows in a
pastrami on rye.

"Didn't I meet you a few weeks ago at that party on
Laurel Canyon?" the photographer guy asked me.

I looked at him. His brown hair was graying around
the temples and at the tip of his head. His brown eyes
looked small, encircled by the big silver wire of his
glasses. They rested on top of a short nose that hooked
under at the tip. His navy-blue hooded sweatshirt hung
loosely around his body. EAST HAMPTON was written across the middle of his chest in a bright yellow.

"Oh yeah, I think you were going when I was coming. I remember your glasses."

"Elliot L."

"I don't get it. Elliotel?"

"Elliot Lieberman. Elliot L."

"Cute. Karrie K. Kline. Just call me Karrie."

"I remember," he said. "Wow. It's freezing on this
sound stage." He smiled. He seemed nice in a benign
sort of way. A little shy. And a little interested.

It was such a fast thing. It took a millionth of a second to tell if someone was interested. It was always nice.
Always flattering. But so far, always Not Right. I had

been feeling blue since Jane left as well as a little gun-shy. The photographer guy smiled again. This time with meaning.

Oh, God. Did I even want to start? Did I want to make pleasant chitchat for a few minutes so he would say something and I would say something else and we'd exchange last names, numbers and nights we were free? Did I really want to venture out on a date and talk about where we grew up, where we went to school, where we should eat.

"Yeah," I finally said. "It is kind of chilly."

"What do you do here?" he asked. At that moment The Famous Television Star approached me. "Well, hello there. It's you. You're here. How are you?"

Before I could answer he said, "In this episode Harry's going to say he needs to hire a new waitress." The Famous Television Star gave me a look that seemed to say, "And if you play your cards right, it could be you."

The photographer hung back and observed. Sort of summing me up. Assessing.

"I mean the casting people will like that you were in that Starkman play," said The Famous Television Star. "Yes, it's a very good thing you were in *Eat That*."

"*Eat This*," I said.

"Dinner isn't for a while yet," said Elliot.

"You mean I can audition?" I asked The Famous Television Star, completely ignoring Elliot. "For the waitress? For real?" I was very excited. I wondered if it would be a recurring role, or a series regular. I saw the picture of the entire *Deli* cast on the cover of *TV Guide,* and the little interview written in italics, my name bolded in black.

"I did one of his plays. A decade ago. Did we talk about that? Well, you probably remember the name of it better than me. What was it?" The Famous Television Star scratched his head looking for the answer. *"Second Calling,"* he said, snapping his famous fingers.

"I saw you, I told you," I said, relishing the memory of how I had treated myself to that matinee on spring break. "I was home from college. Took the train into the city from Queens." Saying the word *Queens* in California suddenly brought forth a longing for the borough I had never dreamed possible, but now with the bigger possibility of winning an Emmy looming beside me, it disappeared rather quickly.

"Yes," he said. "Us kids from Queens need to stick together!"

This was too much! The Famous Television Star was flirting with me. I was surprised he had called again after the weird night at his house, and even more surprised he invited me to the taping. He was obviously oblivious to any oddity during the evening we had spent together. I didn't know why The Famous Television Star was suddenly being so attentive and helpful, but I sure was swept up by the attention. The photographer looked on. He seemed to be too.

"We need you for a rehearsal," called a voice to The Famous Television Star.

"Expect a call and have a good time tonight," said The Famous Television Star. Then he disappeared toward the set. I climbed up to the bleachers to take a seat. The actors had disappeared to their dressing rooms as everyone went to their places.

"Wait!"

I turned around to see Elliot standing below the bleachers looking up at me.

"I'm Elliot, remember," the photographer said, handing me his card. "I'd like to go out with you, but not if you're dating him. I couldn't compete with that."

My, that was unexpectedly sweet. And candid. And real.

"Uh, thanks, Elliot." I took his card and saw two phone numbers. One area code was 213 and the other one was 212.

"You still have your place back east?" I asked.

"Yeah," he said. "I'm bicoastal, but I'm thinking of moving back."

"Maybe we can go out sometime," I said.

"What about him?"

I remembered the night The Famous Television Star pawed me!

"Just friends," I said.

"Good to have friends in high places," said Elliot, looking up at me in the bleachers. "Maybe I'll see you again."

"Yeah, maybe. Maybe I'll see you here," I said, hoping The Famous Television Star needed a waitress just like me.

There's No Place Like Home

It was lunch hour on the set of *Deli*. I took a walk on the lot. My first TV gig. The audition came a few days after I'd been to the taping. Because I was a friend of The Famous Television Star I was able to read directly for the casting director and the producers. They loved that I had played a waitress in *Eat This*. Once a waitress, always a waitress. They called that day and offered me the role of Penny. Initially it was a role—it had scenes, a story, a plotline and everything. We'd been rehearsing all week and now I was down to three lines. The way I saw it, I was being paid about $200 a word. It was a lot less than I had hoped for, but I was happy for my first TV gig and my first television credit.

I walked across Solar Stages, past the commissary, past the sound stages, past the souvenir store, past the little bungalows used for offices. It was Hollywood as I knew it. From pictures. From movies. I thought of all the magic that happened on these lots. Or, at least what audiences perceived as magic.

As I took a step, I took a step back. It was amazing. Here I was in California, on this lot because I was actually employed here. I stopped walking, looked in front of me and saw The Big Picture. Los Angeles may not be home in my heart, but it was home for now. I wanted to lay this life next to the one in New York. I just wanted to take a look. Try them both on and see what they felt like. I wanted to be in two places at the same time.

I clicked my heels together three times. "You could go home anytime you want." The voice was weak. I looked down. I didn't have the ruby-red slippers. I looked down at the scuff marks on my black heeled loafers, tripped and missed a step. My foot almost buckled under as I knocked against something. I looked down and saw my foot bang up against a curb. It looked very urban, very familiar. Like a New York City curb. I turned the corner and I was home. I had stumbled onto a street that was designed to look like my hometown. The streets looked like Hell's Kitchen. Right near the theater district.

It was thrilling to walk down a sidewalk and see brownstones and fire escapes and garbage cans. There were cracks in the sidewalk and hydrants on the streets. I could practically smell the city.

The sidewalks turned into cobblestones. I came upon a shopping district. There were vendors selling their wares. Tourists could go into these stores and buy little souvenirs.

I passed a bakery, a shoemaker, a market and a haberdashery. I was elated. Olde New York. I expected to see Fanny Brice run out of a building, singing "I'm The Greatest Star." I swung around the street lamps, contemplating breaking into song myself. I felt like Julie Andrews with her arms outstretched on top of the Austrian Alps. Her hills were alive with the sound of music. My hills were alive too. Only mine were made of brick and cement.

I savored each step. Each step was a piece of home. I ran across the street to check out the other side.

"What's doin', Cookie? Tips and all?"

The voice stopped me cold. I looked behind me. No one was there. An odd feeling washed over me.

"So…it's a delightful day, isn't it, Cookie?"

I looked up and saw a man standing in front of me. A butcher. In front of a butcher shop.

"Are you hungry? How about a nice rib steak?"

The friendly man wore a long white apron that tied in the back.

"Are you an actor?" I asked him.

"No."

"Well, you're not a turn-of-the-century butcher…"
There was something eerie. Something else. I knew I
wasn't frightened. Not exactly. "Are you?"

The man looked like a character actor. Late sixties,
overweight and bald. He pulled a cigar out of his apron
pocket.

"We're hired by the studio," he explained. "You want
to come in and see my store?"

The bells jingled as I opened the wood-and-glass door
and entered a store best known to me on New York's
Lower East Side. Sawdust covered the floor and the insides of the glass counters housed lots of fake red meat.
Specials were listed on the walls and a cash register was
perched on the little table in the front. The man sat down
on a small red stool and propped up a chair for me. I sat.

"This is fun," I said. "It's very cool."

"I like it," the man told me. He took out a lighter and
lit the cigar. He took a long puff.

"Can I see?" I asked, pointing to the gold lighter with
the small black insignia.

"You never saw a lighter before, Cookie?" he asked,
holding it up for me to see.

"It looked…familiar," I said, my insides tightening.

"So what brings you over here? Did you lose the
tour?" He propped the stool against the wall and leaned
back. I figured it could be a little lonely for him and he
wanted some company.

"I'm on lunch hour," I said.

"Oh, do you work in the office? Bookkeeping?"

"Bookkeeping! No, I work on one of the shows."

"Are you one of those production assistants? A script girl?"

"No, I'm on that new show *Deli,*" I said, only too aware that I didn't have to worry about instant fame in Hollywood. "I play a waitress."

"An actress!" The butcher perked up. "Oh boy oh boy oh boy. What are you doing over here? Slumming!"

"Visiting. I'm from New York."

"Oh yeah, pussycat? I'm from New York too!"

"Really!" I felt a sense of relief. New York. That must be it. The familiarity of New York faces. Knowing he hailed from back east made his pet names acceptable. Even enjoyable.

"Where are you from?" he asked.

"Manhattan," I said. "Upper West Side."

"Nice. I had a little business up there once. Long time ago. Coffee shop."

"Oh yeah?"

"Yeah, but I lived around the whole place. Born in Brooklyn. Lived for a while in Queens."

"That's funny," I said. "That's where I'm from. My folks still live there," I said, feeling more and more comfortable with the stranger. The butcher. The strange butcher.

"Yep, another life ago," he said.

"Feels like that for me too," I said, glancing at my watch.

"You got to get back?" he asked.

"Yeah."

"Will you visit me again?" he asked. His blue eyes danced like a child's.

"Sure," I said. "Maybe tomorrow."

"Okeydokey..." He paused. "What's your name, Cookie?"

"Karrie," I said. "What's yours?"

"Carrie," he repeated.

"What's yours?" I asked.

A tour group walked into the store.

"Never mind. See ya!" I called, making my way through the T-shirts and the instamatic cameras.

I walked back to the sound stage. I only had two days left till the taping of *Deli*. What would happen next was anybody's guess. The Famous Television Star had been very happy for me when I got the part. He asked me to dinner the first day. He didn't want to go out and invited me back to his house. Over dinner he became very parental and angry with me. I made a salad and asked if he'd like me to toss it.

"There's no such thing," he said. "It already is a tossed salad."

"I know," I said, "but it's what you say when you put on the dressing. You say you're tossing the salad. Do you want me to toss the salad?" I asked.

He told me I didn't know correct grammatical usage and opted for an untossed salad and a bottle of Wishbone Italian. Then he told me I talked through the whole meal and didn't eat and that's why I was so thin. I, in fact, have mastered the art of talking through the whole meal while eating everyone under the table, and that and my metabolism is the reason why I'm so thin. Or so fat, as I had recently learned. Then he started the barking again. Not up for being bitten, I quickly got myself out of his house and home in my car.

That was on Monday. By Tuesday he was cooler. When I returned to the set yesterday after meeting the butcher he was a little more chilly, and now, the day before the taping, he was downright cold. It was clear that I was supposed to do something I hadn't done. He wasn't going to tell me. I was being punished and I would have to guess. My guess was sex. I guess I was supposed to have sex with The Famous Television Star because he helped get me a job. I didn't do what he wanted. I passed up sex on the casting couch and went straight into the doghouse, though it was the doghouse that made me pass up sex in the first place. Not having sex on Monday was probably what shredded my part by Tuesday. I walked into my dressing room and threw down my purse. I stared at myself in the mirror. I thought I looked the same as always, except for the neon sign over my forehead that was no longer invisible. It was danger zone red, it was flashing and it said, Boy, Are You Naive!

I picked up my bottled water and took a long slug, knowing within a day there'd be little to no complications on the work front, or any front for that matter. Whatever. I didn't want to get a role that way, and I didn't want to have sex with The Famous Television Star.

"There's nothing like the smell of a good cigar!"

The butcher's voice popped into my head later that night when I drove home. His words triggered something in me that hadn't gone away. Something about that butcher made me want to cry.

"There's nothing like the smell of a good cigar!" rang in my ear as I drove past the Hollywood Bowl. I had gone to visit him today on my lunch break and, again, our visit was cut short by another tourist group that stomped in. I watched him entertain them. In his own way, he was quite an actor.

I needed to get back to him. I didn't know why. Tomorrow was my last day. I didn't think I'd have time. Tomorrow, I thought as I accelerated to the middle lane. Tomorrow I will make the time to see the guy again.

Climbing out of the car, I heard the chimes gently brush together. The breeziness of the sound fused with the lightness of the jasmine as I turned the key in the door. As usual, my roommate wasn't home. I went out back and slid the glass door open. I walked out to the deck to get a glimpse. The sun was setting over the hills. I went back into the kitchen to pour myself a glass of wine when I heard talking.

"Hi. It's Elliot. Karrie, are you there?" I heard his voice coming from my machine. I hadn't even heard the phone.

"Hi," I said, picking it up.

"I just wanted to see if we can get together soon," he said.

"Sure," I answered. "But let's wait until the taping is over, okay?"

We made plans for next Friday, a week from tomorrow. Enough time, I hoped, for me to have my head back together.

"Oh, wait," said Elliot. "I may have to change that. I might be going back east for a shoot on an independent movie. I'll know tomorrow. It could be a couple of months. Then I'd be back here."

"Or I'll be back there," I said.

"Do you want to just go out now? Tonight?" he asked.

"Okay," I said, then instantly realized that tonight was probably not good. I thought about how reticent I'd felt to date him when we met. All week, though, he had been really nice. However, the complications with The Famous Television Star and the intrigue with the butcher were haunting. Better to wait, I thought as I went to step on the brakes.

"Elliot, you seem very nice and I would like to go out with you, but as far as tonight goes..."

"Do you want to cancel?" he asked.

"We don't have a plan to cancel," I said.

"Do you want to make a plan and cancel?" he asked. "I can do that."

"Do you want to cancel?" I asked, thinking this was his way of getting out of it now that I sounded tentative.

"No," said Elliot quickly. "I want to see you. I just thought that... Never mind. What do you want to do?"

Okay. I decided to go. "Eat," I said.

"Oh."

"You'd rather not?"

"No, just..." said Elliot. "I never know where to go."

"Oh. Well, there's not exactly a shortage of restaurants in Los Angeles."

"Should I pick you up?" he asked.

"Sure."

"Or maybe we should meet and have two cars."

"That's fine," I said.

"No. Maybe I should just pick you up and we can take my car."

"Okay, let's do that."

"Or...you could pick me up and we could take your car."

"Or we could each rent a car, meet in San Diego, and eat there."

Silence. I was waiting for a laugh. Well, maybe not an out-and-out guffaw, but perhaps a chuckle.

"Umm…" Elliot was pondering something. "Let me pick you up," he said slowly and deliberately.

"Okay." I gave him the address.

"In about an hour?"

"That's good. See ya."

"Yeah," he said. "See ya soon."

"Elliot."

"What?"

"Can I tell you something and you won't be upset?" What was I doing?

"I can't promise," he said. "What?"

"I can't go out tonight," I finally and simply said. I really could not go out with him tonight. "Tomorrow is the taping, I need to get some sleep and I've got a lot of things on my mind."

"Okay," he said without missing a beat.

I wanted him to say something now to smooth it over so I wouldn't feel bad, but I knew he felt rejected so it wouldn't be forthcoming. Not from him. I hadn't meant to hurt his feelings.

"Elliot. Thanks for asking and I'll see you tomorrow. And listen—"

"What, Kar?"

He was already calling me Kar, like he'd known me

for years. A familiar term my family and close friends used. It was sweet.

"I'm holding you to next Friday if you don't get that job. And if you do, I expect to see you when you get back!"

He laughed. I could tell he didn't know whether or not to believe me, but he chose to because it made him feel good. It would have been okay for Elliot to trust his instincts, because though it might have often been to a fault, I did not lie.

We Have So Much in Common

The Next Night
Hollywood, CA 1997

It was the day of the taping for *Deli*. I got to the lot early. Thought I'd look up Mr. Butcher, for lack of a better name. Maybe he wanted to come to the show that evening. I waved to the guard and drove to my parking spot. The routine had become familiar and for me that made it all the more enjoyable. The sun was shining, the lot overflowing with the business of make-believe.

I walked over to my favorite New York street and sprinted down the cobblestones until I came upon the butcher shop. The little bell jangled on cue as I made my way inside. He was sitting there eating a bag of potato chips and smoking a cigar.

"Well, look who's here," he said with childish delight when he saw me. "I never thought I'd see you again, Cookie. I figured you forgot about me."

"I haven't at all."

"Sit down," he offered, bringing over a wooden folding chair. "So, what's doing. Tips and all?"

I laughed and got that feeling again.

"My show tapes today," I told him. Actually, tonight's the last taping before the hiatus. You want to come?"

"You want to have me to your show? Well, that's very nice of you, Cook—Car—" He paused a second. "You don't mind me calling you Cookie, do you?"

"Nah," I said. "It makes me laugh because I have an aunt by that name."

"Oh yeah?" he said. "I knew a Cookie once. Long time ago. Nice girl. Yep. Hmm…" He looked somber as the thought took him back to wherever he went. "What stage do you do your show?"

"We're on nine," I told him.

"Sound stage nine," he repeated as if he were mentally writing it down.

"Great," I said, glancing at my watch, making my way to leave. As I got up from the chair I realized I still didn't have the butcher's name. I needed it to put him on the list to get into the taping.

"Oh! Can you give me a piece of paper so I can write your—"The phone started ringing and interrupted me.

"Wait—" he said, going to answer it. He walked behind the old-fashioned counter and picked up a modern cordless telephone. I sat a moment hoping he would be brief. "Hello. Yeah," he said. "For a minute."

I looked around the little shop. There were photographs of him posed with famous people who had come by. There he was in each and every shot, a cigar in one hand, the other around some television celebrity and a grin across his face like a boy who had made his parents proud.

"I sent it over three weeks ago. What do you mean you didn't get it?" I overheard him say.

I got up from the chair and walked to the window so I wouldn't appear to be eavesdropping. However, the store was tiny and there was really no escape but out. And looking at my watch, again, it was telling me that was where I needed to be headed.

"You'll have the money. I gave you my word. What else do you want?"

I looked in the butcher's direction, trying to get his attention.

"This is going to be a while," he told me. "I'll see you at your show."

· "Yeah, but…"

"This is business," he said, gesturing to the phone. "What?"

"Uh, I don't have your name," I said. "To get you on the list."

"I know everybody, I'm okay," he said, taking a puff on his cigar. He turned his back to me, resuming his conversation. "So what do you want me to do?" I heard him say quite loudly.

I made a dash for the fake cobblestones, and walked briskly over to work. An uncomfortable feeling settled itself below my neck. I wished I could shrug it off. I decided it was for the best that he had no name. The whole thing was disturbing and for what? It wasn't as if there had been any—

"Karrie! Earth to Karrie. Helllll-o!"

I was waiting in the wings, waiting for my touch-up. I was so absorbed in my thoughts I didn't even notice anyone talking to me.

"So, what have we got?" asked Artie, applying blush to my cheeks. "What amazing things are you up to Miss Guest Star of the week?" he asked, putting down the makeup brush, unclipping hot rollers from my hair.

"Let's see," I said, leaving the butcher shop for my *Deli*. I skimmed my Xeroxed pages, looking for lines spoken by Penny. "I don't order the corned beef on rye with mayo, but on white with mayo!"

"'That'll go over big!" He smirked.

"Right. People on both coasts will laugh, and everyone in the middle of the country won't get it. It'll be like that scene with Woody Allen in *Hannah and Her Sisters* where he pulls out the mayonnaise and the crucifix and the audience didn't laugh."

"Are you kidding? Where'd you see the movie?" said Artie, expertly moving the strands of my hair into something wonderful.

"Idaho!" I said. We both laughed. Artie originally hailed from East Meadow, Long Island.

"And now let's bring them out for you to meet," the comedian announced to the studio audience.

That voice sounded familiar. I hadn't been listening to him before. I'd been too wrapped up.

"Who's that?"

"There's a new warm-up comedian tonight."

"Oh yeah?"

"Yeah. Well, hello, gorgeous!" Artie said to me as he dabbed on the last bit of lip gloss. "Come on, let's take a peek and watch the new guy."

I listened behind the *Deli* set to the maniacal applause of the studio audience while the new warm-up comedian introduced the *Deli* stars. L.A. was about instant gratification. Out here you took your curtain call before and after the show. I scanned the audience, and wondered if the butcher had made it. As we were about to start and I stepped on my mark, the new warm-up comedian waved to me. Dressed in a pair of black jeans, a gray T-shirt and a black-and-gray tweed jacket was Jack Whitney, waving to me with his right hand and holding a mike with his left.

My smile grew bigger, broader and finally stayed falsely fastened to my face as Jack took his place up in the bleachers. I smiled and applauded and wondered what he was doing here. How did he get here? On my show? Our relationship flashed through my mind like the coming attractions in a movie. I was well over Jack, but seeing him here made me feel queasy. For goodness' sake, it was not the time to be thinking about Jack. I needed to shift my attention back to the taping.

I looked around and watched the studio audience screaming from their seats, thrilled to see live and in person those fabulously funny people who come into their living rooms every Tuesday night. My three lines had shrunk to one line and a word. The Famous Television Star had cut the exchange between us. Elliot had snapped pictures of me all week, unaware of the backstage drama lurking behind my perky smiles. I thought I had tonight under control until Jack turned up. I wasn't familiar enough with doing a TV show to deal with any real familiarity. It was just breeding contempt. I could feel the air deflating from the free-floating balloon of me.

The taping went by in a blur. I felt robotic, but delivered what was needed. After the final bows, I left the sound stage. I zipped down the hall to my dressing room as quickly as possible.

"Karrie, wait up."

Jack's voice stopped me in my tracks.

"Hey!" I said.

"Where are you running? No hello?"

"Hello!" I said, turning to face him.

"How are you?"

I didn't answer. I didn't know.

"Don't you think this is pretty amazing! Us. Here. L.A.! Same show and everything!"

"It's amazing," I said. It was. It was very amazing. And I wasn't very much in the mood for it.

"Umm, look…" I continued. "I've got to pack up my stuff."

"Yeah," said Jack. "The producer said he'd use me on *Cousins Club.* This warm-up stuff pays really well and…"

I saw The Famous Television Star at the end of the hall. I had to catch up with him before the night was over. If I could just make that right.

"Jack, I'm sure we'll talk soon. I've got to run now." I went to kiss his cheek but wound up patting his shoulder instead.

"Okay. I'll call you."

"Great," I said, gliding past him down the hall. "See ya," I yelled behind me.

"Yeah," he called back. "Maybe the three of us can have lunch."

"Three of us," I said, stopping dead in my tracks. "Who's the third?"

"Carla," Jack said. "We're engaged. Now, isn't that amazing!"

"Oh! That really is. I'm happy for you both," I said cheerfully. Automatically. Not meaning happiness. Not meaning harm. "Look. Take it easy. Give my best to Carla," I shouted as I ran down the hall and collided into his famous chest.

"Oops! Hi. Going to Nelson's for a drink?" I asked.

"Going back out for a pickup shot."

"After."

The Famous Television Star looked at me.

"Where are you going after?" I said.

"Going, going, gone," he said, motioning his famous hand through the air like an airplane.

"Oh. You're flying out tonight?"

"No. I'm flying over to Nelson's to get myself a drink!"

"So maybe I'll see you over there."

He looked at me, saying nothing.

"You know, this show has really been a good thing for me. And it's been great working with you and..."

He waved his right fingers and dismissed me as he headed back to the set.

An alarm went off inside me. I bet The Famous Television Star would blackball me. I'd never work again in L.A. or New York for that matter. No. Wait. I wasn't important enough. None of this was important enough. I should just go out for a drink. I was being paranoid. I would go out.

I wasn't going out. I was going to pack up and go home. No. I would not be afraid. I would go out. But just for twenty minutes. Or ten. Just long enough to be seen. I wanted everything to get fixed tonight and it wouldn't. I wanted to know what was going to happen to me and I couldn't. So everything was unsettled. So my destiny hung in the air. What was I so upset about? My destiny was always hanging off something. There was a knock at my dressing-room door.

"It's open," I called out.

"Surprise!"

The tanned faces of Millie and Henry stood before me.

"Ohmygod!" I screamed, jumping from the chair, throwing my arms around them. "What are you doing here? How did you...?"

"Well," my mother began, taking off her jacket and tossing it over the club chair. "When you told us the show might not be picked up we figured we'd better come out and see you now," she said.

"We wouldn't miss you in your first television show," said Henry, smiling broadly.

"I know, but you had that trip to Vegas," I said. "That's why you couldn't come."

"Henry suggested—"

"Your mother thought of it too. We both decided—"

"We both decided," said Millie, "we could fly down from Vegas, see the taping—"

"Take you for a bite to eat," said Henry.

"And then fly back!" said Millie.

"Wow! You've become such jet-setters since you retired," I said. "I'm glad you did. How did you get in? How'd you know where to go?"

"Jack had called a few weeks ago and asked for your number out here." Millie knew everything and looked like it. "Well, he turned out to be good for something."

"Very nice young man," said Henry. "But just as well. What's yours is still out there."

"Did you talk to him too?" I asked.

"No. Mother did," said Henry. "Why?"

"You didn't get him this job, did you?" asked my mom, moving a pile of workout clothes on the chair so she could sit. "Here, Henry," she said, patting the crown chair, showing there was room enough for two.

"I'll stand," he said.

"Here," I said, pulling out a folding chair from the vanity under the makeup mirror.

"I'll stand," he said, waving it away with his hand.

"It was a coincidence," I told my mother. "I can't get him a job. I can barely get me a job. Did you talk to him tonight?" I asked.

"We went over at the end but he was with the fiancée, so Mother and I felt funny."

"She doesn't look so great, huh?" I asked.

"I don't want to talk about them," said Millie. "What's done is done. What are your plans?"

"They'll want her back," said Henry, reaching into his inside jacket pocket for a cigar. "She'll be back on the show," he said, changing his mind and putting the cigar back.

"You never know," said Millie. "Listen, it's a miracle anyone ever gets a job in this business. Who says they'll even want the show back."

"It's a good show," I said. "I figured you'd like it. A Jewish deli, Harry, the people who come to the deli… It's fun."

"I want to know why they portrayed the parents like that," said Millie, picking up the Calendar section of the *L.A. Times* that was lying on the floor by the chair.

"Like what?" I asked.

"Jewish," she said.

"That's what they were supposed to be," I answered, folding the flaps on my cardboard box. I had accumulated a lot of junk in just a week.

"But who's like that?" asked Henry. "We don't know people like that. Do we know people like that?" he asked my mother, reaching for the paper.

"Like what? I'm reading that. Here," said Millie, handing him a different section. "No, we don't know people like that. Nobody talks like that either."

"Like what?" I asked.

"Like the way they talk," said my stepfather. "They finish each other's—"

"Sentences," said my mother. "And they never know what anybody's talking about. Right, Henry?"

"What?"

"He never listens," Millie said to me. "They make them come off as stupid and I object to that."

"Don't you think it's funny?" I asked Henry.

"I, myself, thought it a little offensive."

"I most definitely thought it was offensive," said Millie.

"Well, I thought it was funny," I said.

"Karrie, if you come back next season, tell the writers about us. Model the parents after us," suggested Henry.

"They always do that to the Jewish people in the movies too. I don't know why," said Millie, shaking her head. "Remember *Hannah and Her Sisters?* Woody Allen is never nice when he writes a script."

"Well, I think it's funny. And quite honestly, endearing. It was just meant to be funny," I said.

"Well, it wasn't," said my mother, rising from the chair. "Maybe that's why your show's on hiatus."

"It's not my show and it's not my hiatus."

"Whatever. So. Where can we go to eat?"

"Is there a good Jewish deli in this neighborhood?" asked Henry. "I could go for a nice tongue sandwich. Your show got me in the mood."

"You want to try Mexican or Japanese? Something different?"

"I don't need different," said Millie. "I know what I like."

"I know what I like too. Come," said Henry, walking to the door.

Henry opened my dressing-room door. The butcher was standing there in gray polyester pants, a yellow Lacoste cardigan and his trademark cigar.

"Hello, Cookie!" he said.

Out of his butcher garb I almost didn't recognize him. My mother, however, did.

"MEL KLEIN!" she screamed, before collapsing into Henry's arms.

"WHAT!!?"

I looked at Henry looking at my mother who was looking at—

The butcher.

Mel!

My—

My—

My whatever was still standing in the doorway, smoking his cigar.

"Look who's here!" said Mr. Butcher. Mr. Mel. "It's Millie! I'd recognize you anywhere. How about that! Never thought I'd see you again, kid. Boy oh boy, what a surprise." Mel spoke as if nothing unusual was going on. He stepped into the room and walked over to a nearby ashtray.

"What are you doing here?" Millie asked Mel, lifting herself from Henry's arms and straightening out the waistband on her black nylon pants.

"I was invited," said Mel, pointing to me. "You haven't changed a bit," he told Millie.

I stood very still, first staring at Millie and then staring at Mel.

"By who?" Millie asked him. "Who invited you?"

"Boy oh boy oh boy oh boy," said Mel. "You really haven't changed a bit." He took a puff on his cigar. "And you still look pretty good, too. You always looked great, Mil. You were a good kid."

"You know him?" Henry asked my mother.

She frowned. I frowned. Henry looked at me. I looked back at my mother. We frowned together. Henry reached into his jacket and took out the cigar.

"Want a light?" Mel asked him, reaching into his pocket and pulling out his lighter.

"Oh," said Henry, a little startled. "Very kind of you, thanks," he said, puffing the cigar into the flame Mel offered. It was odd enough watching the two men smoke their cigars, but seeing that lighter made the familiar feeling rush through me again. It must have rushed through my mother too.

"Let me see that!" she said to Mel.

He handed her the lighter. Millie took the metal

piece in her hand and turned it over. She read the inscription aloud.

"To M. With love, M. May, 1956."

"Who's M?" Henry asked.

"He is," I said.

"So then, who's M?" Henry asked again.

"I guess she is," I said, pointing to my mother.

"You always had good taste," Mel told my mother, reaching for the lighter.

"Wait a minute. Let me see that," said Henry, taking it from Millie.

Henry turned it over in his hand.

"That's you?" he asked Millie.

She nodded.

"And that's…you?" he asked Mel.

"Yessirree," he answered.

"Oh God. Oh my God! Mel Klein! *That* Mel Klein!!" said Henry, as if hearing his name for the first time. "Wait! You've been in touch with him all this time?" Henry asked me.

"No," Millie answered for me. "She hasn't seen him in thirty-five years. I know that. But he says he was invited here. How could she invite him? She doesn't even know him."

I had been standing against the vanity of my makeup mirror. Earlier tonight when I had felt anxious I had stared at my reflection in that mirror. The round makeup lights turned into colored balls and a clown juggled all of my emotions. A clown named Mel. And here he was. Standing right in front of me. Right in front of the makeup mirror with the makeup lights that looked just like ordinary, round lightbulbs. And I stood in front of them. Looking. Watching. Absorbing.

"I haven't seen who in thirty-five years?" Mel asked Millie. "You? I tried calling you once from Des Moines, you hung up on me."

"Please," said Millie. "Running away to join the circus. You leave a wife and a four-year-old to go play games…"

Henry wiped his forehead with his hankie while taking really big puffs on his cigar. Millie kept bobbing her head as she spoke to Mel. I stood watching as she kept on talking.

"…years and years and never took any responsibility," she finally finished.

Mel shrugged.

"You seemed to have done okay, kid," he told my mom while flicking ashes from his cigar.

"Jesus Christ Almighty," Millie cried, flailing her arms in the air. "Who is that, Mel?" she asked, pointing to me. "Who do you think she is?"

"This is a little actress friend of mine who invited me to come to her taping. Isn't that right, Chippie?" he asked me.

"What do you know about her?" Millie asked.

"What do I know? What's to know?" said Mel. "She works here on the lot. So do I," he said with great importance. "She came into my store, we talked, she asked me to come here."

My heart was beating faster.

"What do you know about her?" Millie asked again.

"She's an actress. What's to know?"

Millie wouldn't let him off the hook. He thought about it.

"Let's see. She's from New York. Queens. Like us," he said to Millie. "That's all. Oh! She has a relative named Cookie, like your sister-in-law. Sy's wife, right? She was a good kid, too," Mel said.

"What's her name?" said Millie, pointing to me again.

"Carrie. That's your name, right, Cookie?" He looked at me.

I nodded. I felt sick.

"Karrie what?" asked Millie.

"You know, I don't know. I left my seat before the curtain call. I don't know. What's you last name, Cookie?" he asked me.

"Tell him your name," said Millie.

"Kar—" It felt as if my mouth were coated with cotton. "Karrie Kline."

"What a coincidence," said Mel. "I'm Mel Klein and that's Millie Klein, well, it was—now it's..."

"Eisenberg," said Henry.

"Thanks. Eisenberg." Mel looked at my mother and Henry and then to me. "How do you know them?" he asked.

"They're my parents," I told him. "Well, actually that's my mother and that's my stepfather. My real father left when I was four to join the circus."

"So, you're not an Eisenberg?" he asked.

"No. My name's Kline. K-L-I-N-E. For the stage. But my real name's K-L-E-I-N. Karrie's a nickname for K-A-R-E-N. I'm Karen Klein."

He looked at me a long time before he spoke. He looked a little incredulous.

"You're telling me you're my daughter?"

I nodded my head and lifted my eyes.

"Oh boy oh boy oh boy," said Mel. "You know something...you're a big kid. I remember a little girl. Look at this! How do you like this!"

It was now my turn to look incredulous. I stared at Millie and Henry who were doing the incredulous thing as well.

"So what do you know, I'm a father," Mel announced, puffing on his cigar as if the nurse had just told him "It's a Girl!"

I couldn't speak. I had always wondered what it would be like to see him again. On some level I had thought he must have died. I had thought that years and years ago the guy walking the high wire must have slipped, fallen on top of Mel and the impact of his body must have caused Mel to die. He had to have been dead all these years. He had to have been. Because if he wasn't, how could he have had a daughter and never cared to find out who she was?

"Well, if I knew my daughter was a big-shot actress, maybe…" Mel didn't finish the sentence. Even he must have caught how awful it sounded.

Since there was nothing anyone could do to make it better, we all chose to do nothing. I looked at the group in my dressing room. My mother and her two husbands. Henry. He was an honest man. You always knew what you would get with Henry. No surprises. Mel was another story. As a young man Mel was full of big ideas. Hopeful. Promising even. But I couldn't imagine Millie with him. She was so straightforward. Always called a spade a spade. Mel was a character. Someone you'd chat with behind the counter of a deli or a bakery. Someone you'd talk to because you were sitting in the back of his cab. Someone you'd cross paths with who belonged to someone else. He was not someone who made you. Not someone you shared a gene pool with. And not someone whose personhood would be consoling on dark days when you felt a little frantic that the apple didn't fall that far from the tree. Some days were really dark, black because I never knew just where the apple was falling from. Now I knew the exact location.

"So, Cookie, say something to your dear old dad."

"I don't feel like it."

"What's the matter, Chippie. Aren't we buddies? Pals?"

"I think you're a better friend to a stranger," I told this clown. This butcher. This phony. This father.

"Come here," said Mel, moving toward me.

"Leave her alone," said Millie, walking into us. Creating a small circle. A triangle. The three of us. The family. The family I never knew. The family that never was.

"Mil, calm down," said Henry, pulling my mother to him. I walked a few steps to my left. To that circle. That family. The family I knew for close to thirty years. The family that was normal. The configuration that enabled me to introduce friends to My Parents. To bypass explanations of runaways, and circuses, and why there was only a mom on open school night and how despite everything, I really was so well-adjusted. The family that was real, and really existed on the inside as well as the outside. Even when I didn't know it.

I knew it now.

"You don't want to talk to me anymore?" asked Mel. "What did I do?"

"Nothing. That's the problem," I shouted. "You did absolutely nothing!"

I slammed the dressing-room door behind me and ran out into the hall.

"Look what you did now!" I heard Millie say.

"She'll calm down," Henry was saying.

I ran down the hall to the water fountain to splash some water on my face. I wasn't feeling so hot.

"Come here, I want to talk to you," I heard Mel say from behind me. I jumped. Water dripped onto the floor.

"What?"

"I want to talk to you."

Mel stood close to the concrete wall. I looked behind him but saw no sight of Millie or Henry.

"What?" I repeated.

"Listen…" He shifted his weight from one foot to the next. He was wearing a worn-out pair of Nikes. "I never meant to hurt anyone," my father told me. "I…uh…I thought about you, you know. But I figured your mother would take care of things. She always did. You didn't turn out so bad. Am I right?"

"And if my mother didn't take care of things, then what? If I didn't turn out so great, then what? Did you ever care to find out?"

He didn't answer me.

"Did you marry? Do you have any other kids you don't know? What have you been doing?"

"This and that. There was a woman…. It didn't… What's the difference? I never forgot your mother. What a woman. What a figure on her!"

"Then why'd you leave?"

"I left because… I left."

I laughed.

"What's so funny, Cookie?" he asked in a singsong tone.

"It's unbelievable."

"Yeah. Hey—pretty unbelievable, huh!" he said as if it were a good thing. A funny thing. A thing to be appreciated.

"I've got to go," I said.

"Wait a minute. Can I ask you something first?"

The tone of his voice stopped me. It was serious. It was with intent.

"What is it?"

"Listen. If it's not too late I want to… I know you probably hate me, but maybe… I don't know. Maybe…"

"Why?"

"Why?"

"Yeah," I said. "Why?"

"Why not?"

Too much he wasn't capable of. I wanted to crawl under the water fountain and sleep for six months. I felt tired. Exhausted. Drained. I'd comply. Who knows? This guy. My father. Maybe.

"Okay," I told him. "I'll talk to you again. We'll see."

"Give me your number, okay?" Mel asked, reaching into his pocket and pulling out a small blue spiral note-pad with lined paper and a pen. "Here." He handed it over to me. "Listen," I heard him say, as I leaned the note-book against the wall and began writing. "Can I ask you something?" asked my father.

"Sure."

"What do you make on a show like this?"

"It depends on your deal. I'm just a guest star."

"Ten thousand a week?"

"The regulars do. Some a lot, lot more. I didn't make ten thousand."

"What'd you get? Seven? Five? Less? What?"

"Yes. Less. Around that. Around there. Around some much smaller number."

"Even if you made three thousand it's a lot. You must have made a few grand on that play. The commercials. That's a lot of money."

"So."

"So, listen. I have a great opportunity to go into business with a fellow out here. He's from England and wants to open an English pub out in Santa Monica. He wants me to be an equal partner, but I don't have to put in equal money. He wants me for my expertise, you see."

"Your expertise on English pubs? What do you know about English pubs?"

"Listen, I know a lot. And I've been waiting for my chance, you know. This is my chance for my ship to come in. Now, I told him I already sent him the check."

"Yeah, I heard."

"I was supposed to have the money but someone didn't get it back to me yet. That's okay. It'll be coming soon. Now all he wants from me is ten thousand dollars.

Ten thousand dollars, Cookie, and I'm an equal partner.
This is my shot!"

"Well, good luck to you. I hope it works out."

"Listen, don't go. If you can give me the money I'll
be able to pay you back next week when I get what
I'm owed."

"Tell your English friend to wait till next week."

"He's already been waiting a month because he wants
me so much. But I only have till the end of this weekend. Then I'm out."

"I'm sorry for you," I said, ripping the paper I wrote
my number on off the pad and stuffing it into the pocket
of my jeans.

"You're not going to give me the money? You
wouldn't do that for me?"

"No," I said. "I am not going to give you the money.
I am not going to give you ten thousand dollars. Are you
crazy?"

"I'll give you a percentage. It's a great investment for
a young girl like yourself. Besides, what's ten thousand
dollars to you? You're rolling in it."

"I'm what?"

"Sure, you have plenty. You have your mother there and
Eisenberg. Sure. I see the diamonds on her hand. Around
her neck. What's a little loan to you for your dad? Can't
you do that for me? This is my last chance for my ship to
come in. I need you to help me. It's my last chance, Karen."

The rumblings started in the bowels of my stomach. They inched up higher and higher until they moved into my throat and cried out of my mouth. My body convulsed and the sounds I heaved moved deeper and darker and louder and harder. I was shaking. I was screaming.

"Stop hurting me," I pleaded. "Please stop hurting me. You've been hurting me all these years."

"Take it easy, take it easy, kid," said Mel. "How am I hurting you all these years? I never even saw you!"

"That's how, goddammit!"

Millie and Henry came rushing down the hall from my dressing room.

"What'd he do?" she hollered, taking me into her arms.

"I think you'd better go," Henry told Mel.

Mel peered over to me.

"Sorry, Cookie," he said. "I never meant to hurt anyone."

I didn't look up. I was sobbing into my mother's bosom.

"Boy oh boy," I heard him say as he walked away. "Yessiree, Bob."

You Should Be So Lucky

Presidents' Day
West Hollywood, CA 1998

"I'm not sure if there's anything I can eat here," Elliot said after studying the menu of a trendy Melrose Avenue restaurant. Two girls in their early twenties walked by dressed alike in black miniskirts with matching combat boots and pierced ears, noses and belly buttons. Elliot had called last week when he returned to L.A. after three and a half months in Trenton, New Jersey, working on a low-budget indie film about a young magician from a Chinese family.

"It's got Italian food and some American food and fish," I said, glancing at the menu. We had been standing there long enough for me to memorize it. "What do you want?"

"Well, I think I want Italian food," he said. "No Chinese. I ate so much Chinese food the past few months. Too much. It almost ruined it for me. Let's have Italian."

"That's a good start." We had already read menus at a Thai restaurant in Hollywood, a Japanese near Universal, a Mexican place on Santa Monica and two other Italian places within walking distance.

"You want to go in?"

"Well, we have to do valet parking." The car was parked in a resident parking spot that expired momentarily.

"So?"

"They charge three dollars plus tip. It's not the money…"

It never is, I thought.

"…but the principle of the thing," said Elliot. "I think this menu's okay though. Unless—"

"What?"

I hadn't gone out on a date since that awful night of the taping. I spoke to my mom and Henry daily for a while, and went to see them in Florida over the holidays. My perspective had finally shifted. The past was no longer the unknown. Mel was no longer fiction. It was not what I would have chosen for myself, but when I woke up that next morning the sun still shone and I was still me. For the first time I understood those age-old adages, *The truth sets you free* and *What doesn't kill you makes you stronger.*

"No, this'll be okay… I guess," said Elliot.

"You want to go to a deli in Studio City?" I asked.

"No, that reminds me too much of New York, and I really hate New York."

"Okay, I've just made an executive decision, Elliot. We eat here. Bite the bullet and pay for the parking. You practically spent that in parking meters tonight."

His face lit up. "You're right! I never thought about it like that. Okay."

Elliot headed to his car to drive it around the back. Maybe all he needed was a voice of reason and three good rationales a day.

"See, once I make a decision I'm like a new person. It's just making it. I'm much better out of New York too."

"Oh. You mean like... here? You mean this is good compared to the way you usually are?"

"Oh God, yeah. You're really lucky you met me out west. Believe me."

"I can see how lucky I am."

To my surprise, I was happy to hear from him when he called. I wanted to like Elliot. When he picked me up this evening I actually felt a little flutter when I opened the door. His warmth was appealing, and I liked his brand of quirky. He had a nice body, nice, gray curly hair and a nice, cute smile. Those initial moments were great. And then...

One moment Elliot would seem fine. Relaxed, happy,

even confident. Then he'd be overpowered by insecurity.
For every moment I found him attractive, his indecision
would obliterate it. Then he'd regroup, say something
oddly charming, and I'd forget and find him attractive
again. It went back and forth and back and forth. I became so immersed after an hour's conversation with Elliot, it felt like the indecisive one was me.

Elliot handed his car keys over to the attendant. He
looked back several times on our way into the restaurant.

"It'll be okay," I said, walking into Tre Colores.

The place was spacious with white linen tablecloths
and black rattan chairs. Black candles adorned the tables.
There were a few oversized modern art paintings hanging on the wall. Primary colors in wide strokes shot
across the canvases. The floors were a high-glossed wood.

"This is really pretty!" I said as the waiter showed us
to our table.

"It's okay," said Elliot.

"Very striking, don't you think?"

"I don't know. I don't pay much attention."

I ordered a glass of Pinot Grigio, Elliot had a Coke.
I dipped the sourdough bread in olive oil, Elliot asked
the waiter for butter. I had an endive, radicchio and ar-
ugula salad. Elliot had more bread and butter. I had
shrimp, artichokes and leeks in a cream sauce over hay
and straw pasta. Elliot had spaghetti with marinara. Everything was so good, so delicious, I enjoyed being there.

Maybe it was the wine, but I was enjoying being there with quirky, wacky Elliot L. I was having fun. Something I could see Elliot tried to take in small doses.

"Oh, my movie is postponed," he told me while I ate my stemmed strawberries.

"Oh really?" Elliot had just gotten another job. I knew he was doing publicity stills for a new action film in Detroit. He worked a lot and spent a lot of time on the road, but said he wanted to have a girl waiting in the home port. Hmm…that arrangement could work into a good thing. Uh-oh! I went to instant rewind and erased that thought, but it was too late. There it was. The defining moment of the ambivalent relationship. Yikes! I took a gulp of my decaf cappuccino.

"Just a week," he said, taking a bite out of his chocolate cake.

"Is it good?" I asked.

"Yes. This is."

"Can I have a bite?"

He looked at me.

"A bite for a strawberry?"

"Well, I told you I don't like strawberries when you asked to share them before. Only watermelon."

"Uh-huh."

"But you can have a bite. But not too big, okay? This is the first thing I'm eating tonight that I'm enjoying."

"Everything here is great," I said.

"Well, maybe I just have higher expectations of things than you do."

"Maybe I just know how to enjoy things more than you do."

"That's not true at all," he said, cutting a small piece of cake and putting it on my plate. "I'm going to be making so much money on this film, it's obscene. And so you know what?"

"What?"

"I'm going to take a vacation before the job starts and then, again, after."

"Oh, so you won't be staying in L.A. the extra week."

"Nope. I'm back to my studio apartment in New York."

"Thought you hated it there. Why don't you move out here? There's more work."

"Are you kidding! I hate it out here. No place good to get a slice and a Coke. And that's all I want to eat out here. That's my L.A. lunch. EVERY DAY. Slice and a Coke. Slice and a Coke, and I'm happy."

"But I thought you hated New York."

"I do. But there's no other city where I could live."

"Boston?"

"Too cold."

"Chicago's great. And there's work."

Elliot looked at me cross-eyed. "That's really too cold."

"D.C.?"

"I love it there. Lived there for five years."

"Move back."

"Too humid."

"I know. San Francisco!" I announced as if I had just pressed the correct buzzer on a game show.

"Umm," he said, formulating just how he'd reject that. "Too west coast. I'm an east coaster."

"I thought you hate it there. You said you hate New York."

"I know, but I like the east coast. And I have my studio apartment. Fifteen years. Boy, I'm almost forty-five years old and I still live in a studio. I want a one-bedroom."

"You said you're making a ton of money. Move after the Detroit job."

"Are you kidding? I have a great deal. Besides, I like to be able to see everything in one room. It would be weird to have to walk from the living room to the bedroom. Don't you think?"

"I think you could get used to it." I looked at Elliot for a few moments. "Maybe not."

"I'll take this whenever you're ready," said the waiter, dropping the black leather billfold containing the check on our table.

"I'm going to treat," said Elliot, reaching for the check.

"Well, thank you," I said, watching him take out his Visa card. "That's very nice of you."

"You know what I really hate," he confided as he mentally tallied up the bill. "It's women that spend the whole evening talking about how independent they are and what great jobs they have and how they make great salaries, and then when the check comes they want nothing to do with it."

"Oh. Well… Thanks."

"I can treat now, but I don't want to always treat. Just because I'm a man, it's not my job. Because you're a woman it's not your job to cook and clean."

"Well," I said, "maybe to clean."

Elliot looked blankly at me.

"You think so?" he asked.

"Was a joke."

"Oh," he said, thinking it over. "Well, I'm glad one of us is funny."

I looked at him, wondering which one he meant.

"Me!" he said, getting up from the table. "I'm the funny one. I have a great sense of humor."

I said nothing as I picked up my purse.

"I know it's a little intimidating," he said.

"You know, Elliot, you are pretty funny."

"I bet you look great in a bathing suit," he said, walking out of the restaurant.

"Only bikinis," I said, knowing I didn't, but figuring he'd never find out.

As we took a few steps I felt him put his hand on the nape of my neck, moving me in the direction of the parking attendant. A tingling sensation flushed over and through me. To my astonishment, his touch felt good. Really good.

We climbed into the car. He faced me as he turned it on. Elliot touched my cheek and rubbed his hand down around my neck. I was filling up with the delicious anticipation of touching and being touched. And that made me crazy. How could this person who was so antijoy have this luscious touch?

We drove up Franklin, over Laurel Canyon, and twisted through the back streets to Coldwater. The stars were out, the air was sweet and my juices were flowing.

"Maybe I can call you after I'm done with Detroit," he said, shutting off the motor. "Are you staying out here?"

"I have no idea," I said. L.A. and I were beating to the sound of different drummers. Thoughts of leaving were becoming my constant companions. Once again I felt change looming in the air, but I'd think about that later, I thought while unbuckling my seat belt. "Where are you going on vacation?" I asked Elliot. "The one you want to take next week."

"Let's see," he said, unbuckling his with one hand, sliding the other one down my neck. Again. "I want to go to Club Med. It's easiest, but I don't know exactly where."

Elliot lifted my hair and began rubbing the length of my neck down to my shoulders. They were practically bare as I wasn't wearing my blazer, leaving only the thin straps of my sundress. I felt my body relax as I anticipated his hands gently moving down my back.

"What have you looked into so far?" I asked, feebly attempting to get him off my back and back on Club Med.

"Everything," he said.

"And…" It came out a little husky.

"Well, it's hard."

"Lots to choose from, huh?" I sighed. He was moving his hands up and down my back in an even rhythm. He'd start with the palms of his hands pushing toward his fingertips.

"It's just that I don't like humidity and I don't like charters. And I don't like families, but I don't like just singles."

He was touching my skin with the tippy tips of his fingers. It was so light, so tantalizing, and so unexpected I was practically drooling. Elliot was negative. He lacked joie de vivre, most social graces and was ridiculously indecisive. Yet his touch was incredibly sexy. I guess everyone had to have some redeeming qualities. I debated if I wanted to reap the benefits of his.

"Go to Cancún," I said, turning to face him, breaking the spell.

"I'm afraid to drink the water in Mexico."

There. That was a stupid thing for him to say. I would just have to listen. I was sure Elliot would say several more stupid things and then he wouldn't be sexy anymore.

"Turquoise!" I suggested, amusing myself and laughing, the motion causing the strap on the right side of my dress to fall off my shoulder.

"I thought about that," said Elliot, seizing the opportunity, "but I don't think there's enough…"

Enough *what???* I thought. I knew it would be ridiculous. I hoped he'd say it and say it fast because the tips of his fingers were leaving my shoulders and delicately making their way over to my collarbone.

"Shade," he said. "Somehow I think in Turquoise there would be too much sun."

That was ridiculous. It was stupid. It was really dumb. But it was too late, because I couldn't help but inch my body a wee bit closer to his during the whole collarbone thing, which somehow caused the other set of straps to fall, and Elliot immediately caressed the other naked shoulder, so I inched even a wee bit closer and that was when he finally said *shade,* and I thought that there was plenty of shade in Turquoise, I mean there were umbrellas to sit under in Turquoise, but by that time my body was saying *all systems go* and the tips of those fingers had found their way underneath the fabric of my dress, which wasn't all that difficult to find, and by the time they were swirling themselves slowly atop my, yes, heaving bosom—what can I say?—there was nowhere else to go but down. Elliot gently pinched the tip of my nipple. We kissed.

I resisted it at first. Like a dieter resists a tempting piece of delicious cake. I'll just lick the frosting. I'll only have a taste, well, maybe a bite....or two. Half. Just half of the piece. Okay. The whole piece. But just this once. Like a present to me for...for what? For today. Because... Because I say so and I'm here now and why not? Besides, who was I kidding? I had made my decision over the cappuccino.

Our mouths were pressed against each other's, while our tongues explored each other's lips and our bodies connected over the gearshift. The top of my dress had fallen down. His hands were warmly touching me. My hair, my face, my shoulders, my arms, my breasts, my back my...my...my, oh my!!!

"You want to come in?" I breathed.

Elliot smiled in response.

We entered my house. I turned on a little light revealing the living room.

"This is cute," said Elliot.

I walked through the French doors in the living room into the small hallway that connected to my bedroom. I lit a peach-colored candle sitting on the wooden dresser.

"See," said Elliot following me, "I could live here because—"

Don't speak, I thought.

"—you can see the kitchen and the bedroom from the living room—"

DON'T SP—

"—so it's not exactly—"

I grabbed him by the shoulders, pushed him down on my bed, took his hands and placed them around me. Then I kissed him so he wouldn't be able to talk. As long as he didn't say anything we'd be okay.

I pulled off his T-shirt and brushed my hair against his chest. It was smooth, kind of strong…well, strong enough. He unzipped my dress as I kicked off my shoes. I lay over him on my bed with nothing on but my lavender satin panties. I loved those little dresses. They felt so light and sexy on, and were so easy to take off. Somehow I felt the evening never would have gone this way had I elected to put on a pair of jeans.

Elliot pulled his off. He wasn't wearing socks. He pulled me into him and pressed hard against me, underwear to underwear. His hands covered every area surrounding the purple panties. I moved up and down along his legs, his stomach, his back and his front. I started to pull down my panties.

"Don't," he said, stopping my hand. "Let me do it, Karrie. It's part of my pleasure. Don't take away from my pleasure." He pulled down my panties and I pulled off his briefs.

So, he liked chocolate cake and sex. An interesting combination I've experienced many a night. Usually on my own.

I have a theory that people are in my bed as they are

in life. So what I was actually experiencing here was potential. Elliot had the potential to really live life, but instead he chose to give his tickets away. I had been around
long enough to know not to spend the night falling in
love with his potential, but not so long as to give up what
potentially could be some night.

His hands found their way to the areas that had been
unexplored by the presence of the panties. The barrier
was now gone and opened a whole new horizon.

That touch. The tippy tips of those fingers in, out, and
around the tippy tip of me. Ohh! Oohhh! OO…!!

"I want to be inside you," he said.

…hhhh…NOOOO! I thought.

"Right now?" I asked, trying not to lose it, to hold
on to it, to…

"Yeah," he said, still touching me.

"Umm," I said, figuring out what I wanted to do. I
knew I wanted to have sex, but I didn't know if I wanted
to have Sex. He had told me at dinner he'd been tested
last year and hadn't dated anyone since. Still. Emotionally, I was… I was… I was wondering if I had any—

"But I don't like to use condoms," he said. "And I did
tell you over the salad—"

"I remember," I said, thrusting my body into his fingers, into the palm of his hand. I leaned over him on all
fours, his hand still intact, my mouth very available but
facing in the opposite direction of his. DON'T SPEAK,

I thought. Don't talk to me about condoms or salads or apartment layouts or—

"Do we have to use a—"

I laid my body over his, giving him something else to do with his mouth. My mind shut off as my mouth was now occupied too.

Our bodies moved in sync, over and under each other. On our sides. Moving and breathing and heaving and panting and… And… AND…

…YES!

"Oh God!" I moaned. "Ohhh, Ohhhh, God!" I breathed out.

Elliot had pulled away the moment before. If not for that and the obvious telltale signs, I never would have known he experienced anything.

"Kar, come here," he finally said, pulling me into him and holding me around my waist. "That was great," he said.

"Oh yeah? Better than the chocolate cake?"

He waited a moment. "I'll have to think about that."

I laughed.

He looked.

He wasn't joking.

A Eulogy for Henry

My Fortieth Birthday
West Palm Beach, FL 1998

Henry and I first met when I was four years old and getting my tonsils out. Coincidentally, his niece, Robin, was also having a tonsillectomy and was in the crib next to me. Henry came to the hospital to visit Linda and said hello to me. I looked at him and said, "Daddy, Daddy, take me to the bathroom."

"I'll take you to the bathroom, but I'm not your daddy," he said.

"Yes you are. Take me."

Henry had just had a hernia operation and couldn't lift, so he got someone else to take me. But he checked on me the next day, and the next, and as fate would have it, seven years later he did become my dad.

There are certain people you feel you know the moment you meet them. I believe this was true of Henry. One would immediately sense his warmth, goodness, likeability, generosity, kindness, honor, integrity and of course, his humor. He was always there with a joke, a funny response, a look. Henry had certain standard lines you could count on. Often when we'd go out to eat I'd have trouble deciding what to order. Henry would tell me, "Take all the time you want, Kar. Just remember I have someplace I have to be tomorrow."

He would lend a helping hand to anyone, put others' needs ahead of his own. Everyone adored him. In the hospital this past week the nurses fought over who got assigned to take care of him. Henry genuinely liked people. He would stand out in front of the apartment building in Queens, smoking a cigar and greeting people. The mayor! However, his priorities were clear. Family, family and family.

He took on any role—son, husband, father, grandfather, brother, uncle, in-law—with complete pride and love. I remember the special relationship he had with Grandma Rose who always said, "He's not a son-in-law, he's a son."

When Henry began to court my mom I was just a little girl, but I remember seeing the change in her. He rode into my mother's life like a knight in shining armor. The love of her life. His love enriched all our lives.

Earlier this week he was so sick. A stroke. We thought he was going to make it, but he didn't. That last day me, Mom, Lenny and Sharon all gathered round him. He asked my mom to take out his tuxedo. Miraculously, Henry sang:

After the ball is over—
After the break of dawn—
After the dance is leaving—
After the songs are gone—

Henry may no longer be with us in the physical sense, but his songs will never be gone. They will resonate in our hearts, uplift our spirits, and sing out the love now, forever and always.

I love you, Dad.

The Wedding

Father's Day
Brentwood, CA 1998

He asked me to go to a wedding. That was a good sign. Most men I date don't even know what one is. We knew each other from a class. An improv class. We were improvising a scene about a couple on a first date. Unfortunately, they were on a bad one.

That night after class we had California cuisine pizza. Over the pizza Marcus was eager to please. He told me all about his faithful friend and companion, Wilbur, a big black Lab. He complimented my looks and my acting. He was an actor, too, and had done a spy series in Canada. He played a bad guy.

When he dropped me at home that evening, we lingered in his Jeep in my driveway. Marcus leaned over to kiss me, and started to rub my neck. His fingers went deeply and directly into my pain.

It was surreal to have been in Florida burying Henry. The place didn't feel like home, but the people did, surrounded by close friends and family who had relocated. Jane had been a great support and flew down to Florida. William was there on business, and they came and paid a shiva call. Fred called often, and with his recent development that he would be moving out of my apartment and into his very own lease come July. Did I want him to line up another sublet? Elliot was still in Detroit with the action film. We spoke several times and he was as compassionate as Elliot could be.

When I returned to L.A. after Henry's funeral, I knew the decision to stay or to go would be imminent. It felt even harder to be there knowing Millie was alone. New York was much closer to Florida than California. I spoke with my mother every day. As she said, she had "what to do" with so many activities in her Florida development. The days were busy, but the nights were bad.

Now I was back, parked in my driveway, sitting in a Jeep, getting my neck rubbed by a guy who'd been on a spy show. Three thousand miles away from real life. Marcus's hands made me forget everything. I was feeling relaxed, feeling better and that's when he asked me to go to the wedding. It was ten days away. I immediately said yes. I am sucker for a good neck rub.

That weekend Marcus took me out for prime rib. We drank a lot of wine. Not only was Marcus good at neck rubs, he was even better at kissing. I liked kissing Marcus. I'm pretty verbal. My mouth does a lot of moving. And since we never really laughed, I preferred us kissing to talking.

Three days before the wedding Marcus took me to Jerry's Deli after class. Pastrami and chicken soup brought back memories of childhood. Not just mine. His.

"My parents visited me at a sleep-away camp in New Hampshire when I was eleven," he told me. "It was visiting day and they brought me my favorites." Marcus was opening up. I thought learning about his youth would bridge the gap between us.

Marcus was calling me daily. He was attentive, He was trying hard, but something was off. I knew a lot of it was me. I was not ready to start a relationship and had told him. Marcus insisted he just liked my company and wanted a date for the wedding. As long as I had agreed to go, I wanted it to be nice. I wanted us to be able to enjoy ourselves and for it to be pleasant, even fun.

Marcus looked superserious as he started his story about his parents and the camp. He was always superserious. "My father unwrapped pastrami sandwiches and chicken soup he brought from the local deli at home," said Marcus, his thick eyebrows furrowed together. How serious could a story about a delicatessen be? Marcus really did look like he could be a spy, I thought. Tall, intense, handsome and bald.

"How nice," I said, thinking about Henry, thinking about Mel and imbuing Marcus as a man from a perfect suburban childhood. A childhood inscribed with sleep-away camps, delicatessens and love.

"I didn't want to eat it," he said. "I only wanted pizza."

"Kids."

"My father screamed at me in the cafeteria. He humiliated me."

"What did he do?"

"He told me I was stupid!"

"That's awful." I tried to picture an eleven-year-old Marcus resisting chicken soup and pastrami on rye in a rustic cafeteria, while a man who looked a lot like Marcus does now was calling him stupid.

"My father always hated me!" Marcus spewed out the words with venom. It may have been thirty years ago, but either Marcus was reenacting the scene or he just wasn't over it.

Don't say anything, Karrie. Just listen. Don't give advice. Let him vent and let him know you're there to listen.

"Aren't you going to say anything?" asked Marcus.

"I would like to hear more." Yes, that was warm and diplomatic.

"Well, he screamed at me in front of everyone. It was a public place."

"That must have been horrible for you," I said.

"I can't believe how much he hates me. What do you think of that, Karrie?"

"Do you really think your father hates you?" It was just a question.

"Absolutely. He has a lot of problems."

"It sounds it. Is it possible he takes them out on you?" I thought it so sad that this forty-one-year-old man felt detested by his father.

"Yes, of course, it is."

"So maybe he loves you, but he has so many problems he can't express love. What's it like between him and your mom?"

Marcus banged his hand on the table. The salt shaker fell over and some of the chicken soup spilled.

"If I tell you he hates me, then he hates me. Goddammit!" Marcus's voice was attracting a lot of attention. I was very aware of how Marcus felt when he was eleven, since he had just done to me what his father had done to him. "Just listen to me," Marcus had shifted his voice into a loud stage whisper. He pounded his hand on the table again. "Would you just listen!"

The waiter caught my eye, but suddenly Marcus was quiet, and the waiter chose to ignore us and carry on.

"I'm sorry," Marcus said quickly, regaining his composure.

"It's okay," I said, regaining mine. I obviously was not good with bad stories about men and their fathers. I now understood how Marcus's passion went into acting and animals and kissing. Anything but laughter. Nonetheless, this wedding thing with me and Marcus was not going to be. I had to get out of it.

"I know it's this weekend," I said to Marcus when we pulled up to my house and were sitting in his Jeep. "But I think it's best I don't go with you to the wedding."

"You're kidding," he said. "I'm counting on it. I have no one else to take."

"I'm sorry," I said. "But you scared me." I thought I should be very honest with him. Direct. "This—us—it's not going to work. I can't. I already told you what's been going on with me, so I'm not in a great place. I can't go with you to this wedding and I don't want to be misleading."

"Please come to the wedding," said Marcus. "I'm sorry about what happened in the deli. When I talk about my father… I'm in therapy, you should know… I—I…like you. Please. No strings. I understand. Just come with me to the wedding."

There was no neck rub. I was just a sucker. I went to the wedding.

I chose to skip the ceremony and met Marcus at the reception. Thought I'd take my own car, meet him there, be independent. Just a few hours. It'd be okay. He and I were clear. I knew what it was like to go to a wedding alone. This was a nice thing to do. For Marcus. I would survive. Unless they served chicken soup and pastrami.

Driving up the Canyon, I envisioned an intimate breakfast wedding. An outdoor tent, classical music and assorted sandwiches cut into quarters. I walked into the wedding scene of *Goodbye, Columbus* at eleven o'clock on a Sunday morning. Glitz. A band. Fortunately there was no deli. Instead, this morning, we were served a soup to nuts dinner.

Marcus was asked to help usher the guests to the correct room and table. As I milled about, people asked, "Whose side are you on? The bride's or the groom's?" I was on Marcus's side. His left to be exact. When I was introduced to the groom I found myself suddenly wrapped up in Marcus's arms like I was a gift. His.

"Should I hold on to this one?" he asked his newly wedded friend. "I think I will. What do you think?"

I escaped to the ladies' lounge. I looked in the mirror and asked myself just exactly why I thought that going to the wedding of people I didn't know with a man I didn't like was ever a good idea. At this point, I already knew it was not a good thing for me, and it certainly would be less of a good thing for Marcus.

Significantly annoyed with myself, I found my place at Table Nine. It was the friends table. Couples. The television producer from Brooklyn spoke to us first.

"So," he began in his deregionalized accent. "Do you two live together, are you married, or what?"

"That's his significant other," answered the scientist from Pasadena who had never met me or Marcus before in her life.

Everyone at the table was married except for me and Marcus. They smiled at us with "You're Next!" shining in their eyes. Weddings bring out the happy in people happy in love, and the angst in the rest of us. I looked to Marcus for a moment of shared angst, only to see he had embraced the role of Happy that Table Nine had cast him in.

The music saved me. *Hava Nigilah!!* We danced the *Hora*. Around and around in circles, stamping my feet, kicking my heels. I loved the *Hora*.

"We need eight strong men to lift the bride and groom in the air," called out the band leader. "Four men to a chair."

Up in the air they went, the new husband and wife. They were laughing through terrified eyes as everyone danced around them. I went back to the table. I did not want to look. I could only remember the story of Rabbi Bernstein's daughter. At her wedding reception, her husband of forty-five minutes was accidentally dropped during this ritual. He remains a cripple, she remains single.

"Let's dance. A slow one," said Marcus, sneaking up behind me. His eyes were suggestive as he led me onto the dance floor.

"The food," I said, watching the waiters bring my breakfast of baked chicken, candied apples and a potato concoction.

"It'll wait," he said, and pulled me close. "You look very delectable," he murmured in my ear.

The closer Marcus tried to get, the farther away I went. I had agreed to be his date, not his love. I suppose my acceptance of his invitation, despite the conditions, led him to believe anything was possible. Especially at a wedding. I knew nothing between us was possible and had no appreciation for the situation I had put myself in. My eyes welled up with tears. I wished the happy was being brought out in me instead of this angst. This yearning to feel what the bride and groom were feeling.

"Are you sure you're okay?" Marcus asked. The band was playing a medley of New York songs that reminded me of my parents.

"I'm just homesick," I said. I was. It had been two years since Millie and Henry's retirement to Florida. It hadn't really affected me, living in L.A. So what if the Queens apartment was gone. Manhattan was my home. It still was, but now home looked a little different. Although I was an adult, Henry's death marked the end of an era, the end of childhood.

"Ohhhh," Marcus said, pulling me closer. I closed my eyes and for a brief moment let it feel good to be held. But the dance ended, and my eyes reopened.

When we got back to the table, the champagne had been poured for the toast. Marcus entwined his arm around mine and looked into my eyes.

"To—" he said.

"Making money," I said against the clash of our glasses.

He looked disappointed. I didn't blame him. So was I.

"What?" I asked, putting him on the spot. Half hoping to have it out and finished. At that moment, the bandleader requested all single women line up to catch the bouquet. Everyone at my table urged me to go.

"No, thank you," I said. "This sort of thing really isn't for me."

Marcus strongly urged me to go.

"I hate this stuff," I said to him in a harsh whisper. The whole table was watching.

"Be a sport," he said. "Come on, be a good sport."

The photographer came up behind me and pulled at my hand.

"Are you single?" he asked. He must have spotted my neon sign. "Come on," he said, pulling me up on my feet. "You may get lucky."

I turned to Marcus for help. What was I thinking? He grabbed me from the other side. "Do I take this to mean that you think that we…"

"It means I'm embarrassed," I said. "Take it to mean I'm embarrassed."

Somehow Marcus equated opening my arms for that

bouquet with opening my arms to him. The photographer led me to the dance floor. Marcus and the people at Table Nine were rooting for me.

I stood in the center of the room, mortified, while the photographer snapped away at me, the mother of the bride, a woman from England, and a seven-year-old. The seven-year-old caught it.

I went back to the table. A piece of wedding cake decorated the plate in front of me. I certainly was not going to take it home and hide it under my pillow. I sat quietly and ate it, while Marcus tried to catch the garter.

It was ending. Goodbyes. Good wishes. The staff breaking down the tables. The last dance had been danced, and there was…singing? I hadn't recalled a singer all day.

Night and day, you are the one—

I looked up to see Marcus crooning on the microphone from the bandstand. The woman next to me noticed.

"He's singing to you. Pay attention," she advised.

I tried.

Spend my life making love to you—

He sang the lyrics directly to me. My cheeks were flushed. I felt like an impostor who was highly imposed upon. I stayed put. It would be over any minute.

"You have a good voice," I told Marcus five songs later.

"I want you to have the centerpiece," he said. It was pretty. Roses. Pink and red.

"You take it," I said. "I'm going away for a few days. It'll die."

"No. I wanted you to have it." Marcus insisted.

In the parking lot we passed the happy couple loading the presents in their Honda.

"It was great meeting you," said the groom. "I hope to see a lot more of you," he said, emphasizing the words *a lot*.

"Good luck," I said, and slunk away.

Marcus and I said goodbye at my car.

"You're sure you don't want to come to the afterparty with me? It'll be even more fun than this was." He just asked. He wasn't insistent. Marcus had finally backed off. This time I just declined. The wedding was over and so were we. I thanked him and drove off.

The roses filled my car with a wonderful scent. The sun over the mountains shone brightly. "I Love To Cry At Weddings" from *Sweet Charity* hummed inside my head as I waited for the light to turn green. Jane had called yesterday to announce that she and William were engaged. She asked me to be her maid of honor. My best friend was getting married. Jane was very excited. Even though we were older than the typical age of most blushing brides, her engagement brought up the same emotions. Giddy, girlish, hopeful and proud. I wondered what that felt like.

I allowed myself to daydream about the kind of wedding I would like to have. Away from the pressure of the wedding, and the misfit of me and Marcus, I allowed myself to daydream. I indulged the fantasy of being married on a beach in the Hamptons, or California, or Coney Island. In a synagogue or a beautiful old mansion. I wondered what I would wear. I pictured my family and friends dancing the *Hora* around us. Happy. I hoped everyone there would be in a place where my wedding brought out the happy in everyone invited. That there would be no angst.

I allowed myself to think of actually meeting the man I would fall in love with and marry. Who was he? Imminent or far away? How would we meet? Was he out west or back east? And before that thought was fully constructed, I knew I would return home to New York. As soon as possible. Now. So...that's how decisions were made, I thought. Picturing myself back east, being with a man I could truly care for, brought forth a feeling of peace, but just as quickly came the sinking feeling that it was all so remote, rapidly replaced with yearning.

My mother had felt that way once. Then she married Mel and had a daughter. Then she divorced and felt that way again. Then she married Henry. Now she was grieving, but it was possible one day she would feel that way again. She might yearn for someone, someday, again.

"One day you'll be married, you'll be settled...." What did that mean? Once it got settled, did it really stay settled? I hoped I would be given the opportunity to find out. It was one thing to date and another to marry. I'd met men to date, not men to marry. Though I supposed it depended on what you needed. There were all kinds of men and all kinds of marriages, which often led to all kinds of divorces. I wanted it to work out. There were no guarantees, but deep in my gut I would need to emphatically feel that it could. I would know when it was right, I thought. Just as I've always known that it was not. I would allow my instincts to guide me. My instincts.

Me and my instincts were forty and still single. It seemed impossible that could have happened, but it did. In fact, the evolution felt fairly normal. Normal. What was normal? Individual, I thought. Your own normal. Tomorrow night Marcus could tell another woman his delicatessen story and they could fall in love.

I didn't know for sure what my normal was or who would be my normal. I only knew where my normal would be. I knew that whoever he was, I wanted him to be back east. I wanted him in Manhattan. Near Central Park and the 42nd Street Library. Near Lincoln Center and Chinatown. Near Millie and Jane and Fred. Near seasons and a slice and an egg on a roll. If I stayed out here any longer, I would have to hire a tutor. L.A. was a language I could not learn. I would give my roommate notice, sell my car and get a bunch of cartons. I would tell Fred not to find a sublet and fill out a change-of-address card at the local post office.

The sudden curve in the road took all my attention. My body stiffened, and I shifted my focus to the narrow road of Beverly Glen, thinking how much easier it will be to stop pumping gas and buy a subway token. I turned the wheel, making my way down the twists and curves of the canyon. The sun was shining and the smog had lifted. I could see the snowcapped mountains. And though I appreciated this beautiful Southern California day, I had the unshakable feeling that whatever was meant to be, my normal would always include fire escapes and taxis, subways and cement, skyscrapers, doormen, walking and weather.

How Personal
Do You Want to Get?

Halloween
Columbus Avenue, NYC 1998

I met him through *The Personals*. I knew by his ad I would be attracted to him. Don't ask me how. I just did.

Theoretically, I could have been attracted to everyone in *The Personals*. If you've been wondering where the crème-de-la-crème of New York City are hiding, I'll tell you. *The Personals*. It's filled with handsome, stunning, gorgeous people. Everyone claims to be so good-looking, it is a major cause for alarm to read an ad where someone would merely describe himself as attractive.

Always feeling *The Personals* had value but were in all probability not for me, I had never answered ads. But after returning from Los Angeles, I felt differently about a lot of things. One was that I felt open to trying some main-stream dating opportunities I had always thought were good for other people, but not me. While waiting for my appointment one morning at the dentist, I picked up a copy of *New York Magazine*. After being informed that a woman my age had a better chance of being hit by a truck than falling in love and getting married, I began to peruse *The Personals*. Everyone sounded amazing! I thought I'd give it a try. Over a three-month period I answered, by way of a written response and photo, about twenty ads. I received eleven phone calls, spoke to all of them and chose to meet two of them, only to return to my original feeling that *The Personals* had value but were in all probability not for me.

Then I read his.

EYE DOCTOR TURNED SPORTSWRITER
Handsome, successful, fit, Jewish 41 wants pretty, verbal, evolved, smart, funny, trim woman for love, marriage and family.

The ad actually told me more about me than him, but I answered it anyway. It sounded a lot like the other nineteen ads I'd answered, but for one difference. This time I knew I'd be attracted. I think the word *verbal* turned me on.

When Rob and I spoke, he told me I was one of only two women he called out of almost two hundred responses. There was one other but he answered her by mail. She lived in Minnesota. It wasn't the long-distance call that was the deterrent. The woman was incarcerated and didn't have a phone.

"She really sounded sincere," said Rob, his voice kind of nice with an interesting rasp. "I just wanted her to feel hopeful."

"I didn't think they got *New York Magazine* in prison."

"Oh, you wouldn't believe some of the letters I got," he said. I could almost see the frown in his brow.

"So tell me how I cut through the hundred and ninety-eight."

"The photos eliminate most of it," said Rob, stroking my ego like the ears of a cat. "But you wouldn't believe it. Most people can't write, and so many women sounded so desperate. Pages and pages of their whole life's story."

My response to him included some information about my statistics, my interests, my favorite things to do, and a current list of the contents of my refrigerator.

Rob told me he lived on East 76th, ran the marathon, had a car, had never married and had never done *The Personals.* We made plans to meet the next evening for dinner at a great French restaurant on my side of town, right near my apartment.

"Do you want to know what I look like?" he asked.

"Well, enough to recognize you."

"But don't you want to hear about my looks?"

"Not really. I mean you look how you look. And ultimately what you say doesn't matter," I said.

"You mean that looks don't matter?"

"They do in that there has to be attraction. There has to be chemistry. And all that happens in person. It's not about words. The phone can be really misleading."

"This has been a great conversation," said Rob. "You have to admit it's great."

"It's very nice and I look forward to meeting you."

"Why can't you just say the conversation's great? Why can't you just say it?"

I thought the conversation was nice. Nice enough to choose to meet. Considering we had absolutely no context, I guess you could say it was really nice. The talk was easy and he got my references. I got his. There was a little laughter, a little buzz. But I was always aware of one major thing. I didn't know who I was talking to! I honestly didn't know what we would feel. For real. In person. I had learned my lesson on the other two dates about creating pictures in my head with the safety of the phone. Especially with a stranger. Therein the obvious success strategy of the 900 number.

"I could be falling in love with you over the phone," said Rob.

"Oh God, don't say that," I said.

"Why not?"

"Because we don't even know each other. We've never

even met. We have to meet and see what it feels like. Let's just keep it light and meet tomorrow."

There was a giant pause. I knew it wasn't one of the good ones.

"You know, I don't want to hurt your feelings," he began, "but I don't think you should tell me how I should be. If I want to be excited I will be and you can be cautious, but don't put your stuff on me," he said, surprisingly nicely without any edge in his voice.

I took a breath. Oh no! Was this another nutcake? Should I bail? No. I wanted him to turn out to be somebody. Maybe it was me. Maybe I was the nutcake because I was too cautious. I was in the middle of my first crisis with this man and I couldn't picture his reactions because I didn't even know what he looked like.

"Okay," I said as if I was letting him into some secret place. "This is a great conversation, Rob. Now please tell me what you look like."

"So you *are* interested!"

False alarm. I got it. I inadvertently hurt his ego. He thought I was disinterested as opposed to self-protective.

"Well," said Rob. "I'm about six foot one with brown curly hair and brown eyes. And how will I know you?"

"I'll be looking for you. And you have my picture."

"Right. Yeah, I liked that picture. That was a great dress. Really caught my eye," he said, lightening up.

The photo was taken out in L.A. I was wearing a very

retro dress. It was short, tight, sleeveless and shiny with silver, black and orange numbers chaotically written all over it.

"Well, you sound cute too," I conceded. I wanted to like him and I wanted him to be great, but I really needed to stay low-key. I didn't want to build it all up, just in case it all came tumbling down.

"You know, tomorrow's Halloween," said Rob. "Wouldn't it be funny if I paid some unattractive guy twenty-five dollars to say he was me tomorrow night?"

"Honest? I don't think that would be funny at all."

"Believe me, I don't know exactly how to say this so it comes out right, but I'm pretty sure you'll be attracted to me. Seeing your picture we, uh, kind of look like people that would…you know, go together."

I felt myself flush. I knew he was right. I mean I had known it when I first read the ad and saw the word *verbal*.

"Do me one favor?" requested Rob. "If you're attracted to me, tell me I was right."

The next evening I strolled south on Columbus Avenue wearing the black Benetton miniskirt Jane had given me for my birthday, and a black leather jacket. I couldn't help but wonder if I was off to dinner or the beginning of a future, though I hated when I'd think that way. It made me feel like such a vulnerable girl. I was realizing to a great extent I was. We all were.

I got near the restaurant I saw a man about six feet

tall standing outside. He was in an old black wool jacket and had long curly hair. Dark brown. Or was it dark red? No. Dark brown. A beard. And he was waiting…for me! He waved. I pointed my index finger at him in a motion that said, "Hey!" It was either very cool or very not.

"Hi!" I smiled.

"Hi," he said, leaning over to kiss me on the cheek. "You look fine."

"Oh," I said, wondering why I wouldn't. Did I tell him something? Maybe I said something about going to bed too late, not getting enough sleep, something, who knows.

"There's a slight change in plans," he said.

I noticed the rasp in his voice sounded a little deeper than on the phone. I really needed to get a new cordless phone.

"What?" I asked. Rob seemed a bit sloppy. Or was it just Bohemian? I'd have to see. I was glad I was self-protective and hadn't gone too far on the greatness of our conversation.

"My office is having a party downtown," he said. "There's lots of people and food. If it's okay, I figured we'd go."

"Oh, sure," I said. I had expected something else. Something a little more…something. Upscale. Polished, maybe? I was surprised he thought we'd fit together. I was disappointed. Disappointed with him. Disappointed with *The Personals* and really disappointed I wasn't going to eat at the French place. "It's fine," I said, thinking maybe it would be better to be with a group after all.

"I just have to check my car," he said, walking to the corner of 75th Street.

"You're lucky to have that car," I said. "Did you drive here?"

"No. I walked."

"From 76th?"

"75th."

"Don't you live on 76th?"

"75th."

"I thought you said 76th and…" I didn't know. "Anyway, the car…"

"It's being worked on. The mechanic is working on it on the street. I've known him a long time. I trust him."

"Oh. That's why it's over here," I said. I knew he lived on East 76th. Well, okay, East 75th, and he must have driven across town to park it over on the West Side so the mechanic could work on it. Then he walked over to meet me.

"I couldn't sleep last night," he told me. "And I wanted to get up and run today too. Too tired."

"That's a drag," I said. "And you ran the marathon and all. That's pretty amazing. I was impressed when you told me that."

He looked at me with uncertainty. I suppose I wasn't what he'd hoped for either.

We crossed over to 75th Street. There was the mechanic working on his old burgundy Chevrolet. Even the car was not as polished as I'd imagined. I checked my watch. This was going to be a long night. Rob talked to the mechanic, and I wondered if I should suddenly remember something or get a headache.

"Okay, let's go," he said, taking my hand. "I'll get a cab."

"Aren't you going to take the car?"

"Why would I do that?"

"Because then you have to come back here."

"I have to come back here anyway."

"You mean to take me home?"

"No. I live here."

What was this man talking about? Did he think he wouldn't get a parking spot and wanted to cab around all night? If he wasn't going to use the car, why didn't he have the mechanic work on it on the East Side? And he just said he lived… What?

"You live on the East Side," I said.

"No, I don't. I live here on the West Side."

"No, you don't."

"I live right here," he said pointing to a brownstone off Columbus on 75th.

"You do? How could that be?"

Wait. Wait a minute. Things were clicking in place. Nothing was wrong but nothing was right. Was it possible…?

"What's your name?" I asked.

"Phil," he said.

"Yeah, yeah. Trick or treat. Come on. Really. What's your name?"

"Phil."

"I get it! It's that twenty-five-dollar thing, right? Right?" I could see by the way he looked at me there was no twenty-five-dollar thing.

"Are you really Phil?"

He nodded, leaning up against his car with ownership. His car. His name. Uh. Oh.

"You mean... You're not Rob?"

"You mean... You're not Jill?"

"Jill? Who's Jill?"

"I'm supposed to be on a blind date at Chez Maison at seven-thirty," said Phil.

"*I'm* supposed to be on a blind date at Chez Maison at seven-thirty. But not with you! And now we're *both* late!"

Phil and I ran back to Chez Maison. I was light as can be. It was a movie moment. A second chance! Let Jill go to the party downtown. Let Jill go drive around in the dilapidated Chevy. I was getting a second chance. I approached the restaurant and saw no one outside. There was, however, a man standing at the bar.

"That must be Rob," said Phil, looking around for Jill who was obviously very late. "Oh, listen," he said, reaching inside his pocket. "If it doesn't work out with him, here's my card."

I threw it in my purse, ran inside and saw not a cute guy standing at the bar, but a really cute one! Handsome in fact. Polished. In a suit. A beautiful suit. I ran up to him, panting. Out of breath.

"Are you Rob?" I asked, holding it for a second.

"I thought I saw you walk by about ten minutes ago, but you were with another guy so I figured it wasn't you."

"It was!"

I was giddy as the waiter seated us. A cozy table in the corner. Wine. Candles. Rob. Our own romantic comedy unfolding before our very eyes. I loved it!

"You're right!" I said, my voice blowing through the flame of the candle. "You were right. I am attracted you. You're really good-looking. I am attracted to you." I could now say in person what I could not say on the phone. I was infinitely more relaxed, not to mention re-lieved I wasn't spending the evening with Phil.

We ordered. Rob was nice. Reserved. Yes, much more reserved than last night on the phone. Uncomfortable? No. Well-mannered. That was it. But? No. Nothing. Things were going fine. Great. He was… I was… Well… I was trying to figure out why a guy like that in a city like this needed a personal ad.

"How did you know?" he asked.

"How'd I know what?"

"Last night? That I was safe on the phone and it would be different in person. You're very attractive and everything. I'm just… Well, I'm not as comfortable in person as I was on the phone."

"Oh?" I said, trying not to choke on my Caesar salad. "Funny. I feel better. I'm a people person," I said, feeling before the coffee was poured I'd know how this fellow fit into *The Personals*.

And I was right.

Now I must tell you I didn't need to be right. It would have been okay for him to be fabulous and for me to be hypersensitive to all the nuances and have been wrong. But as it turned out, I was right.

Rob told me all through the entrée, steak au poivre for me, coq au vin for him, about the horrible relationship with his parents. How alone he feels in the world. How in forty-one years no one has ever understood him. How he and I had a connected conversation on the phone last night and that hardly ever happens. No one really knows him. And no one ever gets him.

"Just my friend Elizabeth and my therapist," he said.

"And how long have you been with your therapist?" I asked, starting to feel more like that than his date.

"A year."

"I see."

I picked at the apple crumb cake and drank a little decaf. I was disappointed again that evening, but at least

I was disappointed by the right man this time. The good news was that Rob felt he knew how to connect with people now. His life was improving because he now knew how to connect and make good relationships.

"Well," I said. "That's great. And as you feel more nourished by these new relationships in your life I'm sure all your relationships will get better. Why, as you grow to be happier and see things through happy eyes, it's possible that your relationship with your parents might even improve."

I smiled at him. He sat back and looked at me. I was sure he was thinking what a perceptive and compassionate woman I was, and I was thinking I didn't know how to tell him I really wouldn't be turning out to be the one he'd be bringing home to meet the dysfunctional parents.

"I can't believe you did this to me again," Rob finally said.

"Did what?" I asked, thinking I had done something good. Something very, very good.

"You put your stuff on me again. And you judged me. I just told you my parents are not good for me. Maybe the best thing for me is not to have a relationship with them. Maybe the best thing for me is to lead my life and have nothing to do with them. What do you think about that?"

I recognized this road as I had, unfortunately, been down it before.

"I'm sorry," I said, apologizing because it was obvious

he was in deep pain, and it was obvious it was time to go home as soon as possible. "I thought I was being nice. I really didn't feel I was judging you, but if that was your experience of it," I said, carefully using appropriate shrink jargon, "I apologize. If I sounded anything, it was probably a little Pollyanna. We all have our problems, but it's nice when people can get along with their parents."

"Just because it's your fantasy to be with someone who likes their parents, don't put that on me. You have made me very, very angry," said Rob in one of the least angry voices I'd ever heard. "As a matter of fact, this is the angriest I get."

"Listen," I said. I was trying to be careful. He wasn't fooling. I knew he was fragile, but he was way out of line. "I was not trying to judge you or tell you what to do. If anything I felt a little, well, you know… I'm hearing about all your negative relationships within the first hour of a first date. A blind date no less. From an ad. It's just kind of uncomfortable. Kind of like a red flag."

Rob smiled. Good. He understood. I had gotten through to him. Okay, we weren't going to walk into the sunset together, but at least we could peaceably walk out of the restaurant.

"Well." He shook his head, still smiling when he finally spoke. "You have taken the most sensitive issue of my life and judged me on it and told me I was a red flag and wouldn't be a good spouse or father. Thanks. Thanks a lot."

We left. He insisted on walking me home. I wanted to leave him at the restaurant, but he looked sad and I felt awkward and guilty, so I agreed to let him walk me the few blocks. I figured him in too much mental pain to inflict any physical kind. It's a pity, I thought. He was cute. Kind of bright. And maybe he just needed... Maybe if we went out again... Maybe... Maybe not. No. He's wrong for you, Karrie. Wrong. Wrong, wrong, wrong, wron—

"Good night," said Rob. "So... It was..."

"Yeah. It was a....a nice—a...interesting...evening. Good night."

My head was reeling when I plopped on my couch. I sat there catatonic for more than an hour pondering the awful evening. I decided what was most awful was that I really wanted to like someone like Rob, if only Rob was someone like Rob instead of who he turned out to be. Okay. Over. Next!

Two days later Rob called me for another date. He immediately noticed the hesitation in my voice.

"No secrets," he said. "Tell me what's going on."

And I did. I told him. I told him he's attractive and nice and bright, but maybe...he should get to know someone, oh, just a little, before putting all his dirty laundry on the table. Especially someone he shared no context with. I told him we saw the world too differently and I didn't think we made the right combination. After hearing this he asked if we could be friends. I, for lack of wanting to say anything else difficult, said I was always up for taking a walk in the park and getting an ice cream.

"That's much different though," he said. "Much easier. Not as intense. Not like a relationship. Not like a marriage."

"Excuse me, but I think when you meet someone from an ad you have to start at the beginning," I told him. "You can advertise for a marriage but it doesn't happen because you meet in a restaurant and pour out your life stories. It's earned. And it takes some light walks in the park, some ice cream, maybe a couple of movies, some fun and time. Mainly it takes time."

Rob didn't know if he wanted to be my friend after all. He had to process the information and get back to me.

The next evening I was on the East Side, running down Third Avenue to catch the crosstown bus, and I passed a man on the street. I didn't recognize him at first. He was in sweat clothes and seemed a little uncomfortable in his own skin, but I stopped and called out, "Rob?" The man stopped. It was him.

"So, this is what we look like not dressed up," I joked, looking at the sweat clothes I was also wearing.

Another chance, I thought. Another chance to rewrite this movie. To rewrite the ending. We chatted a few moments about the weather, the day. There was no epiphany, no meeting of the minds, no nothing. Just some pleasant on-the-street conversation with someone you know you will never see again.

That weekend was Jane's birthday. William invited us out for a birthday dinner at a Spanish restaurant downtown. They were living in the West Village, and planning a spring wedding. Fred came as my "date." I was hoping to hit it off with Rob and bring him along too. Alas… Anyway, this was familiar and fun. Jane and Fred had become friends with each other through being friends with me. I always loved how people's social circles expanded that way.

"Don't ask," I said to Fred when he did. However, Fred had just broken up with a computer analyst he met Salsa dancing by the fountain in Lincoln Center over the summer. Fred was artsy, but had a real penchant for guys who weren't.

"Okay. What happened?" Jane looked so happy with William.

"I want to know too," said William, feeling a little left out.

"Well…okay."

I told the *Cliff Notes* version. "I had a blind date… I showed up at Chez Maison…yada, yada, yada…and then I said, 'You're not Rob?' and he said, 'You're not Jill?'"

Ba–dum–bum!!!

Uproarious laughter.

"What a story!" said William.

"And you really didn't know?" asked Fred.

"What were you thinking to fill in the blanks?" Jane was into specifics.

"I guess I found out you can fill in anything, if what you really want is to make something fit," I said. It was true. But I had nailed my last square peg into Rob's round hole.

"What if there was no Jill," said Fred. He was such a disbeliever! "What if Phil was just trying to pick you up?"

"Did you actually see her?" asked William. He was a lawyer. He needed proof.

"Maybe she looks just like you," said Fred. "Call Phil and find out. You have to find out what he was thinking."

"If this were a movie you'd fall in love with Phil," said Jane.

"Oh, but it's not a movie. Believe me!" I said. "I wanted it to be, but it's not."

"You have to find out about Jill," said Fred. "You have his card. Call him. I'll do it with you. We'll do it tonight! Come on."

"I love the way you're so adventurous with my ridiculous love life, Fred!"

"Do you still have the card?" asked William. He needed hard facts.

"I put it in my purse." I reached down under the table to get it. I hadn't looked at it since tossing it in there that night.

"Let me see," said William, taking out his glasses to get a good look.

I produced a white, slightly crumpled business card that said:

PHILIP BLAKEMAN
CityLife Realty
520 Broadway
212 555-3857

William read it aloud.

"OHMYGOD!" shrieked Fred. "Phil Blakeman? Real-estate agent? Lives on 75th and Columbus? That Phil Blakeman?"

"Yes," I said. "Yes!"

"Reddish curly hair?"

"Yes! That's him. You know him?" I asked, thinking I really messed up on the hair thing but, I swear, it was only in a certain light it looked a little red, otherwise to me it really did pretty much look brown.

"That's the guy who got me my apartment. Oh, Karrie, he's crazy," said Fred. "One night he asked if I would meet him at his building when he was taking me around to show me places. I think he lives with his parents. I rang the buzzer, but he lived on the first floor of a brownstone. The stereo was blasting and his father ran out to the stoop and screamed at him. 'Phil! Take out the GARBAGE, Phil! Take out the goddamn GARBAGE!' I think he was stoned when he showed me the place. That's probably how I got such a good deal," finished Fred.

"This is incredible," said William.

"Amazing," said Jane.

"Always happened to you!" said Fred.

I punched him. "Stop it. This isn't funny anymore. I have to change my karma."

Everyone looked at me. I glared back.

"This is not a joke. I have to figure out how to change it."

We all sat in silence for a second.

"Well, it's my birthday and I'm hungry," said Jane. "Who wants to share the bouillabaisse?" I shifted my attention to food, guaranteed nourishment, while I contemplated my bad boyfriend karma.

After dinner, on the way to the subway, we passed a spirits shop on Christopher Street.

"Hey, you guys, I'm going to say good-night and duck in here," I said. "Anybody want to come?"

Fred had an audition in the morning and passed, and Jane and William clearly had better things to do!

"Happy Birthday, Janey! Next year when we celebrate you'll be married!"

Jane sang in response.

Sadie, Sadie married lady—

We all hugged good-night and I ran inside and bought a special candle and a book on karma. I read the book on the #1 train all the way back up to 79th Street. I kept the brown paper bag holding the candle tightly tucked inside my purse, and my purse tucked inside my coat. I did not want to expose it to life. I was afraid any vibrations might collect like dust all over this candle I was going to use to perform a ceremony to change my karma. My boyfriend karma needed changing. And fast!

They all thought it was so funny. It was hilarious! If you were someone else, not me. There was obviously a hole in my karma and it was so big all the good boy-friends fell through it. I needed to patch it. Sew it up. Make a pocket that was big enough for a great, big boy-friend to land.

I entered my apartment and headed straight to my bedroom. I closed it behind me and hinged the pine shutters. I opened the night table and pulled out an old candy dish I'd been using to hold my bracelets. As I un-wrapped the candle, I could already visualize the wax dripping down onto the glass dish and creating a brand-new karma, while I creatively visualized exactly what I wanted. I would do everything the book said.

I turned the radio to New Age jazz. There was a me-lodic piece with a slightly morose feel to it playing on the air. I turned the volume down low. Then I took out a match and lit the candle.

For a few minutes I just looked into the flame and stared. Then, slowly, I circled my hands over the candle. It began to feel like the ritual that I watched Grandma Rose perform on the Sabbath. The fear of sacrilege soared through me, so I tried to incorporate Grandma Rose's movement into something larger. I circled the candle three times with my arms. I moved them to the side then I flung them up. Up, up, up. My palms open to the heavens.

"Heal me," I cried to whomever was listening. "Please. Heal my karma now!"

I repeated it several times, growing more and more impassioned.

"Dear God," I said. "Take out your sewing kit and mend my karma. Sew it up. Sew it up for me. For single women everywhere."

Then I did it again. I stood. I added shoulders, head movements. It was New Age choreography. A modern dance piece. Performance art.

"Heal me. Heal my karma," I said, my hands overhead, my torso spinning front and back and back and front. "Heal me. Heal my karma."

I turned the music up full volume. The tune had changed. Whatever was playing now sounded like a chase scene from a James Bond movie. I kicked my right leg up, as high as I could. I was a Rockette! A Radio City Rockette! My childhood dream. I would make it come true now. My hands sprung up, I kicked my leg up high, higher, highest while the music blared.

"HEAL ME, GOD! TAKE THE DARKNESS AWAY! SEW THE HOLE IN MY BOYFRIEND KARMA!"

My leg came down hard and fast as my ankle knocked the candle on the floor. The flame went out as it landed on the blue carpet, singeing it slightly. Some of the wax dripped onto the carpet.

"And the weather in New York tonight is kind of ominous," the late-night radio DJ sleepily said, overlapping with the end of the last song. "Fifty degrees, dark clouds and a chance of a midnight rain. So if you're going to be out late, grab an umbrella. But tomorrow should be crisp, cool and sunny, a perfect day."

See. It was okay. It would be fine. It was already working, I thought while I sat on my bed, staring at the carpet and waiting for the wax to dry.

32

Putting Back the Pieces

At work. I had a part-time job planning the holiday party for a sound studio where I auditioned frequently, and was often lucky in getting radio work. Since the studio didn't have the space to give me an office, they literally gave me an old laptop computer they otherwise would have disposed of. I could create my own minioffice just by plugging the thing into the wall. This was my first entry into the world of computers, and plugging the thing into the wall was about the extent of my computer literacy.

Flipping through the Rolodex on my computer. Place the cursor. Left click. Scroll down. Like magic. Names.

First names only. Did I forget anyone for the studio's Xmas gift list? Scrolling down, scrolling down. Maurice, Chelsea, Doug, Chris, Henry...

Henry.

It's not my Henry. It's another. A voice-over actor. A forty-five-year-old. A person who's alive. Not my Henry.

Life is going forward. Full speed. Thanksgiving. Then Christmas. New Year's Eve. Valentine's Day. One holiday after another after another all happening without another. Henry was gone, and the holidays kept coming. Didn't they know this year was different?

An odd time now. I forget. Not dead, just gone. When I pray, I ask God to watch over my mother and Henry. When people ask who lives in Florida, I say my parents.

I stared at the computer, placed the cursor before the H of Henry and clicked. I highlighted it. The arrow moved around the name. Across the top. Around to the bottom. Henry Peerce would laugh to know of this computerized massage of his name. His Henry. His Henry isn't mine. Where is my Henry?

I talked. To his name. To him. I told Henry I was alone in the studio and I missed him. I told him about work and a callback for a commercial. I told him they're finally going to paint my bathroom, and I told him about Mom. He asked.

"How is your mother?"

Henry knows what's happening here. He tells me. He's

up to speed. He is positive. He is at peace, but he is sad he's not here with us.

"What can I do, Kar? It's not me, it's the man upstairs."

I moved the cursor over his name and cried. I said the mourner's *kaddish* for him at a Bat Mitzvah last week, and cried. But lately I have been busy and energized and so happy to be back home in New York, there's been no thought to cry.

"You're a young girl. You've got to live your life. I wouldn't want you to sit around staring at the four walls."

"*I* would," I told Henry. "If I died, I'd want everyone to stop everything and miss me forever."

"You're still young yet, you'll see." He laughed.

Things are changing for me. I don't know where it's leading, but I feel the changes. The energy.

"Are you doing this, Hen?"

"I'm trying. I'm trying. I predict wonderful things. I still think you may wind up in California yet."

"No more California. Not permanent. That's finished."

"Whatever."

The office lights in midtown Manhattan shine through my window. It is only six o'clock. It felt like midnight.

"They're all going to Evergreen tomorrow for Thanksgiving dinner," I say. "Sammy's thrilled."

"I'm sure he is. My brother having everyone to *his* development, to dinner at *his* clubhouse. Him and that clubhouse."

"Did I tell you they wouldn't let me in for lunch two weeks ago when I was down visiting with Mom. They said no tank tops. It's Florida. It's hot. What are you supposed to wear? I was in a sundress and sandals. I looked nicer than everyone wearing T-shirts and shorts."

"What can I tell you? Sammy loves it over there. He has the golf."

I hear a siren sixteen floors below. The sound jumped higher and higher up Fifth Avenue. It gave me a jolt. I must go. I must go to the bank the gym the liquor store and the florist. I must go. I turn off the radio. I must keep moving. I must go.

File. Exit. Yes. I want to save.

"Night, Hen."

Yes. I want to exit.

"Night, Kar."

Yes. Yes. Log off. Shut down. Wait.

It's now safe to turn off your computer.

During the fifteen months that ultimately led to my stepfather's death, it felt as if my family was falling off a cliff in slow motion. It seemed impossible to me that if Henry died, the rest of us would land.

Within those first months after his death, the pieces of the puzzle no longer fit the same way. In the spaces between my visits to my mother in Florida and my time home in Manhattan, I was taking in the new design.

* * *

My mother is alone.

When we get off the phone and I know there's no Henry in the house with her, I hurt. I hurt for her as a daughter. I hurt for her as a woman.

"I wasn't a person my whole life until I met Henry," my mother said the day after his death. "For years I wasn't a person. I was an individual, but not a person. And I'll never be a person again."

I said nothing. What was she talking about? She is a person, she is an individual, and now she is a *widow*. I hate that word.

"The widows do very well down here," Aunt Cookie said as she arranged the nova and sable on platters for the *shiva*. "When we go out there's a table for couples and a table for widows. They all dance together. They're great."

The widows table is to that generation what the singles table is to mine.

"Aren't there any *people*, Ma? Men and women who are single by choice, or divorced, or widowed, or people who are married. Couples or widows, what is that? Your generation is weird."

On Henry's deathbed he asked my mother to fold and pack the laundry. He had to catch a bus. I learned later in reading that travel metaphors are the way the dying say goodbye. They see the beautiful place, they are signaling they are ready. Dead people they know are beckoning them. Ironically, they are not alone. Henry asked my mother to pack his tuxedo.

His tuxedo. Whenever I had a date Henry would say, "So, Kar, should I get out my tuxedo?" For many years it was funny, but it became tiring. It became a goal, the goal, the validation, the raison d'être. No one saw me. My accomplishments, my life. They saw a woman alone.

After his death, I watched as my mother walked around their Florida house, seeing it for the first time as only hers. She touched tables and pictures, opened closets, saw clothes.

"Henry's tuxedo," she cried. I saw the bow tie and the cummerbund. "He was saving this for your wedding," she said. "And you disappointed him."

She was off to the next room, the next memory. My eyes opened wide. I knew this was funny but I could not laugh. A few weeks before, when death was something off in the distance and unimagined, I was visiting from L.A. We were all out on the sunporch. Henry was smoking a cigar. My mother was eating candies.

"Millie, I'm still walking Karrie down the aisle, but if you keep eating like that we're going to have to roll you down."

I wasn't dating, and I didn't know he'd be dying but somehow I knew acutely in that moment that Henry would never walk me down the aisle. I felt sadness and regret for what never happened. An unrealized dream. However, I had never dreamed of anyone walking me down the aisle. I wanted to live for me and give myself away.

"It's a different life when you have somebody," my mother often tells me. "Without a mate it's just busywork."

That negates my life. That negates hers.

I will be with my mother in Florida for Thanksgiving. I will be with my mother because all the couples are going away. She and Henry had made a reservation, but it has been canceled. I do not want my mother to be alone.

I see Henry. In jeans and a sweater. Strong and vital. *Kib-bitzing*. Smoking a cigar. My mother's husband. Her best friend. Her lover. They created a bond, a life, and now the man is gone. As a woman overly sensitized to separation, seeing my mother make this adjustment hurts.

"This is what happens," my mother says. "This is life. At some point one partner will outlive the other."

Whenever and however we get down that aisle, at some point someone will no longer be a person.

"Do you think he knows we're here?"

My mother and I were staring at Henry's grave. It was her birthday. Unlike the day of the burial, surrounded by people, chairs, a tent and tears, it was just my mother and me looking at the ground. There was a small sign that identified him until the headstone arrived.

"Yes," I told her. "I do think he knows. I feel him around me. Don't you?"

"No," said my mom. "Do you think I'll ever get used to this?"

I didn't answer. Or maybe I did. I just felt the same me-and-my-mother-staring-at-Henry thing I felt that long week in the hospital. My mother and I sat in chairs and stared at Henry in the hospital bed. Waiting for him to recover from the stroke. Now we were sitting on a marble bench in a Florida cemetery, and we were staring at the ground. Still waiting. For what?

My mother stares at days ahead without a child to raise, work to show up for or a husband to go away with. Retired days without her companion. Days that may never hold affection and romance. We went shopping. I got black pumps and a sheer skirt and a lacy black top.

"I don't want to get dressed up anymore," my mother said. "For who?"

I cried that night in the bathroom in Florida. The beautiful bathroom with the immaculate white tile and ceramic fish on the wall. I cried MOS as they say in the movies. Without sound, so she would not hear.

I had rubbed my mother's back. We lay on her bed on the peach-and-lavender sheets, and we laughed and chatted like schoolgirls. It was fun and she was warm. The schoolgirlish camaraderie occurred because Henry is gone and that made me cry. I cried because I had missed that girlfriend warmth the years she was a Sadie Married Lady, and I was not. I cried because one day I might be and she probably will not. She lay in bed alone without her husband and best friend. I missed her husband who was my stepfather and my friend. I cried because it's forever different and changed and would continue to change. I could count on things changing. A lot of it would be good, but a lot of it would not. It would be out of my control, and that made me cry more.

My mother has joined a bowling league and two card games. She is having ladies over for lunch on Thursday. She is scoping out the Couples vs. Widows situation in retirement communities. She is doing a lot of driving again and we are planning a trip to Europe, a place she claimed she never wanted to go because Henry didn't want to, but it turns out to be a place she wants to go to very much. Time with family. Movies and dinners and time at the pool. I think her phone rings more than mine does. As lonely as my mother is, she keeps moving. So her different life is moving forward.

And my same life is moving forward differently. It has been six months since Henry has gone. I am back east, and I am back. I am focusing, and making plans and looking ahead. And as each event manifests, I think of Henry. I think of Henry. I think of him as I say the mourner's *kaddish* in my new clothes. I think of him as I feel determined not to waste the time I am given here. That makes me feel some control. Makes me feel happy. Lately many things make me happy. But feeling happy makes me feel sad. I feel sad he's not here to see the things that would make him happy.

"But it's because of him," my mother said today on the phone.

Yes. It is because of him. I believe this is true. Because he does know we're here. So when the pain comes I feel it. I trust that if I let myself feel it, overwhelming as it can sometimes be, I can count on the fact that it, too, will change into something else.

In Motion

33

St. Patrick's Day
Baltimore, MD 1999

"Take me down to the Harbor for dessert. Bring me to your old apartment in Mt. Vernon when the streets are dark. Ride the elevator to the thirteenth floor to the bar of The Belvedere Hotel. And when no one is looking, kiss me. In the elevator. Now. Kiss me today. Then introduce yourself. Tell me your name. As if for the first time. Tell me yours. I'll tell you mine."

I said this in my head. Images from fourteen years ago had washed over me as soon as the Metroliner pulled into the Baltimore station. We had met by chance, a lifetime ago, when I was in town shooting a commercial. Now I was back doing regional theater, playing a woman who had a twenty-five-year relationship with a man only one weekend a year. The same weekend each year. It was serendipitous to do the role here. In Baltimore. It made me remember. I felt the images with force and texture. I felt them in the Harbor. Near the Monument on my way to Eddie's to buy groceries. And most powerfully on the corner of St. Paul and Fayette when I went to the post office to get stamps. These memories. First memories of him.

He remembers these memories the most. He remembers what happened on his home turf. He always remembers the beginning. And so he remembers the potential.

I remember other things. Things that happened in places where I lived. My studio apartment in New York. The first time. A bottle of wine. Velvet pants. A bad complexion. Little Italy. A white skirt. No socks. Upper East Side. A black dress. No panties. Los Angeles. A weird play performed in a bar. The hotel downtown. A haircut. A car accident. Margaritas. Too many.

For me, life was breezy. For a young actress, Baltimore was a greater distance from New York than L.A. For him, it was building. In Maryland. In the District. As a journalist. Politically. Personally.

I called only once and asked to visit. I couldn't. There was someone. But he still saw me. Then he married. And still attempted to see me. I could no longer see him. Not that way. But what other way was there? So there wasn't.

I'd been feeling lonely. In Baltimore. I liked the work.

It was a good play and a good part, but it only had a cast of two. I was on the road with just one other guy. The actor was quite nice and wasn't gay, but he was married. Going out for drinks with the cast after the show had its pitfalls, especially on the nights someone couldn't make it! Not to mention the cast parties were very, very small.

Elliot had passed through Baltimore on his way to Houston doing a two-week shoot on a local TV show. We spent a lot of time together. Elliot was still Elliot, but seeing him reopened my desire to be seeing someone. And there was someone. Nearby. Doing a play where I shared someone's husband one weekend a year was, perhaps, an omen. In the play it was not immoral. It was not even hurtful. I picked up the phone book. I turned pages. I looked under the T's. Tuck—Tucker—Tuckerman—Tuckman. Michael & Sue.

And though I had never returned his calls all those times he tried, he returned mine when I called from my high-rise apartment on N. Charles Street in Baltimore. We spoke. Then we talked. And then we saw.

We saw each other in D.C. and Fell's Point and Federal Hill. He saw me in pink and black dresses. I saw him cook me a restaurant-style meal in my kitchen in the corporate housing high-rise. I saw him stifled and he saw me probe. Then there was nothing more to say. So we danced.

And then he saw me. Maybe for the first time. With

eyes open, aware, wanting and sad. And for the first time I saw him. So before he went home I agreed to sit in the black swivel chair and let him kiss my breasts.

"Oh, you're so beautiful," he told me. "Remember how you make me feel," he told me. "Remember you're very desirable. Remember this always. Take this with you."

He talked erotically. Sexually. And then he talked.

"We have emotions for each other," he said as I rode down in the elevator with him responding to my uncharacteristic silence. And that was said and so it was all said. So we said goodbye. But he called the next day to say hello.

I wanted to put it on its proper shelf and leave it to collect dust. But now I was sad. I walked to the Harbor wrapped in a trench coat. Black scarf almost covering my red hair. Sunglasses covering my eyes. I looked at the water and wondered. I called my voice mail to see if he had called. Pulled off the dark glasses so I could see the numbers better. Blue eyes and pale skin reflected back in the metal of the pay phone. Was I being dramatic? I was Holly Golightly. Eating breakfast at the Harbor instead of Tiffany's. I strolled up Pratt. I went to work. I forgot.

But that night when I walked into the empty high-rise apartment on N. Charles the feeling came back. And then so did he. Because he had called to say he was thinking about me. That he had returned from the Pentagon and was thinking about me. His marriage had not been good, he confessed. They were separating. He would be in touch. But most of all just wanted to let me know he was thinking about me. Bye. He said that too. He spoke with breath in his voice.

I went to sleep. At five-fifteen I woke up. On fire. Hot. Because I wanted him to touch me. I was sitting in the black swivel chair, naked, touching myself. He was watching. My body lay across the butcher-block counter in the kitchen. He was sitting on a stool. Watching. I was dripping. In the dark I picked up the phone and pressed the lighted numbers.

"You have no new messages and one saved message. To listen to new messages press one."

I reached between my legs.

"To listen to saved messages press six."

I pressed six.

"Hello. I just called to say hi…."

My hand swirled.

"…thinking about you…"

Touching my wetness.

"…separating…will be in touch…"

Pushing into myself.

"…mostly wanted to let you know I was thinking about you."

I put my hand deep and pulled it out and moved it over me.

"…mostly wanted to let you know I was thinking about you."

358   *Laurie Graff*

I put my hand in deeper. I pulled it out and moved it over me some more.

"To repeat this message press six. To exit the system press nine."

I pressed six.

Wet. Intense.

I pressed six.

Touching. Reaching.

I pressed six.

Reaching. Pushing. Moving.

I pressed six. I pressed six. I pressed. I—

"Are you playing a game?" he had asked that night in the kitchen. Me reading aloud a sexual passage I asked him to create on my laptop computer. "It's okay if you are, Karrie. Are you?"

"Yes, I am, Michael," I said, looking straight into his eyes. "No, I'm not, Michael," I said, shifting them down while I kept on reading.

I am reading now. My laptop computer is on the bed. The bed in Baltimore. It is another passage. It is a story about a married man and a woman. And she reads to him on pages she saved on the hard drive. And he does what the man in the story does. It is instructional. It is happening now.

She kneels over her laptop on all fours, reading about the man who is licking her from behind. And as she reads the man is behind her, licking. She reads about the man who is spreading her lips as he moves the computer to the side to feast on her. And the man moves the computer as he eats. She picks it up to read about the man taking himself and putting a piece of him inside her, but she cannot find that section. It is gone. It is deleted. It's not happening. Was it ever there?

"There's a theory that everything we think about actually happens," he had told me that night. After the reading. After the black fettuccine and scallops. After the dance. "Those thoughts are laid out next to your life as a separate reality that also is happening."

Maybe he would separate from his wife and maybe he would not. It would remain to be seen. But it did not have to be seen to exist because I knew, right now, we were both thinking it.

And so it was happening. Now.

Unscrambled

Liberation Day
NYC Underground 1999

I walked to the IRT on 79th and Broadway with a lilt in my step. Who cared that it was a Monday morning? Who cared that I was back from Baltimore and once again unemployed as an actress? I didn't even care that I was shlepping all the way down to Fulton Street in the height of the morning rush hour to audition for an an-imatic radio demo that would hardly pay, never air and I would most likely never get, because sounding like a six-year-old Japanese boy was hardly my strength in the world of voice-overs. I was a few weeks away from my forty-first birthday, still single and I didn't even care about that! I had a lilt in my step. I was happy. I was transported to a wonderful place inside my mind, because I was thinking about my love affair.

Oh, yes. By the way, I had been having a love affair. A real bona fide, secretive, passionate love affair. With my old flame who was now brand-new. Tuckman came through. He and Sue had separated. It'd been going on since the middle of the run in Baltimore. Not only that, he had a monthlong assignment in New York and he'd been staying with me! It was perfect. Well, okay, he was still married and still conflicted and perhaps rebounding so it was not nearly that perfect, that easy or that trite. I knew he and Sue were in touch and not eager to officially call it quits, which led to complicated emotional undertones, but it was still going on and I was kind of thrilled.

I drank my small Tall Coffee of the Day cup of Starbucks as I walked south on Broadway, passing Staples, GNC and Parade of Shoes. I caught my reflection in a mirror showing through the glass window of Filene's Basement. Although I was running late, I stopped. I was pleased. It was a beautiful day. The sun was shining, the weather had turned the corner on spring and was sitting on the edge of summer. I had dressed quickly. A pair of jeans, black clunky shoes without socks and a tight black T-shirt. I clipped little butterfly barrettes in my hair, threw a jean jacket between the straw straps of my new summer basketlike pocketbook, locked the door to my apartment and was off. Seeing my reflection in the window was fine. I was no longer in my twenties or my thirties, but it didn't look or feel as I had suspected it would back in college. In many ways it felt just the same. I liked that, I thought, and I crossed Broadway to make my way downtown.

I bought the *Daily News* at the newsstand in front of the corner church before taking the stairs down into the subway. Fred thinks I should grow up and read the *New York Times.* I used to. But I missed the comics, the puzzles and the daily horoscope. I not only enjoyed reading the *News,* I had finally mustered the courage to carry it out in the open. The paper smashed against me when I got on the #1 running local. Everyone shoulder to shoulder at each other's throats. Oh, I felt lucky that most auditions never began before ten, usually keeping me safe from the crunch of the morning rush hour. At 72nd Street I switched for the express, and got my leg caught in the closing doors. A cop suggested I pull it out, and I suggested the conductor open the doors so I could. Waiting for the express train to arrive, I caught my breath, and looked forward to getting a seat and unscrambling the four words of *The Jumble* before I got to my destination. I would save the final puzzle for the ride home.

The #2 express was also crowded, but at least I got on. I stood with the newspaper squashed against my chest again, happy to be wearing black so the newsprint wouldn't show. I stood like that while we traveled downtown in the underground tunnel. I transported myself out of the subway, closed my eyes and imagined my lover pushed up against me, instead of all those New Yorkers. It made me light and woozy. A few seats appeared when the subway stopped at 34th Street. I went for it. Carrying the oversized basket pocketbook in front of me I tripped over it in the process, but I was finally seated, ensconced between a man in a yellow Hawaiian shirt wearing headphones, and a very huge woman in a lime-green dress, I opened the paper. I had arrived.

That's when he spoke.

"Most people would say excuse me. You know that." His voice was deep and stern. Accusing. Why?

"What did I do?" I asked. I turned my head ever so slightly to this man seated next to me. The one in the Hawaiian shirt. But I didn't look into his eyes. I wasn't interested. I was trying to turn P-C-E-E-R into a word. So far all I had was PE-REC.

"You tripped over me," he said.

"Oh. I was unaware," I said, seeing the word now as PEER-C.

"Most people would say they're sorry."

I didn't answer. PREE-C. I stared at rearranged letters.

"Well, I don't hear you apologize to me now," he said in a low, antagonistic snarl.

CREEP. Good. Got it. I moved on to V-A-C-H-O.

"Well, now I don't like they way you're speaking to

me," I said, ending the conversation, looking at the word as OH-CAV.

I wasn't getting too far with that, and decided to move on to G–I–L–O–O–G when I heard, "Thank God for women like you."

That was weird, and I didn't turn my head to look at him.

"It's women like you that keep me single." I moved my eyes down the page to R–T–B–F–E–E.

That's when I heard him say, surly and sultry, "Bitch."

I'm in trouble now, I thought, and looked at everyone on the train. Everyone had a seat by now. We were approaching 14th Street. No one was standing, and no one seemed to be listening.

He was looking at me. Mean. I didn't look back, but I could feel the heat of hostility. I thought I should move away, but I didn't want him to watch me. I didn't want to antagonize him further. I thought, He could come right over to me, look into my eyes and follow me off the train. It made me kind of scared. I decided to stay still. I closed the newspaper and started to read from the beginning. MURDER IN THE PARK was the headline. I began turning the pages one by one, figuring out what to do.

"Look at you," he said after the doors closed, letting the people off at Union Square. "You are past your prime. This is the best you're ever gonna look, and you ain't ever gonna look any better."

Today was Amy Fisher's first full day of freedom, I read. She was twenty-four years old. Seven years in jail and she was still in her prime. What would this man have said to her if she had tripped on her pocketbook on the way to a seat? Why was he seething? Why did age have anything to do with this?

"You're never gonna get a man," he taunted.

Why did this man hate women?

I was not changing my seat. I was not giving in. I was not past my prime, I was in it. I had spent the night with my lover, and I had no doubt I was deeply and satisfyingly in my prime. I was being attacked for being a woman without a wedding band, for reminding him of a woman who had turned him down and just for being a woman. I was not moving.

I had been scribbling the jumbled letters all over the margins of the paper. OH CAV quickly, clearly turned into HAVOC. I continued to read.

It was Liberation Day in France, the paper said. There was a photo-op of smiling faces on the Champs Élysée where it intersected with the Arc de Triomphe. Paris gets it, I thought. They understand women and passion and sexuality and aging. Like a good wine, it got better with age. I was improving with age. I knew it, and dammit, I would not let this Hawaiian Shirt get to me. I read the paper and stood my ground.

Basketball Hall of Famer Oscar Robertson would be

signing his new book at the NBA store. *Hurrah At Last* would have its first preview at the Gramercy Theater, and spring fashions would be modeled at Kingsborough Community College. These events would take place today, and I would not move. At Chambers Street I would exit the train and make a left into the next car. I would fake him out, but I would not move. I would stand my ground. For me, for single women, for aging and for possibility. I would travel one stop from Chambers to Fulton, solve the puzzle, relive my lover's touch and ponder the possibility of a happy ending.

A happy ending. I turned the pages hoping to find an article entitled BALTIMORE JOURNALIST LEAVES WIFE, but it did not exist. I knew that answer would be formulated soon. My head wanted one thing, but despite my bliss, my heart said another. I took comfort in knowing I did not need to solve that puzzle now.

"Bitch," I heard again as the train stopped at Chambers. I got up, with dignity, and executed my plan. He called after me, but I pretended not to hear. The next car was less crowded and I had my choice of seats. I territorially claimed the two-seater in the corner, and placed my pocketbook next to me as a sign that no one was permitted to sit there.

The indignities spoken by Hawaiian Shirt coated me like the yolk of an egg. I tried to peel it off. It was still a beautiful May day. I had a seat and half a cup of Starbucks left to enjoy the rest of the ride. A breath of relief wafted over me as I returned to G-I-L-O-O-G and R-T-B-F-E-E.

Would I tell my lover this story tonight? I wondered as I wrote LOGO-GI in the space above today's *Cathy*. My eyes jumped from one animated square to the next. As Irving told Cathy how women and cars are models that got traded, the word came together. GIGOLO! One more to go. TREE-F-B I wrote, feeling that any week now Tuckman would know for sure if he would stay. I could feel his lips on the nape of my neck while I stared at FRET-BE. BE-FRET. A chill went down my spine. BEREFT. I got the last word.

We were pulling into the Fulton Street station. I turned the page to close the paper and saw the horoscopes. If I was fast, I could read it before I had to get off. My eyes scanned the first column. There it was. I saw it at the bottom.

GEMINI (May 21–June 21) Turn your observation powers up to 10. You'll see what others miss. Don't be afraid to rock the boat. Arguments and discussion help you articulate ideas. If you refuse to accept the short end of the stick, that certain someone will stop trying to give it to you. A short romance has ended, but friendship comes out of it.

We pulled into Fulton Street. I got up. I waited for the doors to open. The train stopped. So did my heart.

I Can Do That

Martin Luther King Day
My Kitchen, NYC 2000

It was snowing!

"You have fun skiing, Miss Karrie?" Gomez, the superintendent, held the door open for me as I walked into the lobby, shook the snow off my boots and leaned my skis against the wall so I could unlock my mailbox.

Central Park had been transformed into a winter wonderland, and I got to see it all on my cross-country skis. The restaurant at the 72nd Street Boathouse looked like a resort in Vermont. People all bundled up in colorful ski jackets and sunglasses stood outside sipping hot chocolates while their skis were propped up in the snow and kids sat on top of their sleds. We had gotten eight inches, and I loved every one of them.

"I had a blast, Gomez! Do you like the snow?"

Gomez pointed to the shovel and the salt he was holding in order to clear the pavement in front of our building.

"I like it better if I am you than if I am me," he said, and exited the double doors.

I collected my mail and saw a letter from the unemployment office. We'd been having an electronic fight the past few months. Apparently, their Touch-Tone voice mail system and my personal accounting system were at odds. Trying to straighten anything out with the unemployment office was always more trouble than it was worth, but I needed the money so ultimately it was worth it. I tore the letter open and read without surprise there was still no resolution to the ongoing saga.

Back in my apartment I received a message that I had a callback for a regional theater job in Pittsburgh that would last ten weeks. I calculated that if I got the acting job I'd barely earn enough money to pay my New York rent, but I would become eligible for medical benefits and a new unemployment claim. Heigh-ho, the glamorous life!

I'd called the unemployment help line for help that never came. The phone would ring and ring and no one ever picked up. If people who work for unemployment ever become unemployed, they should most definitely not consider joining the ranks of 911. I now contemplated a way to get someone's undivided attention, having spent close to an hour on several occasions pressing every number on the keypad, and listening to the same Muzak I heard when trying to get a bus schedule. And then I had a brainstorm. A new and revolutionary way to communicate.

Snail mail.

Karrie Kline
219 West 78 Street, Apt. 3G
New York, NY 10024

NYS Dept. of Labor
PO Box 555
Albany, NY 12212

To Whom It May Concern:

I called in for unemployment benefits this past November 5, 1999 and the recording said that was my last day and they had expired. According to my perfect records I was only paid for 23 weeks and not 26.

In addition, you had contacted me to point out an overpayment. The letter you sent stated I would lose eight days of benefits if you did not hear from me within ten days, but I responded within two. You said I would receive the balance of that money at the end of the claim. It is now the end of the claim. When can I expect to receive the last three checks that will officially end the claim? When can I expect to receive the balance of the overpayment money that is due at the end of the claim?

I am enclosing copies of my pay stubs to show you exactly the checks I have received. I would greatly appreciate your reviewing my claim and rectifying the situation as soon as possible.

My best wishes for the upcoming holiday season.

Sincerely,
Karrie Kline

* * *

The next day I found out I did not get the job in Pittsburgh, but I had an audition for another one that would be for three months in North Carolina. I loved to act but hated having to go out of town to do it. It was affecting my passion and making it a little droopy. This felt a bit startling, because as far back as always I knew I wanted to act.

The defining moment was in the fourth grade when Joni Wolf came up alongside me in the coat closet. She hung her coat on hook eighteen, and mine was on twenty. Joni slipped her arm through the sleeve of her blue-and-white hooded ski jacket and turned to me.

"You know who you remind me of?" she said.

I waited with bated breath. Joni Wolf was the unofficial leader of our clique. What she said could propel me to the innermost point of that circle.

"You remind me of *That Girl*," she said as she zipped up her jacket.

"Oh!" I practically gasped. "Really?"

That day I practically floated down the cement streets of Queens Boulevard all the way home. All I truly wanted was to be Ann Marie. I had grown up wanting to be *That Girl*, but I wound up being this one! Stranded again without an acting job, not to mention no Donald and no Daddy, I wondered if it was time to consider doing something else.

I thought of those books that said what you liked to

do for a hobby could turn into a whole brand-new career. I mentally put together "my favorite things" and at the top of my list was talking, quickly followed by eating. And then I got it! I knew what I really wanted to do. I really wanted my own talk show. *This Girl! My Morning Show.* In the 8:00 a.m. time slot. Right before *LIVE with Regis and Kathie Lee.* I wouldn't have to leave town. I wouldn't even have to leave the apartment. It would take place at my house. In my kitchen. Every morning the doorbell would ring, and I'd open the door and all my guests would arrive at once. And every morning I'd still be in my bathrobe. Running late.

"Oh! I wasn't expecting you," I'd joke. "I'm running a little late. Just go in the kitchen and talk amongst yourselves while I get dressed," I'd tell my celebrity friends. "There's bagels and coffee. Make yourselves at home."

Then they'd sit at the kitchen table, read the paper aloud and chat while I went off and got dressed. And I don't think I'd *always* return in some fancy outfit or a business suit. After all, it was a morning show and it was amazing that I was even up. No, sometimes I might just wear some sweat clothes or jeans. If I had a cold I might even do the show in my pajamas and not even comb my hair. If I was really under the weather I could do the show from my room, my guests sitting on the edge of my bed handing me tissues when I had to sneeze. But on regular days, I'd sit around the kitchen table with Kevin and

Julia and Tom and we'd watch film clips of their latest movies and shmooze.

"You want another bagel?" I'd ask Julia. "Maybe just a half? I have sesame."

And she'd say, "No, I really shouldn't."

And I'd tell her, "Don't worry, you can afford it."

Maybe the phone would ring and I'd cover the receiver and say, "Excuse me. It's my mother from Florida. I have to take this." Then I'd go off and talk to my mom while Meryl poured refills on the coffee and opened her wallet and showed pictures of her kids.

As kitchens in New York tend to be quite small, I couldn't have too many guests on at once. However, with a show coming live from my apartment there would be all kinds of exciting cameo appearances. For example, the buzzer might ring and it could be the postman telling me there's a package too big to fit in the mailbox, or the Chinese laundry delivering the dry cleaning. Or the super could just drop by to fix that leaky faucet. I would invite Gomez to sit down and offer him some coffee, and he would probably look to the camera to wave hello to his family.

If the show caught on and I made a lot of money I'd buy a car. Then, on alternate days, the show could take place in my brand-new four-door car. I would be able to have three celebrities on at once. I, of course, would be in the driver's seat. We would sit in my car and banter while we drank our coffee to go and waited for a spot to open up across the street. The alternate side of the street parking days would be most exciting. Sanitation trucks would come by picking up the garbage and creating tons of noise, and I'd have to shout from inside the car, "Dustin, I'm sorry. You'll have to talk a little louder. I know about your theater training. I know you can project." And Dustin would take a deep breath and talk very, very loud in his great theater voice about his most recent movie and then we'd cut to a commercial.

I liked this idea a lot. I thought it was a format that could really catch on! As I got ready for the North Carolina audition I thought about it more. And when the director said, "Thanks for coming in!" and I knew I didn't get the part, I thought about it again. I was still thinking about it the following week when the mail arrived and I finally got a check from the unemployment office paying me the full amount they owed! My letter had worked! Someone had read it and responded. I felt powerful. And right after that I heard the news. Kathie Lee was thinking of leaving the show and they were starting to look for a replacement. With the great success of the unemployment letter I saw my moment and seized it.

Karrie Kline
219 West 78 Street, Apt. 3G
New York, NY 10024

Mr. Regis Philbin
WABC-TV/LIVE with Regis and Kathie Lee
New York, NY 10023

Dear Mr. Philbin,

Can I call you Reege? It's just that I feel like I know you, and that's a good thing considering that I am writing to ask if I can be your new co-host when Kathie Lee leaves the show.

Now, who am I, and what makes me think that you would even give me a look when Susan Lucci, Linda Dano and Cybill Shepherd all want the job. And Lisa Ling is "chomping at the bit for it." I know this for a fact, because I read it in the Post on the checkout line at the Associated on Columbus Avenue while I was waiting to ring up my eggs. And I thought, forget Susan, Linda, Cybill and Lisa—they already have jobs!

From the enclosed picture and résumé you can see I'm an actress. And although quite popular in some social circles, I'd have to admit I am not as well-known as Susan, Linda, Cybill or Lisa. Yet it might be exciting to see a brand-new face. A complete unknown. And after the first week that would all change. It would be a big media buzz. The actress that no one knew, but they should have because she has warmth, charm, wit, wisdom and she and Reege get on so well. And she's real. "When we tune in and see Regis bantering with Karrie Kline, we feel like we can relate, and that makes us feel very included." —Liz Smith

Unlike Kathie Lee I don't have any kids to talk about, I'm single, but I do think after a short time on the show my social life might quickly improve. I might very quickly get a famous boyfriend, so in the mornings when you would turn and say, "Well, Karrie, what did you do last night?" I'd have exciting stories to tell. Who knows—maybe I'd even marry and have a few famous kids. Hey—I might be able to get married on the show. How's that for ratings!

When I watch you with people, Mr. Philbin, I see your gift of making people light up with you. Will you meet me and see if there are any news signs?

Thanks so much for your time and consideration.

Sincerely,
Karrie Kline

P.S. Please note I have included you as part of my Work Search while collecting unemployment insurance. Should someone from the Department of Labor contact you, I would greatly appreciate if you would let them know that I did write to your office seeking employment.

I never heard back from Regis, or for that matter Gelman. And though I am still waiting, it hasn't stopped me from writing letters or dreaming. I don't need permission, and the tickets are free.

Modem Operandi

I read in the paper that a woman was raped by a man she met on the Internet. This is exactly why I refuse to buy a modem. I first heard the story at Elliot's. We were watching TV in his living room, well, not living room exactly. We were in the main room of Elliot's studio apartment that via the placement of his gray ultrasuede sectional sofa became a living room, and we were watching the eleven o'clock news when I heard it.

"See," I said to Elliot, who was online at the time and paying little to no attention to me. "See what can happen. This is why I'm so antitechnology."

"It has nothing to do with technology, Karrie. It's just

another way for crazy people to be crazy. But you need to update. You need to be online. I'm looking on eBay now. You really need a modem."

Elliot was supposed to buy one for me. Well, not buy exactly. Research it so I could buy it. Not that he should have bought it for me. But he never bought me anything. Except food. This began on our first date, three and a half years ago, when we met in L.A. He would pay for dinner one night a week when I would see him. Then he felt his job was done. In a sense, I suppose it was. Elliot and I were ships that sporadically passed in the night and then wound up spending the night. It had been going on the past few years at different intervals that would last a few nights, a few weeks and once for a stretch of a few months. We were in the few months stretch now. Our boats were docked at the same marina, but they weren't moving in any direction.

It wasn't smooth sailing, but since we'd been spending so much time together we were trying to head into the sunset, or at the very least drift without anyone falling overboard. However, Elliot and I didn't brave our storms very well. We didn't weather them either.

One Saturday after our weekly dinner date we walked into a Korean deli on our way back to my apartment. Elliot picked up a box of Animal Crackers.

"Are you going to pay for these?" Elliot asked at the checkout counter. "We are going back to your apartment."

"I hadn't planned on it," I said, looking at the red box of animals wrapped in a thin white shoelace string.

"I just spent forty bucks on dinner," he said. "If you're not going to pay I'll put them back." He began walking to the cookie aisle.

"Give me," I said, grabbing the shoelace string from his hand. "I'm not making an issue over a dollar thirty-nine." I paid for the crackers. We argued outside the Korean deli in front of the lemons. We broke up. Then Elliot came over, ate the Animal Crackers and spent the night.

After we broke up—yes, technically we broke up but in reality who could tell the difference—Elliot bought me a CD.

"You'll really love this," he said, buying me my very first gift now that we were over. It was a collection of Andrew Lloyd Webber songs. If he knew me better he'd have known I didn't love it. If he knew me better he'd have known I did not get excited about Betty Buckley singing "Memory," and Donny Osmond's rendition of "Close Every Door." And if he really knew me he'd have known that in addition to not wanting the CD, I did not want the modem. He wanted me to have the modem. But he didn't really know me. So he kept shopping.

He called his ex-girlfriend, a real ex, to convince Sherrie to sell me her modem. Sherrie also had an old laptop, but she was able to go online. She had met a guy dating online and now Sherrie was getting married. He thought she would sell her modem cheap. He thought she wouldn't need it anymore because Barry had moved in with a diamond ring for Sherrie, and a computer and modem they could share.

"Sherrie's modem will be ideal. Perfect for you," said Elliot. "It's really slow, but you don't need anything great."

Was he talking about himself? Maybe I didn't want something really slow and not so great. Maybe I needed something new and great and fast and expensive.

"Okay," I said. "Whatever you think."

I had decided I wanted the modem. I wanted a new one, an old one, a slow one or a fast one. I wanted one I would like, that I wouldn't like, that would work, or not. I wanted Elliot to want to do something. Something for me. Even if it was something I didn't want. And I wanted Elliot to pay. I wanted that most of all.

Sherrie had yet to call Elliot back, so he took a delay tactic. He insisted I needed to add more fonts to my computer. He had a disk he had purchased.

"I'll give it back to you after I load it in," I said.

"You can keep it," said Elliot. "I'll give this to you. It's yours. It's already in my computer and I don't need it anymore. Besides, if I want it back I'll just ask you for it."

He was so proud. The breakup thing was going so much better than the going-out thing, but like I said, who could tell the difference.

Every morning after we broke up, Elliot would wake up, read the *New York Times* and call to give me modem updates. He'd read different consumer reports and compare. In between modem research he would watch the Finance Channel to see how much money his stocks were making. In between the Finance Channel and modem research he would eat his three meals. The New York lunch was now a tuna take-out sandwich, and dinner was take-out Chinese, but breakfast was the most important meal of his day.

Breakfast was a bagel and coffee. Every morning Elliot would leave his studio apartment, walk to the local bagel bakery, purchase one poppy-seed bagel and a container of coffee. He would bring the bagel back to his apartment, slice it, put it on a plate and smear it with Temp-Tee cream cheese. Then he would pour the coffee into a mug and complain that it was cold.

"Why don't you get a coffeemaker?" I suggested.

"No. I'm just one person. I don't need it."

"How about a microwave? You can heat up coffee in thirty seconds. You can heat up everything."

"No," said Elliot, "I can't get a microwave, or a coffeemaker, or even a toaster oven."

"Why not?"

"Well, I might get married one day and she might have those appliances. Then we'd have two."

Elliot had just turned forty-eight. He had never been

married. He had never lived with anyone. He could not spend two consecutive nights with any woman he was dating. Elliot could barely spend the one night a week he'd spend with a woman he was dating, because he could barely move from his studio apartment. On a priority list of all of Elliot's problems, having two sets of appliances did not rank high at the top.

Sherrie finally called back. She was keeping her modem. She and Barry would have two. One fast and one slow, but two modems. Elliot called to relay the bad news.

"I'm sorry," he said. He sounded very upset. More upset than when we broke up. "I really thought she would sell it to you. I thought I could get it for fifty dollars."

"Well, I have gone into a few computer stores," I told him, "and new modems—oh, for laptops they're called cards—are only double that."

"They're not a hundred, they're more like one-thirty, or one-forty!" he said, pleased to top me.

"But there's a rebate of thirty or forty dollars," I said. "If Sherrie's modem can't work out, I have a choice. And I can get something brand-new and better."

"Well…which one would you buy?" he asked.

"Any one. What's the difference?"

"Not much," said Elliot, "but I still need to do more research. It takes a long time to buy these things. A very long time."

"If there's no discernible difference, why should it take

such a long time to make a not so important decision?"
I asked.

Silence.

"Don't you think it's safe for me to just plunge in and buy one of the top three models that are shown?"

"I need to do more research."

"It's a month since we broke up, Elliot, and you've put more energy into a nonexistent modem than you ever put into us."

Silence.

"What are you learning? What do you need to know to pick one modem over another?"

"Not much. It's all about the same."

"So then, pick one for me to buy. Make a decision, Elliot. Help me. I'm going to buy a modem. I'm going to buy one today."

"Oh."

"So...?"

Dead silence. The same dead silence I'd hear when I'd ask if he'd like me to cook us a great dinner or go out, when he wasn't sure what to do. The same panic when he'd have to choose between two movies he claimed not to care about seeing. The same intense angst as when he actually had to make a reservation and select one B&B in Lenox over another. That decision practically threw Elliot over the edge. That's what happened next.

"Okay, I have an idea," said Elliot. "Don't buy the

modem today. Just wait a little. I have something really good. Trust me. You're really going to love this."

Elliot had wanted to see the leaves change in New England and suggested we go to the Berkshires for a weekend. I was thrilled. It would be fun. It would be normal. It was filled with promise and potential. It was something Elliot would do for me and for him. For us. For several weeks Elliot surfed the net looking for the peak leaf-changing weekend, peak area and the perfect B&B. It made me feel good, and he was feeling good too.

Elliot set a date and made a reservation at a B&B up in Lenox a week in advance. Columbus Day weekend. That whole week he called daily. He was very excited about the trip. We both were. Elliot phoned the night before and told me to be ready ten sharp the next morning. He'd pick me up in his newly washed car. All systems go. No hitches. I was psyched. Saturday morning the phone rang at nine.

"Good morning!" I said. "I just got out of the shower!!"

"You sound perky," said Elliot.

"I am. This will be fun. I'm all packed, just have to dry my hair, and I'm ready to go at ten."

"You don't have to rush," said Elliot, "because we're not going. I woke up today and I don't feel like driving. I'm just going to lose the money on the room. Unpack. We'll do something in the city."

"What are you talking about?" I said. I was shocked. Aghast. Disappointed. "What are you so upset about that you're actually willing to lose the money on the room?"

"It's my phobia," he said.

"Which one?"

I cajoled Elliot out of the barriers of his mind, out of his apartment and into his car with an overnight bag packed in his trunk. Having found a choice parking spot on my block, Elliot came inside and sat down on the couch filled with glee, as if doing something very naughty was really very, very nice. We analyzed his selective traveling phobia for hours, dissecting all the details of his two bad relationships, three missed trips and four years of high school over five refills of Zabar's blend coffee, where the beans were specially ground for my Braun ten-cup coffeemaker with the reusable gold filter.

We went. We left at one. Once on the road, Elliot was on a high.

"Wow, I can't believe I'm going. You should give up acting and become a shrink. Of course we're going to miss the whole day because we won't arrive now until dinner, but I did really good, don't you think?"

As we traveled north on the Henry Hudson Parkway, I kept waiting for an apology or a gesture or any sentence that would acknowledge that what he had put me through all morning was selfish and unpleasant. But the only thing forthcoming was his delight and extreme pleasure at the fact that he was finally executing his plan. There was no thought to my feelings. After two hours in the car listening to Elliot's self-congratulatory conversation, I felt my best alternative would be one of positive reinforcement. I thought having a wonderful time together would speak volumes. I joined in singing the last verse of "Put On A Happy Face" from *Bye Bye Birdie,* let go of my hurt and dropped it.

We arrived in Lenox after four. We stopped to take a short hike in the woods before it got dark. Elliot was right, we had just about missed the day. But there was still enough light for him to take pictures. The leaves were spectacular! The dominant color was yellow, surrounded by orange, gold, auburn and green. He moved a few inches at a time in a circle, and said when the photos were developed I'd be able to paste them together and create a circular montage of the mountain where we were standing. When we were losing the light we drove off to check in.

We parked in the gravel driveway in front of a charming blue-and-white clapboard house and were greeted by Maxie, a big, friendly wheaten terrier. The innkeeper had hot ciders and scones waiting for us in front of a roaring fire in the cozy New England living room. This B&B was not just beautiful. It was perfect! Then we went upstairs to our room. I was completely delighted. Our room was quaint and so romantic. The wall-paper was a sweet floral with pale pink-and-green roses. The sitting room had two wing-back chairs and a chaise longue in a corresponding pink-and-green stripe. A delicate brass lamp sat atop the antique maple dresser, and the king-size four-poster bed reflected back in the antique mirror attached to the wall.

"Come take a bubble bath with me, Elliot," I called out from the pink-and-white-tiled bathroom. I poured bath oils into the tub, stacked the thick white towels on the edge of the pedestal sink, lit a votive candle the B&B had supplied on the glass shelf above, stripped off my clothes and lunged into the sudsy water.

"Wow," said Elliot when he came into the bathroom. Only my flushed face and red hair were visible, as my body was covered with white bubbles illuminated through the candlelight. "Let me get my camera," said Elliot, and returned to snap pictures of me in the tub.

"Come in with me," I said, finally after he finished the roll of film. I reached my hand out of the tub to reel him in.

"Stop, Karrie," he said, pulling away and leaving the bathroom. "Don't wet the equipment."

I dried off and wrapped the big white bath towel around me. Elliot had left his wire-framed glasses on the shelf. I put them on, brought the candle out and placed it on the end table next to the bed where Elliot, exhausted, was napping.

"Undress me," I said to Elliot, wearing just the towel and his glasses.

"I'm tired," he said, rolling over and turning away.

"Elliot…" I said, turning him over.

He looked at me and laughed. "You look pretty funny in my glasses. Wait, let me get my camera."

After photographing me in the towel with his glasses he photographed me without the towel in his glasses. Then, like in the movies, he unpinned my hair and let it fall, removed the glasses, pulled me down on the bed next to him and we made love.

After a wonderful time—making love, after all, was our best event—Elliot said he had another surprise for dinner. Later that night I was seated next to him in the prettiest country restaurant ever.

"I knew you'd like this place," he said, showing off while drinking Merlot and reading the menu through the light of the blue taper candles on our table. They were perched in crystal candlesticks on top of the lacy table- cloth next to the old-fashioned mismatched china.

We ate duck and veal and talked and laughed and smiled and held hands and kissed over dessert and kissed again and again as we walked to the car. And that night, after we made love, my head rested against the soft down pillows and I felt completely content. I was so pleased with myself for figuring it out. I worked through Elli- ot's problem with him and then through actions, not words, showed him how wonderful it was to enjoy being with someone intimately. Without expecting it, we had taken a surprising turn and turned into a relationship. A real one, and possibly a good one too.

The next morning he got up early and met me downstairs for breakfast. Three other couples were staying at the B&B. Everyone was married, but us.

"You live together, right?" asked a somewhat nosy housewife from Smithtown, Long Island.

Elliot's response was to ask her to pass the croissants, while I politely shook my head no and asked her the ages of her children.

We tinkered in and out of a few stores in town buying jams and homemade candles, and each time I went to hold Elliot's hand he pulled it away. He took more pictures, but none of me. When I stopped and asked a man in town to take one of us, he said he didn't want anyone to touch his camera.

The ride home was fraught with tension. But for little quips and uninspiring observations here and there, from Elliot's end there was no talking, no *kvetching* and no Broadway show tunes. The lack of complaints and *kvetching* was the most alarming. When we crossed to our side of the New York State border, Elliot finally spoke.

First he itemized the weekend and talked about how it was too expensive and although it was nice, it wasn't really worth the money.

"What was the point of that dinner last night?" he asked. "You could have made the same thing for a lot less money. I would have been happy just to go to Denny's," he said, "but I was trying to be nice."

"Well, you were, Elliot, and it was all wonderful," I said. I paused. "Wasn't it?"

"I'm not going to come through for you, Karrie," Elliot blurted out, sighing deep with relief because since yesterday morning he'd obviously been trying to cancel not just the trip, but the relationship. "I don't think I'm ever going to come through for anybody unless something really life-changing happens to me, or someone is so special and so perfect I just can't help myself."

"*I'm* not special enough for *you?*" The second the defensive words were out of my mouth I regretted them, but I couldn't believe Elliot would say that to me. Say, It's me, it's not you. Say, You deserve someone wonderful because you're wonderful and I'd just be holding you back. Don't tell me you're waiting to meet someone really special. How mean. How gross.

"I'm sorry, Karrie. You are special. Really special. I can't believe you have the patience to put up with me. It's not you, it's me. I just want you to be free to meet someone wonderful because you're wonderful, and I don't want to hold you back."

Be careful what you wish for. It still hurt and it still felt gross.

We spent the rest of the drive hashing out our on-again off-again relationship from Los Angeles to New York through Pittsburgh, Detroit, Houston, Baltimore and for the fun of it threw a few more cities into the mix. We laughed we got sad we got close he changed his mind then changed it back. We talked I cried Elliot changed his mind he wanted to try I said yes he said no he changed his mind he changed it he changed his mind and changed it back. We'd been driving south on the Henry Hudson Parkway. The 79th Street exit was now in sight. We would be over very, very soon. He was making a mistake he thought, maybe, maybe not, yes, maybe, maybe not, may—

The traffic light turned red on Riverside Drive.

STOP! STOP! **STOP!**

We were now parked in front of my building. I stared straight ahead and looked out the window. "This is enough, Elliot," I said. "This, right here, right now is the end of the line. The very, very end. In fact, I think it'd be best if you never contacted me again."

"Karrie, don't you think that's a little drastic," he said, delicately touching my cheeks and sliding his fingertips gently down my neck.

"No," I said, removing his hand and reaching to get my bags. "It's necessary. We're toxic for each other. It's just a fix and it never fixes anything. We gave it a real try. Thanks for the memories. Have a good life. Now let me just get out of here in one piece." I unlocked the door on the passenger's side, but Elliot's hand reached out to stop me.

"Don't go like this, Karrie," he said. I searched his eyes a long time waiting for his next move. I was completely sucked in. "Oh," he said in his standard Elliot whine, "I don't know what to do now. What should I do, Karrie? What should we do?"

That was it. Really. The last piece of the very last straw.

"Goodbye, Elliot. There's no good way to do this."

I walked out onto the street and didn't look back, but then he tapped my shoulder and was standing behind me.

"What? What do you want now, Elliot? You want to suck the blood out of me?"

"The modem," he said. "I still want to buy you the modem. I promised."

"The hell with the modem. I don't want it. I never wanted it."

"Let me at least do that for you, Kar. It'll make me feel better. I feel so guilty. I feel so bad."

"Do you want this relationship, Elliot, or not?"

"No," he said without faltering. "But I don't want to feel bad."

"Work it out," I shouted. "Please let me go, Elliot," I said, walking quick, quickly, quicker to the steps of my building. "Don't buy the modem, don't buy me anything.

Thanks for the weekend. Goodbye," I yelled as I opened the door to the vestibule into my lobby. "Goodbye."

It was over, but I thought about Elliot constantly. It would have been nice if we could have stayed friends, but we never stayed friends—we became lovers and we never stayed lovers so we couldn't be friends. I stayed home watching television most nights and became increasingly aware of hearing the words *dot com* at the end of most commercials. The same thing was happening on the radio. Dot com. Dot com. The world of cyberspace I was so reluctant to enter was beckoning.

A few weeks after our weekend, I was killing time between auditions, wandered into a Comp USA and made an impulse purchase. Not a modem. Oh, no. A computer. A completely brand-new computer with a printer included in the bundle! Windows Millennium loaded with every conceivable program, plus Internet access, an internal fax and an internal modem. I purchased it in half an hour. After I had it installed—I paid a computer expert to do it—I surfed the net for photographers' Web sites. There is was. Just as I had expected.

www.elliotclick.com. Scanned onto the screen was the circular montage of the leaves we saw on the mountain in New England. They were vibrant and beautiful, full of color and changing.

Shiksa Syndrome

Counting the Omer
West End Avenue, NYC 2002

I always wanted to stand up in temple and scream, right in the middle of the rabbi's sermon. It started back in Hebrew school when I went to Sabbath services. Every Saturday, like clockwork, six and half minutes into Rabbi Bernstein's speech I'd start to squirm. I couldn't stop. The only way I could divert my attention was to focus on boys. I'd look around and stare at every boy in my class. I studied the lapels on the dark green suit Lee Loran was wearing, and the gold braided trim on Craig Schneider's blue velvet yarmulke. I watched Howard Siegel listening intently; his face scrunched, and his tortoiseshell glasses propped up on the bump of his nose. Howard's

Bar Mitzvah was just two weeks away, and he was still having trouble learning his *haftorah* portion. I, on the other hand, had just won the *dovening* contest. I was able to pray really fast and read the most Hebrew words per minute. I was top in my class, popular with the boys, and the only girl. I was a bit of a show-off.

Rabbi Bernstein's *tallit* was wrapped around him like a big white cloak. He held the tassels in his hand, and stroked them as if to signal he was winding down. There was still time for me to scream. Make a scene. Be noticed. For Rabbi Bernstein to really notice me. What if I stood up on the pew and just let one rip? What would happen? It seemed exhilarating, fabulous and…nuts! I would have been removed from the synagogue, most probably on a stretcher. And for certain I would not have been allowed to be Bat Mitzvahed. Forget the scream. Nobody wanted to be Bat Mitvahed more than me.

"Okay," said Rabbi Bernstein. "Will the boys who are concluding today's service please come up to the pulpit."

I watched them go. Richard, Steve, Matthew, Gary, Todd.

"These students are top in the class," he told the congregation. "Only the best students are invited to conclude the services."

The best *boy* students, is what he meant.

Every Thursday, at five-fifteen, Rabbi Bernstein came into our Hebrew school class. He was an imposing presence with a voice that boomed.

"So, who's coming to services this *Shabbos?*" Rabbi Bernstein said the word *Shabbos* like a Shakespearean actor performing in the round. You just knew he loved hearing himself talk.

We all raised our hands.

"Good! And who wants to come up to the pulpit with me and conclude the service?" It was an honor to sing and doven the prayers. Rabbi Bernstein had divided the prayers into five parts, giving several kids a chance each week. Rabbi Bernstein thought he was fair. Almost everyone's hand shot up. Including mine.

"Very funny, Chaya," he'd say, calling me by my Hebrew name. The "Ch" was pronounced like you were clearing your throat. Rabbi Bernstein made a really big sound whenever he said my name. It rhymed with Sky, plus the addition of the preposition "a." My Hebrew name meant life, and I liked it. A lot.

"Now," continued the Rabbi, "are there any boys who are as enthusiastic as Chaya?"

The short answer to his question was no. No. There were no boys as enthusiastic as me. And there were no boys as good. Their voices were croaking and cracking. Mine was soft and clear. I knew every word. I was letter perfect. For God's sake, I had just won the *dovening* contest. Didn't that count for something?

"Why not me, Rabbi?" I asked. "Why?"

"Chaya, you're a girl."

"So what? I like when girls mix with boys. I'm not an Orthodox Jew. None of us are." Our temple, in Queens, was called Conservative, but it was filled with people who were not religious. Mainly Reformed. Traditional, really. Cultural. A bagel and a shmear.

"Chaya, you're a girl. A girl's place is in the kitchen. Not on my pulpit."

That was enough to make me scream. Okay, I thought, just wait until my Bat Mitvah. Just wait. I'll dazzle them when I sing my *haftorah*. But when I became Bat Mitzvah, I was not allowed to doven. Not allowed to sing, to chant my beautiful *haftorah*. Rabbi Schalet made me read it in Hebrew. Unembellished. Plain. I could not stand front and center next to the Torah. I was off to the side where the president of the congregation stood to announce who was born, who died, and who to contact from The Sisterhood if you wanted to help coordinate the Penny Social.

I was denied my full rite of passage, the honor I had been working toward for four years. By my last year of Hebrew school I became bored and angry. I brought unkosher White Castle hamburgers to Hebrew school. I met new boys in junior high and non-Jewish ones in high school. I stopped going to temple altogether. I went away to college, and away from the Jewish religion.

After graduation from college I began working professionally as an actress. I did a lot of commercials and would take pride in the fact I looked very P&G. Procter and Gamble. I did spots for fast foods as the all-American counter girl serving up burgers and fries and a big, toothy smile. I was the young housewife who got the kids out of the pool just in time for a big, cool, sweet summer drink. "I don't look Jewish," I would boast every time I booked another spot. "I can pass," I'd say. People actually thought I came from Pennsylvania.

One day I told my acting teacher about a monologue I did for an audition. It was a role I had played a few summers before in stock.

"Why did you do that? That's not a part for you, Karrie," he said in his singsong New York whine. "She's a Southern girl from Arkansas. A swimmer. You're a Jewish girl from Queens. Why didn't you do something from Elaine May?"

"Elaine May! Don't you know I do commercials? People think I'm a WASP. I have blue eyes, a fake nose, and a born-again Christian boyfriend from Virginia."

But my teacher believed in atavism. He wanted to get you to play parts that pulled from your background and your roots, before moving you on to other roles. He sent me out to the hall to prepare for a part I was having trouble nailing. The play was about the Holocaust.

"Go outside and think about how your grandmother would feel if you married someone who wasn't Jewish."

I stood alone in the prop room and thought of Grandma Rose singing solo in her Cantata at the temple. Her pride when I read the prayer book out loud. I remembered the peace I felt sitting next to her on the piano bench, singing "Sunrise, Sunset" while she played the vocal selections from *Fiddler On The Roof.* I was called back into the class and did the scene. In character as a young German woman, I spoke of my conflict of always wanting to marry a Jewish man, as my family wanted for me, but being so blinded by love I no longer cared. My emotional life propelled the words of the playwright, and turned my performance spontaneous and free. As a repressed German Jew, I was riding an emotional wave in a way I would never ride it. And yet all the feelings were coming from the core of me. I connected to a passion I no longer knew existed.

The born-again Christian boyfriend and I broke up. I bought a menorah and stopped celebrating Christmas. Yiddish words found their way into my vocabulary…I thought I'd *plotz!* At family gatherings, when we were ready for dessert, I'd put on my best New Yorkese and ask, "Who's a cawfee, who's a tea?" I was back. In the fold. Ready for a Jewish man.

I came back, but since I'm back it seemed that every Jewish man I knew wanted a *Shiksa.* Okay, I'm exaggerating. Every creative, funny, Jewish man I could like now wanted to connect with a *Shiksa!* And the uncreative, unfunny Jewish men, who always wanted to connect with a woman, wanted me.

I dated men in the first category many times. It was so comfortable and so easy they'd leave. In a quest to find a *Shiksa*. A *Shiksa* who would not innately understand them. A *Shiksa* who would have to learn that all holidays start on the night before, which is probably why the prayer book is read backward. A *Shiksa* who's worth fighting over with Mother.

"Maaaa! Megan would make a wonderful wife. Just like you. She'll learn how to make chicken soup and light the candles. She's crazy about me, Ma."

Of course she is. Megan's no fool. Everyone knows Jewish men make good husbands. If they don't, their mothers will kill them.

Now, I haven't had any boyfriends in the second category—the uncreative, unfunny ones—but I've met many of these men, if not all of them, on blind dates. Bad blind dates. In a million years, who could have ever thought this could be someone for me—blind dates. These men also like me. My most memorable was with a man I was fixed up with out in Los Angeles.

During the years I lived in L.A. trying to work in television, I fortunately got work in commercials. The first commercial I did was for a well-known copy machine. I was the secretary that kept making copies on the amazing copy machine, even as the office building was being confiscated. At the audition, all I had to do was make-believe I was making copies. I moved three pieces of paper back and forth, up and down. Brilliant! After I booked the commercial, the production office called and asked if I was afraid of heights. What did making copies have to do with fear of heights?

"Well, the copy machine will be on a six-foot-high platform that you'll have to stand on. Can you handle that?"

Sure, I could handle that. It was a national commercial. I could handle a seven-foot platform. I could handle a ten!

The shoot was in downtown L.A., smack in the middle of the biggest office buildings and heavy traffic. After waiting in the trailer for more than five hours, they were finally ready for me. The production assistant, makeup guy and wardrobe woman escorted me to the location that looked like a construction site. I looked up and saw the platform with the copy machine. It wasn't six feet high, it wasn't ten, it wasn't even twenty. It was estimated about forty-five feet high in the sky. They fitted me with a harness, attached me to a pole and raised me into the air. I was connected to the copy machine that stood on a little crag of a platform. A stuntman in a hard hat swung over me in the sky. He tipped his hat and waved. I looked down. I thought I'd throw up.

"Now, when I call action, make copies." The director was on a megaphone shouting his direction up to the heavens. "Action!"

The wind was kind of fierce and the papers were blowing. I was harnessed to the stupid copy machine, scared out of my mind. I pretended to make copies, the efficient secretary. The one micromoment of feeling some control was destroyed when, suddenly without warning, water spurted over me and I was surrounded by pyrotechnics. I didn't flinch. I didn't do anything but make the damn copies. All I wanted was for them to get the shot and get me down.

When it was finally over, I was back in the trailer. Shaking like a scared puppy, and holding in my tears. The copywriter, who I'd met once in New York, came over to me.

"Wow, that was great. You should have seen it. Way cool."

"Yeah. It was something," I said.

"Hey—I've got a cousin out here. A podiatrist named Glen. Helluva nice guy. You seeing anyone?"

I should have known. Instead, I met Glen in Santa Monica at the Third Street Promenade. He was one of those men who looked as if his beauty regime was more intense than mine. Pressed khakis, designer shirt and a manicure with clear polish.

We sat down at an outdoor café and ordered decaf cappuccinos. Glen looked into my eyes and said, "I'm so glad you're not a Jap. I want a Jewish woman, but not a Jap. I want someone successful who has her own thing going, but who's not materialistic. But not so unmaterialistic that she wouldn't know the right clothes to wear, or the right schools to send the children. That's important to me. I'm ready for intimacy. What's your game plan?"

That made me want to flee. But I had learned in college how to get a guy like that to flee first. I met my first boyfriend in the Catskills. We were both waiting tables on summer break from college. I was a sophomore and Kenny was a senior. At the end of the summer, Kenny, who was thrilled to be dating un-Jappy waitress me, took me to the city for a night on the town before we returned to our perspective schools. We went to see *A Chorus Line* on Broadway, and had dinner at a great Italian restaurant in midtown. I had hardly ever been treated like that; I really liked Kenny and had a wonderful evening. Kenny, on the other hand, thought the food so-so, the show boring and the parking too expensive.

Not up for a nightcap, Kenny and I left Manhattan and drove across the Fifty-Ninth Street Bridge. It was all lit up with that incredible cinematic view of the skyline. I pointed out my high school in Long Island City, just behind a factory, when we got to the Queens side of the bridge. Kenny said nothing until he dropped me home in Sunnyside.

"You're kidding," he said when he pulled up to the building I had grown up in. "You can't really live here. It's so—I knew you didn't come from a house, but this!"

"Yes, this is where I come from," I said. "It's not a

house on Long Island but…" I felt embarrassed even though I knew Kenny was the one who should have been. Until that moment I had really liked him. I didn't want it to be over.

"Well," I said, "at least you can see I'm really not Jap."

"Yeah…" Kenny furrowed his brows. He considered. "But you want to be an actress after graduation. I always picture an actress sitting on a park bench alone on Thanksgiving eating chicken. Boy," said Kenny, looking at the stoop I had sat on for hours as a kid hooking potholders. "This neighborhood is depressing. My ex-girlfriend was a Jap, but at least Linda came from a house with a pool."

I thought of Kenny as I stared into my cappuccino and attempted to end my date with Glen.

"I don't have a game plan," I told Glen. "I sort of go with the flow. Kind of Queens thing."

"Oh right," he said. "You're from back east. My grandparents lived in the Bronx."

"Yeah, it's the same."

"You couldn't have lived like they did," said Glen. "They lived in this brick apartment building with fire escapes and maybe just one tree on that whole ugly cement block."

I nodded in agreement.

"You, uh, didn't grow up like that. *Did you?*"

"Exactly."

"Oh," he said. "It's getting late. Check, please." I watched Glen signal the waiter by scribbling an imaginary check in the air. That hand motion was probably Glen's sport of choice.

The moment I got home, I scrambled through my phone book and called up all my ex-boyfriends to see if they'd broken up with Courtney, Kirstie or Kimberly. What were these men doing with women who sound like they should be on *The Young and the Breathless,* dating men named Travis or Sumner? Not "Mitchell Weintraubs" from Flushing, Queens. In the yard, after Hebrew school, was anybody singing:

Arnie and Shannon, Sittin' in a Tree
K-I-S-S-I-N-G.

Certainly not. Not when Arnie just asked Esther to sit next to him at his Bar Mitzvah.

Brooke Morgan, a new female friend I'd met in acting class since I'd returned to New York, told me that she is dating a "Mitchell Weintraub" now. Not only that, she's begun taking Intro To Judaism classes at the synagogue. I've been her partner on two field trips. One to the Jewish Museum, the other to a Friday Night Shabbot Fest. Brooke thought this would be a good place for me to meet a man. A win-win situation. A non-Jewish man who could be attracted to me, and really wanted to be Jewish.

Please! There were no single men converting. Only women. *Shiksas* getting ready to convert for the cute cool

Jewish men sitting next to them. Men don't convert. Why should they? They're in demand. Women want to marry them. And women can be so accommodating.

"What is going on?" I asked Brooke.

"Who knows," she answered, her long blond hair dancing under the fluorescents. "It's probably a new trend. I always seem to do things when they're in."

The only man there who could have possibly been interested in me was the rabbi, but he was already married. To an Israeli. Forget she's not Jewish from New York, she wasn't even Jewish from this country.

Then one day I was getting cash from an ATM at the bank on 72nd and Broadway. There was a long line and the cute guy in front of me, in the gray sweatpants and green scrubs, turned to ask if I thought they were giving the money away. His eyes were huge, and a deep chocolate brown. He had a quick laugh and a wonderful smile.

"Only on Tuesdays," I said.

"Then I guess we're out of luck. It's Saturday. A day of rest."

I looked at him and said nothing, just computing his last remark. Saturday, day of rest, Sabbath… Jewish, not religious, I decided. He mistook my silence for something else.

"I mean a day of rest for Jewish people. I'm sure for you it's Sundays."

"Oh, actually I'm—"

"It doesn't matter what you are, I just mean that you

don't look like you're Jewish," he said, cutting me off. "Sorry. What were you saying?"

I quickly assessed the situation and made a snap decision.

"Just that actually I'm...not an avid churchgoer," I said, actually not lying.

"Well, actually I'm not an avid templegoer. So it seems we've got a lot in common." His smile turned into a grin. His name was Alan Greenberg. He was adorable, a budding opthalmologist and, in my analysis, suffering from a severe case of *Shiksa* Syndrome.

Alan made plans for a dinner date. I rushed to the nearest pay phone and called Brooke. She was very excited.

"This is much better than the Intro To Judaism classes," she said. "Stick with this. And don't tell him you're Jewish. Don't *ever* tell him!"

That day before our date, I de-Jewished my apartment. I put away my menorah and the pewter Sabbath candles handed down to me from Grandma Rose. I buried my prayer book in my underwear drawer. I threw the borscht and frozen blintzes down the incinerator, and put a stick of butter in a dish out on the kitchen table. I tacked a St. Christopher medal over my desk, and haphazardly arranged a couple of Mass cards on the coffee table. Faceup was the Prayer to St. Anthony that said, "O St. Anthony! Saint of Miracles! Saint of Help! I have need of this special favor." I figured, why not? Then I said a prayer. On bended knee I prayed to God.

"Dearest God, please forgive me for what I'm doing. It's not because I don't love the Jewish religion, but because I do. I swear Alan would never have asked me out if he knew I was a member of his tribe. Once we're in love, I'll tell him everything. You know how much I want a Jewish family. I just need a little help to get there. Besides, worse comes to worst I'll convert."

Alan and I went out. It was perfect! We laughed and talked. It was comfortable and warm. He held doors, paid the check, helped my with my coat and like a gentleman, kissed me good-night. It was a stupendous kiss. He made plans to see me again.

"Boy, this was great," said Alan. "This was so different from being with a Jewish woman."

"How?" I was really curious. Even though I knew I was lying about being a Jewish woman, the fact was that Alan had just been on a date with a Jewish woman.

"Well, for starters a Jewish woman would want you to pick her up and take her out and pay for her, and at the end of the evening she'd just kiss you good-night and then expect you to ask her out again."

"Yeah…" I was baffled, as the details of our date matched that exact description. "And that's different from this date because…how?"

"Because they expect it and you don't."

"Oh. I see."

But all I saw was *mishigos*. Craziness. *Shiksa* Syndrome.

Of course they expect it. All women expect it. Jewish *and* non-Jewish alike. Brooke Morgan expects to be treated well, her relationship was flourishing. Jane Murphy expects to be treated well, now she and William were married and wanted to have a baby! Women expect to be treated well—at least we all hope to be. So what was really different?

I was the same with Alan as I always was, with the exception of sharing my Yiddishisms and taking the Jewishisms out of my family stories. It made them a little more generic and a lot less funny. Was less funny better? Was it about being too funny? As a Gentile woman my behavior was golden, as a Jewish one it would have been considered spoiled. What was that? Who were these men really fighting?

I considered Brooke's Star of the Show theory. She says men want to be the star of the relationship, and they prefer the woman to be a bit in the background, a little bit less. I disagree. I don't think all men want that. And if they do, what then? It's hard enough being all I can be, without figuring out how to be that but less. Most important, I aimed for more, not less.

However, Brooke's advice was working. My relationship with Alan blossomed. I thought it could be love. So did Alan. So much so, he invited me home to his parents for Passover.

"Have you ever been to a Passover *seder* before, Karrie?" he asked at dinner one night at my apartment, after he polished off my home-cooked macaroni-and-cheese casserole, three-bean salad, two Pillsbury crescent rolls and a Jell-O pudding five-minute banana split for dessert.

I was so excited. So was Brooke. She took me shopping to Laura Ashley on Columbus Avenue where I splurged on a whole new outfit. I wore a mauve-and-teal green floral dress with jagged white lace trim around the capped sleeves and the hem. A pale green headband pulled back my fake red hair, and a thin strand of fake pearls hung loosely around my neck. We arrived, me holding two dozen yellow roses in my right hand, and Alan's hand in my left. I pretended it was my first *seder.* Ever.

It felt wonderful to be there with Alan, and his warm and welcoming family in a beautiful Upper West Side apartment. From the moment we had arrived I knew this was home to me. The family, the smell of the holiday, the table set with the good china, the plush sofas holding members of the Greenberg clan. Warmth, laughter and that *heimishe* spirit.

"Welcome, dear," said Honey. His mother winked when she took my coat. She was svelte in a cream-colored dress.

His father wrapped his arm around me and walked me into the huge living room. Sol Greenberg was a radiologist. He wore wired glasses and a knowing expression.

"You seem to fit right in. She'll be a convert before you know it," he said aloud to anyone listening.

Alan held me tight. It was perfect. He could be accepted, yet rebellious. I still hadn't figured out exactly whom he was rebelling against, but I was part of the stand. His *Shiksa*. His love.

We sat down to the beautiful *seder* table to tell the story of freedom. I knew this was where I always wanted to be. Sitting next to a man like Alan, in a home like this, with a family like the Greenbergs, in my favorite city. It was happening for me. It was too good to be true.

His father invited all the men to say *kiddush*. One by one, each man stood to say the blessing over the wine. Alan, his brother Joel, his cousin, his father, his grandfather. With each new man I had the same recurring thought. I could do this better than all of them! I swallowed it. I'd come this far, I couldn't blow it now. I smiled at Alan. I pretended to study the *haggadah* as if I'd never seen the Passover story book before. Then his dad turned to me.

"Not easy this Hebrew. You think you can do it?"

I giggled. It was just a joke.

"You could never learn this," he continued. "It's in the blood. It's difficult."

I stopped giggling, but I smiled. It's not that difficult, I thought. Anyway, what was he doing? Teasing? I knew he wasn't challenging me. What if he was?

"I sent my two boys to Hebrew school, but not my Betty. Maybe I was wrong. Things are different now. But at the time, I thought, What did she need to know this for? Am I right?"

I looked at Betty, but she didn't hear. She was busy getting her two-year-old to stop playing with the *matzohs*. I was holding on, but just by a thread. Here I was in a situation I'd dreamed of all my life, and I wasn't able to be me. Tonight was the night to tell the story of freedom, but here I was in a mess. A slave to a lie. I missed being Jewish. I missed being me.

"Danny, you want to give it a try before we move on?" Sol turned to his son-in-law, Betty's husband.

"What the heck?" Danny said, as he stood holding the cup of wine. "Bear with me. You know I only learned what I had to for my Bar Mitzvah. I'm not that good with this." He began. Tentatively.

Sav... Ray... Me, no, *Ma,* no wait, *Mo Rrrrraaawww Noo...*

I fidgeted with the silverware while I listened to Danny abort the Hebrew language. Sitting at the *seder* table with Alan's family brought up the same frustrations and yearnings I had felt at temple all those Saturdays, when I had to listen to Jonathan Weiser make the same mistakes on the verses of *Anim Z'miros,* all the while knowing I could have easily sung the whole thing, crystal clear, perfect... And then it hit me, like two tons of bricks.

It was Hebrew school over again!!!

I stood. I wasn't planning to get up, it just kind of happened. I held the glass of wine in my right hand. It was trembling. I opened the *haggadah* to the page with the blessing. Alan was staring at me in amusement. I caught Sol's eye. He looked right into my soul. His dad was no dummy. Everyone else looked on. Boy oh boy. This is a live one, they must have been thinking. What's she going to do, this *Shiksa* actress?

It was quiet at first. Like a hush. The music was soft as it came out of me. Slow and deliberate.

Sov-Ray Maw-Raw-Nawn V'ra-Baw-Nawn V'ra-Bo-Sai—

Everyone laughed.

"What a quick study ya got there, Alan!" his uncle Herb said. "You just picked that up, huh! That's really something."

"How sweet of Karrie to learn this for Alan," said his mom. Honey motioned for me to sit. The show was over. "How fun having an actress here."

But I didn't sit. I looked over at Sol. Again. His eyes said, Keep going. I did.

Baw-Ruch A-Taw A-Do-Noi—

Elo-Hay-Nu Me-Lech Haw-O-Lawm—

Bo-Ray P'ree Ha-Gaw-Fen—

Each word was a visit to the culture I'd been missing all these months. My volume increased. I continued, gaining confidence. The Hebrew words rolled out of my mouth like my native tongue. I felt free. The music soared from my soul. At some point, without realizing it, I must have put the *haggadah* down and was singing from my heart. The long prayer had been committed to memory since Hebrew school. I used my hands and *dovened* as if I was the Cantor at a congregation. Notes were sustained, I modulated my voice and sang the octave higher. I couldn't stop myself. I was showing off. It was the Bat Mitzvah I never had.

She-He-Che-Yaw-Nu, V'Kee-Y'Maw Nu—
V'Hee-Gee-Yaw-Nu, La-z' M'an Ha-Zeh—
"*Aw-Mein,*" his grandfather sang quietly.

Silence. There was a long, a rather long silence. Then applause. Loud applause. For me. I soaked up the attention; the actress I was, and forgot how I got to this moment, until in my glee my head snapped around and I saw Alan. My smile froze when I saw the unbelievable horror in his eyes.

No one moved. Alan could not shake the look of horror. I felt kind of sick. On the other hand, I knew I had never sung the *kiddush* better, and even had a few new ideas on how to build the middle section.

"So," said Sol, surveying the situation. "I guess you're not a *Shiksa.*"

I looked into his eyes. They were twinkling and compassionate.

"**Why did you do this to me?**" said Alan. "**How dare you!**" He sprang up from his seat.

"I… I'm sorry…. I just…" We were standing there at the *seder* table. I was so embarrassed and desperately hungry.

"Just tell me why," said Alan.

"I really liked you, I mean just so much, Alan, and I didn't think you'd let yourself fall for me if I was Jewish. I think you've got a little *Shiksa* Syndrome. I don't think you like dating Jewish women."

"Hallelujah!" said Honey. "I've been saying that for years but no one ever listened to me." She smiled at me with female camaraderie. "You two are already an item, and now it turns out Karrie is Jewish. I think she was very smart. Everything is perfect now."

"Perfect?" Alan was enraged. "This is awful. I was falling in love with Karrie but now it's over."

"I know I betrayed you, Alan, and I'm sorry. But I promise I'll never lie to you again about anything. It was just that day, at the ATM, I thought—"

"I'm not afraid of your betrayal. I'm not even blaming you for that. It's just that…"

"What? What???"

"I don't want to be with a Jewish woman, and I wanted to be with you."

"But I'm right here and I'm still me."

"It's not the same anymore. Jesus," he said, walking away from the table. He stopped under the archway of the dining room and turned to face the group. "We were so good together. I was so excited about tonight. I was hoping to marry you. I was even going to ask you to convert." With that, he turned his back and left the room.

"I'm so sorry," said Honey. "I liked you, *Shiksa* or not."

Sol came up and gave me a hug. "He's my son, but I don't understand him. Does anyone here understand him?"

His brother Joel, a psychiatrist specializing in phobics, took my hand and led me into the den. As I put on my coat to leave, he squeezed in a quick session.

"I've been thinking," said Joel, assuming a position at his father's desk. He propped his elbows on top of the desk, took off his glasses and wiped the lenses with the end of his shirt. He spoke deliberately. "Alan's a great guy, and you're right about him. *Shiksa* Syndrome is only a symptom of something bigger. F.I.R.O. Fear of Intimacy with the Right One. The only way he might have been able to commit was to think that all along you were just a sweet little *Shiksa*. But you're a smart Jewish girl. You were able to pull this off. Forget it, *now* there's too much threat."

With that the door opened and Patty Murphy-Greenberg stuck her naturally red head and God-given pug nose inside.

"Honey, are you almost ready?"

"Could you wait at the door?" Joel halted his wife, pointing with his hand.

"I'll be right there," said Patty, waiting for her husband by the door.

He looked back at me and spoke quietly. I had to strain to hear.

"In the future, when you meet a guy you like, don't tell him you're Jewish until the ring is on your finger. I know what I'm talking about." Joel stood up indicating our session was over. "Coming, hon."

Joel dashed over to his wife. I watched them embrace while I tied the belt on my trench coat. Patty looked over Joel's shoulder.

"Good luck," she mouthed to me as I slid past them and out the front door.

I walked down Broadway, turned east on 78th Street and walked down the stairs to my building. The night replayed itself in my mind like a movie. I thought about what I did and why. Just how much of yourself do you have to give up for a relationship? Patty was raised with Easter-egg hunts, and pancakes on Christmas morning. Joel won't allow them to have a tree, and insists their children will be raised Jewish. Patty will never get to share those idyllic pieces of her childhood with her children. However, she seems happy. Life with Joel Greenberg was apparently worth it to her. I could not imagine wanting any man so much that I would deny my Jewish identity for him. I thought of the ceremonies of my childhood I would want to pass on.

When I was thirteen, I must have gone to more than twenty-five Bar Mitzvahs. I remembered how happy

Howard Siegel turned out to be at his. There was a great celebration downstairs after the service. We all gathered around Howard to say the prayer over the *challah*. The dough of the bread was braided, and at least three feet long. Just as we were about to begin, Rabbi Bernstein tapped me on the shoulder. "Chaya," he said, "will you go in the kitchen and bring out the cookies while the boys say the prayer?" I could be relegated to the kitchen then, but now I was able to make a choice. Suffice it to say I would never take Joel's advice.

Weeks passed after the *seder* and instead of missing Alan, I just felt stronger and happier and enjoyed becoming reacquainted with myself. And then I did two things that made me very happy. First, I went to my hairdresser and had her dye my hair back to its natural color. The red would be replaced by my not-so-boring-looking-after-all brown hair. And then I did something even better. I went back to temple.

I discovered a temple on the Upper West Side that was right up my alley. I remembered at the *seder* how much I had loved to *doven,* and now I could do it every Friday night. The congregation was huge and exuberant. So huge, in fact, on Friday nights there were two services held simultaneously—one in the synagogue, and another in a church that they shared. The rabbis were young, open-minded, political, progressive, and—this was amazing—both men *and* women! People danced during the service. And the music! The tunes to the prayers were new to me, but still had that magical, melodic dissonance. Musicians played the services on an electric keyboard, with Congo drums and mandolins. The Hebrew words fell exotically from my lips, and the sound of more than six hundred congregants singing together was glorious. When something was unfamiliar, I just listened. The music was a comfort and my thoughts became the lyrics.

Tonight during the service, Rabbi Claudia announced that it was the last day of the Counting of the Omer. She said that on the second night of Passover, an *omer* of barley was brought to the temple as an offering, and each day would be counted for the next seven weeks until the arrival of Shavuot, the holiday that commemorated the giving of the Torah. Apparently God could not give the Torah right after the Passover Exodus, and wanted the Jewish people to go through a period of "spiritual accounting" for the next forty-nine days to be sure they would not squander the opportunity. Rabbi Claudia said the Omer period is one of reflection, a time of heightened spiritual sensitivity and growth, and she said to remember you are not competing with anyone but yourself.

I didn't know it, but from the second night of Passover through tonight I had been counting. I offered up my red hair, my Laura Ashley dress and my delusions of being Mrs. Alan Greenberg as not to squander my opportunity. The unique opportunity to be brown-haired Karrie Kline from Queens, who lived in Manhattan and pursued her dreams. With authenticity.

After the service I stuck around and socialized on the steps of the temple. It was a little reality check, and felt like a singles bar without drinks. In honesty not all that much fun. I used to love hanging out with the boys after services when I was growing up. When it was easier to talk. Easier to flirt. In the mode of true authenticity I chose to leave and go home. I fled down the steps and as I was about to turn the corner, I was surprised to hear someone call me name. My Hebrew name, that is.

"Chaya?" The voice boomed. For a second I thought it was Rabbi Bernstein. "Is that you, Chaya?"

I turned around and faced a very attractive man with dark curly hair and glasses, who kind of reminded me of a boy I once knew from...

"Wait," I said. "Don't tell me. Your Hebrew name was Barukh, right?"

He waited. He watched. He sneezed.

"Ohmygod, I remember. Gazoontite, Barukh!" It was my turn to imitate the voice of our infamous Rabbi. "You always had a cold. Bruce Feinstein. It's you, right?"

"Yeah. Allergies. So... Karen Klein. Winner of the *dovening* contest." He laughed. "To be honest, you sang better than all of us. You look great!"

"Thanks." I smiled at him. "Karrie Kline. Kline like Kevin."

"Married?"

"Nope. Stage name. Single."

"Good!" Bruce smiled.

"Last I heard, you moved to Boston," I said.

"Just moved back."

We stood there smiling. He motioned to walk and I followed. We took just a few steps rounding the corner on 86th Street, when Bruce brought me over to a very attractive brunette and a darling little girl.

"Allison, I was right," said Bruce, pulling my arm over to the brunette. "It was her. Karen, I mean, Karrie, meet my wife, Allison, and my daughter, Emily."

"Hi," I said, extending my hand and smiling as graciously as all my acting training enabled me. He was married. Shucks! "Nice to meet you," I said, smiling even more. "And nice to meet you too, Emily. What a pretty hat you're wearing!"

Emily smiled shyly and hid behind her mother's skirt.

"Bruce said he recognized someone from childhood and I thought…yeah, right! But he was." Allison smiled at him with affection.

"We just moved back from Boston and heard great things about this temple and wanted to check it out," said Bruce. "I want Emily to be a part of a community. And I want to make sure as a girl she's welcome."

"Well, she sure will be here," I said, looking at him and his lovely family.

"We're going to go out for dinner somewhere, you want to come?" he asked.

"Come, Karrie," said Allison. "I'd love it. I need to make some girlfriends in the city."

"Is it okay with you, Emily?" I asked.

She came out from behind her mother's skirt, nodded her head yes, and then hid behind her father's back.

"Come here, you," said Bruce, picking Emily up in the air and placing her on his shoulders.

"Ooooo, Daddy," she squealed.

"Which way?" Bruce asked.

I pointed south. We started down West End Avenue deciding where to have dinner that night, and again the following Friday. Allison was already making a mental list of available men she knew for possible blind dates. Would I be interested?

"We could double," she said, "so it won't be *that* bad!"

"Oh—you'd be surprised!" I said, and we all laughed. But I was already looking forward to it. They were nice, I was feeling good and I was hopeful I would meet someone who would let me conclude the services.

In Search of the
Regular Ultimate Hold

Fourth of July
East Hampton, NY 2003

I was having a hair-spray crisis. For as long as forever, I had been using the same brand of hair spray. Cheap stuff. Regular hold. Unscented. It's the best. It always worked for me. Suddenly the packaging is different, and so is everything else. Not the price, it's still cheap. But there's no more Regular Hold. There's Extra Hold, Extra Extra Hold and Ultimate Hold. I tried all of them and couldn't figure out which one was really mine. Regular Hold in disguise.

I was on my way to the Long Island Railroad to spend the weekend in East Hampton. If I missed the next train I'd have to wait two hours. I had stopped at three discount drugstores along the way to Penn Station, and came up empty. As a concept, I hated hair spray. I just needed that quick little squirt to keep down the flyaway ends. It seemed I'd have to do without, until I saw an up-scale beauty supply store. I went inside and told them my problem.

"I know vat yu need," said the saleswoman. She was tastefully made up, and wearing a metal bracelet with a turquoise stone that took up almost half of her left arm. She brought over a small bottle and, before I could say a word, spritzed my bangs.

"What is this?" I asked. It was a fresh scent, very light. I liked it.

"Thees is very special spray. From aloe plant. No chemicals. I luf it."

"How much?" I asked. It would be great to be able to get the hair spray and make the train.

"Feefteen dollars. Very reasonable, for thees."

"Fifteen! I usually pay like two."

"You get vat you pay for," she said, taking the spray away.

"Wait!" This struck a chord. That was Henry's motto. In honor of my stepfather, whenever I was able, I'd buy top of the line. I was making a big splurge for thirteen dollars. I could handle it. Maybe the discontinuation of the regular cheap stuff was an omen of better things to come. "I'll take it!"

I studied the bottle of hair spray on the train while I wrote in my journal. The man next to me thought I was a hair-spray specialist writing a consumer report. I wish. I was writing about my anxiety over the upcoming weekend. My plans with everyone had fallen through. Rather than stay in the city alone, I chose to brave it and go to the Hamptons alone. Originally, I thought Fred would come out with me, but his new boyfriend had a house in the Poconos and he really wanted to be with Sean. I was happy for him, but disappointed for me. There'd been a lot of that going on lately. I flipped through the pages of my journal, reading my entries on life's most recent changes.

July 1st, 2003

Recurring frog dream again last night! Not surprised! Hamptons this weekend. Thank God my apartment situation is squared away and I can stay. One less thing to worry about.

June 25th, 2003

Brooke called to tell me that she and her "Mitchell Weintraub," whose name I still can't believe actually is Mitchell Weintraub, just got engaged! He popped the question at the River Café over the weekend. She said it was super romantic overlooking the Brooklyn Bridge. Good thing she loved the view because she's leaving Manhattan and moving into Mitch's Brooklyn Heights brownstone on Clark Street. I have dinner with Brooke at least twice a week. With them moving in together and planning a wedding, how often will I see her now?

And Jane's not available these days... Oh well, at least Fred is still planning on Fourth of July with me in East Hampton.

June 12th, 2003

Oh my God! Jane had the baby! She and William have the most precious little baby girl. She is 7 lbs, with William's blue eyes and Janey's dark hair. They are naming her Eve. Eve Marin Harris. I told them I'd come downtown and baby-sit when they feel ready, and they told me they were saving the news till it was definite, but they were closing on a house in Ridgewood, NJ and would be moving out of the city this summer. I spend so much time with them. Things will be so different now. Jane and I will always be close but... I can't believe I have to deal with them moving. I'm still recovering from Marcy's wedding!

June 1st, 2003

If I knew the day I met Marcy in day camp in 1970 that it would result in being dateless at her wedding where the only people I knew were the women who snubbed me at her shower, I never would have become her Swim Safety Buddy. I can't believe I lived through that wedding today! Marcy and Martin tied the knot in an intimate little affair for 200 at the Woodmere Jewish Center in Five Towns on "The Island" where Martin was raised. Marcy's from the Bronx, but I doubt she'll ever admit that to anyone again. When I asked if I could bring a date she said, "Sorry—only the people who have a significant other can bring someone." The prize for not being in love was going to the wedding alone. I understand the expense, but I couldn't believe that Marcy, who had cried on my shoulder for years, had the nerve to tell me that she had survived being miserable and dateless for many a wedding and so would I. Next time I'm in this situation I will definitely be smart enough to get myself out of it. The lowest moment was when the band played their first slow tune and the five couples I was seated with got up to dance, leaving me all alone at the table with the baby green salads and forlorn looks from the waiter. What a comfort when Marcy told me after the wedding cake ceremony that there were a dozen "no shows," and had I called her that morning I could have brought a date after all. Now why didn't I think of that???

May 28th, 2003

Last night I dreamt about frogs. AGAIN! All these guys I've dated show up in my dreams looking like frogs. It's so strange! When I first had the dream the other night it was kind of a nightmare, like being a Holocaust survivor of bad dates trapped in a frozen pond, but the dreams keep changing and its become kind of sweet. Last night I dreamt I had one shoe and I was going through all my shoeboxes looking for the mate. But instead of shoes, every box had a pair of frogs. I finally found one but it wasn't a good match or a great fit. The next thing I remember was being somewhere bright and pretty where there were rows of new shoes and I had a choice.

* * *

I felt pleased to read that last entry. I had been thinking about those frogs, those guys, those dates, those men,
so much since my forty-fifth birthday they had taken on
a life of their own. A cast of fictional characters that
were, at the very least, entertaining! And I needed to entertain myself because I knew just how strange East
Hampton could be.

The last time I was out was a handful of summers ago,
when I had bought a few weekends in a summer share
house after moving back from L.A. I fell hard for the
dunes and the white, sandy beach, but the scene was not
for me. I flunked Hamptons 101.

Most of the people had been going out there for
years. They had already dated each other, and as no one
formed any permanent connections, they were now recycled, and circulating through each other again. The
men gathered around to check me out because I was new
blood, or so the women made sure to tell me. They gathered around me too. Not because they wanted to be-
friend me, but to make sure they got to keep the recycled
guys for themselves. If any two people did want to date,
they had to go ALD. Hampton code for After Labor
Day. This was explained to me by Chet. "No guy wants
to give up a night in the Hamptons to go out with
someone, when they might be able to meet someone
else. Dates have to wait to happen in the city, ALD."

The system of Circulation and Recycling was in business. The other thing circulated and recycled that summer, was a copy of a bestseller that contained rules for catching a husband. However, only the women read it, leaving the men even more clueless than usual.

According to that book, women were not to talk to men first, call them, call them back, go Dutch, open up, rush intimacy, take the lead, talk about life in any serious way, or stare. I definitely agreed with the staring thing. On the other hand, who was I to talk. Suffice it to say, a book like that should have been enlightening, or at the very least required reading for a gal like me.

Despite all the good advice, women in East Hampton, including *moi*, did not embrace those rules. Despite reading the very methodical chapters on How To, almost religiously every Saturday night women in East Hampton rushed home from the beach, blew-dry their hair, put on OUTFITS, and drove out to Happy Hour in East Hampton Point, where they broke the rules before they began just by buying their own drinks and talking to men first.

And the men obliged the women in breaking the rules by not buying them drinks, not talking to them first, and then not even asking them out. Not even ALD. I encouraged the women to stay home. Memorize the book and boycott The Point. But this didn't work because summer shares are very expensive, and no one wanted to go back to the city feeling they had left any stones unturned. I never went to The Point, feeling that for me, it would be pointless.

Then, one particularly dreary day, I ran into Elliot by the bicycle stand at Main Beach. We talked, but hadn't seen each other since we'd both returned to New York from L.A. I told him I was having trouble with the social scene, and he told me I was the cutest girl on the beach. So I called him up and started to date him. Instant Fix. I looked for a chapter on this, but it did not exist. I was breaking a rule so big, it didn't even fit in the book. Especially since I reconnected with Elliot in the Hamptons, where I should have been breaking rules trying to meet new men at The Point, but instead I began meeting new men through Elliot, which was a good thing because I didn't talk first, but a bad thing because it seemed like I was in a serious relationship when, in fact, I knew I was not. Had I known what was in store for Elliot and me, I might have truly reconsidered the book. In retrospect, I should have crammed it like it was the SAT of dating, highlighting in yellow the chapters most applicable: Don't Rush Into Sex, Don't Date Him If He Doesn't Buy You A Romantic Gift For Your Birthday, and NEXT! Dealing With Rejection. Seems the only rule Elliot and I got right was Don't See Him More Than Once A Week. But now that was all water under the boardwalk.

When I arrived at the train station in East Hampton,

I was careful to not get caught up in eyeing the women who were being met by men, and caught a cab directly to the beach instead. It was a glorious day. The water ahead sparkled, and my feet brought me close to the ocean as they plodded into the cool sand. I picked a perfect spot, threw down my knapsack, and settled into my sand chair.

It was delicious. I gazed at the ocean, basking in being out there again. I was pleased I had come alone, and was able to enjoy my own company.

"Hi!"

"Hey, Karrie Kline! Long time no see."

"You know her?"

"*You* know her?"

I turned my head and faced my worst nightmare. Three men I had dated were sharing a blanket, and ohmygod, *Elliot* was coming up from behind on my right, making the fourth. Elliot had never contacted me again after our weekend in the Berkshires. It was the only time he ever listened to me.

"Hi... Hi... Hi... Ohhhhhhh..."

How could this happen to me? Seeing them all together like that was unnerving. Did they talk about me? Did they compare notes? No one was talking now. *Everyone* was staring, but the only one unnerved was me. And Elliot.

"Karrie. Hi. Do you want to talk to me, or should I

go away?" he asked. Elliot was wearing bright green Speedo water shoes, and was carrying his knapsack and the wheel to his ten-speed bike. I looked at Elliot and then back at the other men. I had not kept in contact with any of the men, and now I was remembering why. I acknowledged my all-male Beach Blanket Bingo.

Publicist Jay Kohn. Jay was partially responsible for my reconciliation with Elliot. Jay pursued me under the guise of being completely into me, but tortured. He would charm me, woo me, practically seduce me—until I would respond. That's when Jay would let me know he was pining for another woman, and relationships and feelings could only result in pain. I was always sucked in. During The Summer of the Share, Jay had offered to drive me out one weekend. After making the plans, he never called me back. I wound up taking the train out and running into him that night at a bar. Instead of being embarrassed, he was charming, lovely, fraught with pain, and willing to make it up to me. A few weeks of trying to keep up with that drove me crazy, and back into El-liot's arms at the bicycle stand.

Next guy up was Bill, Ad Man, Marder. Bill was my ex-boyfriend Elliot's ex-girlfriend's ex-husband. Bill ran into me in Central Park when I was running the reser-voir. It was during one of the periods when Elliot and I were on the outs. Bill and I had a few great dates run-ning, lunching, dining and necking. Four weeks later, I received an e-mail from Bill telling me he had gotten back together with his girlfriend. In addition, his affiliation with Elliot made him feel bad about dating me. He didn't want to be responsible for breaking The Guy Code. That's listed in the handbook alphabetically, after ALD.

Producer Pete Tannenbaum was on a beach chair behind Bill. I had met him after services on the steps of the temple. After half an hour of glib chitchat, I found out Pete worked at the same ad agency as Bill. And if that was not enough of a coinky dink, somewhere after Running With Bill and before Real Breakup With Elliot, Bill had even spoken to Pete about fixing him up with this actress friend of his. That turned out to be me. How lucky I had thought I was, to have met Pete on my own. I had thought it was "meant to be."

Pete and I dated for several months, until he came by to tell me he had started seeing another woman and wanted to consummate their relationship that week on Valentine's Day. He was not breaking up with me, just redefining our relationship. How we were to continue was completely up to me. Pete said all the options were mine. Anything I wanted was possible except for dating him, or no longer seeing him. He would not tolerate losing me. Pete told me he wanted me in his life forever. As a postscript, Pete let me know he had had difficulty dealing with my age right from the start. I'd soon be forty-five, and Pete was forty-four. Pete was upset that later in the year, he, too, would be forty-five. It wasn't me, it was him. I was great, the number was trouble. It was his problem, and to show me how sincere a guy he really was, Pete continued to send e-mail and cards. Too bad for Pete he never got a response.

The revolving door had stopped turning. When a relationship did not, could not work, it was over. I did not need to keep juggling. I did not need to keep all the balls up in the air. Sometimes they just fell and rolled away never to be seen again, and that was okay. Looking at these four guys on the beach, I only had one question.

"What are you all doing here?"

"We all share a house," said Elliot. His eyes were full of innocence and guilt.

"Oh." I got my answer. I walked across the beach to the pay phone, realizing this was when a cell phone would come in handy. I wanted to talk to my mother.

Millie was on her way out to bowl when she picked up.

"Is everything okay?" she asked. "I thought you were out in the Hamptons. What is it? I'm running out."

"Are you okay?" I asked. I wasn't going to confide in her, but I needed to hear my mother's voice. I was always concerned for my mother.

"I'm fine. The women had a breakfast this morning. I'm going bowling now. Your uncle is a doll. I needed a special bulb for the light fixture, and he dropped everything and drove me to Home Depot. Sy also fixed the garbage disposal for me. Everyone has been terrific. A lot of couples are going to dinner later. The men always want to pay for me, but I'm not their date so I like to take care of myself."

"They pick you up, right, Ma? They drive?"

"Of course, Karrie. They watch out for me. Just like Henry did for anyone in my position."

My mother sounded good. My mother generally sounded better than I did. "I don't dwell" was Millie's motto, and it often rang in my ear. It had been five years since Henry's death, but sometimes I still found it inconceivable to understand how she was able to live with the loss yet get on with it. I assumed it had something to do with faith, acceptance, and feeling like you had really been loved. I had a lot to learn from my mother.

"Are you okay?" I asked again. I knew Fourth of July was a holiday when Henry liked to grill, and they always had a big barbecue with their friends and neighbors.

"I'm okay. Even though it's been years, you don't forget. But I don't like to talk about it. I don't air my problems to everyone. Everything's fine. I'm busy. I have plenty to do. Enjoy yourself, Karrie. I love you."

As I walked back to my chair, I thought about the end of Henry's life. But not the negative parts. The love. The closeness. Being there for Henry, and even ill, how Henry was there for us. We were there for each other. I thought of all the friends and family and people who went out of their way to take care of my mother and me. I knew what that was. I knew very well, because in addition to my friends, the people in my mother's life were in mine too. I had that caring in my life; I always have.

I looked at the beach boys sitting together, laughing in the sand and realized I didn't need anything from any of them.

"Where're you going?" asked Pete. "Hang for a while. We can catch up."

Bill's girlfriend was lying next to him. He only had eyes for her.

"Maybe I can give you a lift back to the city," said Jay. "I can't promise anything, though, but I can leave you my number and you can call me."

"No thanks, guys. I'm fine." I was. My sand chair was over my shoulder, my thongs were in my hand, my knapsack was on my back, and my head was finally screwed on straight.

Elliot caught up behind me.

"Wait," he said, stopping me in my tracks. "I think about you a lot, Kar. I never call you, though, because I know I frustrated you and I just don't know what to say. You're the one who's good with words, not me."

"Thanks, Elliot. It's okay. No hard feelings." I looked at him and felt relief that I did not feel compelled to fix it, get him to talk, or get it to change.

"Your hair is different," he said. "It's brown."

I pulled the black scrunchie out of my hair and shook it loose. "It's my natural color," I said. "You like it?"

"I like it a lot, Kar," said Elliot, smiling at me, making me feel a warmth I knew wasn't from the sun. "I like it. Better than the red hair."

"Good!"

"Although…" Elliot took a step in and paused. "Maybe I like the red better. Oh… I don't know now. I think the brown. No. The red. I miss the red."

"Oh, Elliot," I said, looking down from his confused face to his green Speedos. "Listen, be careful in the ocean. Avoid live fish and sharp rocks. Take care of yourself, El."

All I wanted was a new, clean, clear spot on the beach.

I picked a perfect one, threw down my knapsack and settled into my sand chair. It was delicious. I gazed at the ocean, basking in being out there again. I was pleased I had come out alone, and was able to enjoy my own company. When the sun began to recede, I called a cab, checked into the motel and took a walk before dinner.

The town of East Hampton was lovely. The shops on Main Street were beautiful. I saw a great pasta bowl, two terrific white shirts, and a pair of sandals. Short on cash, I was in Look Don't Buy mode. The name of the store on the corner caught my attention. Paw Prince. As I got closer, I saw it was a pet store. I ducked inside Paw Prince knowing there would be no temptation there.

I browsed through the aisle that held sunglasses, hats, raincoats, and sweaters for your pet. It was more like shopping for a child than a dog. A dog. That's a responsibility, I thought. And not cheap either. I was not into this. It was not for me. I was going back to not buying at a boutique, instead of not buying at a pet store.

"Excuse me! Owwww—" I was walking out of the store, and the man behind me accidentally stepped on the back of my shoe.

"Oh, uh, sorry," he said, exiting with a huge bag of dog food.

I leaned up against the window to rub the sole of my foot. Looking down I saw the big, dark chocolate-colored eyes of the sweetest little Maltese looking up at me. Staring. I stared back. For the moment I was hypnotized.

"Can I hold him?" I asked the owner, hobbling back into the store as quickly as my hurt foot would take me. I felt slightly frantic someone might get to him before me.

They placed him in my arms. The little ball of white fluff laid his head on my shoulder. He was warm and cuddly, and fit right into the side of my neck. What a cutie, I thought, before I went to return him. But somehow I didn't move.

I looked at the dog for a moment. He was staring again. He looked smart and interested. I felt like he was assessing me.

"Hello," I said in a singsong voice. "Do you like me?"

He let out a little bark. Yes, he was saying. I do. I kissed his nose and he smiled. His mouth opened, his pink tongue wagged up and down, and he kissed me. The little puppy licked my nose.

"How old is he?" I asked.

He'd be three months that Tuesday.

"How much is he?" I asked.

I blinked. I blinked again. He was expensive. He was way more than a thousand dollars. But he was so soft. Ah, but he was not short-term. He would not be leaving in two to three months. He was going to be there. Every day. In a regular way. He was commitment. He was responsibility. And in no uncertain terms, he was love.

But it was too much commitment, too much responsibility and too much money. Just too much! I went to return him to the store owner, and looked into his eyes once more. He was talking to me. I felt it. He was it. He was the one. Oh yeah, I knew this and I was scared because I wanted him, and I was afraid I could not make that commitment. And then the lightbulb went off. No one had ever made a commitment to me, but then, I hadn't made one either. I held this dog in my arms. His warmth radiated through me. I reached into my beach bag to get my wallet, and the hair spray fell out. The fifteen dollars I had spent in the morning was nothing compared to what I had the feeling I was going to do next. This dog was not the cheap stuff. He was the real stuff. With a regular, unsticky, long-lasting hold. What was I waiting for? I whipped out my credit card, and he was mine.

The little dog and I traveled back to the city on the Long Island Railroad, the dog silent in a cardboard carrying box for animals. When we got to the Upper West Side, I took him out.

"This is Broadway and this avenue is Amsterdam," I said, pointing out the sights while holding him in my arms. "This is the neighborhood deli, and this is your new house." I showed him the building. "What do you think of the art deco tile in the lobby?"

Gomez was busy mopping the floor.

"You bought a dog, Miss Karrie?" the superintendent asked, looking from the pup back to me. "You make sure he doesn't pee in the lobby, okay?"

I filled a laundry basket with towels, a ticking clock and a few soft furry toys Paw Prince had sold me. For the next few days the nameless white dog did not make a peep. He ate his meals and peed on the newspaper, but mainly he looked at me through those luminous eyes that said, "Who are you and where am I?"

By Monday, I went to bed sad. I was thinking I had made a mistake.

"Hey, you," I said. "You were so happy in the pet store

when we met, I thought you'd liven up the joint. Are you unhappy here?"

I awoke the next morning and greeted the dog with abundant energy.

"Happy three-month birthday," I said, picking up all five pounds of him and kissing his cold little nose. "Did anybody ever sing you a happy birthday song before?" I asked. He looked at me with the same hopeful, quizzical luminous stare.

"Well, you are in for a treat." I picked up his front paws and as I sang the Happy Birthday song, I moved them from side to side.

Happy birthday to you—

Happy birthday to you—

Happy birthday, dear...

Oh my. Of course this dog was confused. He didn't even have a name. He didn't know where he was but he didn't know who he was either.

Happy birthday, dear...

Something would come to me.

Dear...

Something would come soon.

Dear...

Something would—

Dear Charlie!!!!!!

He started to jump. To smile. He began to wave his paws and dance! I sang the birthday song over and over and he danced throughout. Every time I sang his name he let out a bark, jumped a little higher and waved his paws a little harder. Charlie had found himself, and Charlie had found home.

Charlie and I have been having a ball. He is so full of energy and curiosity and love. My apartment is filled with another life. He is my buddy, he is my baby, and we belong. I see his little face when I say good-night, and the first thing when I awake. Charlie makes me laugh. He is hard work that comes easy.

The gifts I received for my little puppy could not have been nicer if I had actually given birth! A check from Grandma Millie, a plaid fleece winter coat from Fred, a yellow slicker from Jane and William, and a blue crocheted *yarmulke* from Brooke and Mitch. "For his Bark-Mitzvah," she wrote in the card.

Last week Charlie went to his first singles event. "Singles and their Pets" was a PR event sponsored by a pet product manufacturer. Charlie and I waltzed through the revolving doors of an upscale Central Park South restaurant as if we lived in Paris, and joined our party in the private back room. Waiters served water and treats to the dogs, cocktails and hors d'oeuvres to the singles. Goody bags filled with pet paraphernalia lined the perimeter of the room. Comics and soap stars were hired to entertain, and pet-sitters were there to give the owners a chance to mingle and meet. Upon returning from the ladies' room I couldn't readily locate Charlie. Then he jumped up behind me, held on his leash by Carmen, one of the pet-sitters.

"Your dog is very popular. He was pulled outside for a photo-op with James Whelan from *All My Problems.* Charlie's very gregarious and gets along well with others," she said. "I think he'd do very well in doggie day care." And Carmen handed me her business card from Happy Pets Day Care & Grooming. At the end of the evening Charlie won the grand prize in the raffle, a gift certificate to the Pet Bowl and a "Day at the Spa" at Canine Ranch. All three places just blocks from my apartment! And then a reporter interviewed us. That weekend, Charlie and I were in the paper!

Navigating the treacherous singles scene had perks for Manhattan-based actress Karrie Kline, who brought her adorably scruffy Maltese, Charlie. Kline would not come if this were just another singles event. "I figured if I don't like any of the people, at least I'd be with Charlie," she said.
***Daily News*—"Critters" Section**

But in the neighborhood, Charlie has earned a reputation all his own. Everybody knows Charlie! He'll hit it off with a dog, and its owner will want to arrange a play-date. He'll hit it off with a man, and they'll talk to Charlie's owner and want to arrange a date-date! After the episode with the weird, unemployed bartender and his mean pit bull, I had to teach Charlie it was good to be open but he had to learn to be discriminating. If he was to continue to introduce the two of us, his judgment needed to improve. Last week we were taking a walk, and Charlie dragged me up to a great-looking guy at the 79th Street bus stop. Two great-looking guys, in fact. The dark-haired guy and I spoke. Then the other one abruptly said good-night and left his cute dark-haired buddy at the bus stop with Charlie and me. The guy asked if he could walk with us. As we walked, I gave Charlie a little wink. He was learning quickly. Charlie is very obedient.

When the guy from the bus stop, Jeff, finally called and asked me out I said yes. He appeared warm, sincere, humble and a little shy. Sunday, he and I will have dinner and take in a movie.

I expect it will be a lovely evening. However, it's all right if it is not. I have love in my life. Romantic love will find me when it chooses. Besides, whatever the evening has in store, I'll still need to come home and walk Charlie.

39

The Water in the Walls

New Year's Eve
Brooklyn Heights, NY 2003

The guy from the bus stop was cool. Definitely cool. A musician. Piano. Classically trained. Hip, humble and *heimishe*. Like someone I already knew. I ran into his friend, Keith, on the street the night after Charlie and I had met them.

"Your friend, Jeff, walked me and my dog for like thirty minutes," I said. "He told me he was ambivalent about buying his apartment. Something about pipes bursting in the halls."

"Broder is Mr. Ambivalent," said Keith, calling Jeff by his last name. It sounded ultracool to me. Keith was out tonight with another musician friend. He introduced me to Mickey who was carrying a bass guitar. Keith was an actor, but he obviously befriended a lot of musicians. "Broder's ambivalent about everything, but he's a kick-ass keyboard player."

It had only been twenty-four hours at that point, but Broder hadn't called. Actually, he hadn't even asked for my number. But I felt I had a lot of information. Jeff hadn't asked for my number, so there could have been an ex lingering in the background. If so, I doubted it was anything serious since Keith had left him to walk with me and Charlie, urging Jeff to make a move. But obviously time was not of the essence. And Jeff was ambivalent.

Two and a half weeks later Jeff called, having looked me up in the phone book, and we went to dinner and a movie. It was a lovely evening and all my instincts about him appeared to be correct, but I added into the mix that not only did it feel like Jeff really liked me, he looked at me as if I could be it. "I think he wants to fall in love with me," I told Jane a few weeks later, after Jeff and I took a VHS Test.

Jane and I developed a theory years ago, that the first video two people rent ultimately winds up dictating the nature of that relationship.

Dazed and Confused. Jay Kohn. *The Abyss*. Elliot L. I'll say no more. *The English Patient*. A spurt of passion, followed by something monotonous and boring, resulting in two people traveling off in different directions. That was Michael Tuckman. What relief when he went back to Baltimore to reconcile with Sue. *Midnight in the Garden of Good and Evil.* Seemed like a good story was about to begin, but it turned out to be empty, shallow and meaningless. My time with Mr. Monogamy, Pete Tannenbaum.

Jeff and I rented *The Opposite of Sex.* Fun, engaging, original. The characters go on their individual journeys, to discover that they finally are ready for the opposite of sex. Love.

I liked him. His talent and compassion. His looks, his point of view on the world, stories about India and his family. I liked his tastes and his smile, his generosity and his laugh. I liked his dark curly hair, his mouth, and how his voice sounded like velvet, as musical-speak of the fifties slid off his tongue.

I liked him so much. And I liked how he liked me.

When we saw each other I felt him totally attentive to me. Enveloped by me. He got me. He thought I was beautiful. Sexy. Smart. Special. This is it, I thought. Jeff is it.

But I was going away on Labor Day to Missouri to do a play for six weeks. And time felt precious. And Jeff got mixed up in time. He dissolved into it and floated inside it, till the tide of time rolled in and washed him onto shore. The precious dates before Missouri got canceled, abbreviated, shortened. There were less than I had wanted, but each was wonderful and built on the one before.

My last day we had planned to get together in the early afternoon, in order to spend as much time as possible since I was leaving early the next morning. Jeff called every hour on the hour starting at noon, giving me updates on a flood in his newly purchased co-op. The pipes from the upstairs apartment had burst, and the water dripped through the ceiling, sliding down his bathroom walls. Jeff finally arrived just after 10:00 p.m. Enough time for saki and sushi, edamame and goodbye.

After dinner he held me in front of my building. Both of us in denim shorts and white tank tops.

"I want to make love to you," he said. "Do you want to make love to me?"

I was dying to make love to him. Every pore and every sense inside me was screaming to rub up against and inside him.

"Yes," I said. "Yes."

But Jeff hesitated. And then so did I. And it was already midnight and I had to be up at five.

"Come to Missouri," I said. "Come."

"Maybe I will," said Jeff. "Maybe I will."

In Missouri our contact dropped off. I thought it might be best to leave it that way, but it picked up again after a few weeks, and then again when I returned to New York.

"I wasn't ever pulling away from you," Jeff told me that Sunday afternoon in October, the first time we got to-

gether when I was back. We took Charlie to a Halloween party at the dog run near the Museum of Natural
History and dressed him up as a pirate. The black patch
on his eye looked cute, but he couldn't see so I had to
carry him in the costume parade. Charlie didn't win any
prizes nor did he get an honorable mention, but we all
had fun. Jeff came back to my apartment. We lit a few
candles, put on the classical station and lay down on the
couch. It felt like home to be back in each other's arms.

"This is powerful," I said as he kissed me. We decided
our kisses weren't just kisses, but explosive expressions of
emotion. "I know we're on the same page physically, but
are we emotionally?"

"Yes. Definitely. This is potentially great," he said. "I
was thinking that all day. When you were away, I was just
going over what I really needed in my life. You know
how you can have a lobster dinner, but do you really want
one now…or do you want a couple of Whoppers first?"

I waited. I wanted to hear the "specials."

"I want this," said Jeff. "I want to focus on this. We'll
talk daily. I'll call. You'll call. We'll be exclusive. I want to
focus on us. Yes. And I'm glad we talked. Now I'm not
that nervous about asking you out on another date. Now
I'm not nervous at all."

That was easy. We expressed our feelings, we wanted the
same thing, and now we were together. Jeff called. We went
out. It was wonderful. We became lovers. But. But. But…

It was wonderful, but it was halting. It was starting. Stopping. Starting. Stopping. No, it never stopped, it just…lapsed. There were lapses between the times in person. But the times in person were so connected. Emotion and flow, synchroneity and interest. Jeff said he would cook for me, and we would take a bubble bath. Go to temple and light the Shabbat candles. Jeff wanted to buy me a vase, and have me meet his family. Have massage night with special oils. He said we'd go skiing and stay at a B&B in Vermont. He was going to play the CD he composed, and sing to me while we sat at his piano. Jeff wanted to drink wine, and make love to me while I held on to the posts of his bed.

Jeff was cleaning his apartment and getting it ready. I would wake up next to him. In his bed with the wood posts. Down the hall from the kitchen with the dumbwaiter and the living room with the grand piano. I could imagine everything, and feel how perfect it would be. He asked if I'd help fix up his apartment. The apartment I never saw. Jeff and I had lots of plans. And Jeff did not follow through.

Thanksgiving weekend we made love one last time, for after that he stopped calling. Jeff called to cancel a date, and suggested we postpone. The relationship is what I heard him postponing. And, as usual, I was right.

Almost a month passed before there was any word from him. Then, the day before New Year's, a letter arrived in the mail. Jeff apologized. For not communicating, calling, writing or visiting. For stopping. He had "things in his life" he was having trouble dealing with. He had "unresolved issues" with his ex-girlfriend. His ex. Ah…never underestimate one's first instincts, I reminded myself. He thought I was great, but he wasn't ready. He thought that maybe at a point in the future we could be together. He left the door open, he took all the blame, and he signed off.

Happy New Year!

I was sick. Hurt. Devastated. Disappointed. Angry. Humiliated. Lonely. Sad. Depressed. Confused. Horny. Empty. Disillusioned. Pained. Frustrated. Hanging. Opened up and suspended in air. An overripe libido, an aching heart. Bloody, warm, slit through the middle. Waiting. Wanting. Worried.

"Relax," said Jane. "He'll be back. You'll see. You have to let this die so it can be reborn. He will be back. You get yourself together so you will be ready. So you won't be anxious when he returns. He needs to win you back. You take care of yourself."

And I did. I got in shape. I went to the gym. I swam. I did yoga, I did Pilates. I learned to swing dance. I did radio spots and network voice-overs and national television commercials. I got a contract role on *All My Problems* and the lead in a new Broadway show. I threw Charlie a one-year birthday party and got him in a national TV and print campaign, his face on the can of a major dog food. I bought a new wardrobe. I went to the Bahamas. I went out on dates. And just as I was about to kiss someone new, the phone rang.

"Hey…hi…it's me. Jeff. Jeff. Broder. How are you? I'm… I'm… I'm not so great. I miss you, Karrie. I miss you a lot. I think about you. Yeah, like, a lot. I think I was scared, but… I'm clear now. It's cool, and I'm…I'm ready. Yeah. I'm ready to be with you, Karrie, for real. Is it too late? Let's talk soon. I'll call you."

I didn't return his call, but I didn't kiss the new man. Jeff called again.

"Hi. I hope you're well. I hope you got my message. I'm going to call you again. Get a good night's sleep, Kar."

I didn't return his call. The phone stopped, but the buzzer rang. Three dozen roses in yellow, red and white came by messenger with a card that read, "Please. Jeff xxx."

It started out slowly. It started over for the first time. Jeff called me every day. Plans were made in advance and were unaltered. We saw some good movies and a wonderful play. Jeff cooks a mean chili, and his voice sways inside me like silk when he *dovens* in temple. I made my sourdough French toast and read him poetry. I had to work hard to keep up with him when we ran the reservoir. We got a tennis permit in the park. We both really liked the new exhibit at The Metropolitan Museum of Art, and I flipped when he played his CD and he'd written me a love song. We have massage night regularly, and the keys to each other's apartments. We hold each other all through the night and make love like a beautiful duet. Charlie has adjusted to the routine of the three of us, and Jeff loves him too. Oh, he loves me. Jeff told me he loves me.

And now I will tell you something. I'm lying. I'm lying here in my bed wrapped in a wisp of a white silk robe making this up. It is New Year's Eve day. I got the letter yesterday. When I received Jeff's message after Thanksgiving, I knew I'd never hear from him again. His letter was a surprise, but the real surprise was that I was fine. I had let go of him before the letter arrived. I had really enjoyed Jeff and I was more than hopeful, but his behavior was not that of a grown-up man who wanted a grown-up relationship. I needed to explore it with him so I'd feel satisfied with whatever the end result would be. This was it, and I was satisfied.

I would not respond to the letter. I would not be in touch. Jeff and I had felt more than promising, but the vapor evaporated. Like water in a vase that kept the flowers blooming, but never was refilled.

Tonight is New Year's Eve. Brooke and Mitch are having a dinner party in their brownstone in Brooklyn Heights. I will be going, and I'm bringing Charlie and Fred. Jane and William are bringing six-month-old Eve. Millie is in Florida, and my mother told me that tonight she has a date! Her first since Henry died.

I lie in my brass bed on my blue-and-white-striped Laura Ashley sheets looking up, watching the ceiling fan spin while Charlie naps on the pillow next to me. I have to get up and get ready for tonight. It will be a brand-new year in a matter of hours. Who knew what would be in store? Life continued to surprise. Each thread helped weave another picture that created its own tapestry. Its own design.

One steamy summer night I was walking my dog and a stranger opened me up. I remember the feelings with joy and not pain, because I enjoy remembering. It is winter. Spring is coming, and soon it will be summer. I can already feel the warmth penetrate through me. I can taste the texture of the passion that awaits. I am here, I am ready and it is coming.